THESE ARE
THE WOMEN IN WHITE—

DR. REBECCA DALTON, CARDIAC SURGEON
One half of a celebrated husband-and-wife heart transplant team, she watched anxiously as her career soared and her marriage floundered.

HELGA SUNDBERG, TOP NURSE
"Unflappable," they called her. And so she was, the very model of the cool, capable professional —until surgeon Mike Raburn entered her life.

CAROLYN PAYSON, NURSE
She grappled with a momentous, life-and-death decision as she watched her father die the slow agony of Huntington's disease.

**DR. VALERIE LeMOYNE,
CHIEF ANESTHESIOLOGIST**
By day, a brilliant and respected woman of medicine. By night, a relentless huntress whose insatiable hunger for men drove her to almost any lengths.

DR. KAREN FLETCHER, HEAD PATHOLOGIST
She exercised her keen mind and flaunted her petite body in cold pursuit of professional success.

The continuing saga of the women in white— their trials, their triumphs, their families, their careers, the men in their lives.

Frank G. Slaughter

Women
In
White

PUBLISHED BY POCKET BOOKS NEW YORK

POCKET BOOKS, a Simon & Schuster division of
GULF & WESTERN CORPORATION
1230 Avenue of the Americas, New York, N.Y. 10020

Copyright © 1974 by Frank G. Slaughter

Published by arrangement with Doubleday & Company, Inc.
Library of Congress Catalog Card Number: 73-83673

ISBN: 0-671-82849-5

First Pocket Books printing February, 1975

10 9 8 7 6 5 4

Trademarks registered in the United States and other countries.

Printed in the U.S.A.

Women
In
White

Chapter 1

JUNE IN MIAMI is much like midsummer farther north, with the difference that the constant sea breeze, sweeping westward across the towering skyline of the famous resort hotels marking the Golden Strand of Miami Beach, plus the sparkling blue waters of Biscayne Bay separating the two cities, tempers both heat and humidity to a pleasant, languorous warmth. The rustle of palm fronds is a constant soft obbligato beneath the more strident theme of automobile motors, the deep staccato roar of motorboat engines, and the higher-pitched whine of jet airplanes beginning the descent to Miami International Airport, one of the busiest in the country.

It was just a quarter to three on a Tuesday afternoon when Helga Sundberg left the rear entrance of Bayside Terrace. The former luxury hotel had been converted to apartments when four blocks of prime bay-front land just north of downtown Miami were turned into the sprawling new Biscayne University Medical Center, with the twenty-story hospital tower its central point. Inhabited largely by the faculty and staff of the center, the old hotel stood in the midst of a tropical garden surrounding the swimming pool where a few of its residents fortunate enough to have the day off were splashing or sunning.

Crossing the putting green beyond the pool, Helga didn't bother to think how nice it would be to swim or lie in the sun; there would be plenty of time for that over the weekend, when she would be off duty from Friday night until Monday afternoon. Immediately ahead was the daily reality of her job as nursing supervisor in the combined medical Intensive Care Units of the great hospital during the eight hours between three and eleven that always brought a succession of small crises, and sometimes larger ones, when the decisions and prompt actions of a highly trained and resourceful ICU nurse could easily make the difference between life and death.

Across the green spread of lawn separating Bayside Terrace from Biscayne General, Helga could see the three-to-eleven shift coming on duty, a brigade of women in white converging upon the towering citadel of the great hospital in a thrice-daily assault. At the concrete marquee over the main entrance, the purring engine of a city bus spilled a barrage of exhaust fumes into the atmosphere as it disgorged a chattering bevy of women in all sizes, shapes, ages, and variety of uniforms. Behind the bus a taxi slid to a stop and five nurses emerged, scrabbling in handbags for change to pay the driver. In the line of cars waiting to approach the marquee a husband, eager to relinquish a white-clad wife and thereby gain eight hours of relative freedom, honked his car horn impatiently. And from the multilevel parking garage across the boulevard, lines of nurses in white nylon, attendants in pink or blue, cafeteria personnel in pale green, and an occasional visiting doctor in summer seersucker converged upon the crossing lines or waited for the light to change.

Reluctant to leave the sunlight for the atmosphere of tension that invariably greeted her when she opened the doors to the main ICU section which, with the adjoining Emergency Department, occupied the rear half of the hospital's ground floor, Helga Sundberg turned away from the main entrance. Following a graveled path, she skirted the bulkhead separating the water from the garden, her goal the Emergency Department entrance at the rear of the hospital.

Tall, blonde, blue-eyed, Helga was vigorously alive with the healthy beauty of her Nordic heritage. Her body, too, in a white orlon pants suit, was as symmetrically proportioned as if her measurements had been calculated by a computer, instead of being the result of a casual encounter between sperm and ovum, each bearing its varied quota of the ultra-microscopic genes that control heredity. What was more, like the healthy human animal she was, she ate what she wanted when she wanted it and had never been sick a day in her twenty-five years of vigorous and uninhibited living.

Pausing for a moment on the bulkhead, the tall nurse watched the joyous leaps of mullet in the bay that stretched here for almost a mile between beach and mainland. No one knew just why a distinctly lower-class fish like mullet—whose major claim to immortality was the fact that, fried in hot fat with a corn-meal-based delicacy called a "hush puppy," it turned into a dish fit for the gods—chose on bright warm days to quit its normal watery environment in ecstatic leaps that often carried it as much as three feet into the air before falling back with a splash. Unless it was from the sheer joy of living or, perhaps more likely, while playing a game of hide-and-seek with some finny predator beneath the surface.

On a solitary concrete piling, barnacle-covered where it jutted from the water as the sole remains of the pier that had served the hotel for a promenade in better days, sat a morose-looking, sleepy-eyed pelican. An almost grotesque gargoyle in repose, it turned into a thing of startling grace and beauty when, with a few flaps of its wings, it rocketed upward, to plunge in an arrow-straight dive into the bay. Seconds later the grayish bird emerged, flapping awkwardly toward its perch upon the crumbling piling, water streaming from its beak around the silvery body of the fish it had captured for its dinner and which, once again perched on the piling, it proceeded to devour with almost obscene relish.

Nearer the bulkhead, where the mud-sand bottom had been laid bare for a few feet by the receding tide, fiddler crabs scurried about, each carrying a single huge claw before it, like a small boy stumbling reluctantly toward his weekly music lesson, bearing his violin case before him. And in the shallows a few snowy egrets stalked majestically on pipestem legs, spearing an unwary minnow or a small scuttling crab every now and then with rapierlike bills.

Where a side path joined the graveled walk that followed the bulkhead, Helga turned reluctantly away from the water, intending to enter the hospital through a door beside the circular drive and ambulance unloading platforms at the entrance to the Emergency Department. The sound of an automobile horn blaring in frantic haste and the anguished squeal of brakes and tires stopped her short, however, as she was opening the side door of the Emergency Room. Turning toward the source of the sound, she saw a station wagon, driven so fast that it barely managed to negotiate the circular drive giving access to the ambulance unloading platforms, come to a screaming stop.

The woman driving the wagon piled out in frantic haste and fell to one knee, only managing to save herself from sprawling full length on the cement by catching the side of the ramp. Helga instinctively started down the ramp to help but the woman waved her back.

"I'm all right, nurse," she said, recognizing Helga's white uniform. "It's my little girl. She's choking to death!"

Moving quickly to the door of the station wagon, Helga pulled it open. The child lying on the front seat appeared to be about four. Her lips and ear lobes were dark from what Helga recognized immediately as the cyanosis of oxygen lack, her skin was dusky from the same cause, and her chest heaved as she tried to suck air into her lungs but without avail, obviously because of an obstruction.

"She was gulping a wiener," the mother started to explain but Helga didn't stop to listen. Picking up the limp burden of the child, she ran up the ramp and through the swinging doors into the Emergency Room itself.

The place was oddly deserted for an area that was usually busy. Helga understood the reason, when she glanced through the door of the small surgery at one side of the Emergency Room and saw the familiar stocky form of Dr. Michael Raburn. The Surgical Fellow, who was also director of Emergency Services, was bending over a wound he was suturing and a spattering line of tiny bloodstains across the front of the surgeon's gown told Helga he was coping with the serious emergency of a cut artery. Dr. Nolan Gaither, the interne on duty in the ER, was also gowned and gloved and stood across from Mike

Raburn holding a forceps ready. The seven-to-three nursing supervisor was standing by too, ready to hand the surgeons whatever instruments or dressings might be needed from the sterile reserve table that was always kept set up in anticipation of just such an emergency as they were treating now.

Recognizing that she could expect no immediate help from the ER crew, Helga moved quickly with her burden into the nearest of the half dozen examining-treatment cubicles lining the side of the main Emergency Room. Draping the small form of the child over the examining table, head downward, she gave her a sharp whack between the shoulder blades, hoping to jar loose the bread or meat, which both logic and experience with this not uncommon Emergency Room problem told her was obstructing the opening into the larynx called the glottis and blocking the entrance of air into the lungs by way of the trachea, or windpipe.

When a second whack, even harder than the first, still brought no results, Helga knew more drastic measures must be taken and wasted no time in calling for help. Lifting the child, she stretched her out on the table, this time on her back, with her head hanging over the end in a position designed to facilitate exposing the glottis, if possible, and removing the obstruction.

"Can I do anything, Miss Sundberg?" A student nurse had appeared at the entrance to the cubicle.

"Keep her neck hyperextended," said Helga and, relinquishing the child's head to the nurse, looked for the laryngoscope and tenaculum forceps that should have been on the small table in the corner. They weren't there, but something else was—a sterile needle-catheter setup used for starting continuous intravenous injections, the whole enclosed in a transparent plastic envelope. And with it, Helga saw a chance to save the child, whose feeble attempts at respiration had now all but ceased.

Mike Raburn had lectured briefly only last week on a recently reported method of by-passing the obstruction in cases such as this by means of just such a needle-catheter as lay on the table. And as she started tearing open the plastic protecting it from contamination, Helga's mind was rehearsing the steps he had outlined at the monthly conference of the ICU and Emergency Department staff, comprising the most knowledgeable group of people in dealing with life or death situations at the entire medical center.

While Helga's left hand explored the child's Adam's apple—the cartilage box protecting the larynx and vocal cords—the fingers of her right hand were busy removing the needle-catheter, with its plastic disposable syringe attached and the point of the needle encased within the nylon sheath projecting perhaps half an inch beyond the tip of the catheter. Feeling along the series of cartilage rings of the trachea, she located the cricothyroid membrane just below the Adam's apple. And setting the point of the needle against the now dark blue skin of the unconscious child's neck, she angled it downward about forty-five degrees before thrusting the point through the skin, the lining membrane, and into the trachea.

A quick pull on the plunger of the attached disposable syringe brought air into the barrel, confirming that the needle point had penetrated the respiratory tract itself. Holding the shaft steady, Helga pushed the needle inward about another quarter of an inch, before starting to work the nylon sheath that almost covered it down over the point now resting inside the respiratory passage.

When she withdrew the needle from inside the catheter, leaving the latter in place, air immediately whistled through it. But, knowing more would be needed if the near asphyxiated child were to be saved before oxygen lack endangered vital brain tissues, the nurse took down the emergency oxygen tube hanging from a hook attached to the wall panel in each of the cubicles.

The open end of the oxygen tube slipped over the plastic flange at the outer end of the catheter without difficulty. When it was secure, Helga reached for the control valve on the wall beside the oxygen supply and began to turn it slowly. In his lecture, Mike Raburn had emphasized that the valve must be opened carefully, lest the pressure from the main supply of oxygen piped throughout the hospital overinflate the lungs and damage the delicate air sacs.

As Helga listened to the hiss of the gas through the catheter into the little girl's respiratory passage, however, something Mike had failed to mention happened. When the positive pressure built up in lungs straining for air suddenly exceeded the atmospheric pressure forcing the meat fragment against the glottis, the end of the wiener popped from the small throat like a bullet, splattering with catsup and mustard the white uniform of the student nurse who was holding her head. At the same moment the little girl gave a gasping cry, sucking air into her lungs along with the oxygen that was whistling through the catheter. Almost immediately, too, the color of her lips and skin began to improve rapidly as the vital gas passed through the lining membrane of the lung air sacs and into her bloodstream, where it was absorbed by the hemoglobin in oxygen-starved red blood cells.

"Your baby's going to be all right," Helga assured the mother, who had stopped crying and was watching with fascinated eyes the tense drama being enacted in the narrow cubicle.

"Is—is that the piece of meat?" The mother pointed to the section of wiener resting in the lap of the student nurse.

"The cause of all the trouble." Helga picked up the small fragment. "When I gave her oxygen through the small tube, it blew out the obstruction."

"But it's so small. How could anyone choke to death on something as small as that?"

"What happened, Miss Sundberg?" Six feet two, with the broad shoulders of the All-American fullback he'd been at Harvard, Mike Raburn stood in the entrance to the cubicle. He had stripped off the sterile gloves he'd worn during the surgical procedure, but still wore the operating gown, with the line of small bloodstains across the front from the spurting artery he'd been forced to ligate.

"She just saved my daughter's life, that's what," said the mother. "Where were you, Doctor?"

"He was operating," said Helga.

"On a severed artery," Mike added.

"She aspirated part of a hot dog." Helga wondered why

7

the tips of her fingers had started to tingle. "There was no laryngoscope around, so I used that needle-catheter technique you lectured on last week."

"I'm glad to see it works so well. We'll leave the catheter in awhile, but I'll cut down the oxygen." Mike reached up to the control valve on the wall panel and closed it slowly until the hiss of gas through the catheter was barely audible. "Don't want to overinflate her lungs." When he turned to face Helga again, he reached out suddenly, however, and took the flanged connection of the catheter from her hands. "Wait in my office, Miss Sundberg," he said.

"I'm late for—" Helga shook her head to clear it, and didn't succeed. "Yes, Dr. Raburn," she managed to say.

"Take this tube, Miss Stern," she heard him tell the student nurse as she stumbled from the cubicle, but his voice sounded strangely distant. Nor could she understand why her legs felt as if the muscles were gone and why the white tiled walls were swinging slowly in a wide arc. She didn't even realize Mike Raburn was just behind her until she felt his hands beneath her elbows guiding her through a door and easing her into a comfortable chair in his office.

"Don't try to get up," he said firmly. "Back in a second."

When he returned he was carrying a mug of steaming coffee from the urn that stayed hot night and day in the utility room.

"Drink this," he commanded, handing it to her, "all of it."

As Helga obeyed, a wailing cry came from outside the office, followed by the unmistakable sound of vomiting. Mike left and when he came back perhaps five minutes later Helga was finishing the last of the coffee. He took the mug from her and put it on the desk.

"Is the little girl okay?" Helga managed to ask but the voice that spoke sounded only faintly like her own.

"Fine. She emptied her stomach and was still yelling, so I removed the catheter. What about you?"

8

"My fingers still tingle and I feel like I could pass out any minute."

"You realize what a chance you just took, don't you?" His voice was suddenly harsh and accusing. "That procedure's so new it was only reported in the *Journal* of the AMA two weeks ago. You didn't wear sterile gloves either and there was no sign of antiseptic on the skin of her neck."

"What the hell did you expect me to do?" The unjustness of his accusation brought a sudden surge of anger. "That girl was dying."

"I know." His voice had changed again and Helga suddenly realized that her anger had quite washed away the feeling of faintness. When she looked at Mike, too, she saw that he was smiling and wondered how she could ever have thought him ugly.

"Damn you, Mike Raburn," she said.

"That's better," he told her.

"What happened to me anyway?"

"Stress reaction. In order for you to cope with a life or death situation promptly the way you did, a lot of adrenalin had to be pumped into your bloodstream from the suprarenal glands. When the emergency was over, you didn't need the extra adrenalin any longer but it was still there and your body reacted to it."

"Then you deliberately made me mad just now so I would burn it up?"

"Right."

"That was a dirty trick. If you weren't so darned big, I'd sock you."

"Be my guest." He turned his face so his jaw was exposed.

"And break my hand? No, thank you."

When he turned to look at her again, there was an odd look in his eyes, as if he were seeing her for the first time—and liking what he saw.

"How long have we known each other?" he asked.

"Almost two years. Since Carolyn and I came here from Brazil."

"Brazil?" He frowned. "What in the world were you two doing there?"

9

"Nursing in a mission hospital."

"You—a missionary?"

"I said I was nursing—and no cracks about my being better suited for the role of Sadie Thompson."

"No cracks," he promised. "I was just thinking that for the past two years I've seen you only as a tall, beautiful broad who's also my best friend's girl."

"I'm nobody's girl, except when I choose to be. Besides, Ed Vogel and I broke off two weeks ago."

"He didn't tell me—but then I guess being dropped by you isn't something a man would boast about. What happened—if that's not being too inquisitive?"

"Ed and I had gotten to where we were taking each other for granted. When that happens you either break off or get married—and I'm not ready for that."

"I'd have thought Ed was the sort of doctor a nurse would marry."

"He is, but I've seen too many of these medical center marriages turn sour after the husband finishes a residency, or a fellowship, and goes out into practice."

Mike Raburn frowned. "Maybe I'm dense—but you seem to have left me somewhere."

"Ed is to cardiology what you are to surgery—the hottest young doctor on the staff. Even if he stays here and goes into the Private Diagnostic Clinic—"

"The nearest thing to private practice a faculty member can have," Mike interjected.

"Exactly. Actually it wouldn't make any difference where Ed goes, though. A good doctor in private practice jumps into an income bracket he never even dreamed of being in, with all the fringe benefits."

"Membership in the country club, Wednesday afternoon golf—"

"Plus nurses and technicians, to say nothing of divorcees and debutantes on the make," said Helga. "Of course if his wife has taken care of herself and still makes the right sort of a production out of their love life, she may be able to hold him against that kind of competition. But you've been around the medical scene long enough to know it doesn't usually happen that way."

"We see 'em in here every few days with migraine

headaches, colon spasm, or an overdose of morphine snitched from the husband's medical bag," he agreed. "They exhaust themselves at the wheel of a station wagon, taking the kids to speech class and ballet school, or working with the medical auxiliary because they think it will help their husband's practice."

"But when hubby comes home at night, what does he find? A tired wife who doesn't feel like taking a bath and dousing herself with perfume before putting on the sexiest lounging pajamas she can buy and making like Cleopatra giving Julius Caesar the hots."

Mike suddenly doubled up with laughter. "You're making Shakespeare turn over in his grave," he protested.

"Old Shakey knew enough about human nature to bring a sexy Mark Antony on the scene just about the time Julius' prostate was making him get up two or three times a night," said Helga. "But the reverse happens in a lot of doctor marriages, when hubby starts watching the women in white who run the average medical community. Unless she's a knockout, a wife in a plaid skirt and loose sweater can't compete with a nurse or technician in tight-fitting nylon, or even a secretary in boots and a mini. Before she even knows it, wifey finds herself on the losing end of a divorce."

"Are you going to be the *femme fatale* who takes him away from his wife?" Mike asked.

"I don't fool around with married men," Helga said indignantly. "I'll go on having my fun until I'm about thirty-five then I'll pick me a successful doctor of forty-five or fifty whose wife is dead or who's been divorced."

"What about love?"

"Love is for youth—what I'll be looking for is security and affection. I'll be a damned good wife, too, so even if the upkeep is high, he'll be able to afford the sort of bargain he'll be getting. I'll see that we have only upper-echelon friends and in a pinch I might even become president of the medical auxiliary, when he's elected to head the state association. But the most important thing is I'll keep myself so desirable that he'll be eager to come home at night. And when his sexual vigor starts to wane, I

11

know just the sort of hors d'oeuvres that will make his gonads shift into high."

"Stop it!" Mike protested. "You're making me look forward to growing old."

"And I'll be looking for employment if I don't get over to ICU and relieve Carolyn."

"Tell her I kept you. Today you're a heroine, I'm going to nominate you for a Carnegie Medal."

"ICU nurses don't get medals. You ought to know that."

"Or Emergency Room surgeons." His craggy face softened once more into a smile and his dark eyes were warm enough to step up her pulse a beat or two. "It looks like we'll just have to organize a mutual admiration society—and come to think of it, that's not a bad idea."

"Roger." She stood up, swaying a little. But when he reached out to steady her, she pushed his hand away.

"Keep your paws to yourself, Doctor," she said with mock severity. "I never play around on duty."

"For which that little girl out there can be thankful. I guess that makes us two of a kind, Miss Sundberg—and a rare kind at that."

II

In the office of Dr. Jeffry Toler, provost of Biscayne University Medical School and chief administrative officer of the new university medical center, Dr. Rebecca Dalton put down the magazine she had been holding, but not reading, when the door to the outer office opened. Slender, auburn-haired and of medium height, Rebecca was as distinctly feminine, and as forthright, as her biblical namesake. The starched long white coat she wore was emblematic of the medical faculty, and the coiled tubing of the stethoscope peeping from a side pocket indicated that her field was medicine, not surgery. At thirty-two, she was already an associate professor of medicine in the school and a highly respected cardiologist in her own right, as well as a beautiful and highly sensitive woman who was also deeply troubled.

"Forgive me, please, Rebecca." The two doctors were

friends of long standing and Jeffry Toler's voice was warm as he came over to where she was sitting and bent to kiss her cheek. "Manning Desmond collared me in the parking garage as I was coming back from Rotary. Your division chief can say less in more words than anyone I know."

Rebecca smiled. "Dr. Desmond taught me more about the human heart than all the doctors I've studied with put together so I can forgive him the verbosity."

"I would be more inclined to call much of it verbiage," Toler said somewhat dryly as he took the tall chair behind his desk and swung it around to face Rebecca. "I imagine you already saw this," he added, opening the afternoon edition so she could see the headline: JURY EXONERATES DR. DALTON IN HEART TRANSPLANT DEATH.

"I missed the radio announcement but it was all over the hospital immediately."

"I'm not surprised. My secretary always knows what's happening around here long before it comes to my attention."

"Dr. Desmond called me before he went to Rotary, Jeffry. I imagine he talked to you about Dr. Barrows' application for retirement."

"The request will be presented to the joint meeting of the Hospital Board of Directors and the Executive Committee this afternoon at five. Manning tells me Jake Barrows has been having angina ever since that coronary three months ago, so there shouldn't be any hitch."

"The medical indications are perfectly clear," she agreed.

"Did Desmond tell you he plans to recommend to the Board this afternoon that you be raised to the rank of full professor and appointed chief of the Cardiology Section?"

"Does it have to come right now?" Rebecca asked quickly. "I'm only thirty-two and you'll be promoting me over several older heart specialists."

"None of whom are as capable as you—or want the job."

"Lately I've been wondering just how capable I really am, Jeffry. It seems—"

13

"If you're blaming yourself for part of what happened to Ken, don't. Lots of husband-and-wife teams—"

"I was still largely responsible for selecting the cases for those heart transplants. Which makes me equally responsible with Ken for their deaths."

Caught up for perhaps the hundredth time in the past six months by the memory, and the horror, of what had followed, Rebecca turned to stare unseeingly at the large picture window behind the administrator's desk. And recognizing the source of her agony, Jeffry Toler didn't intrude into her thoughts immediately but removed his pipe from his coat pocket and took his time about stuffing and lighting it.

Nobody understood yet, although intensive research was being pursued in dozens of medical schools throughout the world, just why lymphoid cells in the body of a person saved from death by the transplant of a heart or other organ from another so often invaded, and sought to destroy, the very organ that made continued life possible for the recipient. And so no one had really been able to explain why the series of heart transplants Dr. Kenneth Dalton had performed so brilliantly over a period of about a year had suddenly begun to die, one by one, six months ago from the mysterious process called rejection.

As an expert cardiologist, Rebecca Dalton was quite aware that death always watched over the shoulder of a surgeon in the cardiovascular field, where Ken had already achieved a string of brilliant successes even before he started transplanting hearts. One slip, a moment's lessening of the surgeon's confidence in the skill of his own hands, even a minor failure in the complex armamentarium of technical aids that made such surgery possible, and death was always waiting to step in.

Two years ago Ken Dalton had startled the surgical world and the press alike by performing fifteen heart transplants in succession, without a single death on the operating table or in the early postoperative weeks. As head of the Cardiac Research Laboratory and one of the

14

chief heart specialists at Biscayne General, Rebecca Dalton had personally selected the cases for transplant and evaluated the chances of failure. Not from the operation—for Ken Dalton had already honed his skill to a degree of perfection that had earned him a reputation for technical excellence equal to a DeBakey, a Shumway, or a Cooley—but from concomitant disease of the liver or other organs that made success unlikely.

The Emergency Room at Biscayne General and other neighboring hospitals had been the main source of donors and the case from which the court test sprang had seemed typical enough—at the start. Kept breathing mechanically by a resuscitator in the hands of the alert crew manning one of the crack Fire Department Rescue Squad units, a young woman with a massive brain hemorrhage from an automobile accident had been rushed to the Biscayne General Emergency Room from the Golden Glades Expressway.

Her heart was still beating when she was brought into the hospital, proving that it at least was alive. Not so, however, the brain, for the electroencephalogram, taken routinely on all such cases since Ken's spectacular success with heart transplants had created a continual demand for donors, had shown no action currents—the ultimate proof of brain death. While Kevin McCartney, the prospective recipient, waited, his failing heart barely able to maintain enough circulation to keep his brain alive, a frantic search for relatives of the doomed hemorrhage case who might give permission for the transplant had been carried on, with no result.

Three times the respirator had been stopped for five minutes, the period agreed upon in most hospitals as establishing death, but spontaneous respiration had not occurred and the brain waves, too, had remained nonexistent. Yet each time the respirator was reactivated and oxygen once more moved into the red blood cells by way of the lungs, the girl's heart had continued to beat—proof positive that it alone still possessed life. Finally Dr. Adrian Cooper, professor of forensic pathology in the medical school, and county medical examiner, had determined

15

officially that death had occurred and approved opening the otherwise dead body to remove the heart.

It had been one of Ken's most exciting and brilliant operations, Rebecca remembered. An hour after the first incision, Keven McCartney's new heart was beating strongly in a body revitalized by its presence. The postoperative course had been equally rapid and free from complications, too, and for the past year Kevin had been able to work part time as bartender in the Dolphin Lounge adjoining Bayside Terrace.

His testimony, plus that of the staff and Rebecca, had destroyed the contention of the plaintiff—a brother of the accident victim—that she had been technically alive when her heart was removed. In the face of the barrage of expert testimony brought to bear by the lawyers Jeffry Toler had employed on behalf of both Ken and the hospital, the jury had refused to believe that there had been any life in the body of the dead girl, save only her heart, now beating strongly in the chest of Kevin McCartney and thus saved from death.

Long before the case had even come to trial, however, the gulf developing between Ken and Rebecca had widened when earlier transplant cases, for whose escape from imminent death he had been so highly praised at the time of the original surgery, began to die from rejection.

"Did Ken call you from the courthouse?" Jeffry Toler's question shattered Rebecca's painful reverie.

"I haven't heard from him since I testified at the trial," she admitted.

"I was hoping—" Toler broke off speaking: the look in her eyes had given him the answer.

"The next move is Ken's," she said. "I've done all I can do."

"If he wasn't such a good friend, I'd have tried long ago to knock some sense into that hard head. Or maybe, since I'm a friend to both of you, I should still give it a try."

"You can't help the situation, Jeffry—not while Ken is

convinced that I've gone farther in the medical side of heart disease than he has in the surgical."

"Hell!" Toler exploded. "Ken did some of the earliest transplants in this country and at one time was almost as famous as Christiaan Barnard. If you ask me, it's his ego that's to blame."

Rebecca shook her head. "The real trouble between Ken and me isn't ego, Jeffry. It's his conscience."

"How can that be, when he's always given his patients the best he has—and then some?"

"Ken's convinced that fourteen transplant cases died because he let enthusiasm get the better of his surgical judgment. I don't agree, but I'm sure his unconscious mind still blames me for encouraging him to operate on some patients he wasn't sure about."

"All of them lived through the early weeks after surgery."

"Until rejection killed them, yes."

"Then how could he blame you?"

"I'm not much on psychiatry, but I do know that the unconscious isn't always rational."

"I guess the story of your and Ken's marriage isn't so different from some others I've seen in the medical field, at that," Toler conceded. "Both of you were top rank in your fields—until Ken stumbled and decided he was out of the race."

"I've tried to tell him he isn't, but he won't listen."

"In a contest between husband and wife for success in their careers, it's usually the woman who drops out—to have babies."

"We tried, but with no luck."

"Your fault—or his?"

"Neither, according to Jerry Singleton. He says my reproductive system is absolutely normal, and Ken has enough active spermatozoa to impregnate every female in sight—"

"That might just start to happen, you know. This place teems with attractive single women, divorcees, and wives looking to better themselves."

"For God's sake, Jeffry!" Rebecca's voice rose to an almost hysterical note as the rigid control she'd been

17

exercising over her own fears on just that subject suddenly snapped. "What else can I do?"

"You don't have to be letter perfect in everything."

"Suppose I interpret an electrocardiogram wrongly and some poor devil dies of coronary thrombosis, when he could have been saved by pumping heparin into his bloodstream to keep a clot from forming?" Rebecca demanded heatedly. "How long do you think I could live with myself?"

"I guess you're right. But it's hell to stand by and see two of the finest doctors I know of in their fields beat their heads against a stone wall—especially when I know you're eating your heart out into the bargain, Rebecca."

She reached across the desk to squeeze his hand in a gesture of gratitude. "I can at least thank you for caring, Jeffry."

"What do you want me to do about putting you up for promotion this afternoon? If you hold back, people will start jumping to conclusions."

"That I'm trying to save Ken's face?"

"What else? And frankly I don't think that would make the situation between you any better."

"Go ahead, then. Ken's on the Executive Committee, so he'll know about it anyway." She stood up. "I'd better get to work."

"I'll call you as soon as the meeting's over—not that there's any doubt of the decision."

Toler accompanied Rebecca out into the corridor and stood watching her thoughtfully as she walked down the hall, slim, proud, and very lovely, with the afternoon sunlight pouring through the window at the end of the corridor turning her auburn hair into a golden aureole. As the elevator door opened she turned with a parting wave in his direction, before stepping inside.

Back in his office, he turned the afternoon edition over and sourly studied the second-section headline: COUNCIL FINANCE CHAIRMAN ATTACKS HOSPITAL BOARD IN ROTARY SPEECH.

It was bad enough that he would have to watch Ken Dalton's face that afternoon, when Rebecca was promoted

18

to a position in the Medical Department comparable to Ken's own status in Surgery, without having to listen to the fulminations of a politician like Ross McKenzie for an hour.

Chapter 2

THE CLOCK over the main console of the nursing station said five after three and Carolyn Payson, nursing supervisor of the Consolidated Intensive Care Section, comprising the Medical, Pediatric, and Coronary Intensive Care Units for reasons of efficiency and the most effective use of highly trained personnel, was still on duty. She was considering calling Helga Sundberg at their Bayside Terrace apartment in the unlikely possibility that the other nurse had overslept, when the chime of the Patient Distress Alarm sounded.

One of the world's newest and most sophisticated hospitals—in both construction and function—Biscayne General had been carefully planned to make the maximum of expert care available to the sick or injured. The Emergency Room and adjacent Observation Ward, with the main waiting room and business office, occupied half of the first floor, the rest being devoted to the Intensive Care Units. Concentrated in one section were the expert nursing care, constant physician supervision, and highly sophisticated patient monitoring systems so important in all cases where a life was in jeopardy—whether a child in respiratory distress or a heart threatened by the closing of one of its own arteries from coronary thrombosis.

A glance at the flashing red light on the Patient Selector, with its eight numerals and control buttons, told Carolyn the alarm had come from Cubicle Four, occupied by Carmelita Sanchez. And a flick of a switch produced the sharply delineated wave pattern of the electrocardiogram

19

(ECG in correct parlance instead of the more commonly used EKG derived from its original German name) upon the master oscilloscope screen of the large monitor before her.

The select group of ICU nurses were so highly trained in cardiology that they were generally able to interpret an electrocardiogram more quickly and correctly than the average doctor. And as Carolyn watched the moving point of light outlining the ECG pattern upon the sensitized ground-glass screen of the monitor, she saw that, although the patient's pulse rate was somewhat increased, the heart function was still essentially normal—for one who had been in coma three weeks from the often fatal serum hepatitis.

From the elevation of the nurse's station, Carolyn could see all eight cubicles making up Section One of the ICU, a general-purpose medical ward for critically ill patients, as distinguished from the adjoining Coronary Intensive Care Unit, abbreviated naturally to CICU. And through the open glass door of Cubicle Four she could also see that the nurse bending over Carmelita Sanchez showed no sign of alarm.

Pressing the switch of the two-way communication system beside her, Carolyn spoke into the microphone. "Temperature rising, Ella?"

The startled nurse jumped, then leaned over the bed to speak into the grilled front of the internal communications unit on the wall. "Up half a degree, but there's no change otherwise."

"That was enough to set off the PDA. I'll call Dr. Vogel."

Switching the controls of the monitor screen back to their usual function of recording the vital signs, Carolyn reached for the telephone to call the Medical Fellow in charge of the intensive care patients in that category.

"Please ask Dr. Vogel to call the ICU," she told the paging operator.

"Dr. Vogel's out of the hospital for a few minutes, Miss Payson, but Dr. Raburn is taking his calls. Shall I have him call you?"

"Please." Carolyn knew that, although Carmelita San-

20

chez was technically a patient on the medical service, Mike Raburn had been interested in her ever since he'd performed a liver biopsy shortly after she was admitted to the hospital.

The phone at Carolyn's elbow started blinking moments later. When she picked it up, Mike Raburn's voice sounded in her ear.

"Trouble, Miss Payson?"

"Carmelita's temperature is rising again, Doctor."

"Any of her family there?"

"Only her fiancé, Miguel Quintera."

"Tell Miguel I'll be over to see Carmelita as soon as I'm free; this place has turned into a madhouse again. You'd better put the top half of the cooling blanket on Carmelita, too, but tell Miss Sundberg to watch her temperature closely. It goes down pretty fast with both blanket layers operating."

"Right." Carolyn hung up the phone and passed the order on to the nurse who was specialing Carmelita Sanchez.

Transferred from another hospital in coma two weeks ago, at the insistence of her fiancé upon his arrival in Miami from Spain, where he was a first-year medical student at the University of Madrid Medical School, the lovely Cuban girl was already in an advanced stage of serum hepatitis.

Although the virulent and often fatal liver infection was almost always contracted through transfusion with blood containing the dreaded Australian—shortened to Au—antigen, Carmelita had been inoculated with the virus accidentally. A graduate laboratory technician, she had been taking blood from a patient with the disease when a defective syringe broke, sending a sliver of bloodstained glass into her hand and inoculating her with the deadly Au virus.

Every available weapon had been used in Carmelita's behalf. Large amounts of glucose had been given intravenously to shore up the failing liver and provide much-needed calories to combat those being used up because of the steadily rising temperature. With repeated blood transfusions in large volume, the staff had sought to dilute the deadly virus to a point where the girl's own antibody-producing forces would be able to overcome the life-destroying agent.

But all measures had been to no avail and day after day the young Cuban first-year medical student had sat beside his fiancée or paced the nearby ICU waiting room, his dark eyes wordlessly accusing both doctors and nurses of a failure of which they were already disturbingly conscious, both his presence and the quietly breathing body of the lovely dark-skinned girl a constant reminder of their own helplessness.

"Was that the Patient Distress Alarm again, Miss Payson?" the soft voice of Miguel Quintera, who had been watching TV in the small staff lounge, asked at her elbow.

"Carmelita's temperature rose a little," Carolyn told him. "Dr. Raburn ordered the top of the cooling blanket put on."

"Why does he not come to see her?"

"He's tied up in the Emergency Room but will come up later."

"It doesn't matter." Quintera turned away, his slender shoulders drooping with weariness and loss of hope. "She is dying."

"Something may still happen to save her," said Carolyn. "Don't give up."

But even as she spoke, Carolyn Payson recognized that her voice carried no conviction. For who knew better than she that there were cases where no hope existed, either now or ever, no hope except the blessed relief of death that stubbornly refused to come?

II

"Female coming in," Dr. Valerie LeMoyne called out as she opened the door to the doctors' lounge adjoining the Operating Room Section on the third floor. "Keep decent."

"Be with you in a minute, Val." Dr. Jerry Singleton appeared briefly in the doorway leading to the shower and locker rooms. He wore a towel around his mid-section and

22

his dark wavy hair was damp from the shower. "I want to talk to you."

Moving to the window, Valerie LeMoyne lit a cigarette. Of medium height, she was dark-haired, svelte, and inclined toward somewhat severe fashions bought during an annual vacation on the Continent. Today she was wearing a white nylon pants suit, but with her usual degree of chic.

Val's rise to professor and chief of the Anesthesiology Section at Biscayne General had been meteoric, since she'd come to the United States from Paris and the Sorbonne ten years ago for a residency in her field at Duke.

Jerry Singleton appeared a few minutes later. In double knit blue slacks, a bright blue shirt, maroon sports jacket, and white Italian shoes of soft leather with a crepe sole, he was as fine a specimen of genus *Homo medicus* as one was likely to see—a fact of which Val LeMoyne was physiologically quite aware.

"Without that shapeless hospital gown you insist on wearing at work, you're a very handsome woman, Val." Moving over to where she was standing by the window looking at the street below, he took one of her cigarettes and lit it for himself.

"Since nylon was invented," she said, "women in white have had a distinct advantage over others."

"It does give a better idea of what's beneath while still not removing the excitement of learning for yourself."

"Is that why you and Kay broke up?"

"The divorce was Kay's idea, not mine, but I can't really say I'm sorry; life is harrowing enough for a surgeon without a wife to nag him when he's late for dinner. Besides, Kay had worked enough in a big teaching hospital as a volunteer before we were married to know what goes on in one of the most highly sexed atmospheres existing anywhere—except maybe in a brothel. She refused to believe I wasn't making out on the side."

"Weren't you?" Val's tone held a tinge of mockery.

"Actually, I wasn't. I tried to convince Kay of that, even offered to leave the university and go out into private practice—"

23

"Where you would have made twice what you make here."

"And more. But I also like teaching, which was something else Kay couldn't understand. I guess because her father's a gynecologist who has made a fortune out of small fibroids."

"To a hysterectomy-minded surgeon they're worth their weight in gold," Val agreed.

"Until a patient drops dead on the day she's leaving the hospital, like the one I lost last week," said the surgeon glumly.

"Nobody can prevent pulmonary embolism, Jerry—just like we still don't know how to prevent the occasional anesthetic death for no reason anyone can find. They're simply hazards both surgeons and anesthesiologists have to face."

"Still, if I hadn't operated on that one, she wouldn't be dead."

"You're not going to let an unavoidable death throw you the way Ken Dalton has let those transplant deaths do him, are you?" she asked sharply.

"No." Jerry Singleton unconsciously straightened his shoulders, which had slumped momentarily. "Like you say, embolism is a normal hazard of even the simplest operation."

"Cheer up," said Val. "You've got a lot to live for, my friend. Just think of all the pleasure you're giving the women you go out with. And when you marry—"

"Oh no! I'm not putting on the ball and chain again."

"That's what you're saying now. But from what I've seen of divorced men, it takes about a year for them to finish sowing all the wild oats they'd been dreaming about while they were married. Then they settle down and marry again, usually to someone very much like the wife they divorced."

"God forbid! Besides, Kay divorced me—"

"That doesn't make any difference. Still, you might be the exception. Certainly you're much too handsome and sexually attractive for anybody to believe you could really be a family man the second time around, Jerry. And from

24

the hospital scuttlebutt, you've given what was obviously a natural talent for seduction quite a high polish."

Jerry Singleton grinned. "I have to do something in my spare time, and I don't like golf. Come to think of it—and this isn't the first time—why not join me in an exciting and tempestuous affair? I could show you some of the things I've learned."

"I came into the lounge for a cigarette, Jerry, not looking for an invitation to seduction."

"I know you like scuba diving. Why not go to the Keys with me this weekend?"

Valerie LeMoyne stubbed out her cigarette in an ashtray on the window sill before she answered—and hoped he didn't notice the sudden trembling of her hand.

"You're very sweet and very attractive, Jerry," she said on a deliberately casual note. "But I was badly hurt once, there's even a small scar left."

"Scarred hearts thrive on moderate exercise, my dear. All cardiologists recommend it."

"Fair enough," she said. "Will you give me a rain check?"

"Of course."

"I'll let you know Thursday evening." Val looked at her watch. "It's time to start the next case. Good hunting, Jerry."

III

Dr. Karen Fletcher finished her daily thirty laps of the Bayside Terrace swimming pool and climbed the ladder to the rim of the pool. Pulling off the rubber cap that had protected her silver-tinted hair from the water, she shook the silky pile loose until it tumbled about her shoulders. Moving to a beach chair, she picked up a large nubby towel and began to rub her body dry in the nylon tank suit that was almost as revealing as its absence would have been, not at all unconscious of the admiring eyes of a pair of medical students who had been dozing beside the pool until she came out and started swimming.

At thirty, Karen Fletcher had already achieved many

25

of the goals she'd set for herself long ago, when she left the small Midwestern town that was her birthplace for college—and never returned. Already a championship swimmer in high school, she'd been able to parlay an athletic scholarship into a college pre-med course. And the decided flair for bacteriology and pharmacology she'd shown in college courses, plus her emergence as a serious contender for Olympic honors in swimming, had guaranteed her medical school tuition.

From there, Karen Fletcher's rise had been meteoric, for the most part because of a real ability and flair for the fields of pathology and toxicology, but to some extent because a petite beauty, whose pocket Venus proportions were exquisitely perfect, was enough of an anomaly in the musty basements of pathology laboratories to be notably distinctive. Assistant professor of pathology four years out of medical school, she had come to Biscayne University Medical School as an associate professor two years before.

When Karen bent to pick up a comb that had fallen out of the folded towel, one of the watching students gave a shrill whistle of appreciation.

"Cool it, fellows," she said. "The university frowns on faculty-student fraternizing."

"There's nothing fraternal about what I'm thinking right now, Dr. Fletcher." The shorter one, a merry-eyed Cuban, grinned impudently. "Is it true that you won a gold medal in the 1967 Olympics?"

"It was '68, Mendoza, don't make me any older than I am." Karen picked up a short terry robe from the chair and slipped her arms into it, hiding her torso but leaving the superb legs of a championship swimmer fully exposed.

"To me you're the epitome of the eternal female, Dr. Fletcher," said the dark-skinned Mendoza. "It's too bad you're a pathologist and all that loveliness has to be wasted on the dead."

Karen laughed as she picked up the magazine she had brought out with her, in case she felt like reading after her swim. *It has never been wasted yet, my friend,* she thought. *And never will be—not since the day I discovered how really valuable it is.*

Halfway across the stretch of lawn between the pool and the rear lobby entrance to the Terrace, where Karen had an apartment, she came around a jacaranda bush that was a mass of violet-colored flowers and stopped suddenly to keep from running over a small boy of perhaps five. Squatting in the middle of the graveled walk leading from Bayside Arms, the large, less expensive garden apartment complex a good block away, to the old hotel and the hospital, he was panting audibly. But even if she hadn't recognized the boy, the odd ducklike posture and the bluish tint to his lips, ear lobes, and the skin of his torso, exposed by the brief shorts that were his only garment, would have told her medically trained mind that he suffered from congenital heart disease.

"Hello, Dr. Fletcher," said the boy, smiling.

"Are you all right, Dale?" Karen had recognized the small son of Peggy Tyndall, the physician's assistant who was also chief technician in the Cardiac Research Laboratory.

"I'm okay. Just stopped to get my breath."

"Do you have to rest more often lately?"

The tendency to squat suddenly at play and rest long enough to breathe freely again, plus the cyanotic hue of skin and mucous membranes, were characteristic of a heart malformed long before birth and unable to pump enough blood through the lungs to supply the body's need for oxygen.

"Maybe—when I run a lot." Dale jumped to his feet. " 'Scuse me, Doctor. I gotta go."

"Where?"

"To see Kevin, he gives me beer."

"To a little boy like you? I can't believe it!"

Dale was gone, running toward the door leading into Bayside Terrace and the Dolphin Lounge, where Kevin McCartney was bartender. After a moment Karen followed but stopped at the door of the dim-lit lounge when she saw Dale climb confidently upon a stool at the end of the bar.

"There's my boy!" Kevin McCartney's rich Irish brogue came to Karen's ears as she watched. "What'll you have?"

"Beer," said Dale. "In a frosted mug—and one for Dr. Fletcher."

"Dr. Fletcher?" Kevin squinted toward the door. "Oh, hello, Doctor. I didn't see you."

"I followed Dale—when he told me you gave him beer."

Kevin laughed. "It's root beer. He likes it in a frosted mug—Western style. Can I get you anything?"

"No, thanks. I've been having my daily swim."

"Bet you could win another gold medal if they were staging the Olympics now. I watched on TV when you won in '68."

"I doubt that I'm in championship form right now, but thanks anyway," said Karen. "You see Dale often?"

"Nearly every day. Why?"

"Would you say he's getting more short of breath lately?"

"I'm okay, Dr. Fletcher," said Dale. "Next year I'm going to school. And when I get older, Dr. Dalton is going to operate on me, so I can play baseball like the other boys."

"I think you're right, Doctor." Kevin spoke softly. "But I didn't want to worry Peggy by mentioning it."

"I'll talk to her," said Karen. "Right now, I'd better go up and get a shower before this air conditioning gives me a cold."

"Any news about Dr. Cooper?" Kevin asked.

Two years away from retirement, Dr. Adrian Cooper, professor of pathology and head of the department, as well as medical examiner for the county, had been felled by a massive stroke, leaving him paralyzed for the past two months. As his second-in-command, so to speak, Karen Fletcher had headed the department with her usual efficiency, though on a temporary basis, ever since.

"I'm afraid it's not very good," she told Kevin.

"Too bad. He's a fine man."

"And a great doctor," Karen agreed. "So long, Dale."

"Good-by, Dr. Fletcher," said the boy as he climbed down from the stool. "Thanks, Kevin."

"Any time, Dale."

"*Madre de Dios!* What a woman!" Mendoza, the Cuban student, had entered the lounge by the side door and taken a stool at the far end of the bar. "Did you look at those gams, my friend—and what goes with 'em?"

"I gave up them games when Dr. Dalton put the new heart inside my chest," said the bartender. "What'll you have?"

"Beer to cool my fevered thoughts. Did you ever see as much woman crammed into such a small package?"

"We Irish don't waste time makin' over women the way you Latins do." Keven grinned as he slid a tall stein of beer down the polished bar so it stopped directly in front of Mendoza. "We prefer the 'How 'bout it, babe?' approach. You'd be surprised how often it works, too."

"I'm not surprised, we Latins use it too," said Mendoza. "Know what the students call Dr. Fletcher?"

"I can imagine—but what is it?"

"The Black Widow."

"Why? She's certainly not black—"

"And not a widow, either, as far as I know. But something about her tells you, if she'd ever let you make love to her, she'd eat you alive."

"I suppose you'd like to be eaten?"

"You gotta go sometime." Mendoza shrugged. "And what better way?"

"I guess you've got a point there," Kevin admitted. "But she's a good doctor, isn't she?"

"I don't know how she'd be in practice, but as a pathologist she's tops. In fact she's so good as a teacher that for a little while you even forget she's a beautiful woman—and that's saying something. The students have started a pool on whether she'll take Dr. Cooper's place—for good."

"How are you betting?"

"On her, of course. That baby can have anything she wants—including me."

"Even if you're eaten up?"

29

Mendoza shrugged and drained the stein. "Like we were just saying, what a way to go!"

"Wait a minute," said Kevin, and Mendoza stopped in the doorway. "You're practically a doctor, aren't you?"

"Only one more semester to go. Why?"

"Did you see the boy that was just in here?"

"Sure. I've examined him in the Cardiac Outpatient Clinic, too."

"What's the outlook for him?"

"Not bad—with luck. He's got what's called the tetralogy of Fallot, which means the blood channels inside his heart are pretty well crossed up. Dr. Helen Taussig and Dr. Alfred Blalock in Baltimore worked out an operation years ago that corrects most of the trouble. It isn't very dangerous, either, but most heart surgeons nowadays like to wait 'til the child is around seven or eight, when the heart is large enough for them to use open heart surgery and they can do a better job. The risks aren't much greater than the Blalock-Taussig operation then either."

"And afterwards Dale will really be practically normal?"

"Almost as if he'd been born that way." The Cuban gave Kevin an appraising look. "How about yourself, friend?"

"I'm fine, just fine," said Kevin heartily. "Going fishing tomorrow, down at Marathon."

"The boat my family escaped in from Cuba landed at Marathon. I was only a boy but you can bet heaven won't look any better than that place did after five days at sea in an open yawl."

IV

"Sometimes I wonder whether I'm really cut out for this business," Mike Raburn told Mrs. Faye Connor, three-to-eleven nursing supervisor for the Emergency Department, after talking to Carolyn Payson. "I'm always letting people I can't do anything for make me feel guilty."

"That's what makes you stand out from the average run of doctors like a diamond in a ten-cent-store ring," said the veteran nurse. "The Cuban girl again?"

"And the medical student she's engaged to. Every time I make rounds and stop to see her, he looks at me like he expects me to pass a miracle and cure her."

"That's what you get for building up the kind of reputation you have around here. What's happened to Carmelita now?"

"Her temperature just set off the PDA. Second time today."

"I've never seen anyone as deep in hepatic coma as she is come out of it. Have you?"

Mike shook his head. "Never. I'm getting so I hate to even go by the room. She's so pretty, even through the jaundice, and Miguel's so young—it sort of gets you to look at them."

"You could pass 'em up, you know. She's really on the medical service."

"Yeah. But I still go, maybe because I'm nothing but a sloppy sentimentalist at heart."

"Not at heart—all heart," the nurse corrected him. "Which reminds me—when are you going to get yourself a girl?"

"When I can find somebody who sees the beautiful spirit behind this mug of mine. Not thinking of getting divorced, are you?"

"If I were twenty years younger, I might. Now get out of here so I can do some work."

A tall interne in rumpled whites appeared at the door of the nursing station. His face was flushed with annoyance. "A Negro woman's out there with a little boy, Mike. She won't let anybody see him but you."

"Coming, Dr. Gaither." Mike winked at the nursing supervisor. "At least somebody loves me."

"Don't go fishing for compliments. Everybody at Biscayne General loves you, Dr. Raburn, and you damned well know it."

In the cubicle to which Dr. Nolan Gaither directed Mike, a tall, striking-looking Negro woman was standing beside the examining table, holding the hand of a boy of perhaps six who lay upon it. The child appeared to be unconscious but every few minutes he cried out and clutched at his abdomen, before lapsing into stupor again.

"Rachel Gates!" Mike Raburn's voice was warm. "What's wrong?"

"Thank God you're here, Dr. Raburn," said the mother. "Joe told me any time we got into trouble and I couldn't get our pediatrician, to come to you."

"This is Big Joe Gates's wife and his son Joey; they're old friends," Mike told the interne. "Dr. Nolan Gaither, Mrs. Rachel Gates."

"I'm sorry if I seemed huffy, Dr. Gaither," said the golden-skinned woman, "but I was worried."

"It's all right, Mrs. Gates. If I'd known your husband was the Snappers' star forward, I'd probably have given you the keys to the hospital."

"What happened, Rachel?" Mike moved into the cubicle and picked up the boy's wrist.

"Joey went to day camp this morning; it's run by our church and the bus picks him up at eight o'clock. The school nurse called me about an hour ago to say he was complaining of pains in his legs and stomach. By the time I got there he was like you see him now—in sort of a stupor."

"Was he all right yesterday?" The surgeon's big hand had been moving gently over the child's abdomen but lingered now just beneath the rib margin on the left side.

"Joey played ball with some neighbor kids after he came home from camp yesterday. We took Big Joe to the airport later; he's in San Francisco helping negotiate the new contract for the players' union. On the way home Joey insisted on stopping for some ice cream, he's crazy about that peppermint stick flavor at Howard Johnson's."

"So am I—and a few million other people."

Taking Dr. Nolan Gaither's hand in a casual gesture, Mike placed it on the upper left side of the boy's abdomen. The sudden alertness in Gaither's eyes told him the interne had detected the enlargement of the spleen beneath the ribs.

"Take a look at the nail beds, too," Mike added before turning back to the mother.

"Anything else you can tell me, Rachel?" He reached for an ophthalmoscope, hanging from a rack on the wall.

"Nothing that I know of. They said at the camp that he didn't fall or anything."

Separating the boy's eyelids, the big doctor flashed the light into the pupil. It contracted immediately, as it should, so he pulled down the eyelid itself and moved the bright spot of illumination about.

"Look at this," he told the interne, and Dr. Gaither transferred his attention from marking out the size of the spleen on the boy's abdomen with a wax pencil to the conjunctiva—the white part—of the eye.

"There was a report in one of the journals the other day about near obliteration of the capillaries in the conjunctiva," Mike said.

"I see that but—"

"Did you order any blood work?"

"The technician has already taken the blood. It should be ready in a few minutes."

"Mrs. Connor," Mike called to the nursing supervisor, "will you watch the patient while Dr. Gaither and I go to the laboratory?"

"Certainly, Doctor."

In the Emergency Department Laboratory, which had its own staff covering the ER itself, the Acute Observation Ward, and the several divisions of the ICU, a technician had just finished staining a blood smear. Taking the slide from her, Mike Raburn placed it beneath the microscope and focused the instrument carefully.

He already knew what to expect from the history, the fact that little Joey Gates was black, and the near obliteration of tiny blood vessels in the lining of the eyelids—and he was not disappointed. Spread out on the slide in the bright light reflected up through the lens system of the microscope, the normally biscuit-shaped red blood cells showed all sorts of weird configurations instead. By far the larger number were much the shape of an Arab scimitar.

33

"Take a look," Mike told Nolan Gaither, and slid off the stool.

The interne adjusted the controls of the instrument to fit his own eyes. "My God!" he exclaimed. "Sickle cell anemia."

"What you're seeing is a crisis." Mike reached for the telephone. "Not many that severe get well."

"Get me Dr. Henderson—stat!" he told the operator.

Less than a minute after the operator started paging the pediatric resident, Gus Henderson's voice sounded in Mike Raburn's ear.

"What's up, Mike?" the baby specialist asked.

"Big Joe Gates's son is in the Emergency Room with a sickle cell crisis. His nail beds are already dusky from cyanosis—"

"I'm on my way." The telephone clicked in Mike's ear.

"Alert Pediatric ICU that we'll be bringing them a patient in a few minutes," Mike told the interne crisply. "I'll go talk to Rachel."

"It's a severe crisis, isn't it?" Gaither asked.

"That boy's lung capillaries are so clogged by abnormally shaped red blood cells that he isn't getting the oxygen he needs to keep his brain functioning at full steam. So far, there's only enough oxygen lack to cause semicoma but his pO_2 could drop below the critical level any minute and the brain cells start being damaged beyond repair, along with those in his heart, his kidneys, and a lot of other organs. If we don't reverse that process in the next hour or so, Joey will either die or be a vegetable the rest of his life."

Chapter 3

ONLY OCCASIONALLY now was Richard Payson able to hold his head still and keep his eyes focused long enough to read the time of day on the clock above the nurses' station controlling the section of the ICU that included the glass-fronted cubicle where he'd lain for nearly a month. But then time held only one thing for him any more, the five minutes or so before seven in the morning when Carolyn, his daughter, stopped by on the way to her post as morning shift nursing supervisor in the ICU and again during the hour she customarily spent with him at the beginning of the afternoon shift, before leaving the hospital. The flashes of lucidity were farther and farther apart now, too; when they did come, however briefly, his own mental agony and particularly the torture he saw reflected in the face of his lovely daughter were always worse than before.

He'd first realized something was wrong over a year ago, when little things like sudden explosions of temper, of which he was immediately ashamed, had begun to haunt him like specters from the past. He'd not been able to understand the change and only when his signature had started breaking up to a point where the bank began to query him about checks he'd written had he admitted to himself that the strange movements of his fingers, particularly when he was engaged in some activity requiring intense concentration, were more than simply a result of the increasing nervousness that so often gripped him.

The first time he'd really suspected the grave nature of the change within himself was when he'd run to board an airplane and fallen on the dry, non-slippery tarmac. He had experienced real panic then and, on the way back to Atlanta, had consulted Dr. Peter Gross, chief of neurology

35

at Biscayne General and a professor of medicine on the faculty of the medical school. An old friend, Dr. Gross had identified the pattern of progressively rapid deterioration of almost every body function, accompanied by loss of connection with reality at times, as a sinister gift from a forgotten ancestor, the gene of a malignant heritage handed down from person to person.

"Huntington's disease?" Richard Payson had asked when Dr. Gross told him the diagnosis. "What's that?"

"A progressive deterioration of nerve tissue in the brain, first identified by Dr. George Huntington in 1872 as a strange form of chorea. Did you ever see anyone with St. Vitus' Dance?"

"I had an uncle who was the town ne'er-do-well. Everybody laughed at him because he was always shaking and trembling—except when he got drunk enough to go to sleep. Then he only jerked occasionally."

"How old was he?"

"Maybe forty—or forty-five."

"He probably inherited Huntington's disease—we call it H-D now—like you did."

"But nobody else in my family ever had anything like it."

"H-D usually develops late. How old was your father when he died?"

"Not much over thirty-five, he was killed in an automobile accident—" Richard Payson had stopped, aghast. "Are you saying—?"

"The disease rarely appears before thirty-five or forty."

"Then Father could have developed symptoms—if he'd lived long enough?"

"Quite possibly," Dr. Gross confirmed. "The genes sometimes manage to skip generations but, whenever either parent develops the condition, one or more of the children will have it."

"What are the odds?"

"Fifty-fifty at the very least."

"My God! What have I done to my daughter?"

"You haven't done anything to her," said the neurologist. "After all, you had no way of knowing—"

"Suppose I had? What could I have done?"

"Not having children stops the disease from passing, of course. The main trouble is that people who develop H-D in later life cannot know, while they're young, whether they're going to have it or not—since it usually doesn't appear until after their children are born. And by that time there's no going back."

"How much do you suppose Carolyn knows about this —this Huntington's disease?"

"She probably studied it in her nursing courses at Gainesville. Until a few years ago it was barely mentioned, but there's been a lot of publicity since '67 when Woody Guthrie died of it."

"How long did Guthrie know he had it?"

"The first symptoms appeared about thirteen years before his death."

"You mean I may be a burden on Carolyn for that long?" Richard Payson had asked, his voice taut with horror.

"I can't make a hard and fast prognosis, of course. But—"

"I want the truth, please."

"Considering the rapidity with which your symptoms developed—"

"I probably won't last long?"

"That's a possibility."

"And my only hope?"

"Tranquilizers help sometimes and a lot of other drugs have been tried."

"But none of them actually affect the course of the disease?"

"None that we know of."

"It's incredible that a single one of your chromosomes can determine what will happen to you when you're thirty-five, forty, even fifty years old—and condemn your children to the same fate."

"Not all of them," said Dr. Gross. "There's a fifty-fifty chance because, in the production of sperm and ova for reproduction, each chromosome splits."

"I know almost nothing about heredity, so you'd better start farther back than that."

37

"Each body cell is composed of a nucleus of dark material known as chromatin and a surrounding zone called cytoplasm that stains very lightly in a microscopic preparation causing the nucleus to stand out," Dr. Gross had explained. "When studied under a high enough magnification, the nucleus can be seen to contain a skein of chromatin with tiny dark spots along the strands that make it up. The dark spots are the genes that carry all hereditary human characteristics. Every normal body cell —except the sex cells which are specialized for reproduction—has forty-six chromosomes divided into two sets of twenty-three each plus innumerable genes. In the offspring, one set comes from the mother's ovum and the other from the father's sperm cell."

"Are you saying that every cell in a person's body carries genes from both the mother and the father?"

"Excluding the sex cells—yes."

"Then how can anyone escape inheriting every trait from both parents?"

"Because the first body cell—formed by the fusion of the sperm and egg—can have only forty-six chromosomes. Which means that, before the two sex cells unite at the time the ovum is fertilized, half of the chromosomes each of them has are discarded in the form of what are called polar bodies to keep the new individual from having ninety-two instead of forty-six chromosomes."

"Reducing the chance of inheriting a trait like H-D to fifty-fifty?"

"Exactly—unless both parents carry it. In that case, transmission of the disease from parent to child is a certainty—"

"God! What an heirloom!"

"There have been some real dillies in history," Dr. Gross confirmed. "Through Queen Victoria, members of royal families all over Europe wound up being bleeders—suffering from hemophilia. It's transmitted through the female but affects only the male."

"So what do I do?"

"Put your affairs in order—and wait."

"For death?"

"We may discover some way to treat the disease—a lot of work is being done on it."

"That's like having cancer and sitting around waiting for someone to discover a cure before you die. It would seem to be about as futile a reason for living as I can think of."

"We used to think the same thing about people who are prone to attacks of apparently senseless violence," said Dr. Gross. "Then a few years ago we learned that many such attacks are caused by epilepsy limited to the temporal lobe of the brain. The whole picture still seemed hopeless, though, until some brain surgeons started removing the part of the temporal lobe that's involved. Or using a much simpler treatment consisting of putting a needle into the area through a small hole drilled in the skull and destroying that part of the brain either with cold or by electric coagulation. Now a lot of these people can be saved to live useful lives."

"How long can we keep the truth from my daughter?"

"I don't advise it, Richard. Carolyn's a brilliant girl, one of the best nurses we have. Besides, she's engaged, I believe, to a fine young pediatrician named Gus Henderson."

"I know him."

"I don't know what their wedding plans are, but neither of them may want to take the chance of bringing a child into the world with a black gene like the one for H-D as a heritage."

"We'll cross that bridge when we get to it," Richard Payson had said firmly. "I'm going back to Atlanta—to wait. And don't tell her."

"As you wish, Richard. We've been friends too long for me not to want to help you—even though I think you're making a mistake."

"There's always a way out—for me."

"Some people with H-D take it. But as a doctor I cannot countenance suicide."

"Even when it's the simplest answer?"

Dr. Gross shrugged but gave no answer. And, in the end, Richard Payson had not possessed the courage to take his own life, although he cursed himself many times later because of that failure—now that he was no longer physically able to do so.

II

Gus Henderson's examination of Joey Gates was brief. The clumped red blood cells under the microscope with their bizarre shapes that resembled nothing except sickle cell anemia, plus the urgency demanded by the deepening color of the boy's blood, indicating oxygen lack, made rapid treatment imperative.

"You've got a very sick boy, Mrs. Gates," the tall pediatrician told the mother. "He's in a severe sickle cell crisis and we'll have to put him under intensive care immediately—"

"Aren't there some new drugs, Doctor?"

"We'll use the treatment with intravenous injection of urea that you probably read about, even though we're not as sure of its value as we were at first. Even more important, we'll use potassium cyanate, which seems to have even more promise. Right now, though, the sickled cells are sticking together to form masses that clog the small blood vessels of his lungs and other organs, interfering with his getting the oxygen his brain needs. That's why he became unconscious."

"Can't you give him oxygen?"

"We will, as soon as we can get him to the ICU and start—"

"Gus." Mike Raburn's voice was suddenly urgent. "There's another way—the hyperbaric chamber."

"It's never been tried," said the pediatrician doubtfully. "And we need to get the urea and cyanate started right away."

"He can be getting that intravenously while he's in the chamber."

"What are you talking about, Mike?" Rachel Gates asked.

"We have a large tank here called a hyperbaric chamber," the surgeon explained. "Inside it patients with ox-

40

ygen lack can breathe the gas under pressure so more of it gets into the blood."

"If the red blood cells can get through the capillaries," Gus Henderson added.

"Obviously we can't increase the number of cells getting through until the drugs have time to exert their effect," Mike said somewhat impatiently. "But we can still double or even triple the amount of oxygen carried by the cells that *do* get through. And that's certainly worth trying."

"Okay," said the pediatrician. "He's critical enough for desperate measures."

"I'll go into the chamber with him," Mike told Rachel.

"I've had a lot of experience with hyperbaric oxygen in connection with some geriatric work I've been doing, studying its effect on the deterioration that so often goes with age."

"Big Joe and I appreciate what you're doing, Mike," said Rachel. "Joey likes you a lot, so if he wakes up in there he won't be afraid."

"I'll get things going in the Hyperbaric Laboratory." Mike moved to a wall telephone. But he didn't add that, unless the desperate measures they were taking to save Joey's life were able to turn the tide of crisis in the boy's favor, he might never be conscious enough to be afraid.

The pressure chamber was at the end of the long corridor through the ground floor of the Biscayne General tower that also gave access, by a side door, to the main ICU. As Mike was passing the door, Helga came out of it and the two almost collided.

"This seems to be my lucky day," he said. "Are you okay?"

"Sure. Just because my suprarenals overshot the mark doesn't mean my whole endocrine system is permanently out of balance."

"God forbid!" he said fervently, and Helga laughed.

"I learned one thing today, at least; the superefficient Dr. Raburn is also quite human. Where are you off to in such a hurry?"

41

"I'm taking a patient into the hyperbaric chamber in a few minutes."

"Will the pressure be very high?"

"As high as we can stand it. Why?"

"I'm beginning to worry—"

"About me?"

"Of course not, you're indestructible." Her voice had taken on a mocking note. "I'm going to put out a sex alert on the grapevine. If all that oxygen you'll be breathing under pressure has the same effect on you that it has on some of those old fellows you've been taking into the chamber, feminine virtue isn't going to be safe around here for the next three or four days."

III

Standing beside her father, after turning the ICU over to Helga Sundberg shortly after three, Carolyn Payson tried hard to keep from crying—and didn't quite succeed. Even someone living in the midst of a constant battle against death, as she did, could hardly fail to be moved by the sight of her own father lying helpless, his body twitching constantly in the purposeless, uncontrollable movements of Huntington's disease.

She had first learned of his illness about a month earlier when, disturbed because she hadn't heard from her father for some time, she had asked a friend in Atlanta to check on him and discovered that he had entered a nursing home of his own volition. Carolyn had gone to Atlanta immediately and brought Richard Payson back to Biscayne General, placing him on the ICU where she could watch him closely herself.

At Carolyn's insistence Dr. Gross had revealed the details of his earlier examination and the marked progression of the disease process since that time. Until now even Richard Payson's eye muscles were beyond control and his eyeballs jerked constantly when he was awake, gripped by the same malignant force that was rapidly destroying the strong, vigorous man of forty-five who had tossed her in the air as a little girl, catching her when she fell, squealing with delight, in arms that could be as gentle as the touch of the mother who had died bringing her into the world.

Sometimes Carolyn thought her father was still able to recognize her. But more often than not these past weeks, as the destruction of a man by his own genes progressed with inexorable determination, she was sure he no longer even knew her. Only rarely did he speak any more either, and even then the words usually tumbled over each other in an unintelligible jargon that was almost always meaningless.

"Let me die! Let me die!"

The three words—the desperate need they signified penetrating even through the grip of the monstrous evil that had risen from the heritage of past generations to destroy him—kept constantly recurring like a desperate prayer. He spoke them again now as Carolyn stood beside his bed, holding a hand that writhed constantly within her grasp. For once the words were amazingly clear, too, considering the meaningless stream that tumbled from his lips except when he was in the grip of strong sedation. And, hearing again those same three words, Carolyn felt her heart twist in an agony of pain and frustration at her own helplessness.

"I've ordered a sedative," a familiar voice said at Carolyn's elbow and she turned to find Dr. Peter Gross standing there.

At the sight of the neurologist's little goatee and soft brown eyes, warm now with compassion for her, she could hold back the tears no longer and buried her face against the white coat of the older doctor.

"Let it come out, child," he said. "He doesn't recognize anyone now."

"But he can still speak."

"Only because the wish to die is more powerful than anything except the life force."

"I'm all right now." Carolyn dried her eyes with the large white handkerchief Dr. Gross gave her. "It's just that everything's happened so fast."

"No faster than your father wanted it to happen, once he knew the truth," the neurologist assured her. "H-D isn't a pleasant fact to face."

43

"Why must he face it any longer then—when he wants to die so badly?"

"Many sick people say they want to die, Carolyn; you're too experienced a nurse yourself not to know—"

"Surely you don't think he wants to live now?"

"I'm not sure he isn't past knowing what he wants—"

"Let me die! Let me die!" The voice from the bed was a prayer—to God and to those whose hands could play God, at least long enough to deliver a man from torture—and a cry of protest, too, against the crucifixion of the spirit Richard Payson was undergoing.

"Listen to that!" Carolyn seized the lapels of the long white coat Dr. Gross was wearing. "Listen to that and tell me he doesn't know what he wants."

"I've sworn to preserve life, Carolyn—and so for that matter have you. Neither of us has the right—"

"But he was always so strong, so vital. You don't know what it is to see him now."

"We'll make it as easy for him as we can—count on that. It's you I'm worried about."

"I know what's ahead," said the dark-haired nurse quietly. "Quite a lot has been written about Huntington's lately and most of it's in the medical school library. I think I've read it all since I brought Father here."

"Then you realize its place in your own future?"

"It *controls* my future, Dr. Pete. And *has* controlled it, since long before I was born."

IV

Tanks for increasing the pressure under which air was breathed had been used for many years, when deep-sea divers or caisson workers developed complications in their work. The hyperbaric—literally high pressure—chamber at Biscayne General was only a sophisticated version of the older pressure chambers.

Consisting of a double tank with a connecting air lock between, it allowed those involved in treatment or experiments to go from one chamber to the other and had been one of the most expensive single parts of the recently completed hospital. Only a grant from the government, through the Navy, had enabled it to be built at all by the Hospital Board responsible for the giant medical complex on Biscayne Bay.

Occupying a separate room at the back of the squat wing behind the main hospital tower that also housed the Cardiac Research Laboratory, the hyperbaric chamber had thick metal walls interspersed with heavy glass ports. Through them the technicians handling the controls outside, by means of which the pressure was raised and lowered inside the tank, could also watch what was happening inside and carry out immediate measures to release the pressure and enter the chamber, in case of emergency.

The operation of the chamber itself was the province of a specially trained team of technicians, all former Navy diving experts. Two were always on duty whenever the pressure tank was being used. One handled the control panel for the pump that compressed the air inside and the valves by which the pressure could be released; the other technician watched those participating in its use through the main observation port.

Joey Gates, still unconscious, was brought into the Hyperbaric Laboratory on an amazing new stretcher that was practically a portable intensive care unit in itself, developed for handling acute heart conditions. Oxygen from a tank and respirator on the stretcher had also filled Joey's lungs with every breath, while he was being moved from the Pediatric ICU—naturally called PICU by students and staff—to the Hyperbaric Laboratory.

As soon as the boy and Mike Raburn were inside, the metal doors comprising the end of the chamber itself were swung shut and locked into place. Air from the main pump immediately began to rush into the chamber, raising the pressure inside steadily. But since air is only one fifth oxygen and it was vitally important to raise the concentration of the gas in the unconscious child's brain cells as quickly as possible, Mike now removed the mask connected to the oxygen tank on the stretcher, replacing it with a breathing bag and pressure mask drawing from the main oxygen supply of the hospital. Thus, as the pressure inside the hyperbaric chamber was raised, the same effect

45

was exerted upon the breathing bag, increasing the flow of oxygen to Joey Gates's red blood cells and with it the concentration of the vital gas in the body tissues.

"How high do you want us to raise the pressure, Dr. Raburn?"

The voice of the technician from the speaker in the ceiling of the tank was unnaturally loud, shut up as they were in a constricted space. To answer, Mike had only to lift a telephone from its hook on the wall of the tank, within easy reach of the stool on which he was sitting beside the unconscious child.

"Try two atmospheres at first," he directed.

"That should be safe even with him breathing more oxygen."

Mike understood what was troubling the chief technician: the odd fact that the greatest hazard in the use of a hyperbaric chamber was oxygen poisoning, since an overdose of the gas could cause convulsions that were as much of a danger as a lack of the same gas.

"One atmosphere," the voice of the technician reported moments later via the speaker.

"We're okay," said Mike. "You can take it on up."

Gus Henderson had applied a number of delicate sensors to Joey's body, as well as threading a tiny nylon catheter into an arm vein and passing it through ever larger vein channels up the arm and into the chest, where it lay with its tip near the left side of the heart.

Inserting the catheter almost to the heart itself was a precaution taken to prevent irritation of the smaller vein channels leading to it by the urea-cyanate solution being injected to reverse the sickling process in the red blood cells. Flowing slowly from the end of the venous catheter into the large stream of blood being received by the upper chamber of the heart, the atrium, the urea-cyanate solution was less likely to injure the delicate walls of the venous system.

The monitor attached to the special stretcher upon which Joey lay was recording his heart action in a continuous flashing pattern on its small ground-glass screen and at the same time the heart picture was being transmitted

46

by telemetry to a receiver outside the chamber where it could be watched by others. While the pressure inside the tank rose steadily, as evidenced by the manometer on the instrument panel beside the door, Mike carefully checked the intravenous catheter and increased the drip rate in the glass chamber of the IV setup. Still another and larger catheter, placed in the urinary bladder, was showing a steady flow, indicating that Joey's kidney function, a crucial factor in recovery, was holding up satisfactorily.

"Two atmospheres, Dr. Raburn," the technician reported.

"Hold it there for the time being while we give the red blood cells a chance to load up with oxygen," said Mike. "It's hard to estimate the degree of cyanosis with his skin pigment, but I don't think it's getting any deeper."

"Hold on two." The technician moved aside and Gus Henderson's face appeared at the glass port.

"Everything okay, Mike?" he asked.

"It looks that way in here, but he's still unconscious."

"The ECG is coming through fine. How high do you plan to take the pressure?"

"We're at two atmospheres, but it doesn't look as if that's going to do the trick."

"How high can you go before the danger of oxygen convulsion sets in?"

"Probably not much above four atmospheres. Actually, an oxygen convulsion would tell us we're saturating the brain, which is what we want to do, and I could always control it by letting him breathe the air in here and wash the excess O_2 out of his brain cells. But I'd still rather not deliberately throw Joey into a convulsion."

"I just finished talking to Big Joe Gates in California," said Gus. "He was relieved to know the boy is in your hands and said he's coming back as soon as he can get a plane out."

"I think we'll go to three atmospheres now," said Mike. "Can you stick around for a few minutes, Gus?"

"Sure." Then the pediatrician's expression suddenly changed. "Not any more, Mike; they're calling a CODE FIVE for the Emergency Room."

Her afternoon interrupted at the start by the arrival of Joey Gates, Mrs. Faye Connor had just finished reading the seven-to-three nursing supervisor's summary of Emergency Department activities during the morning shift, before sending it on to the Nursing Office, when an ambulance whined to a stop at the loading ramp. Seconds later a Rescue Squad stretcher from one of the crack Miami units burst through the double doors leading outside.

"You don't have to knock the doors down. Callahan." The nurse spoke severely to the tall fireman at the head of the stretcher.

"We've got an OD here that's near term, Mrs. Connor. DOA, too, from the looks of it, but I think I heard the fetal heart."

The cryptic abbreviations told a graphic story, one the gray-haired nurse had seen many times during her years in command of the Emergency Department nursing staff. OD meant "overdose," usually of heroin, an all too frequent diagnosis in what had come to be called the Drug Age, and DOA was the universal term for "Dead On Arrival." But it was hearing the fetal heart inside the mother's body that created the real challenge.

"Over here!"

Mrs. Connor led the way to a plywood-walled cubicle that differed markedly from the rest of the dozen examining-treatment areas making up the main Emergency room. Equipped with the same battery of highly specialized monitoring devices found in the ICU itself, the small room had been designed almost two years earlier in order to provide every facility needed for an immediate evaluation of accident and other cases that might be potential heart donors for Dr. Kenneth Dalton's transplant program.

As the stretcher was pushed into the empty cubicle, the nurse reached for the diaphragm terminal of the phonocardioscope, a modern-day ultrasophisticated version of the simple stethoscope. Separating the blankets over the patient's abdomen, she pressed the diaphragm against the swollen mound and flipped the switch activating the instrument.

Immediately a faint sound, hurried but rhythmic, came from the loudspeaker on the wall of the cubicle, the unmistakable beat of a baby's heart inside the uterus of its dead mother.

"Hold this, Callahan, if we move fast we may save this baby." As Faye Connor handed the fireman the diaphragm, her mind was working like the computer that was the heart of the hospital's complicated electronic system, considering the alternatives at her disposal and discarding them one by one.

Mike Raburn was in the hyperbaric chamber with the Gates boy and so was not available. Dr. Kenneth Dalton was on call for Emergency, but it would take minutes to reach him, minutes the baby, whose racing heart would soon be slowing to a stop unless something was done to free it from the deadly burden of its own mother's body, couldn't afford to lose. Dr. Nolan Gaither, the interne on duty, was putting on a cast in the plaster room down a corridor some fifty feet away, but reaching him would take time. And even then the nurse had no way of knowing how quickly the still not fully trained reflexes of the young doctor could be galvanized into the action necessary to save the baby's life.

Which left only a single alternative, the one sure way to get expert help quickly and the most urgent call that could be sounded over the hospital loudspeaker system. It would bring a CPR—cardiopulmonary resuscitation—team on the double, ready to tackle a stopped heart or cope with any other emergency.

Only a fraction of a second elapsed between the initiation of her review and the motion of Mrs. Connor's hand toward the red button on the wall of the cubicle. No more than a similar fraction later a high-speed tape recorder activated by the red button was locked into the hospital's public address system, abruptly stopping all other use of it.

"CODE FIVE—EMERGENCY!" the rarely heard summons brought every activity in the hospital for a halt for an instant.

"CODE FIVE—EMERGENCY!" The summons was re-
peated and, like Sleeping Beauty at the kiss of the Prince,
everything suddenly began to move again, but on a new
tack, a planned course where everyone knew his or her
job perfectly and needed no time-consuming instructions
before acting.

Chapter 4

MOMENTS before the alarm sounded, Rebecca Dalton had
descended to ground level from the Medical Department
located on an upper floor. Emerging from the elevator,
she was startled to see Ken step from an adjoining one
and, to avoid meeting him, turned toward the Cardiac
Research Laboratory at the back of the building. At the
same moment, however, he started toward the lobby, with
the result that they collided and he was forced to catch
her to keep her from being knocked down. Facing each
other with their faces less than a foot apart and his arm
around Rebecca's waist, they were like two people frozen
in time—until Ken released her and broke the tension of
the sudden meeting.

"I heard the operator paging you for the lab a few
minutes ago, Reb," he said. "Anything wrong?"

Reb was the pet name he'd given her before they were
married. Hearing it now for the first time since they'd
separated nearly six months ago twisted Rebecca's heart
so sharply that she turned away, lest he see the sudden
start of tears in her eyes. And noting her concern, he
reached out to touch her, then dropped his hand.

"I'm sorry," he said softly. "Sorry about everything."

"Congratulations on the verdict," said Rebecca but,
when she saw his expression suddenly harden, was sorry
she had mentioned the subject that had finally caused the
break between them.

"At least it took the hospital off the hook." His tone was harsh now. "But nothing will really be changed until—"

Whatever he had been about to say was interrupted by the announcement from the CODE FIVE tape. At the sound both of them turned instinctively toward the door of the Emergency Department, not much more than a dozen feet away, everything except the urgency of the crisis causing the announcement suddenly erased from their minds.

As the husband-and-wife doctor team burst into the white-tiled Emergency Room, Mrs. Connor looked up from where she was following the set routine in apparent DOAs by applying sensors to the chest of the patient.

"The surgical tray's ready," she reported. "The Rescue Squad just brought her in—DOA, and pregnant. You can still hear the fetal heart on the phonocardioscope."

The question of what should be done in such an emergency had been answered by the Emperor Numa Pompilius of Rome more than seven hundred years before the birth of Christ in what had become known as the *Lex Caesaris*—a decree forbidding the burial of a pregnant woman until the child had been removed from her womb, if possible before its heart stopped beating.

A glance at the girl on the stretcher beneath the glaring white ceiling lights told a graphic and tragic story: the features that had once been pretty but were only pathetic now; the frame of lank blonde hair; the enormous abdomen; and most diagnostic of all, the small dark splotches along the course of the veins visible over both arms and legs—all signs identifying the young mother as an addict, most likely on heroin.

Following a routine Ken and Rebecca Dalton had worked out for the special monitor cubicle, Mrs. Connor switched on the ECG connections she had just made—revealing a flat line for heart action on the oscilloscope screen.

"No heartbeat," she said, and moved on, still following the SOP for such cases, to attach electroencephalographic terminals to the girl's scalp, needlelike sensors used to register electric waves denoting brain activity.

51

The procedure had become routine with all patients brought to the hospital *in extremis,* as a means of determining brain damage—the ultimate cessation of life itself even though the heart might still be beating. In the hectic period when Ken Dalton had performed fifteen heart transplants in one year, the procedure being followed by Mrs. Connor had resulted in the discovery of a number of donor hearts soon enough after legal death to furnish much of the supply needed for the dramatic transplant operations. But for the past six months it had been allowed to lapse.

With only seconds in which to save the child through the age-old procedure of immediate Caesarean section, two things were necessary. One was to determine as certainly as possible, without the electroencephalograph since there was no time for delay, the fact of death by means of the conventional evidence provided by cessation of both heartbeat and respiration. The other was the availability of instruments for the operation and a surgeon capable of performing it.

Fortunately all these requirements were now met by the presence of a surgeon and a cardiologist in the Emergency Room and the failure of the electrocardiograph to reveal heart action in the mother. Ken Dalton pulled on a pair of rubber gloves while quickly surveying the contents of the instrument tray another nurse had already opened upon a table beside the stretcher. Rebecca, meanwhile, was removing the terminal of the phonocardioscope to the patient's chest and placing it over the heart.

"There's no heartbeat," she reported when no sound was heard. "She's clinically dead."

"Somebody call for Gus Henderson and a Pediatric ICU bassinet." Ken was picking up a scalpel from the instrument tray as he spoke. "This baby's going to need all the help we can give it."

With his left hand, he tensed the skin over the mound of the abdomen and, using a long slashing stroke, laid the abdominal wall open from well above the navel to the brush of darkish blonde hair over the patient's pubis. A second stroke penetrated the peritoneal lining of the abdomen, allowing the distended uterus, its muscle almost

52

black now from the absence of oxygen, to protrude through.

Rebecca did not wait to watch, but moved to a telephone.

"CODE FIVE. DR. HENDERSON," she told the operator. "Emergency Room Three."

As she hung up, the call came from the loudspeaker in the corridor outside, the calm voice of the paging operator saying distinctly and clearly: "CODE FIVE, DR. HENDERSON! Emergency Room Three. CODE FIVE! Pediatric Team! Emergency Room Three."

"She can't have been dead long," said Rebecca as the scalpel in Ken's hand slashed into the thick muscular wall of the uterus. "The blood hasn't started to clot."

Separating with the thumb and forefinger of his left hand the edges of the cut he had made into the wall of the uterus, Ken dissected more carefully now, since too deep a cut could damage the body of the baby within the uterus. A sudden gush of yellowish amniotic fluid from the reservoir in which the child had lain, while developing from the union of two cells to the immensely complicated structure of a separate human being, indicated that the uterine cavity was penetrated. And, slipping his left hand inside the uterus with the back of it protecting the body of the child, Ken opened the incision widely enough in both directions to allow removing the infant with the umbilical cord still attached to the mother by way of the placenta. Dropping the scalpel from his right hand, he searched inside the uterine cavity for a tiny foot.

"The baby's still alive," he reported. "I can feel the fetal heart beating against my hand."

"Thank God!" said Rebecca.

Circling one tiny leg with his fingers, Ken pulled it through the incision he had made into the uterus. In a continuation of the same movement, he found the other foot and extracted it, then gently drew the whole body of the child from the mother's womb.

Holding the baby up with his left hand, he gave it a smack across the soles of its feet with his right. A spasmodic contraction of the tiny chest brought a faint cry with initiation of breathing and, picking up a hemostatic

53

forceps from the instrument table, Ken clamped across the umbilical cord which, until a few moments ago, had connected the circulation of the child with that of the mother, bringing it vital oxygen and sustenance until her own heartbeat had ceased.

Gus Henderson had just arrived and was holding a small blanket across his outstretched arms. When the surgeon placed the baby gently upon it, with the hemostat still dangling from the cut stump of the umbilical cord, Gus moved immediately to the special portable ICU bassinet Helga Sundberg had just brought to the Emergency Room as part of the pediatric emergency routine.

"At least it's breathing and its heart is beating," said Rebecca.

"It couldn't weigh over two and a half pounds, so it's definitely premature," said the tall pediatrician. "And from the looks of the mother's veins, that baby's been an addict ever since it was only one cell. Cold turkey is no fun when you're grown; it must be hell when you only weigh two or three pounds."

They all knew what he meant, "cold turkey" was a graphic description of a method of treating drug addiction by abrupt withdrawal of all narcotics. In the excitement of saving the baby, none of them had noticed that, while Ken Dalton was operating, Mrs. Connor had finished attaching the sensors to the young mother's scalp and switched on the electroencephalograph.

"Dr. Dalton! Look!" Mrs. Connor was staring at the small monitor screen of the EEG where, faintly, but beyond any shadow of a doubt, a familiar pattern was plainly visible.

"She still has brain waves." Rebecca's voice was little more than an incredulous whisper. "Which means she's technically still alive."

II

In the hyperbaric chamber, things were going very well for Joey Gates.

"Three atmospheres, Dr. Raburn," the pressure technician reported. "His pulse is slowing on the monitor out here, too."

"Hold at three for the time being, Matt. I think the cyanosis is less marked."

Once again Mike checked the catheters and found both of them open. The bottle of intravenous fluid was almost empty, however, so he changed it for a fresh one that had been put into the metal tank when they first came in, before the air-tight doors were closed.

"Any idea what the CODE FIVE was about?" Mike asked via the telephone.

"A DOA in the Emergency Room with a live baby according to the grapevine. Dr. Kenneth Dalton's doing a Caesarean, I guess that's why Dr. Henderson got the special call."

"Looks like I missed some excitement."

"You have enough," the technician assured him. "Every time I get on my Honda and start home through the expressway traffic, I pray that I don't get tossed off it and brought to the ER when you're not on duty."

A sudden movement of Joey Gates's arm, the one with the catheter in the vein, caused Mike to reach for it quickly.

"Looks like he's coming around," he said.

"His ECG just took a nose dive, too." The technician's voice was suddenly tense. Then it relaxed as he added, "But it's back on schedule now."

"The IV catheter must have moved enough to touch the wall of the atrium," said Mike. "I'll pull it back a little before he's completely conscious."

Carefully he adjusted the tiny flexible tube, withdrawing about an inch of it through the small skin wound where it had been inserted. Pulling the stool upon which he had been sitting closer to the low stretcher, Mike kept his hand on Joey's arm now, lest the boy accidentally jerk the vitally important tube from his arm.

For perhaps a quarter of an hour nothing happened except a gradual slowing of Joey's pulse and respiration, both signs that the strain upon his circulation of trying to supply oxygen to his brain and other important tissues was being lessened by the increased amount of the life gas reaching his body cells. Then, just as if awakening from a sound sleep, the boy opened his eyes.

Mike lifted the oxygen mask from Joey's face for a moment. "How do you feel?" he asked.

"Okay—I guess. Where am I, Dr. Mike?"

"In the hospital."

"Where's Mommy?"

"Outside, waiting. I had to give you a special treatment, so we brought you into this room."

"Looks more like a submarine."

"It's actually a tank where you breathe air under pressure—"

The boy's dark eyes brightened. "Like scuba diving?"

"Pretty close."

"Daddy's going to take me scuba diving when I get bigger. We're going to the Penne—" He stumbled over the rest of the word.

"The Pennecamp Coral Reef State Park," said Mike. "You'll see a lot of fish and some of the prettiest coral anywhere. Now let's put the mask back on and breathe some more oxygen so you'll get well in a hurry. Okay?"

The boy nodded and Mike adjusted the mask.

"Breathe deeply, Joey," he said. "You need all of this stuff you can get."

For another half hour the boy breathed the oxygen while his pulse rate continued to drop and his color improved. Then Mike removed the mask and watched him closely for about ten minutes. When he showed no signs of growing drowsy again, and the monitor indicated no change in heart action, Mike shut off the oxygen valve and picked up the telephone again.

"You can lower the pressure, Matt," he told the technician via the telephone. "It looks like everything's going to be all right."

III

As chief anesthesiologist for Biscayne General, Dr. Valerie LeMoyne was in charge of all resuscitation activities in the hospital. Not only had she instituted the training programs and organizational procedures which made a trained CPR—Cardiopulmonary Resuscitation—team available on instant notice to any section of the hospital but she was personally the head of the most important of them, the one always on call for the Emergency Room and the Intensive Care Units. She had arrived in the Emergency Room barely a minute after the CODE FIVE was sounded, along with Dr. Ed Vogel, Research Fellow in Cardiology and second-in-command on the team, who had just returned to the hospital after a brief absence.

For an instant following Rebecca's dramatic announcement that the supposedly dead patient showed at least a faint flicker of life in the nervous system, everyone in the ER was frozen into a tableau. But when Ken Dalton broke the silence everything began to move again.

"Is Dr. LeMoyne here?" he asked.

"Here, Doctor," Val answered.

"Resuscitation is your field. Take over, please."

"Right," said Valerie LeMoyne crisply. "This looks like a straight line arrest. Do you agree, Rebecca?"

"Entirely."

"Then electrical stimulation is out for the moment and we can best stimulate the heart by direct massage through the diaphragm."

"I'll make room." Ken reached for a scalpel from the instrument tray.

"Put on some sterile gloves, Dr. Vogel," Val directed. "You can employ direct massage while Dr. Rebecca Dalton searches for a vein and gets an IV started."

While Ed Vogel was putting on sterile gloves, Ken's scalpel was moving swiftly at the upper end of the incision, extending it upward to make room for the cardiologist to massage the heart through the lax muscular shelf of the diaphragm separating the chest cavity from the abdomen.

As Ed inserted a gloved right hand into the upper part of the incision, Ken began to remove the placenta from inside the uterus. Scooping out the thick, pancake-like organ with the cut umbilical cord dangling from it, he dropped the specimen into the basin Mrs. Connor held out to him and reached for a needle holder with a long strand of suture material attached to the curved needle between its jaws.

Meanwhile, Ed Vogel was feeling for the base of the heart through the thin muscle of the diaphragm. When his fingers closed around it, he began to squeeze the thoracic organ rhythmically, massaging the muscular wall in an attempt to incite a spontaneous contraction and at the same time duplicating artifically its action in pumping blood through the body to preserve life.

At the patient's head, Valerie LeMoyne had pushed down the jaw and inserted a curved plastic airway to hold back the tongue and create a clear airway to the lungs. When she placed a mask over the girl's mouth and nose and switched on the respirator, the breathing bag attached to it began to inflate and deflate in a steady rhythm of artificial respiration. Thus, with blood being pumped through the patient's circulation and oxygen passing into it from the lungs, the inactive life processes were being duplicated artificially in support of the weak evidence of life still apparent from the flickering pattern of the EEG waves on the wall monitor.

"I can feel the lungs being inflated," Ed Vogel reported, "but no cardiac contraction."

"What about the baby, Dr. Henderson?" Val LeMoyne asked.

"It's alive," Gus Henderson reported from the adjoining cubicle, where he and Helga were placing the baby in the special newborn resuscitation chamber they had wheeled directly into the Emergency Room. "But I don't like the way it's breathing."

"Take it to the NICU and let us know if you need any help." NICU was the cryptic designation of the Newborn Intensive Care Unit.

"We're leaving," said Gus.

Rebecca had been working over the patient's right arm meanwhile, probing for a vein with a needle-catheter set.

"Blood's flowing," she announced when a dark stream suddenly spurted back into the barrel of the attached syringe. "Shall I inject a bolus?"

"Please," said Val. "Ten cc. of calcium chloride and a half cc. of Isuprel."

Rebecca busied herself at the outer end of the needle-catheter setup, injecting the medication before removing the needle and attaching the glass adapter of an intravenous tube to the end of the catheter remaining in the vein. Both powerful stimulants, the entire dose of the drugs was being delivered directly into the heart itself.

"Still no heart action," Ed Vogel reported as Ken continued to close the wound in the wall of the flabby uterus with deep running sutures, using his right hand, while massaging the muscular wall of the organ with his left. Blood surged from the cut edges with each squeezing action by Ed Vogel's hand upon the heart, and Ken was hoping by his own massage to make the uterus itself contract and squeeze down the blood spaces opened by the scalpel.

"The EEG waves are very faint." With the respirator automatically duplicating the act of breathing, Val LeMoyne was able to watch the monitor screen, as well as the other orderly activities going on in the room. "There's apparently some life still in the brain but the pupils are widely dilated, which probably means the brain damage would not be reversible, even if we started the heart."

No one there required an explanation; between a dead patient and one that was little more than a vegetable from brain damage, there was really not much choice.

"I just felt a slight heart contraction." Ed Vogel's voice was suddenly tense. "There's another one."

"Display the ECG on the monitor, please," said Val LeMoyne, and Mrs. Connor moved quickly to switch on the sensors she had placed on the patient's chest immediately after sounding CODE FIVE.

A by-product of the sophisticated space research that enable observers in Houston to watch the heartbeats and other vital functions of astronauts a quarter of a million miles away on the moon, the small sensors could pick up even the most minute action currents of the heart muscle and display them in the form of electrocardiographic tracings visible to all on the small ground-glass screen.

For a moment no one spoke, while all eyes were turned to the monitor. The waves being exhibited on the screen were undeniable proof that the heart had indeed begun to beat, but they also graphically described its character, and the periodic and purposeless contraction of individual sections of heart muscle being recorded had no resemblance to either order or continuity of function. Only one diagnosis fitted that picture, ventricular fibrillation, a dangerous complication that could render even a strong heart quite useless.

"You'd better take over from here." Valerie LeMoyne spoke directly to Rebecca, who nodded and moved nearer the monitor to study the pattern.

"It's fibrillation for sure," she said. "Please inject fifty milligrams of xylocaine through the IV needle, Mrs. Connor. Meanwhile we don't seem to have much choice now, except to zap the heart. Do you agree, Ed?"

"Absolutely."

The ICU interne, who was a member of the team, moved the portable pacemaker-defibrillator he had pushed to the room at the sound of the alarm into place beside the patient. At the same time, Val quickly unstrapped the mask of the resuscitator and removed it, cutting off the oxygen. The quickest way to restore a fibrillating heart to a normal rhythm was to shock it— "Zap!" in medical idiom—with a powerful jolt of electricity delivered to the patient's chest over the heart by means of paddle electrodes. Anyone touching the body inadvertently at the time, however, could receive a powerful wallop, so both Ken Dalton and Ed Vogel stepped away from the table.

"Set the controls at four hundred milliwatt seconds." Rebecca was in charge now and there was no hesitation in either decision or action.

The interne set the controls at the figure she had ordered and placed the paddle electrodes over the heart area, so the current could pass from one electrode through the heart muscle and back to the other, completing the circuit. Devised to stop the heart by the powerful jolt of the defibrillating current, in the hope that it would restart itself in a normal rhythm, the machine was an invaluable tool in controlling a condition which, before it became available, had often caused the death of the victim.

At Rebecca's nod, another member of the team pressed the switch on the defibrillator console and the patient's chest muscles jerked sharply from the stimulating current. When the ECG sensors, disconnected during the zapping procedure, were connected once again, the irregular heart action that had turned the surface of the monitor screen into a crazy jumble of lines was gone—but with it all evidence of function by the organ itself.

"Get ready to start massaging again, Ed," said Rebecca quietly. "We're not getting any action."

Ed Vogel had removed his hand from the heart before the current was turned off and stepped back beside Ken Dalton. Now both of them returned to the table and resumed the work on which they had been engaged.

Three times during the next fifteen minutes, faint contractions of the vital cardiac muscles were started by the massaging action of Ed Vogel's gloved hand through the diaphragm, but each time the result was the familiar jumble of lines indicating fibrillation. Twice, after the powerful shocking current had stopped all contractions, the current was switched to the pacemaker, sending rhythmic jolts of considerably less intensity than the zapping procedure through the heart muscle in an attempt to initiate regular contractions. Each time, however, the result was only another flurry of fibrillation, and after the fourth zapping, even the brain waves had ceased, the ultimate criterion of death.

"In my opinion nothing can be gained by any more shocks," said Rebecca quietly.

"I agree," said Val LeMoyne, "but at least the baby was saved."

"For cold turkey?" Ken's tone made Rebecca wish she could take him in her arms and comfort him. "Maybe it would have been better off if I'd let it die with the mother. This place depresses me. Dictate a summary on this case for the record, will you, Reb? I've done all the damage I can do today."

When Carolyn Payson emerged from the elevator into the hospital lobby, after spending the hour at her father's bedside which had become a daily routine for her, she saw the tall figure of Gus Henderson standing beside a bulletin board. Ostensibly he was reading the announcements thumbtacked there but actually, she knew, he was waiting for her. When Gus saw her, his craggy face broke into a smile and he came across the lobby to take her arm.

"I was afraid you'd already left," he said. "Dr. Dalton did a section on a DOA from heroin—"

"Was that the CODE FIVE?"

"Yes." He held open the door of the Coffee Shop occupying an area just off the lobby beside a covered walkway leading to Bayside Terrace and across from the door connecting the Emergency Department with the lobby itself. The popular restaurant was almost filled with a chattering crowd of students and nurses released from the morning shift but they were able to find an empty booth.

"Anything besides coffee?" Gus asked.

"No, I'm getting too fat."

"On you it looks wonderful. Two coffees—black," he called to Maggie McCloud, the plump, middle-aged waitress behind the counter. "I'll get 'em."

"Two coffees, black, comin' up, Dr. Henderson," said Maggie cheerfully. "How's your father, Miss Payson?"

"About the same, thank you." Carolyn was watching Gus as he maneuvered himself to the counter through the crowd filling the shop. Like many pediatricians, he was a big man but, as she well knew, as gentle as a woman. He came back carrying steaming hot-drink cups.

"I only have a minute, while Peggy Tyndall sets up a tray so I can put some umbilical catheters and an electronic probe into the preemie Dr. Dalton just delivered." Gus slumped comfortably in the booth. "Have I told you I love you lately?"

"Not since last night."

"How about marrying me next week? We could make it this weekend, but I have to work."

Carolyn looked away quickly, but not before Gus had a glimpse of the pain that showed in her eyes.

"What's the matter, darling?" he asked. "Your father worse?"

She nodded wordlessly.

"Anything I can do?"

"No." Carolyn drank from her cup but the coffee was tasteless, like everything lately. Hoping to take her mind off her troubles, Gus said, "According to Mike Raburn, your roommate covered herself with glory this afternoon."

"Helga was late coming on duty, which isn't like her. But she didn't say why."

"Mike said she found a child in the last stages of asphyxiation in the ER and put a needle into the trachea—that new technique he was telling about last week. He was very much impressed."

"Everybody knows Helga's always on the ball. Mike shouldn't have been surprised."

"My guess would be that he's been seeing Helga only as a fine nurse all these months, but for some reason he saw her all at once this afternoon as a woman."

Carolyn smiled. "I remember the day you first saw me as something besides a nursing machine—but then I'd been working on you for a month."

"And think of what I might have missed, if you hadn't."

"I'm not so sure," Carolyn's tone was sober again. "Huntington's disease is hereditary."

"But genetics as a science has made giant strides lately."

"Not with H-D. I've been reading up on it ever since I brought Father from Atlanta."

"It still has to be pretty rare. I don't remember ever seeing another case."

"There may be a thousand in the United States and all of them seem to be traceable back to a small number of immigrants who came over here from Europe nearly three hundred years ago."

63

"But your father—"

"The gene of H-D is a defective dominant, Gus. It can lie dormant for one or even two generations."

"Then what are you worrying—"

"My father's brother probably died of it, too, which could mean that the gene is growing stronger in my family, so our children would stand a fifty-fifty chance of developing it. Would you want to saddle such a heritage on your sons and daughters?"

"There's a simple way around that—don't have any."

"Something could go wrong and—"

"Not if I were sterilized. Cutting the spermatic cords is a minor procedure."

"A man's entitled to have descendants, darling. With the gene of H-D probably already in every cell of my body, I could very well die by the time I'm thirty-five. You could still marry then and have children of your own—healthy ones."

"Look, Carolyn, I love you and I want you with me all the time. To gain that, I'd be willing to give up anything, including having children of our own."

From the loudspeaker in the corner of the room against the ceiling came the calm voice of the paging operator:

"Dr. Henderson—115. Dr. Augustus Henderson—115. Dr. Henderson—115."

"That's the NICU. Helga must have everything ready," he said. "Will you have dinner with me in the hospital cafeteria this evening? I can't get away, with this preemie going through cold turkey."

"Make it about six, if you can," said Carolyn. "I want to sit with my father for a while afterward."

"See you then." Gus stood up and dropped some change on the table. "And don't go moping because you can't have children, darling. After watching what Baby Hornsby is going through on the first day of its life outside the womb, I'm not at all sure this is the kind of world we want to inject a child into anyway."

Carolyn stayed on in the Coffee Shop for a while after Gus left. And when she did leave, her steps turned toward the small hospital chapel, located just off the corridor leading from the main lobby to the banks of elevators.

Moved by her concern for her father, as well as for herself and her own future, she had returned instinctively to the religious training of her childhood. Slipping into one of the pews, she dropped to her knees on a prayer bench and sought words to voice her plea for divine assistance in what appeared to be an insoluble problem—at least within her own competence.

"Can I help you, Miss Payson?" The soft voice startled her and she turned quickly to see the hospital chaplain standing at the end of the pew where she had been kneeling.

"Father Hagan!" Carolyn remembered the Episcopal priest from the week he'd spent on her ward, when changes in a routine electrocardiogram had suggested the onset of a more serious condition. Thanks to Rebecca Dalton's skill as a cardiologist, plus the care given by Carolyn and the other dedicated nurses operating the CICU of the main Intensive Care Section, the attack had been averted.

"I am pleased that you knew where to come for help." The old minister entered the pew and took a seat beside her as she rose from her knees. "And that it's best sought on your knees."

"I haven't been exactly what you might call a churchgoer, Padre."

"Each of us serves God in his own way, Miss Payson. I suspect yours may be more in accord with His will than most."

"I know my job, at least."

The old chaplain smiled. "I, too, can testify to that."

"I only wish the problem I'm facing now was as easy to answer."

"Your father?"

Carolyn wasn't surprised that Father Hagan knew about Richard Payson. Even a hospital the size of Biscayne General was still a small and almost inbred community. "I didn't see his name on the critical list this morning."

"He's not critical—in the medical sense. But if you had known him before, you would realize what it means to see

65

someone with a brain like his shut off from communication with the rest of the world while he turns into a vegetable."

"Is he conscious?"

"Momentarily at times—long enough to beg us to let him die."

"Is that what's troubling you? The question of whether your father should be allowed to die?"

"That's part of it—the most important part." She drew a deep breath, still not knowing exactly how to put into words the conviction that had been growing in her mind since she had brought Richard Payson into the hospital and Dr. Gross had told her the diagnosis.

"I'm not familiar with your father's condition," said the chaplain. "If you don't mind talking about it—"

"I guess I need to share it with someone. So far I've tried to keep everything to myself, but—"

"I'm here to listen and to help—or to pray."

As she described her father's condition, the gradual disintegration of the mind and the personality until he'd become hardly more than a body being torn to pieces by the malignant gene of Huntington's disease in every cell of his body, Carolyn found some of the burden lifted from her shoulders.

"Can nothing be done?" the chaplain asked when she finished.

"Not for my father. But I'm the last in my own family line, so by never bringing children into the world, I can at least stop the gene from being passed on to others."

"You can always adopt a child—"

"That's out too," she said flatly.

"Why?"

"What right do I have to saddle a husband—or the children we might adopt—with a mother who could turn into a gibbering travesty of a human being just when they all probably would need her most?"

"There's an even chance that this won't happen," he reminded her.

"That's still too much of a burden to put on a person you love."

"It's a hard choice—"

"There isn't any choice, Padre. I settled that in my own mind—along with some other things—when I learned the real cause of Dad's illness."

The old chaplain studied her thoughtfully for a moment before he spoke.

"Is there someone you love besides your father?" he asked.

"Yes. Very much indeed."

"Have you told all this to him?"

"Not my resolve to never marry."

"Why?"

She looked up then and he saw that her eyes were wet. But, when she spoke, her voice was well under control.

"I guess I'm enough of a coward not to want to hurt Gus."

"Dr. Henderson?"

"Yes." Then she added defiantly, "Are you going to tell me it's a sin to seize what little happiness I can before it flies out the window?"

"I'm far too frail a vessel to sit in judgment on people who may be serving God much better than I," said the old priest. "But I don't envy you the moment when you must tell Dr. Henderson the truth."

"We've already agreed that we shouldn't have children of our own. Fortunately the rest can wait—as long as the man I love isn't tied to me by marriage."

"What if you should become pregnant?"

"The one-in-two chance of passing a horrible disease like Huntington's to a child would be ample grounds for a legal therapeutic abortion, even if the courts hadn't made abortion in the first three months legal any way. But I'm taking no chances of that either—"

"You seem to have thought this all out," he conceded.

"And you don't approve?"

The priest smiled and shook his head. "A long time ago, a woman was brought to Jesus by people who sought to have him condemn her. Do you remember his answer?"

"No. But then I've already told you I haven't been the best churchgoer in the world."

"Jesus answered, 'He that is without sin among you, let him first cast a stone at her.' "

"Thank you, Chaplain." Carolyn started to rise, but he put his hand upon hers.

"I suspect that you haven't told me the real reason you came here," he said. "Wouldn't you like to?"

Carolyn hesitated only momentarily. "Remember my telling you that Father rouses only to beg us to let him die?" she asked.

"Yes."

"I'm sure some part of his brain still knows enough of what's happening, and what will happen, not to want to put any more of a burden upon me. So if the doctors can't let him die, I don't have any choice except . . ."

"There still may be a way—"

She turned quickly. "What is it?"

"Have you read about the 'right to die' controversy?"

"A little—in newspapers and magazines."

"Some hospitals have appointed committees to decide—"

"When a patient's prognosis is hopeless?" she asked eagerly.

"Yes. It's very new here at Biscayne General—and also very secret for good reasons."

"Tell me about it, Chaplain," Carolyn said eagerly. "Tell me, please."

Chapter 5

HELGA SUNDBERG was bending over the bassinet in which Baby Hornsby lay, giving it oxygen by means of a small mask covering its nose and mouth, when Peggy Tyndall pushed the special cardiac catheterization cart into the NICU treatment room. Located just off the eight-bed ward where newborns with any respiratory or other difficulty were given special care twenty-four hours a day, there was never less than one specially trained ICU nurse to every two small patients in the ward.

Peggy was barely five feet, with a blonde pony tail that made her look like a schoolgirl, and a bright warm smile, in spite of having been widowed at twenty with a child destined to be born six months later with congenital heart disease. As a physician's assistant and chief technician in the Cardiac Research Laboratory, she was Rebecca Dalton's and Ed Vogel's right hand, plus being a favorite all over the big hospital.

"Hi, Peg," said Helga. "Dr. Henderson will be here in a minute."

Peggy busied herself in the corner of the room, putting on the gown and mask required for everyone working in the NICU. When she finished, she came over to the bassinet and stood looking down at Baby Hornsby.

"This the post-mortem Caesarean baby?" she asked.

Helga nodded. "Two or three weeks premature and cold turkey into the bargain. That's some handicap to start life with."

"But he'll be okay when the withdrawal symptoms wear off, won't he?" Peggy's tone was a little resentful and Helga understood the reason.

"Maybe. But it's tough sledding for a while—especially starting off your life without a mother."

"I guess I deserved that," Peggy admitted. "But it's hard not to resent a baby that's normal, when you have one who isn't."

"But Dale will be—when Dr. Dalton straightens out his heart."

"*If* Dr. Dalton straightens out his heart. And right now it doesn't seem very likely that he will."

"There are other cardiovascular surgeons—Mike Raburn, for example."

"I know," said Peggy. "When Dale's father was killed in Vietnam, I felt like my own world had come to an end, but I had to go on. When Dale was born and Dr. Rebecca told me he was a Fallot, I even prayed for a while that he would die—"

"Aren't you glad he didn't?"

Peggy nodded. "I guess I'm just tired and depressed. I was busy the two years it took to get my physician's assistant degree. And after that we had a lot of excitement in the lab working on the artificial heart and hoping we could get one going in time to save some of the transplant cases. I didn't have time to feel sorry for myself, but when Dr. Ken and Dr. Rebecca separated, the artificial heart project fell apart, too."

"Dale's still all right, isn't he?"

"As near all right as anybody can be when three fourths of his circulating blood by-passes the lungs, leaving him with barely enough oxygen to get along. Every time I see him squatting to get his breath, I say a prayer that he can keep going until he's eight or so and ready for open heart surgery."

The door of the treatment room opened and Gus Henderson came in.

"Hi, Peg," he said, reaching for cap and mask before starting to scrub at a sink in the corner of the room. "Got the new gold-tipped electrode?"

"It's on the tray, Dr. Henderson." The diminutive technician removed the sterile cover from the tray on top of the cart. "I think I have everything you'll need."

"You always do," said the pediatrician cheerfully. "If I could depend on everybody around here the way I can on you and Miss Sundberg, things would always go smoothly."

"My, aren't we happy today," said Helga. "Love must be wonderful."

"It is. You ought to try it sometime."

"I just might do that," said the ICU nurse.

Lifting the baby from the bassinet, and carrying the rubber tube connecting the mask to the hospital oxygen supply, Helga placed the squirming newborn on the small treatment table in the center of the room, beneath a powerful droplight. Working swiftly and expertly, she strapped the mask in place with a web strap around the head, then wrapped the baby's body below the navel— where the umbilical stump had been clamped by Ken Dalton and covered with a sterile dressing—in a blanket. Moving to the upper half of the small patient, she seated herself on a stool at the head of the table and, sliding her arms down along the baby's sides, took a tiny hand in each of hers and pinned the small torso to the table expertly with a steady pressure.

Gus Henderson had finished scrubbing meanwhile and had put on a sterile gown and gloves. Moving up to the table, he watched as Peggy Tyndall removed the dressing that had covered the navel and the forceps preventing any backflow of blood. After painting the instrument and the skin around the navel with a clear antiseptic, he draped the area with a small windowed sheet. Peggy meanwhile had picked up a pair of sterile ring forceps from a jar almost filled with antiseptic on the reserve table nearby and stood ready to hand him without contamination anything he needed.

Working carefully, Gus removed the hemostatic forceps that had closed off the umbilical cord. The gelatinous strand containing the umbilical artery and vein had functioned as a life channel during the months the baby had been inside its mother's body, receiving oxygen and food through the cord by way of the placenta, plus the sinister gift of heroin, and ridding itself of the waste products of life by the same route. The constant tremor of the baby's muscles, part of the heroin withdrawal pattern, made handling the three-inch umbilical stump a delicate task, even for Gus Henderson's skilled hands.

"We'll put a number 5F catheter into the umbilical artery first," he said.

"You've always used the vein before." Helga was watching closely and trying at the same time to hold the small writhing body as still as possible.

"The gold electrode goes through the 5F," Gus explained. "That way, it can be put directly into the aorta where it can measure the oxygen tension in the main stream of the circulation."

"While he was speaking, Gus had been carefully threading the polyethylene catheter into the tiny artery, hardly larger than a matchstick.

"That should do it," he said on a note of considerable satisfaction, when about six inches of the small tube had entered the artery.

Picking up a syringe with a blunt metal tip from the tray, he injected clear saline through the catheter and was rewarded by a few drops of rather dark blood from the open end, when he removed the syringe. From the tray, Peggy used the ring forceps to hand him the electrode. Smaller than the 5F catheter, it was also sheathed in polyethylene, but enlarged at the tip, which shone through the plastic covering with a distinctly golden tint.

"Measuring oxygen tension is simple, if this gadget works the way the journal report I read described it." Gus started to thread the gold-tipped end of the electrode into the hollow interior of the 5F catheter he had already inserted. "Once inside the aorta with arterial blood flowing around it, the electrode will give an immediate reading of the blood oxygen tension on a continuous strip recorder. That way we can tell whether the baby is getting too little or too much."

"Too much?" Peggy frowned. "Is that possible?"

"Very much so," said Gus. "We used to give preemies all the oxygen their blood could absorb, but we know now that a lot of them became blind later because of it."

The electrode had been disappearing into the open end of the umbilical artery catheter while they were talking. Now he ceased threading it in and made the necessary connections to the meter whose readings would be faithfully portrayed on the strip recorder. Immediately, the meter began to register the oxygen tension in Baby Hornsby's blood in millimeters of mercury.

"Fifty!" Gus Henderson's tone was grave. "Looks like we didn't get the electrode in a minute too soon."

Without taking off his gloves, the pediatrician moved to the oxygen control valve and adjusted the flow of the vital gas through its bubble bottle meter to the highest level. Immediately the oxygen tension recorded by the electrode deep inside the small body began to rise. But just then the baby grunted, as if it were having difficulty getting the gas into its lungs, and the tension level dived dramatically, to return quickly when the odd sound could no longer be heard.

"Looks like we're in for a rocky time," said Gus soberly.

"I'd better connect the other sensors," said Helga.

"I asked Dr. McHale to come down as soon as he's free. While we're waiting, I'll start an IV."

Her work finished, Peggy Tyndall left the treatment room with her cart. And by the time Dr. Angus McHale, professor of pediatrics, came into the room with its two rows of four special bassinets arranged against the walls, a constant stream of information was being displayed on the battery of monitors above Baby Hornsby's crib as well as upon the master screen at the nursing station outside, easily visible through the glass half walls of the ward. In addition to the vital oxygen tension pattern revealed on the strip recorder, other sensors reported hydrogen-ion concentration, pulse, respiration, ECG, arterial and venous pressure.

"I've just finished inserting one of those new electronic sensors into the umbilical artery, sir," said Gus. "It appears to be working very well."

The older doctor came over to the bassinet and studied the pattern being printed out on the strip recorder. "I wonder how we ever got along before these gadgets were invented and we had to make it with only our five senses to guide us—"

"Plus the sixth sense every good doctor has to develop," said Gus.

"Of course." The relationship between the tall pediatric resident and the professor was without the tension so many older doctors seemed to feel in the presence of younger ones obviously destined for greatness because of superior ability. As the author of one of the most widely used pediatric textbooks in the world, Dr. McHale's position was secure.

"Being premature is hard enough on a newborn," said the professor, "without adding narcotic addiction to it."

"And maybe HMD into the bargain, judging from the sound of its breathing and that low pO_2," said Gus.

Hyaline membrane disease—identified by the cryptic initials HMD—was a killer that annually destroyed some twenty-five thousand newborns in the United States alone, including a son of a former President some years earlier. The combined product of infant lungs failing to expand

73

fully after being thrust prematurely into an alien world, plus the formation within those air sacs of a proteinlike layer of material that seemed to act as a physical barrier, keeping oxygen from reaching the bloodstream and subsequently the body tissues, HMD was the most serious threat to life in these very small patients.

"How much did this fellow weigh?" Dr. McHale asked.

"Three and a half pounds, sir," said Helga.

"We figure it's maybe four weeks from term," Gus added.

"In that case, it may make it. I just saw some interesting figures from New York on the birth rate of these heroin babies—five hundred of them there last year."

"Too many of them die," Gus agreed. "But even so, the mortality has dropped off sharply from thirty-five per cent or more several years ago. Fortunately this one's not having convulsions like some of them do."

"I understand the mother lived only a little while after she reached the Emergency Room," said the older doctor.

"It's questionable whether she was really alive," said Helga. "If Dr. Dalton hadn't been where he could answer the CODE FIVE immediately, this little man would be down in the morgue too."

"I wonder if Baby Hornsby will ever thank Dr. Dalton for it," said McHale.

The baby sneezed and the small blinking light on the minotor marking the respiratory rate suddenly quickened for a dozen or more breaths and the pO_2 level sagged sharply before settling down. About the same time, the rapidly moving line on the monitor screen marking changes in heart function by way of the ECG suddenly skittered almost off the screen.

"Put an extra dose of chlorpromazine into the IV, Miss Sundberg " Gus Henderson spoke quickly. "This could be the beginning of a convulsive state."

As the nurse moved to a cabinet in the corner of the room and took a glass syringe from it, the tall young pediatrician turned to his chief.

"I think we should intubate and put the baby on CPAP before it gets beyond help, sir."

"It's the quickest way to get oxygen into the body," the older man agreed. "That should lessen the withdrawal symptoms, too."

To the uninitiated, the hospital jargon of diseases and procedures labeled by initials would have seemed as untranslatable as Egyptian temple and pyramid hieroglyphics had appeared to archaeologists prior to the discovery of the Rosetta Stone. But to those in the room, CPAP meant Continuous Positive Airway Pressure, a method of artificial respiration almost as new as last week's *Journal* of the American Medical Association.

Devised by the director of a pediatric intensive care unit in San Francisco only a few years earlier, CPAP was a method of keeping the lungs inflated between respirations in babies whose breathing mechanism was crippled by hyaline membrane disease. Keeping the air sacs inflated with oxygen and simultaneously removing most of the waste carbon dioxide allowed the greatest possible amount of lung surface to be exposed to the maximum concentration of breathable oxygen, a vital factor in saving these often otherwise doomed newborns.

Gus Henderson's first act in initiating the somewhat difficult procedure was to put in a call for the chief anesthetist, Dr. Valerie LeMoyne. She arrived a few minutes later, carrying a case containing the tools needed for the difficult job of inserting a tube into the tiny trachea, or windpipe.

"Not another cold turkey, Gus," she said. "Getting a tube into a trachea the size of a pencil is hard enough without all that twitching."

"If I could put a gold electrode into the umbilical artery, you can do this," Gus assured her. "And Baby Hornsby needs it badly."

"We'll give it the old college try," said the anesthetist. "Can you bring the baby's head to the end of the table, Miss Sundberg?"

"Certainly, Doctor." Helga loosened the oxygen mask and removed it. Then, exchanging her position at the head of the table for one at the side, she slid the tiny body, still wrapped in blankets, along the table until the anesthesiologist could draw its head off the end into the best possible position for the extremely delicate procedure. Opening the instrument case, Valerie LeMoyne took out the smallest laryngoscope it contained and checked the battery current to the tiny bulb at its very end that produced the light necessary for visualizing the larynx.

"Watch those parameters, Gus," said the anesthesiologist. "We may be in for a few bad moments while I'm getting a tube through the larynx. And hold the baby steady, Miss Sundberg."

Expertly Val slid the laryngoscope across Baby Hornsby's tongue past the soft palate. When she pulled the handle downward the entire area could be visualized through the metal barrel of the scope. Illuminated brightly by the rice-sized bulb at the far end, the tiny larynx came into full view, with the vocal cords separating as the baby tried to cry.

"Talk about a camel going through the eye of a needle," said Gus as Val reached for the small rubber tube to insert into the windpipe. "After one of these jobs I can almost believe it."

"How about the readings, Gus?" Val asked.

"Everything's skittering all over the place, but we expected that."

With a quick, skillful movement, the anesthesiologist slid the rubber tube through the laryngoscope into the opening between the vocal cords, past them through the larynx and into the trachea. Then, steadying the tube, she removed the metal barrel of the laryngoscope through which she had inserted it.

"Neat! Like always!" said Gus admiringly.

"That was the slickest intubation I ever saw, Dr. LeMoyne," Helga echoed.

It took about fifteen minutes to move Baby Hornsby back to the NICU ward and reconnect the sensors that fed vital information to the monitoring screens and meters at the main control station. When he finished adjusting the somewhat complicated pressure apparatus that controlled CPAP, Gus Henderson stopped in the small doctors' office adjoining the main nursing station to dictate a summary of what had been done for insertion into Baby Hornsby's record.

"Did you know Mike Raburn's been singing your praises all over the place?" he asked when he finished dictating.

Helga looked up quickly from the medication chart upon which she had been noting the orders he'd left for the small patient. "What about?"

"He seems to think you saved a child's life in the ER this afternoon."

"I guess I did. She had stopped breathing."

"Mike doesn't hand out compliments that aren't deserved."

Helga laughed. "At least he noticed me."

"He'd have to be blind not to. And Mike's not blind."

"Did he tell you I almost passed out on him?"

"No, and I don't believe it either. For my money, you're unflappable."

"The Unflappable Helga Sundberg. Somehow the title doesn't appeal to me."

"It must have to Mike. I've never heard him rave over any woman before."

Gus left the ward but Helga remained where she was, staring at the master screen of the monitor before her and seeing the face of Mike Raburn when he'd said, "It looks like we'll just have to organize a mutual admiration society—and come to think of it, that's not a bad idea."

And the more she thought of it, the more it appealed to Helga too.

II

Mike Raburn pushed the special stretcher upon which Joey Gates lay, conscious and bright-eyed with interest in the complicated control panel, out of the hyperbaric chamber—to be greeted with popping flash bulbs and TV cameras.

"What the hell's going on?" he demanded, half blinded by the lights.

"You're a hero," said Gus Henderson. "I've been telling the press how you saved Joey's life by putting him in the chamber."

"And going in with him. That took courage, Dr. Raburn." Mike recognized the decorative woman reporter from the local CBS outlet, Marcia Weston, when she shoved a hand microphone in front of him.

"About as much as scuba diving in the Keys, Miss Weston. I still don't know what this is all about."

"You saved Joey, Doctor." Someone had pushed Rachel Gates from the crowd to stand beside him. "Big Joe and I won't ever forget it."

"Do you mind telling us just how this new treatment works, Dr. Raburn?" Marcia Weston asked.

"Joey here was in a sickle cell crisis, which means his red blood cells had become crescent-shaped instead of looking like biscuits. We think sickling is related to the shape of a hemoglobin-S molecule in the cells themselves, and once they've sickled, they tend to get hung up on each other. Eventually the piled-up abnormal cells block small blood vessels and interfere with the absorption of oxygen in the body."

"Endangering his life?" Marcia Eston asked.

"In time. Joey's cells weren't carrying enough oxygen, so we let him breathe it under pressure in the hyperbaric chamber to increase the degree of oxygen saturation in his blood. It's really just an emergency measure, though; the real treatment is being given by fluid from that intravenous flask you see hanging beside the stretcher."

"What's that—a new medicine?"

"A new use for something the body manufactures all the time—urea. We don't fully understand the process involved yet but injection of large amounts of a urea solution seems to change the shape of most of the sickled red blood cells back to normal so they no longer get hung up on each other. Adding a cyanate compound appears to help even more."

"Cyanate?" The woman reporter frowned. "Isn't that poisonous?"

"What you're probably thinking of is cyanide, a deadly poison, but this is a somewhat different compound. The important thing is that cyanate plus urea—or maybe just cyanate alone, we don't know yet—not only seems to reverse the sickling but, when given in small doses continuously, may keep these crises from occurring at all."

"Then they're actually a cure?"

"To cure means getting rid of the disease, Miss Weston. Keeping up a maintenance dose of the drugs merely cuts down sharply the likelihood of further crises like the one Joey had this afternoon."

"One other question, Doctor," said a reporter at the back of the small crowd. "Isn't sickle cell anemia inherited?"

"The tendency toward sickling of red blood cells under certain circumstances seems to be in the group of inherited conditions," said Mike. "Along with blue eyes, webbed toes, a high-bridged nose—and the Mongolian spot."

"What's that?" the TV reporter asked.

"We Americans have a diverse ancestry and occasionally a remnant of it pops up in what you might call a wild gene. When the Mongols invaded Hungary and Austria in the thirteenth century, they apparently exercised a conqueror's right upon at least some of the female population—with or without their active co-operation. As a result, a few Mongolian genes were left behind and one of them crops up every now and then in the form of a pigmented area at the lower end of the spine—"

"You're pulling my leg," Marcia Weston protested.

"The idea is attractive, Miss Weston," Mike said with a grin. "But the Mongolian spot is a true genetic oddity. You'll find it in any good text on heredity."

Marcia Weston smiled warmly. "I wouldn't think of arguing with a Harvard All-American, Dr. Raburn."

III

As the rest of the press contingent was leaving the Hyperbaric Laboratory, the woman TV reporter stayed behind.

"I occasionally do mood pieces for the Sunday magazine section besides my TV work," she told Mike. "You know, sketches and impressions."

"I've read some of your pieces, they're very good."

"Thank you. I've been planning one on the role of women in a busy medical center."

"Sort of a *Women in White,* like the old Sidney Kingsley play?"

"Something like that, but right now I'm more interested in you." She smiled, a bit archly. "As the subject of a profile, of course."

"Women still run the show around here. We men are only puppets."

"That was to be the tone of my piece but, after meeting you, I'm not so sure. Anyway, how about sitting for my tape recorder sometime?"

"It's okay with me," said Mike. "But you'll have to clear it with Administration."

"Dr. Toler's office called and told us you were taking a desperate measure to save Big Joe Gates's son."

"Are you sure?"

"Absolutely. They even told us to get here on the double, if we wanted to photograph you bringing Joey out of the hyperbaric chamber."

Gus Henderson had been walking ahead of them; now he dropped back to say: "The staff also got word straight from the top to co-operate in every way with the press, Mike."

"I wonder why?"

"After that blast by Ross McKenzie to the Rotary Club at noon today about the hospital budget, maybe Dr. Toler has decided to strike back," Marcia Weston suggested. "Big Joe Gates is a name to conjure with in Miami and the black vote is getting larger all the time."

"Toler's smarter than I realized, when it comes to publicity," said Mike.

"Does that mean I can tag along sometimes?" Marcia Weston asked.

"You should have been here an hour earlier," Gus Henderson told her. "Dr. Kenneth Dalton had to do an emergency Caesarean on a woman who was practically dead from an overdose of heroin, to save the child."

"Did he—save it, I mean?"

"Yes. I've got the baby on CPAP." When the reporter looked blank, he added, "Continuous Positive Airway Pressure. It's a new way of treating hyaline membrane disease."

"Didn't that kill the Kennedy baby?"

"That was years ago. We know a lot more about treating it now."

"Could I see this baby?" Marcia Weston asked eagerly.

"Why not?" said Gus. "Dr. Toler seems to have given the press carte blanche and the ICU is just off this corridor."

"I'd like to see the baby myself, since it was delivered in my department," said Mike.

Helga Sundberg joined them when they came into the main ICU and Gus introduced the two women. "Could Miss Weston see Baby Hornsby?" he said.

"Of course," said Helga. "Mrs. Alvarez is specialing the case."

"Are you in charge of the ICU, Miss Sundberg?" Marcia Weston asked.

"I'm the three-to-eleven nursing supervisor."

"And also a heroine in her own right," said Mike.

"So?" Marcia Weston was interested immediately.

"She saved a little girl from asphyxiation this afternoon," he explained, "using a method we'd never used here before."

"But which Dr. Raburn had described so well in class that I could hardly have failed. He's a wonderful teacher." There was a faintly mocking note in Helga's voice and the willowy TV reporter recognized it.

"You'll have to tell me more about that, when we have our interview, Dr. Raburn," she said. "Sounds interesting."

Mike grinned as Helga's eyebrows shot up. "I'll be happy to tell you the whole story," he said. "Then I'm sure you'll want to go on with your piece on women in white."

"If very many of them are as stunning as Miss Sundberg, I'm sure I will," said the reporter. "I didn't know

81

doctors got to work in such pleasant surroundings—except on television programs."

They were at the door of the NICU and Helga opened it for them to enter the small utility nook where gowns and masks were kept, then followed them in. She helped Marcia Weston put on the required coverings and stood in the doorway, as the three of them moved across the eight-bassinet ward to the newborn resuscitator, where a plump nurse with dark skin and hair was watching the latest addition to the nursery.

"Cold turkey is hard enough to take when you're seeing it for the first time—and CPAP is worse," said Mike. "If you feel like passing out, slump my way, Miss Weston. Dr. Henderson is already spoken for, I'm not."

"Do they all look like this?" she asked. "I mean more like a rat than a human?"

"Most overdose cases do," said Gus. "HMDs usually have a peculiar grunting respiration, too, that's almost diagnostic. But with an intubation tube already in its trachea—windpipe to you, Miss Weston—this fellow doesn't make much sound."

"But the baby isn't breathing! I can hardly see its chest move."

"That's because CPAP keeps the lungs inflated most of the time," Gus explained. "The blood oxygen level is registered on that printer you see by the bassinet."

Mike moved nearer to study the pattern being registered on the moving paper strip of the recorder.

"Looks like close to eighty millimeters of mercury," he said. "What did you start with, Gus?"

"Fifty."

"Hmm! Nice work."

"Credit Val LeMoyne."

"Do you mind explaining?" the reporter asked.

"By keeping the lungs inflated all the time, we raise the blood oxygen level and improve the baby's general condition to the point where it can breathe for itself," the pediatrician explained.

"What will happen to this one after it leaves the hospital?"

"On the basis of statistics, it will probably become an addict."

"Surely that isn't hereditary too."

"No, but the Welfare Department is required by law to offer the baby to the mother or to the mother's family. In the average case it's lucky if it isn't taken—"

"Why do you say that?"

"Any child is better off growing up in foster homes or an orphanage than in a family of heroin addicts. Most of the time the mother doesn't want the baby but too often a grandmother or an aunt does take it. In that case it grows up with the same heritage that produced addiction in the mother and winds up addicted early in childhood."

"How terrible!" exclaimed the TV reporter.

"I guess one thing is worse," said Mike. "Being dead."

At the nursing station, Mike stayed behind while Gus Henderson showed Marcia Weston out.

"I asked Miss Payson to tell Miguel Quintera I'd be up to see Carmelita in a little while, but that was an hour ago at least," he said to Helga. "Did adding the top half of the refrigerating blanket have any effect?"

"Her temperature is down a degree."

"The blanket would do that, but at least it will help Miguel's morale a little."

When Mike and the tall blonde nurse entered the cubicle where Carmelita Sanchez lay, her dark hair spread out on the pillow like a fan, Mike put a restraining hand on the shoulder of the slender Cuban as he started to rise from the chair in which he had been sitting beside the narrow hospital bed.

"Don't get up, please, Miguel," he said. "I just stopped by to check on the refrigerating blanket."

"Her temperature has dropped a degree, Dr. Raburn. Couldn't that be a good sign?"

"As long as her body is capable of any physiological response, we can always hope," Mike assured the girl's fiancé.

"You're a surgeon and Carmelita's Dr. Vogel's patient on the medical service," said Helga as they were walking

83

back to the nursing station. "Yet you spend a lot more time with her than he does."

"Ed's not neglecting the girl—"

"I didn't mean that, we both know he's as good in his field as you are in yours. But we know doctors don't like to spend time on hopelessly ill patients either."

"Nobody likes to be reminded of his failures."

"But you keep coming back and I can't help wondering why."

"I notice that you're always kind and considerate to Miguel, even though it must get in your hair to have him always there in the way," he said.

"My answer is simple. If anybody loved me the way Miguel loves Carmelita, I'd want him to be with me when I was dying."

"Even though you didn't know he was there?"

"I'd know," she said confidently. "There's a special sort of ESP connected with that sort of love."

He looked at her in surprise. "That doesn't exactly agree with what you were telling me not much more than an hour ago about your philosophy of love and marriage."

"I was talking about the future—not the past."

"Then you've experienced this sort of ESP?"

"Two years ago—in Brazil." She studied him for a moment, as if searching his mind and his emotions through the steady dark eyes, then nodded, as if she had learned something from them.

"Carolyn and I went to the mission hospital I told you about just after we got our nursing degrees from the University of Florida," she continued. "We were part of a hospital team from the university, but we stayed on awhile after the others came back. The laboratory chief at the hospital was a very attractive man and I guess what you could call a chemistry developed between us from the start."

"Was he from Gainesville too?"

"No. He'd come to Brazil six months before we arrived, from a position as head biochemist for a firm in the Midwest. I learned later that he had absconded with a lot of the firm's money—Brazil has no extradition treaty with the United States, so it's a paradise for absconders." She smiled, albeit a little crookedly. "By that time, I'd gone off the deep end: paroxysmal tachycardia at the sound of his voice, swooning in his embrace—the whole bit."

"Why didn't you marry him?"

"He finally told me he had a wife back home and three kids. Whatever else I may be, I'm no home wrecker, so Carolyn and I took the next Varig flight out of there for Miami—and landed here at Biscayne General."

"No regrets?"

Helga shook her head. "One thing I don't waste time on is regrets. And now that you've heard the story of my love life, Doctor, you can answer my question about why you keep coming back to see Carmelita."

"I guess it's mostly because I hate defeat but, way back somewhere in my mind, I can't help feeling I've overlooked something that still might pull the girl back."

"Time's getting awfully short," she reminded him.

"That's the hell of it. Suppose she dies and the next day, or the next week, I suddenly remember what it was that escapes me at the moment. If that one thing could have saved her, I'm going to feel guilty for her death the rest of my life."

"So you keep torturing yourself by coming back, hoping that seeing her will blast whatever memory you've lost to the surface?"

"Something like that. I know it sounds foolish—"

"It's not foolish. I'd feel exactly the same way under the circumstances."

"Thanks for understanding. I guess we're beginning to develop some of that ESP you were just talking about."

"What about Joey Gates?" Helga changed the subject abruptly. "How much of a chance would he have had of coming through this crisis if you hadn't thought of taking him into the hyperbaric chamber?"

"Who knows?"

"Obviously his prognosis has been increased considerably because you did, so why not chalk that up as your good deed for the present?"

"You know damned well that doctors don't set quotas—

and neither do ICU nurses. Besides, Gus ordered the urea and cyanate."

"Isn't there some doubt—about the urea?"

He looked at her quickly. "Why do you ask that?"

"I read the *American Journal of Nursing,* Doctor, the same as you read the *JAMA.*"

"There *is* a question about urea, but cyanate seems to have real promise. And if Joey should go into coma again, I can always take him back into the chamber."

"You never give up, do you?"

"Not until they carry me off the field. By the way, will you leave an order for the lab to do a red cell check on Joey's blood about 7:00 P.M. for abnormal cells." He glanced at his watch as Helga picked up the small portable hand keyboard by which she could communicate with the central data storage computer bank. "Four-thirty already? The Emergency Room will soon start jumping with the five o'clock traffic rush casualties. See you later."

"Can I depend on that?" Helga's voice was mocking as she started pressing the keys of the communications instrument.

Mike grinned. "Unless the computer decides to stun you with an electric shock and gather you into its embrace."

"In that case," said Helga, "be sure to hurry to my rescue—so I can slump your way."

Chapter 6

"HERE AT Biscayne General we call it the Moriturus Committee for obvious reasons," Father Hagan told Carolyn Payson. "But medical humor is pretty caustic, so the students already have another name for it—the God Committee. And a more appropriate one, I'm sure."

"Why do you say that?"

"According to our belief, only God can give life, so logically only God should decide when to end it."

"But circumstances alter situations, Father."

"And they're considerably different in the medical field than even five years ago," the chaplain conceded. "Every day you and your staff in the Intensive Care Units keep people living who would otherwise be dead. All of which has given rise to a lot of controversy over the technical question of whether a person with no hope of life should be kept alive against his will."

"I don't see how there could be more than one answer."

"Suppose you were old, yet clinging to life, and your relatives should decide you were too much of a burden upon them?"

"I never thought of it that way."

"Few people do," said the chaplain. "None of us like to be reminded of just how mortal we really are, and the idea of accomplishing one's own death, even at the hands of another, smacks too much of suicide."

"But is letting someone else decide when you shall die—and how—really different from suicide?"

"If the dying person makes the final decision, no—but it *is* still legal," said Father Hagan. "The courts have ruled here in Florida that a person may refuse medical treatment and choose death, when life means only pain and suffering."

"That's exactly what my father does when he begs to die."

"Certainly life can hold out no hope—or pleasure—for him," Father Hagan agreed. "But Huntington's disease is often characterized by severe mental symptoms, even psychosis, so a court might rule that he isn't sane enough to make a choice."

"That would be cruel."

"The so-called 'right to die' controversy arose over that very point. The committee makes the decision for patients who are unable to make them for themselves."

"At the request of the relatives?"

"Usually, but first the committee hears competent medical opinion on whether the patient is actually hopelessly incurable. You work every day within the parameters of living and dying, Carolyn, so I'm sure you can appreciate how difficult that sort of decision can sometimes be."

Carolyn nodded. "When heart transplants were first being done, people doomed by chronic heart disease; some of them hardly able to take a deep breath without severe anginal pain from the effort, were suddenly made whole again—as if by a miracle. But then the whole thing blew up when the transplanted hearts started being rejected by the bodies of the people who received them."

"And the career of a very fine surgeon may have been wrecked because he found himself regarded as an executioner when, a few shorts months before, he'd been hailed everywhere as a savior. If the newspapers were to start mentioning even the existence of a Moriturus Committee at Biscayne General, we soon wouldn't be able to get people to serve."

"In spite of the fact that you're actually being merciful in allowing a hopeless case to die?"

"Who is to say what is hopeless? Dr. Rebecca Dalton told me once that her husband was very near to developing a practical version of the artificial heart, until he started brooding over the number of transplant cases that were dying and stopped his research. Right now I would hesitate to recommend that a patient with advanced heart disease be allowed to die, when tomorrow a mechanical pump may be invented that can take the place of the heart. Such pumps have already worked for months in calves and other animals, you know."

"If you cannot make a decision then, what's the use of having a committee at all?"

"I've asked myself the same question and haven't come up yet with an entirely suitable answer," the chaplain admitted. "But in some degenerative diseases and in many cases of severe brain injury, the patient may be little more than a vegetable, with no hope of improvement."

"You're describing my father exactly." Carolyn put her hand on the old priest's arm in a pleading gesture. "Will

88

you bring his case before the committee, Father Hagan?"

"If you're absolutely certain that is what you want."

"I am," said Carolyn firmly.

"Very well. I'll transmit your request for a hearing to the chairman and you'll be notified when to appear."

"Shall I prepare a plea?"

"We have what you might call a 'devil's advocate'—a lawyer or a doctor—to do that for you."

"What about Dr. Rebecca Dalton, if I can persuade her to plead for me?"

"You couldn't have made a better choice. But let the chairman ask her, it will be best that way."

II

Hospital morgues are generally gloomy places located in the basement of the oldest building connected with the institution. But because Biscayne General was brand new, its basement was brightly lit, well ventilated with year-round air conditioning, and generally cheerful. When Ken Dalton came into Karen Fletcher's office in the Pathology Department at four-thirty, he found her bending over a binocular microscope.

"May I come in?" he asked.

She looked up with a smile. "Of course. You got my message?"

"My secretary said you have information I might want on the Hornsby case."

"I think I have something." Karen's silver-colored hair was gathered into a discreet bun at the back of her neck and she wore flat oxfords, giving her an oddly small and fragile appearance in the freshly starched long laboratory coat she wore.

"I've been running some preliminary tests on the blood of the dead woman in the private laboratory," she added as they moved into the adjoining small room, where a dark liquid was bubbling in a retort. "For heroin or rather morphine, since heroin is changed to that in the body."

"You haven't autopsied her already, have you?"

"Sam Toyota just finished. Anthony Broadhurst called as

soon as the hospital notified his office that the mother had died."

"Why would the State's Attorney be interested in a routine OD? Mike Raburn sees them almost every day in the Emergency Room."

"The police have arrested the pimp and pusher she had been living with. He admitted belting her a few times and, if Mr. Broadhurst can prove that the girl actually died from the injuries and not from an overdose of heroin, it will be murder, not just drug peddling." Karen was working expertly while she talked, decanting a small portion of the fluid in the retort from its spout into a test tube.

"What did Sam find?" Ken asked.

"A couple of cracked ribs, but they weren't splintered and there was no air in her chest, so a punctured lung is out. There were plenty of bruises, too, but none of the abdominal organs. With that pregnant uterus sticking out in front of her, it would have been hard for an attacker to rupture a liver, kidney, or spleen the way assassins kill by rupturing the spleens of chronic malaria sufferers in the Far East, unless he knew just where to strike."

Pouring an equal amount of amyl alcohol into the tube, Karen shook it vigorously, then put it into a rack while she fitted a fluted circle of filter paper into a small funnel.

"I'm extracting some of the alkaloid with amyl alcohol, so I can make the final definitive test," she explained.

"The one *you* reported?"

"I didn't know surgeons read laboratory journals." Her tone was warm and, for the first time he could remember, Ken Dalton realized that, beneath the starched white coat and the horn-rimmed glasses, there was a very beautiful and desirable woman.

The knowledge made him feel a little guilty, and he moved a step farther away. Karen didn't miss the unconscious admission, either, and a faint smile appeared on her face as she turned to lift the test tube, with the alkaloid-alcohol mixture, from the rack and pour its contents into the funnel, beneath which she had placed another empty tube.

"I accidentally discovered the short test for morphine

90

while I was still a medical student," she said casually as she removed the tube of filtrate and, picking a bottle from the rack before her, poured a few drops into the brownish solution.

"Fletcher's solution, my sole claim to immortality," she added on a wry note when the mixture in the tube suddenly took on a deep violet tint. *"Voilà,* as Val LeMoyne would say."

"Of course this isn't a quantitative test," she continued, "but if I'd used exact amounts and put that solution into a colorimeter, I'm sure it would register enough heroin to kill her easily."

Ken had turned and was studying her more closely. "Why did you go to all the trouble of telling me this, Karen, when you could have sent a copy of the report to my office tomorrow, or the next day? And it's your afternoon off, too, isn't it?"

"I changed days when Dr. Toler asked me to take Dr. Cooper's place on the Executive Committee this afternoon," she explained. "And I had to do the tests as quickly as possible, so the State's Attorney's office would know whether to arrest the man who beat up the Hornsby girl."

"But you didn't have to go to so much trouble on my account."

"Mrs. Connor brought the body down and told me what happened. I knew you were disturbed—about everything that's happened, Ken, so I thought I could at least assure you that you couldn't have saved the patient."

"The EEG was positive. What if I had concentrated upon resuscitation instead of drama?"

"Could it really have made any difference?"

"Rebecca was there and could easily have slid a catheter-electrode through the mother's external jugular vein into her right atrium while I was doing the Caesarean. We could have stimulated the heart directly."

"Did she suggest it?"

"No," he admitted. "But neither did I."

"The girl died of respiratory paralysis from an overdose of heroin, Ken; I've just proved that to you. So even if you had kept her heart beating artificially long enough to wash some of the heroin out of her system and allow resuscitation, the damage to the brain cells was already irreversible. All you would have produced would have been a human vegetable the county government would have to take care of from now on, at a time when Ross McKenzie and a lot of other people are raising hell about the cost of operating this hospital."

"We still might have saved two lives instead of maybe saving one."

"Did you read the ambulance attendant's report?"

"No."

"They weren't able to get a pulse in the mother for at least five or six minutes before she arrived at the Emergency Room, and after four minutes of anoxia, the brain cells are usually damaged beyond repair. You're not God to decide who's going to live and who's going to die, Ken. You did what you thought was indicated and you saved a life. What else do you want?"

"Maybe you're right," he admitted. "There was a time when I kidded myself for a while that I *was* God—and look how many people I killed while doing it."

"Down here we live with death every day," said Karen with a shrug. "For my own information as a pathologist, I studied all those hearts you took out when you were doing transplants. Not one of them had more than a year or so to live, even as cardiac invalids, and for most of them it couldn't have been more than a few months. You and Rebecca both thought you were doing the best thing for all of them and your operative mortality was the lowest in the country, so you brought them a skill they could never have found anywhere else."

"Except in Houston—or San Francisco."

"Your operative mortality was lower than it would have been in either place."

"They still died," he said doggedly.

"Because their own bodies fought against the healthy hearts you substituted for diseased ones. You didn't kill those patients, Ken; they killed themselves."

"I tried telling myself that, Karen—and it doesn't work."

92

"For God's sake, why not—when it's the truth?"

"But not the *whole* truth. When the first transplant cases started dying, Rebecca suspected what was happening and warned me, but I had to play my role as the giver of life and keep on operating. After you've been God for a while, it's hard to step down and become an ordinary man again."

"Was Rebecca's warning about rejection the start of the domestic troubles between you?" Karen asked.

"I suppose so; it takes a lot of ego to do any kind of major surgery, particularly on the heart. And it's particularly hard not to resent being shot down by your own wife, especially when you have to stand by helplessly and see people die one by one, after you were warned that it was going to happen and kept on operating."

"Has Rebecca ever thrown it up to you?"

"Reb's not that kind of a wife, but things might have gone better if she had. Then we could have had a shouting match and maybe saved our marriage."

Karen glanced at her watch. "It's almost five. Mind if I go up to the Executive Committee meeting with you?"

"Not at all."

"I know most of the people there will be friendly," she added, "but from what I've heard about Mr. McKenzie's prejudices, he'll probably try to eat me alive."

"Jeffry Toler will protect you," Ken assured her. Then, obeying an impulse he could't have explained, but which Karen quite understood, he added, "and so will I."

At the elevator Karen said casually, "Have you seen Dale Tyndall recently?"

"No. Why?"

"He was going to the Dolphin Lounge when I came out of the pool about a half hour ago. Kevin gives him root beer and both of us are pretty sure he's a little more cyanotic and short of breath lately. You may want to suggest that Rebecca check him over soon."

"I'll speak to her about it," Ken promised. "Thanks for bringing it to our attention, Karen. We're very fond of Dale."

"So am I," she said. "I'd hate to see him get into trouble because we didn't watch him closely enough."

In the Board Room located on the twelfth floor of the hospital tower, the other members of the Executive Committee of the Board of Directors, governing body of the medical center, were already gathered around a long polished mahogany table when Ken Dalton and Karen Fletcher came in. A coffee urn occupied a small table in the corner, with a stack of insulated paper cups beside it, several of which in various degrees of emptiness were beside the board members.

Outside, visible through a large plate-glass window, was a beautiful scene. Sport-fishing boats plowed the bay southward from the ocean-access small-boat channel at Haulover Island toward their berths along the mainland bay front downtown, while water skiers crisscrossed their wakes. A great white ship was putting out of the new Miami harbor, dredged so the procession of cruise vessels that regularly left for the Caribbean and other ports could berth in the heart of downtown instead of the more utilitarian Port Everglades a few miles to the north between Miami and Fort Lauderdale. The new port of Miami had greatly increased shipping in and out of Miami itself, making it one of the busiest cruise ports in the world.

The chair at the head of the table was occupied by Andrew Graves, a local banker who was chairman of the medical center Board of Directors, functioning essentially as a hospital commission for the county. At Graves's left was Ross McKenzie, veteran county political boss. One of Miami's wealthiest citizens, McKenzie owned extensive groves, as well as a large packing house in the surrounding county area. He had been a long-time member of the governing County Commission and chairman of the Commission Finance Committee.

The chair to the right of Andrew Graves belonged to Jeffry Toler, chief administrative officer of the center, his deceptively guileless blue eyes behind steel-rimmed glasses masking a brain that operated like the central computer in the basement of the hospital tower. At his elbow was the secretary of the Board, Helen Gaynor, with a stenotype machine before her, ready to record the business transacted by the governmental unit supervising the vast medical center.

The medical staff of the hospital and faculty were well represented. Dr. Manning Desmond, a florid and rather pompous physician, was professor of medicine in the medical school. Ken Dalton represented surgery. Dr. Adrian Cooper, whose place Karen Fletcher was taking that afternoon, had been, in his capacity as county medical examiner, something of a liaison between the hospital-medical school complex, the county government, and the myriad conglomeration of municipalities that made up the metropolis that was Miami.

Karen looked deceptively small and defenseless when she occupied Dr. Cooper's chair as the at-large member of the small group making up the Executive Committee of the considerably larger Board, now in recess during the hot summer months. Jeffry Toler introduced her to Ross McKenzie, who grudgingly acknowledged her presence with a grunt. And when Andrew Graves whacked the gavel beside him on a polished wooden block, silence fell over the room.

"The June meeting of the Executive Committee, substituting for the Board of Directors, is called to order," he said. "All of you received a Xerox copy of the minutes of last month's meeting. If there are no corrections, I declare them approved as recorded. Mr. McKenzie has asked to be heard first." He turned to the grower. "The floor is yours, Ross."

Ross McKenzie was a sturdy man of sixty-five, with the dour expression of his Scots ancestry as much in evidence as the burr he'd retained, even though brought to the United States when he was only ten. He looked around the table as if daring the others to dispute his right to speak first.

"Gentlemen," he said, ignoring Karen's presence, "I am sure you know that, judging from the budget you have submitted to the commission for the fiscal year starting July 1, this hospital is approaching a severe financial crisis."

"Show me one that isn't," said Manning Desmond.

"With labor costs skyrocketing since the Civil Service Commission allowed hospital employees to be unionized and Congress raised the minimum wage, how could the situation be otherwise?"

"That's not the point, Doctor," said McKenzie. "All of you know I was against building this medical center in the first place. Now that it has turned out to be the white elephant I warned you it would be, don't expect the county government to bail you out."

"Would you rather have a cockroach-infested medical slum, Mr. McKenzie?" Jeffry Toler demanded bluntly.

"My daughter was born in an old hospital and both she and my wife got along all right."

"Twenty years ago all you needed for an obstetric department was a delivery room, a dozen bassinets, and beds for the mothers," said Toler. "The whole thing cost maybe twenty dollars per patient day then but at this moment it's costing over a hundred dollars a day to keep one premature alive in the Pediatric Intensive Care Unit, after Dr. Dalton managed to get it out of the mother's body before it died too."

"Maybe it isn't worth the trouble," McKenzie growled.

"Which would you rather see, Ross?" Andrew Graves asked. "A few dollars saved or babies lost that could have lived? I dare say you'd sing a different tune if your daughter and your grandchild were involved."

"What did the mother die of?" McKenzie asked.

"An overdose of heroin," said Ken.

"Just as I thought," said the politician. "Saving people who will only wind up costing the county thousands of dollars in welfare payments is a waste of time and money."

"Doctors don't equate human lives with dollars," Karen said quietly, and Ross McKenzie looked startled, then shook his head, as he might have done at a vagrant gnat, and continued his diatribe.

"From the looks of this room, none of you have any idea what a dollar is worth—spending a hundred thousand dollars so the doctors who use it can look out over the bay? And that Intensive Care Unit you've got down on

96

the first floor, the equipment alone cost nearly a million dollars."

"Concentrating all emergency and intensive care functions in one area not only makes a lot of sense, Mr. McKenzie, it has also made Biscayne General the most modern hospital in the world," said Ken. "Most hospitals have small intensive care units scattered all over the place, all needing specialized personnel and very expensive instrumentation. By putting everything having to do with intensive care on one floor, we enable personnel to be shifted to fit the greatest need and avoid duplication of monitors and other electronic equipment. And by having highly trained people only seconds away in the Emergency Department, less time is lost when treating life or death situations."

"Why does Biscayne General have to get so many emergency cases, Doctor? They never have paid their way and never will."

"We built this center where it is because it can be reached in minutes by expressways," said Andrew Graves. "One of the attractions this area has for older people is immediate access to expert medical care, and a lot of the older bay-front hotels over on the beach side are full of them, sitting in the sun and waiting to die—"

"What the hell has that got to do with waste in this hospital?" McKenzie demanded acidly.

"If people in those retirement hotels just dropped dead when their time came, it wouldn't be necessary to have a hospital to look after them that's operating in the red— and our students would lose one of the best sources we have for clinical material," Ken interposed. "But old people don't oblige the city fathers by dying that easy, Mr. McKenzie. They have strokes, heart attacks, inflamed gall bladders, and enlarged prostates. Even with Medicare most of them don't have the financial resources to stand a long siege of illness, so it's up to the local government to provide it for them the same way we provide the whole cost to welfare recipients and also make that care easy to reach from all parts of the county."

"Give me one good reason why taxpayers who don't

use charity have to provide for those who do?" Ross McKenzie growled.

"I can give you more than one reason, Ross," said Andrew Graves. "When the occupancy rate in Miami area hotels started falling off because tourists would rather go to gambling casinos in the Bahamas or the Caribbean to say nothing of Disney World and all those amusement complexes being built in Central Florida—the municipal governments in the county were all for turning those hotels into retirement homes and luring old people down here."

"And what can you give them besides the climate that they couldn't have gotten in their home states—without putting a burden on Florida taxpayers?"

"For one thing, we have one of the finest geriatric research programs in the country—financed by the federal government," said Ken. "One of our Surgical Fellows, Dr. Michael Raburn, has been treating a group of older people suffering from a general decline of all body functions because of age and arteriosclerosis until they're almost vegetables with oxygen under pressure in the hyperbaric chamber."

"Another million dollars wasted," McKenzie observed.

"The Navy gave us the chamber and also subsidizes its operation," said Jeffry Toler. "You can't change that to the taxpayers of the county."

"It all comes out of the same pocket," said McKenzie. "Go on, Doctor."

"As I was saying, Dr. Raburn exposes the patients to the highest pressure of oxygen they can stand without convulsions."

"Experimenting, Doctor?"

"Yes, but for their own good. Men and women who shuffle into the chamber like zombies, rarely speaking or showing interest in anything and having to be fed like babies, walk out seemingly rejuvenated, reasonably alert, and even able to communicate and look after themselves. What is more, the effects aren't just temporary but sometimes last for weeks. And when they do start to wear off, another hyperbaric treatment produces a repeat effect."

"Better not force us to discontinue that program, Ross," said Andrew Graves dryly. "We both may be needing it one of these days."

"Speak for yourself," said McKenzie. "I must say I'm pleased to see that one department, at least, is doing something to keep the old and arteriosclerotic alive, Dr. Dalton. You've certainly done your share personally to reduce hospital overcrowding by senior citizens."

The politician's acid comment was like a stiletto thrust in the body; Ken Dalton stiffened and turned white while Karen Fletcher gasped at the bald implication of McKenzie's cutting words. But nobody spoke as Ken rose to his feet, his chair tumbling backward at the sudden movement. Nor did anyone make a move to stop him when he left the room, walking like a man in a trance.

"Well, Ross." Andrew Graves broke the tense silence as the door closed behind the surgeon's back. "With apologies to Dr. Fletcher, I must say that you have just qualified for the title of All-American son of a bitch. Congratulations!"

"I only spoke the truth and everybody knows it." McKenzie showed no sign of either sorrow or resentment. "Dalton's killed so many people that, if they were all women, he could be called a modern Bluebeard."

"Dr. Kenneth Dalton is one of the truly great surgeons this country has produced in modern times," said Jeffry Toler. "I shall make it a point to apologize to him as soon as this meeting is over."

"You won't be apologizing for me," said McKenzie. "If he wasn't guilty, why did he turn tail and run?"

"Probably to keep from killing you," Dr. Desmond observed dryly. "It's a good thing I wasn't in his place. I'm nearer your age, McKenzie, and I certainly would have given myself the satisfaction of slugging you."

"All right, gentlemen," said the politician. "I came here to listen to some concrete proposals for handling the financial crisis this hospital faces—and so far I haven't heard any."

"We gave you our budget for the fiscal year starting in July," Graves reminded him. "What are your suggestions?"

"Cut your operating costs in half by not admitting any non-paying patients except life or death emergencies. And stop teaching a lot of young punks to be specialists, so they can get rich instead of settling in small towns and practicing the sort of medicine that's needed there."

"That makes about as much sense as cutting off your head to spite your face," Andrew Graves snapped. "If you politicians can't come up with a better solution to medical care costs than that, the full medical center Board of Directors will have to request that a referendum be put on the ballot this fall. We'll let the people decide whether they want Biscayne General to stay open and make up our deficits out of tax dollars, or close it and let a lot of people die because they can't get medical care."

"I guess you know what the answer of the voters will be to that question, Mr. McKenzie," said Manning Desmond. "People are proud of this medical center and what it means to the community as a whole. Well over half of our patients are old enough to vote and the rest have parents."

"Is that a threat, Doctor?" McKenzie inquired in a tone of contempt he might have used toward a yapping poodle. "Or a bluff?"

The older doctor shrugged. "Take it whatever way you prefer. But if we're forced to cut down our teaching functions by lack of patients and funds, we'll lose thousands of dollars in research money from government grants."

"Maybe the public would be better off without what you call research," said McKenzie ."I understand that Dr. Dalton learned to transplant hearts by operating on dogs. And I don't have to remind you that at least fourteen people would be alive today, if he hadn't learned so much."

"The patients Dr. Dalton operated on had only a few months or a year at most to live," said Karen Fletcher. "In fact several of them had been a burden on the city for years because of severe heart disease."

"And in the course of performing heart transplants," Toler added, "Dr. Dalton and Dr. LeMoyne were able to work out some important advances in anesthesia for open

100

heart surgery and heart-lung pump operation that will help save many children otherwise doomed by congenital heart disease, as well as older people who will need artificial heart valves and the like."

"Both of the Daltons have learned a lot from studying the problem of organ rejection that will make kidney and other organ transplants more successful," said Karen.

"I'm not here to argue medical questions with doctors; you're supposed to know what you're doing in that field, at least," McKenzie snapped. "I'm just warning you that the Finance Committee will okay the same budget you had this year and not a cent more."

"But you know it takes considerably more to operate this hospital than it did the old one," Jeffry Toler protested.

"You wanted this white elephant and you've got it, Dr. Toler. We aren't going to give you any more money to run it than you had for the old plant, so if you find yourself short before the end of the fiscal year, you'd better buy some padlocks before you run out of money, so you can lock up the place."

"But—"

"What's the next order of business, Andrew?" said McKenzie. "I can't stay here all night."

Andrew Graves looked down at the agenda before him. "The only other item of importance is to approve the retirement of Dr. Jake Barrows for disability—"

"What's wrong with him?"

"Dr. Barrows suffered a severe coronary thrombosis recently," said Manning Desmond. "He has continued to have attacks of angina and in our opinion can no longer function efficiently as chief of the Cardiology Section. I have recommended that Dr. Rebecca Dalton take his place as section chief, with elevation to the rank of full professor."

"Kenneth Dalton's wife?" McKenzie's tone suggested that he couldn't believe what he was hearing.

"Yes."

"How old is she?"

"Thirty-two, I believe."

101

"You mean you're willing to make a woman that young head of the most important section of the hospital?"

"The medical faculty is willing," said Manning Desmond.

"What is it you object to, Mr. McKenzie?" Karen Fletcher's tone was deceptively mild. "Her age—or the fact that she's a woman?"

"Both. Plus the fact that she's Dr. Kenneth Dalton's wife." He wheeled upon Manning Desmond. "Didn't she help decide whether those transplant cases would be operated on?"

"Yes."

"For God's sake what are you trying to do? First you want to promote a woman to a man's job, and then you admit that she's incompetent."

"I have personally examined the hearts that were removed before the new ones were put in, Mr. McKenzie," said Karen. "They were all badly diseased and none of those patients could have lived much longer than six months—if that long."

"And now they're all dead?"

"All but one."

"Your prejudices are well known, Ross," said Andrew Graves severely. "If you would spend a few days observing the work of this hospital closely instead of criticizing it all the time because you didn't want us to build it, you'd know that Dr. Rebecca Dalton is one of the foremost heart specialists in the country."

"While you're airing your prejudices, Mr. McKenzie," said Karen, "I think you ought to know that my assistant, Dr. Sam Toyota, is a Japanese."

"And the chief technician in the Nephrosis Research Laboratory is a Negro, Ross," said Andrew Graves. "I know because he does tests on my grandson."

"You can run a melting pot and a women's lib movement in your school if you want to." McKenzie was closing his briefcase. "But just don't ask me to wheedle any more tax dollars out of the budget than I've told you the commission will give you. Vote me 'No!' on Dr. Dalton's promotion, Andrew. I have another appointment this evening and I'm not going to waste time arguing with you."

Before anyone could protest—and no one made a move to—he stalked from the room.

"Well, that's that," said Andrew Graves. "I guess we have only one choice. I'll initiate a petition tomorrow, asking for medical center financing to be put under a special millage and out of Ross McKenzie's hands."

"The county machine can deliver a lot of votes," said Manning Desmond doubtfully. "And all will be against the proposition."

"We'll just have to deliver more," said Dr. Toler.

"How, Jeffry?"

"Mike Raburn saved the life of Big Joe Gates's little boy this afternoon. The whole thing will be on the six o'clock TV news, as well as in the papers tomorrow."

"And Big Joe is the star black forward of the Miami Snappers." Andrew Graves whistled softly. "Elections have been won with less."

Chapter 7

"YOU LOOK TIRED, darling." Carolyn Payson and Gus Henderson had finished dinner and were sitting at a small table in one corner of the half-empty hospital cafeteria.

"It's been one of those days," said the pediatrician wearily. "Did you see Mike Raburn on the six o'clock news—with Joe Gates's boy?"

"It was on the color TV in the waiting room when I came through. But why Mike instead of you? A sickle cell crisis is a pediatric condition."

"Mike's had more experience than anybody else here with the hyperbaric chamber. Besides, it was his idea to use it and I've got everything I want, except you."

"I thought you'd already had all of me. Or is this some new technique you've learned from Ed Vogel?"

"I'm talking about marriage, darling. The first of July I'll become an assistant professor of pediatrics, with a chance to get in on the income from the Private Diagnostic Clinic. I can pay off everything I owe in my education in a few months and we can start in the black. You won't even have to work——"

"I'd want to."

"Then why don't we get married tomorrow?"

"I couldn't saddle anyone with the burden of my father, Gus. Caring for him since he's been here has already used up almost all the money he has, and I've been putting away everything I can against the time when I'll have to start paying it myself."

"I just finished telling you I'll be in the black soon after the first of July. And my credit's good right now."

"I couldn't let you do that. It wouldn't be fair."

"Not if I'm willing?"

"I'd still feel guilty. Why can't we go on like we have been?"

"That isn't fair to you."

"Have I ever complained?" Carolyn asked.

"No, but——"

"It's settled then."

"I ought to warn you that after July 1 I'll be free almost every night."

"And I'll still get off duty at three o'clock every afternoon," she reminded him with a smile. "In plenty of time to cook your dinner."

Gus glanced at his watch, then reached for the trays they had pushed to one side of the table when they finished eating. "I'd better make rounds——"

"Wait a minute, darling. I want to ask you something."

"Fire away."

"What do you know about the Moriturus Committee?"

"The what?" Then his face suddenly cleared. "You must mean the God Committee."

"It's called that too, I believe."

"Don't do it, Carolyn." Gus's face was etched with concern as he reached across the table and covered her hand with his own.

"How do you know . . . ?"

"You could have only one reason to ask about that committee—your father."

"Then you do know something about it?"

"The whole thing's supersecret, as much as anything in a hospital is ever secret."

"You're not on the committee, are you?"

"No. Who told you about it?"

"Father Hagan. I asked him to call a meeting to consider what to do with my father."

"I still wish you hadn't, Carolyn."

"Why? When Father wants to die?"

"I don't deny him the right to wish for death—or even to take his own life. But—"

"No one else can make the decision for him," she protested. "He can't do it himself and the only words he ever speaks are 'Let me die.'"

"It's you I'm thinking of, darling. I've presented two cases to the committee for Dr. McHale, both of them mongoloid newborns with meningoceles and spina bifida—and both hopeless. You know a lot of those are born with pyloric stenosis, too, keeping anything from getting out of the stomach."

"I've seen several monogoloids in the Surgical ICU after their stomachs were operated on to relieve the obstruction."

"Those didn't have open spinal columns. They're easy enough to save but the worst cases are still practically brainless. The families of the two I presented didn't think it was fair to their other children to try to bring them up and they couldn't afford the cost of an institution. The God Committee approved not doing surgery on them."

"I guess that's why we didn't see them in the ICU."

"There was another reason," said Gus. "The personnel in your department are trained to preserve life, and having to watch a human being die by inches because no food or fluid can enter the body is a very traumatic experience. We just put those two in a separate room on the Pediatric

Ward and tried to see as little of them as we could, but it took them a long time to starve to death and more than once I was tempted to put them out of their misery with a syringe full of air injected into a vein. Believe me, it would be doubly hard on you where your father is concerned."

"I can't stand watching him lie there, Gus," Carolyn protested. "Torn apart by something nobody can do anything about."

"Did you say Father Hagan has requested a hearing before the committee?"

"It's already settled."

"All I can do is hope you won't feel guilty afterward and blame yourself."

"I'd blame myself more if I let him live."

"I guess you would at that," he admitted. "It's a hell of a choice to watch someone you love forced to make. I only wish I could help."

"You can," said Carolyn. "By continuing to love me—"

Gus lifted the hand he was holding and gave it a quick kiss. "There's about as much chance of that not happening as for hell to freeze over—in Miami of all places."

II

Jeffry Toler got Rebecca Dalton on the phone, in the hospital cafeteria.

"Where are you, Reb?" he asked.

"Just finished eating chicken and dumplings, which I can't resist, even though I have to starve tomorrow."

"Can you wait for me? I'm just leaving for home."

"I'll meet you in the lobby. I have to run over to the Terrace for a minute anyway."

"Have you seen Ken lately?" Toler asked when he stopped beside her a few minutes later in the first-floor lobby.

"Not for several hours, since he did the Caesarean in the Emergency Room and saved the baby."

"I heard about that, it took quick thinking."

"Quick surgery, too. I doubt that anybody except Ken, or maybe Mike Raburn, could have moved that fast. But wasn't Ken at the meeting of the Executive Committee this afternoon?"

"He was for a while. But things didn't go well and he left—rather suddenly."

"Do you mean he blew his top over my appointment as professor and chief of the Cardiology Section?" she asked quickly.

"He left before that came up for consideration."

"So he may not know about it yet?"

"He'll learn soon enough, probably has already," said Toler. "This all happened because Ross McKenzie went into one of his tirades. Incidentally, McKenzie also tried to torpedo your promotion—seems to think a woman's place is in the home."

"He may be nearer right than I've ever been prepared to admit, Jeff. At least where my husband's love is concerned."

"I don't think Ken would agree with that, Reb. I'm on my way now to apologize, if I can find him—on behalf of the Board."

"Would it be cricket to tell me just what Mr. McKenzie said?" Rebecca asked, and Jeffry Toler gave her a quick résumé of the events at the afternoon meeting. When he finished, her expression was grave.

"With Ken already depressed over those transplant patients that died, something like this coming right after losing the OD this afternoon could be the nudge to topple him over the brink—"

"You don't mean . . . ?"

"There are other ways of committing suicide, both professionally and physically, than putting a gun to one's temple. I'll have to try and find Ken."

"He's not in the hospital, I had him paged."

"I've got a hunch where he may be." She put her hand on the administrator's sleeve in a pleading gesture. "Let me handle this, please, Jeff. After all, I've got the most to lose."

The Dolphin Lounge had been almost deserted when Ken Dalton came in, just before seven. The pre-dinner drinkers had already moved on and it was too early for after-dinner drinking to really get under way. Ken glanced at the bar with a look that was almost furtive, then visibly relaxed when he saw the familiar stocky torso, broad shoulders, and battered Irish mug of Kevin McCartney above the polished mahogany surface.

"Still here, Doc." Kevin's brogue was straight out of County Cork. "I'm too ornery to die for a long time yet."

"Let's hope so," said Ken, taking a stool at the bar.

Kevin had been his third heart transplant and was now the only living one. He'd been the most difficult one, too, for the only available heart had been considerably smaller than the battered and failing organ removed from Kevin's chest in order to make room for a new central pump. But the delicate job of suturing required to adapt the smaller heart to far larger blood vessels had given Ken the confidence in his own skill that had led to the next dozen operations, with no deaths at the time of surgery or shortly afterward.

Kevin had been visiting in Miami when his third heart attack crippled an already weakened organ beyond repair by the natural healing forces of the body, leaving him the choice of either a transplant or death. Following the successful surgery, he'd stayed on and taken the bartender's job in the Dolphin Lounge so as to be near the doctors and the hospital that had given him life again. In a way, the burly Irishman haunted Ken, however, reminding him of the fact—all too certain since he and Rebecca had pulled Kevin through four rejection crises, each more severe than the previous one—that the Irishman was living on borrowed time.

"Everybody that came in here for a drink before dinner was talking about the baby you saved this afternoon, Doc." Keven filled a frosted stein with draft beer and slid it across the bar to the surgeon. "It must've been a fast job."

"Did they tell you I might have saved the mother, if I hadn't been so centered on getting to the baby?"

"I didn't hear it that way and I don't think many people will see it that way either. How's the kid by the way?"

"Cold turkey, which means about as near having no reason to live as you can get."

"Except one—it's alive."

"That may be small comfort considering what it has to look forward to."

"Don't you believe it. Between livin' and not livin', there ain't no question, Doc. No question at all."

"I didn't know you were a philosopher." Ken took a drink from the stein.

"All the philosophy I need is wrapped up in just bein' alive. The way I figure it, I'm not only keepin' myself alive, I'm also keepin' that girl's heart alive. That makes you responsible for both of us, too. So no matter what anybody says, Doc, you can't do no wrong."

"*Nolle nocere*—do no harm—is the first principle a doctor learns in treating a patient, particularly a sick one," said Ken soberly. "But you're only one out of fifteen, Kevin, and the last one at that. I wonder how many of the others would subscribe to your philosophy."

"You have to look death in the face all the time the way we did to know what it means not to see it staring at you even for one day," the bartender assured him. "Everybody you operated on was lookin' the Grim Reaper right in the eye and, believe me, we were all scared stiff. That's why you've got to go on with that experimental work of yours. Young Mike Raburn tells me you and the missus—"

"Ex-Mrs."

"I don't accept that either. I've cooled too many bottles of Cold Duck for you and Dr. Reb not to know you two make a team. So the sooner you get back together and start your work goin' again, the better it'll be for both of us—and a lot of other people, whose hearts are beginnin' to wear out."

"Got any pretzels?" Ken's tone was almost curt and Kevin recognized that he had touched a sensitive spot—as he had intended.

"Sure, Doc—and the evenin' paper. Why don't you take that booth in the corner? I'll bring 'em to you with another stein of beer."

IV

It was nearly eight-thirty when Rebecca came into the Dolphin Lounge and took a stool at the bar. She waited patiently for Kevin McCartney to finish serving a man drinking beer at the other end of the bar and about a dozen students and house staff members, who had grouped several tables together in one corner of the room near the jukebox and were dancing to the jarring beat of a rock tune.

"That stuff sounds worse than bagpipes." Kevin finally moved along the bar to where Rebecca was sitting. "I left Ireland to escape all that wailin' and it's followed me here. What'll you have, Dr. Reb?"

"I'll try an Angel's Tip."

"Your husband was in here about an hour ago," said the bartender casually, as he poured crème de cacao into a tiny glass, floated about a teaspoonful of heavy cream above it, and then balanced a maraschino cherry pierced with a toothpick atop the whole. "He had a couple of beers and some pretzels."

Knowing quite well why Rebecca had come to the lounge, Kevin had given her the information she wanted without making her undergo the embarrassment of asking whether Ken was drinking heavily, as he had on one or two occasions lately.

"I think Doc comes in here to check up on me, and make sure I'm behavin' myself," Kevin volunteered.

"Are you?"

"Sure." Knowing Kevin as well as she did, Rebecca sensed the overheartiness in his voice and felt a sudden sense of alarm.

110

"I don't remember seeing you in the Cardiac Research Laboratory last month."

"You know how it is, Dr. Reb." The bartender looked embarrassed. "When you feel as good as I do, you forget them things."

"Forget? Or avoid reporting?"

"Why would I do that, Doctor?"

"If you didn't want to remind us that you still need to be careful, you might just not come in for your checkup, fearing there could be some reason for us to really start worrying about you."

"Can't fool you, can I?" Kevin admitted sheepishly.

"Not after what we've been through together."

"How could I forget when you were the one that persuaded me to have the transplant—and Dr. Ken to do the operation—after I'd been given up as a hopeless case by everybody else?"

"I want you to report to the Cardiac Research Laboratory at nine o'clock tomorrow," Rebecca said firmly. "Peggy Tyndall will do an electrocardiogram and some other special tests. I'll probably see you around eleven, when we'll have most of the reports we need."

"Could you make it day after tomorrow?" Kevin asked. "I planned to leave real early in the morning for the Keys and a day of fishing out of Marathon. A guy that keeps a boat down there wants me to go with him."

"All right," said Rebecca. "But no fudging this time."

"I'll be there, Doc."

Rebecca finished the liqueur and pushed the glass and a dollar across the bar. "If you aren't in the lab day after tomorrow, I'll come looking for you," she said in parting.

"Who was that?" the man at the other end asked when Kevin set another stein of beer before him.

"Dr. Rebecca Dalton. She's the chief heart specialist for the medical center and married to the best surgeon in the world."

"Some people have all the luck. But if I owned a looker like that, I sure wouldn't be letting her drink alone in bars."

111

The breeze from the bay had died with the coming of darkness, stilled by the black shadow of a thunderstorm making up to the west over the vast river of grass called the Everglades. The air was hot and muggy when Rebecca came out of the Dolphin Lounge, and particularly oppressive after the air conditioning inside.

The pool between the apartment hotel and the bay front was brightly lighted but only a medical student and his girl were swimming, so she decided to take a dip to cool off before settling down to a couple of hours of reading in the penthouse apartment where she lived alone, since Ken had moved to a lower floor almost six months ago.

In her bedroom she undressed quickly and, noticing a trim blue maillot on a hanger in one of the large zipper bags used to protect clothing from mildew in the damp warm climate of South Florida, took it down. The smell of moth crystals in the fabric was strong, reminding her that she hadn't worn it in a long, long time.

Could it really be the same one she'd bought ten years ago in preparation for that week of happiness they'd spent poking around the island-studded expanse of Florida Bay aboard a houseboat Ken had rented for their honeymoon? They were married the day after receiving their medical diplomas, and with low-paid interneships at the old Biscayne General coming up a few weeks away for both of them, the houseboat had been all they could afford, and all they needed, besides themselves.

Looking back on it now, Rebecca was sure she'd fallen in love with Ken their first day in the medical school Anatomy Laboratory, when he'd offered to help her with the dissection. Pride and the determination to carry her own weight had made her refuse the offer then and she still prided herself that she'd maintained her own personal and professional independence, through ten years of marriage.

Ken had called her "Rebel" that morning but his smile had taken any sting out of the words. And although they had been academic competitors all through the four years of medical school, with now one, now the other leading in the grade averages posted at the end of each year, Ken had beaten her out by half a point in the final months.

During the small amount of free time their studies allowed, they'd been inseparable almost from that first day in the Anatomy Laboratory. The excellence of their class averages had assured both of them of a free choice of interneship appointments, jointly or separately. But, loving South Florida and each other, they'd chosen Biscayne General where they could keep on being together, this time as man and wife—until six months ago.

Nor had either of them changed very much physically, she was sure. Ken worked out daily in the small gym of the medical center Rehabilitation Department and he was still as leanly handsome as he'd been ever since Rebecca had known him. His blue eyes were troubled most of the time now, it was true. And sometimes, when she watched him crossing the stretch of green lawn between the hospital tower and Bayside Terrace, Rebecca could see that his shoulders drooped a little from the burden of guilt he'd taken upon himself, when the list of living transplant recipients had grown shorter almost every week. But when they happened to meet in the course of their daily duties, his smile was still there, even though just seeing it sent a stab of pain through her at the loss of what they'd had for so long together.

Nor had she changed physically, Rebecca assured herself, holding the blue maillot up in front of her body. The breasts were just as high and as proud, although they had felt no lover's touch during the lonely months since she and Ken had started drifting apart. The waist was fully as slender, the hips as sveltely rounded, the thighs and calves as slim as ever. True, she wore her sandy auburn hair short, where before it had touched her shoulders when she let it down at night for bed. But it curled naturally, retaining the same lustrous sheen, even with the passage of the years. And although she had started wearing glasses for reading, the gray eyes were, she was sure, as direct as ever and as capable of warmth.

In a gesture of reassurance, Rebecca stepped into the

blue maillot and, reaching back, tried to slide the zipper upward. It resisted, not, she told herself, because she'd put on weight but from rust, but after a moment of fiddling with the fastener, the metal teeth locked smoothly and she slid it upward. Turning before the mirror, she told herself she could easily pass for the same twenty-two-year-old girl whose entire body had tanned to a golden tint during that week among the unnamed Keys and hidden waterways dotting Florida Bay.

Caught up in memory, Rebecca had almost forgotten for a moment the realities of the present. But a second look in the mirror reminded her that in other than purely physical ways the image reflected there was not the same. The reality of present unhappiness did indeed threaten more than ever now to destroy memories which, with evidence mounting daily that what had seemed at first to be a perfect marriage was apparently winding down to an inevitable end, it seemed foolish to recall. Nothing could really be gained by trying to put those same pleasant memories in mothballs for another ten years, as she'd done with the maillot, she assured herself and, putting a short terry cloth robe over the bathing suit and carrying a towel over her arm, Rebecca took the elevator to the ground floor.

When she looked out at the pool, she saw that the group from the Dolphin Lounge had pre-empted it now and were engaged in a furious game of water polo. Going back to the elevator, she pushed the button for the penthouse floor but, when the elevator stopped, decided to go on up to the rooftop lounge instead, in the hope that the air would be cooler at that height.

A number of lounge chairs and potted palms had been placed on the flat, gravel-studded roof to give the illusion of a garden for those who might want to sun-bathe there by day or make love by night. At this height a light sea breeze was blowing and the wash of the wavelets breaking against the bulkhead was easily audible.

Across the bay the hotels and apartments along the beach formed a pattern of lighted rectangles, while the flowing streams of automobile headlights along the causeways and bridges reminded Rebecca of the swift currents of blood cells through capillaries in the webbed foot of a frog during an experiment she and Ken had conducted long ago in the Physiology Laboratory as medical students.

She'd thought she was alone, until the tiny glowing arc of a cigarette flipped out into space to fall like a tiny shooting star told her someone else had come up here tonight, too, seeking solitude to think. Not wanting to intrude, she started toward the fire stairway to the lower floors but stopped when a familiar voice spoke from the darkness beyond the potted palm.

"Is that you, Reb?" It was Ken.

"Yes. I didn't know—"

"I'm glad you came up, we need to talk."

Rebecca moved to the front parapet where he was standing, a tall shadow against the backdrop of the city across the bay. Like her, she saw, he was in swim trunks and a robe.

"I was going for a swim," he explained, "until that crowd of young people pre-empted the pool."

"So was I. At least it's cool up here. You've lost weight," said Rebecca. "Where have you been eating?"

He laughed a little self-consciously. "Tonight I had two beers and a bowl of pretzels with Kevin."

"I know. He's worried about you—and so am I."

He turned to face her then, three or four feet away, but made no move to shorten the distance between them.

"Afraid I'll start hitting the bottle?"

"That—among other things. Jeffry Toler was looking for you earlier—to apologize for what Ross McKenzie said."

"McKenzie was right, you know."

"He was nothing of the sort," she flared. "Every surgeon loses patients—if he dares to operate and tries to save lives."

"But not every case—you know Kevin's having some trouble again, don't you?"

Rebecca wasn't surprised at the acuity of his clinical instinct. This ability to anticipate trouble, even before it could be discovered by machines and laboratories and other technical adjuncts to diagnosis, was one of the things that made him the great surgeon he was.

"I'm not sure," she hedged. "He's coming to the lab day after tomorrow for a checkup."

"You'll find signs of another developing rejection crisis. Kevin's been trying to hide them by not reporting for checkups. I suspected it, but I was discouraged enough not to insist that he come in—and afraid of what your tests would show, if the truth were told."

"It can't be very far developed yet."

"I agree there, you'll probably be able to pull him through this time. But there'll be others, each a little worse than the one before, until the end."

"They're still doing heart transplants in California, and saving them. Not that I'm critical," she added, when she saw him wince.

"You have a right to be," he said. "My guess is that the California results are produced by careful selection and attention to detail. If I'd gone more slowly and taken the time to try to find a way to overcome rejection, the story might have been different here too. But I had to have more cases than DeBakey, Cooley, or even Shumway in California. We used to say surgeons who always wanted to be operating were seized by the *furor operativus,* but I never thought it would happen to me."

"Is that any reason to be moaning about your failures all the time?" Rebecca was half crying herself. "The man I married wasn't a crybaby—just because he had a run of bad luck. I used to sneak into the gallery of the operating room when you were operating. And when I watched the way your hands moved, I felt like they were moving on my own body."

She shivered, although the night was warm. "What happened to us, Ken? Why did what we had go away?"

He took a step toward her and she caught her breath, waiting for him to take the second step and knowing she would throw herself into his arms if he did, begging him to hold her as he had held her so many times—but he didn't.

"You're a success and I'm a failure, Reb. It all adds up to that and nothing else." The agony in his voice tore at her heart, erasing her anger, erasing everything save the urge to take him in her arms and comfort him in the way lovers have comforted each other in times of stress since time immemorial. Yet from somewhere in the depths of the wisdom her love for him had given her, she knew that if she were the aggressor now, everything would be lost. Only one possible way remained, one hope alone—that of shaming him to anger.

"Did you ever ask yourself which role you began to fail at first, Ken—surgeon or lover?"

"God damn you!" She knew a sudden surge of hope at the anger in his voice and her heart sang a wild keening note when she felt his hands upon her body, ripping away the fabric of the blue maillot, exposing lovely taut breasts and tearing at her body in the desperate urgency of shared passion.

Chapter 8

IT WAS TEN O'CLOCK before Mike Raburn could break free from Emergency and come to the main ICU nursing station. Helga was punching the eleven-to-seven medication orders into the small, hand-held control keyboard by which it was possible to communicate directly with the main computer bank, as well as with the smaller mini-computers used within the unit itself for less complicated operations.

Once the medication schedule was programed, the needed doses would be delivered exactly on time during the next shift from the central dispensing pharmacy by way of the hospital-wide pneumatic carrier system. The nurses on duty would also be warned by blinking lights on the main control panel, until the medication was given and a record of its administration punched into the computer's memory bank and printed on the patient's record.

117

Helga looked up when Mike Raburn stopped at the nursing station.

"Give me a minute to finish these orders and I'll make rounds with you," she said.

"How is Carmelita tonight?"

"Her temperature's going up again, in spite of the blanket. Could you take a look at Joey Gates first? His ECG skitters a little on the monitor every now and then. I suspect the end of that catheter may be touching the atrium."

"You're probably right, I had to adjust it while we were in the tank. Did they get the portable chest film I asked for?"

"A couple of hours ago. The report may be in the data bank by now."

Helga punched in the code number from Joey Gates's chart and immediately four lines of printed words appeared on the storage scope controlled by the computer to display data from the clinical record.

PORTABLE AP AND LATERAL FILMS OF CHEST SHOW TIP OF IV CATHETER AT EDGE OF CARDIAC ATRIAL SHADOW, POSSIBLY TOUCHING IT. LUNGS CLEAR. HEART SHADOW NORMAL.

"There's your ESP again," said Mike.

Helga had finished punching the medication orders into the computer and they were leaving the station. The printed record of the chest X-ray report had disappeared from the screen into the memory bank from which it could be recalled in approximately a millionth of a second if the need arose.

"You almost have to, if you're going to stay ahead of that gadget," she said.

Joey Gates was sleeping and didn't even waken when Mike very gently withdrew the catheter about an inch.

"We'll have a good report for Big Joe when he gets here in the morning," he said. "Let's take a look at the preemie Dr. Dalton delivered this afternoon."

In NICU, Helga filled a syringe with the rich mixture of milk, protein concentrate, and vitamins used to feed premature babies and injected it into the tiny stomach through a small tube that ran through one nostril. As she did so, her body touched Mike's, but neither of them made any effort to break the contact, until Helga moved to the head of the bassinet and flicked a switch to display the reading from the blood oxygen tension electrode inside the catheter that ran through the baby's umbilical stump into the aorta.

"Ninety millimeters," she said. "Looks like this little fellow will make it."

"Marcia Weston wants to do a story on Baby Hornsby," said Mike. "Do you know whether Social Service has anything yet on the mother?"

"She was a college student but dropped out in the second year. Worked up from grass to heroin. Her boy friend was a pusher; they've got him in jail for beating her up but he claims any one of a dozen men could be the father of the child."

"Meanwhile a girl is dead and a premature baby starts life cold turkey with HMD into the bargain. It's a cruel world."

"No crueler than the people who inhabit the globe make it," said the blonde nurse. "Whenever I have to sweat another of these addict babies through withdrawal, I feel like going out and tying one on—and sometimes do."

"No wonder Emergency and ICU have the highest ulcer rate among hospital personnel," said Mike as they left the NICU and moved to Cubicle Four. "If we didn't blow off steam every now and then, we'd explode."

"You don't get rid of that sort of tension at a church social, either."

Mike grinned. "Bayside Terrace seems to provide pretty good facilities for group therapy—not that I get in on much of it."

"I've often wondered why. All work and no play—"

"Makes jack—but doesn't let Jack make much else, I know. But when I'm off duty in the ER, there always seems to be something I need to know more about."

"Like that needle-catheter technique?"

"You were the one who used it."

"I wouldn't have known how if you hadn't spent an evening reading medical journals, when you could have been making out with a willing nurse."

"Between us we saved a life and, according to an oriental tradition, that makes us responsible for it."

Helga laughed. "If you had to be responsible forever for all the people you save, you'd never get much else accomplished."

"Nor you." He was looking at her with the same expression of seeing her for the first time that she'd seen in his eyes earlier that afternoon, when he'd almost had to carry her to his office in the Emergency Department. And she was startled by the sudden warmth it created inside her.

"When I last studied math, two things equal to a third were equal to each other," said Mike.

"I don't think that law has changed."

"Then it looks like we're going to have to be responsible for each other. Right?"

"If you want it that way—in spite of—"

"I said as of now, remember? The past doesn't exist."

"And the future?"

"We'll play that as it happens," he said firmly. "And break clean, if it comes to that. Okay?"

She nodded then looked down at the sleeping Cuban girl. "Half the hospital believes you're in love with her. What are you going to do if she wakes up and decides you're Prince Charming?"

"With this mug of mine?" Mike laughed. *"That* would be a miracle."

"Women patients are always falling in love with their doctors."

"Her fiancé is on the way to becoming a doctor—and a fine young man into the bargain." He looked down at Carmelita. "I've always had a weakness for sick kittens, and this one's the sickest because she reminds me of Juliet. You probably remember the lines:

"Death, that hath sucked the honey of thy breath,
    Hath had no power yet upon thy beauty.

120

Thou art not conquer'd. Beauty's ensign yet
Is crimson in thy lips and in thy cheeks,
And death's pale flag is not advancèd there."

"Stop it!" Helga's voice was husky. "I think I'm going to cry, and my reputation as hard-boiled Helga will be ruined."

"I'll guard your secret," he promised.

"If only there were some way to wash the poisons of jaundice from her bloodstream. And the virus with them."

Mike turned to her quickly. "What did you say?"

"When?"

"Just now."

"If only there were some way to wash the poisons of jaundice from her bloodstream—and the virus with them."

"That's what I've been trying to remember!" he said excitedly. "I saw a reference not long ago to a method of exchange transfusion that substitutes a fresh supply of blood for practically the whole volume of the circulation." He started for the door, then turned back. "If anybody wants me, I'll be in the library—maybe all night."

II

A spattering of rain, sweeping across the rooftop lounge, awakened Rebecca Dalton. Shivering, she quickly put her arms into the terry cloth robe she'd pulled across her body on the wheeled couch after the explosive bout of lovemaking. The torn remnants of the blue maillot lay on the floor beside the stairway leading down to the penthouse floor of Bayside Terrace.

In her apartment, Rebecca stepped into the shower and turned on the water. The body she saw in the full-length mirror on the bathroom door as she toweled herself dry was glowing with life and she felt a shiver of delight at the memory of Ken's hands upon it. As she was dropping a sheer nightgown over her head, the telephone rang and, moving to the bed, she picked it up.

"Reb?"

"Yes, Ken."

"Are you all right? I called ten minutes ago."

"I felll asleep on the roof. You remember how I always did, after—"

"I remember."

"I'll be black and blue tomorrow—but fortunately the bruises won't show."

"That was a low-down trick you pulled on me tonight, Reb."

"I know," she said happily. "But it worked."

"And it doesn't change anything."

"Except that now I know you still love me as much as ever."

There was a silence at the other end of the line, then he spoke again: "It *was* like old times, but the fact remains that you're a success and I'm a failure."

"You're not, darling, either as a surgeon or as a lover. What matters now is the knowledge that you still love me."

"Good night then."

"Good night, darling." She was cradling the telephone when she heard his voice again in the receiver and lifted it to her ear.

"What were you saying, Ken?"

"I almost forgot. Karen Fletcher says she thinks Dale Tyndall is having more dyspnea and cyanosis. Maybe—"

"When did Karen see him?"

"This afternoon, after her daily swim. She asked me to stop by the laboratory and proved to me with some toxicological tests that the Hornsby girl really died from heroin poisoning. We went up to the Executive Committee meeting together."

"That was nice of her." Rebecca's voice had cooled sharply.

"Wasn't it?" Ken didn't seem to have noticed the change. "You'll check on Dale, won't you?"

"I'll set up an appointment tomorrow. I guess it *has* been almost six months since we had him in the laboratory. Good night."

The receiver clicked and she put down the phone. It was a long time before she went to sleep, however, for

Jeffry Toler's words that afternoon kept repeating themselves in her brain:

"That might just start to happen, you know. This place teems with attractive single women, divorcees, and wives looking to better themselves."

And of all of those at Biscayne General, Karen Fletcher was easily one of the most attractive.

III

Carolyn Payson was sitting propped up in bed, reading, about eleven-thirty when Helga Sundberg came into the apartment they shared in Bayside Terrace. The blonde nurse started shedding her uniform on the way to the closet.

"Heavy date?" Carolyn asked.

"No such luck. The guy I'd be dating, if I were going out, just told me he'd be in the medical library most of the night."

"Who was that?"

"Mike Raburn."

"Mike?" Carolyn put down her magazine. "How long has this been going on?"

"Since five minutes to three this afternoon."

Carolyn started to laugh, until she realized her roommate was quite serious. "That sudden, eh?"

"I don't now how it happened myself."

"Maybe if you told me about it—"

"There isn't much to tell. The whole thing has been so fast, I can still hardly believe it isn't a dream. But here goes."

When Helga finished the account, Carolyn shook her head.

"I don't understand it," she admitted.

"Real love isn't supposed to be understandable, is it?" Helga asked. "How was it with you and Gus?"

A shadow passed over the other nurse's face. "That's different; I'm just seizing what measure of happiness I can take now, knowing it can't last. When Father dies, I'll have to break it off in all fairness to Gus. No man with the career he has ahead of him should be saddled with a

123

wife who might be a millstone around his neck by the time she's thirty-five, and unable to give him children into the bargain."

"There's always the fifty-fifty chance that it won't happen that way."

"I love Gus too much to take that risk."

"Any idea what you're going to do?"

"When the time comes, I'll probably go back to Brazil. I enjoyed working in the mission hospital that year after we graduated."

"So did I," Helga agreed. "Until I made the mistake of letting myself fall in love—with a man who had a wife back in the States."

"But you didn't know that," Carolyn reminded her. "And you broke clean and came back as soon as you found out."

"With a few shards of pride intact and a resolve not to let it happen again—but it has. Only this time it's ten times worse."

"Worse—or better?"

Helga smiled. "So much better that it scares me. How could I be around that big lug for almost two years, knowing he's one doctor in a thousand, but not feeling the least bit like falling in love with him?"

"Maybe 'cause you were seeing him only as a doctor."

"Could be. Then one day he looks down at a dying girl, quotes a verse from *Romeo and Juliet,* and bingo, it hits me between the eyes that he's something special—"

"Mike is that all right. But it really started eight hours earlier, from what you told me, with the asphyxiated child."

"What's eight hours—when they make you feel like you're going to die if you don't spend the rest of your life looking after the big lug?"

"I know that feeling," said Carolyn soberly. "So what are you going to do?"

"There's one way to make sure. If I wake up in bed with Mike one morning, listen to him snore, see a day's growth of beard on his cheeks, realize he needs a deodorant—and still want him to make love to me then and there, it's bound to be the real thing."

"Mike doesn't have a reputation for playing around much, which puts him in a class by himself," said Carolyn. "So how are you going to put him to this acid test?"

"I'll make him take me some place where there'll be just the two of us together, no matter how many other people are around," said Helga as she finished buttoning tailored silk pajamas.

"Sounds like the Garden of Eden."

"Could be, I'll know for sure when I give him the apple," Helga laughed suddenly. "And the damnedest thing of all is that right now I wish more than anything else it could be a cherry—mine."

IV

In Apartment 5A, Valerie LeMoyne switched off the television at which she had been looking for the past hour with no memory of what the program had been—and stubbed out a cigarette in the ashtray on the end table. She hadn't really expected, when she came into the doctors' lounge of the surgical suite that afternoon, that the brief conversation with Jerry Singleton and his invitation for the weekend would stir within her such a tangible surge of longing for the embrace of a man, almost any man, once again.

Val knew very well what yielding to the fire burning constantly within her body, demanding the quenching every new affair promised but rarely fulfilled, could mean. That same fire had sent her fleeing in panic from France, lest its demands put her at the mercy of Marcel Thibaut, who had been perfectly willing to share her with others for his own advancement in his chosen career with the French Foreign Office.

She'd been lucky in finding a promising appointment here in the United States and later in Miami, with its constant inundation by successive hordes of conventioneers, anxious for a fling before they returned to their split-level homes all across the country and the wives who strove, but without the skill of women like Valerie

LeMoyne, to keep them happy and contented—and usually failed, as the herd instinct of male conventioneering in places like Miami Beach amply proved. But that, too, had become too risky, with the constant danger of publicity from the occasional police raid designed to assure the public that the law, in its majesty, was zealously guarding the morality of the community.

That Jerry Singleton was the answer to her own particular problem Val had tried to convince herself since his divorce but had held back instinctively until today. Then the craving, stronger than ever in springtime, when all of nature was seized by the reproductive instinct, had sent her to the doctors' lounge, ostensibly for a cigarette, but really because she knew Jerry would be showering there after his last operation. She'd known, too, that he would invite her to spend the weekend with him, just as surely as she knew now that she would accept—and that the affair would almost certainly end as the others had ended, when his prowess as a lover proved inadequate to the demands of her body.

To her credit she usually resisted until resistance was no longer possible, just as she was resisting now. But the very thought of yielding, and what would follow, set Valerie LeMoyne trembling and, moving quickly, she went to the medicine cabinet to count out first one, then two Nembutal capsules. Swallowing them with water, she undressed for the bed whose emptiness the potent barbiturate would shortly assuage with the dreamless sleep of a chemically induced narcosis.

v

Ed Vogel was on call for the ICU and the Cardiology Section, when the telephone rang shortly after midnight in the small room off the Intensive Care Section where the night resident still slept. He'd just come in from a final check of the ward and still wore the short white coat that distinguished the Fellows from the faculty.

"Dr. Vogel," he said.

"There's an outside call for Dr. Desmond, but he's out of the city, Dr. Vogel," said the operator. "The woman is pretty hysterical and asked for Dr. Rebecca Dalton when I told her Dr. Desmond wasn't available."

"I'll take it," said Ed. "Put her on."

"Dr. Dalton?" the voice of the woman on the other end of the line did indeed sound disturbed.

"This is Dr. Vogel, Dr. Rebecca Dalton's assistant. Can I help you?"

"Just a minute."

Ed could hear a man's voice in the background during a brief interchange, then the woman came back on.

"This is Mr. Ross McKenzie's housekeeper," she said. "Mr. McKenzie thinks he's had a heart attack and wants to know if you can make a house call."

"Was the attack brought on by exertion?"

There was a brief hesitation, then she said, "You could say that, yes."

"I'll send a Rescue Squad ambulance to bring him to the hospital."

"B-but—"

"If it's a real heart attack, we can't waste time," said the cardiologist firmly. "The ambulance will be there in five minutes. Don't let him move until they get there."

"Yes, Doctor." Even over the telephone, there was no mistaking the relief in the woman's voice, or the fact that she must be considerably younger than McKenzie.

As soon as he had called the Fire Department Rescue Squad dispatcher and ordered a specially equipped cardiac ambulance with a crew trained in cardiac evaluation and resuscitation sent to Ross McKenzie's house in Coral Gables, Ed rang Rebecca Dalton's apartment. She answered sleepily on the third ring.

"Mr. Ross McKenzie's on the way to the hospital, probably with a heart attack," he told her. "I sent a cardiac ambulance for him."

The telephone was silent for a moment, then Rebecca asked, "Did Mr. McKenzie ask for me?"

"The call was for Dr. Desmond, it came from McKenzie's housekeeper. But when the operator told her Dr. Desmond left the city right after the Executive Committee meeting this afternoon for a convention, she asked for you."

"I'll come right over," said Rebecca. "But Mr. McKenzie voted against my promotion this afternoon, so he may not want me to be in charge of his case."

"Sort of poetic justice for him to have a heart attack tonight, wouldn't you say?"

"I don't have the time to ponder the philosophical aspects of the case," said Rebecca. "When the patient gets there, admit him directly to CICU, Ed, and get an ECG. I'll dress and be there in ten minutes. You'd better start heparinizing him too, just in case this is a coronary."

Ross McKenzie had just been put to bed in the Coronary Intensive Care Unit of the hospital when Rebecca came into the cubicle where he was lying, pale and gasping for breath. One of the night laboratory technicians was connecting him to an electrocardiographic machine. Since it could take more leads than the sensors that fed information into the small monitor screen beside the bed and the larger display scope at the nursing station, the conventional ECG tracing gave a more detailed picture of what was happening to his heart.

Ed Vogel was starting an intravenous into which the blood-thinning agent, heparin, had been mixed, in order to cut down the likelihood of the clot spreading, if one or more of his coronary vessels had been blocked by a thrombosis. The tiny pulse indicator light just below the small screen of the monitor located beside the bed—but opposite the head where it could not be seen by the patient if he were conscious—was blinking so rapidly that the individual flashes could hardly be distinguished from each other. McKenzie himself appeared to be semiconscious.

"How is he, Ed?" Rebecca asked as she came up beside the special bed.

"Pulse volume seems to be good in spite of the rate. I gave him some Demerol but I haven't had time to take his blood pressure yet. From the ECG monitor it looks like an atrial paroxysm."

Rebecca took a stethoscope from a pocket and, putting the tips in her ears, placed the round flat diaphragm on the patient's chest over his heart. She didn't have to explain to either the other doctor or to Mary Pearson, the night ICU supervisor, the danger represented by such a paroxysmal attack. The nurses in the CICU unit were trained to recognize the significance of such complications and to take action quickly when necessary.

Otherwise normal people occasionally developed exceedingly rapid heartbeats, with no permanent damage to the heart if it was controlled soon enough. But in the case of an already damaged heart, this complication could presage a rapid lowering of cardiac output when the heart itself became unco-ordinated as it struggled to keep up with the barrage of stimuli to contract coming from its own stimulus center in the upper chamber.

The heavily muscled ventricles, the main pumping chambers, would then not be able to keep up with the demand and an irreversible loss of co-ordination between the upper chambers—the atria, which received blood from the large veins, and the ventricles, which pumped it out into the lungs and the aorta—could quickly follow. With the heart no longer able to cope with the blood being poured into the right side from the rest of the body and into the left side from the lungs, back pressures could develop quickly. The valves would then be unable to function properly and, when contraction occurred, some of the blood would be forced back through them, setting up a reverse pressure condition, particularly in the lungs, that could quickly lead to serious trouble.

Ed Vogel had been studying the conventional electrocardiogram produced by a metal stylus vibrating against a moving paper strip, as electrical impulses from the heart flowed into the machine from several connections—leads —on Ross McKenzie's chest, arms, and legs.

"The ECG is typical of atrial paroxysm," he said as the two doctors moved from the cubicle to discuss the case where Ross McKenzie couldn't hear. "P waves at the beginning of the heart contractions are sometimes getting in the way of the Ts at the end of the cycle."

"The QRS complexes are intact, so function is still holding up well," Rebecca observed.

"But for how long?" Ed voiced the question that was uppermost in both their minds.

Moving back to the patient's side, Rebecca leaned down until her mouth was near the sick man's ear.

"I'm Dr. Rebecca Dalton, Mr. McKenzie," she said. "How much pain are you having?"

The grower opened his eyes drowsily. "Not much," he said. "But my heart's trying to jump out of my throat."

"We'll control that in a little while," she promised. "The problem is to determine what is behind this attack. Do you object to my treating you?"

"Is anyone else available?"

"Only Dr. Vogel and myself."

"Looks like I'm in your hands." The grower closed his eyes again and a puffing snore escaped from his lips.

"Our best course is carotid sinus massage," said Rebecca. "He appears to have lapsed into coma already so we can't waste time with anything less certain."

"It's hazardous," said Vogel a bit doubtfully.

"So is *that*." Rebecca indicated the rapidly blinking light marking the pulse rate. "If we're dealing with a heart that's not getting enough oxygen by way of the coronary arteries, it can't keep beating very long at this rate without starting to fail."

"I wasn't objecting," said Ed Vogel. "But I'm damn glad you're here to do it."

He didn't need to explain his meaning. The carotid bodies, tiny nodes of very highly specialized tissue, were located on each side of the neck within the forks formed by the division of the two carotid arteries carrying blood to the head, including the brain. Just below the angle of the jaw each carotid divided into two channels, an external branch supplying the face, scalp, and most of one side of the head, plus an internal branch which, penetrating into the skull, brought the major blood supply to each side of the brain.

Known since antiquity, not so much for their presence as for their effect, the tiny nodes of tissue called the carotid bodies—or sinuses—were very susceptible to external force. When pressed upon, they exerted an effect upon the rest of the body so profound that assassins had long ago discovered how, by pressing deeply and quickly

130

upon each side of a victim's neck, to produce uncon-
sciousness and death in seconds.

"We'll need to keep monitoring the heart action while I
carry out the massage, so it's best to do it here in the
cubicle." Rebecca turned to the nursing supervisor. "Can
we move the bed out a little from the wall, Mrs. Pearson?
Just enough so I can get behind it?"

"Certainly, Doctor."

The bed was narrow and on wheels, so the nurse and
Ed Vogel were able to move it far enough for Rebecca to
slip around the end and stand there. Steadying Ross
McKenzie's head with her left hand, she felt along the
neck just below the angle of the jaw with her right hand,
seeking to locate the pulsation of the main carotid artery
there.

"I have the vessel under my fingers," Rebecca reported
after a moment. "Watch the screen, Ed, and tell me
immediately if there's any change."

"Right."

"Give me four seconds from when I say, 'Now,' please,
Mrs. Pearson."

The nurse shifted the watch on her left wrist so she
could easily see the sweep second hand.

"Now!" said Rebecca, as she pressed the artery backward and toward the midline, rolling it with her thumb
against the bodies of the neck vertebrae. Holding it there,
she moved her thumb in a slightly rotary motion that
massaged the pea-sized carotid body beneath.

"Four seconds," Mrs. Pearson reported, and Rebecca
released the pressure of her right thumb.

"No change," Ed Vogel reported.

"I'll try once more on this side, then shift to the other,"
said Rebecca. "Ready again when I say, 'Now'?"

The others nodded and she moved her thumb slightly
again until she could feel once more the heavy pulsation
of the carotid beneath it.

"Now!" she said, and began the massaging movement
once again. But when the nurse called time after four
seconds, there was still no change.

The others looked at Rebecca questioningly, but she
was already seeking the pulsation of the carotid artery on

131

the left side, moving her left thumb about as she felt for it.

"Do you ever do both sides at once, Dr. Dalton?" Mary Pearson asked.

"Not unless you want to murder someone in a hurry," Rebecca said cryptically. "And while you're worrying, you can pray the other artery hasn't been closed up by an atheromatous plaque. In such a case, we could shut down the major part of the brain circulation and create the same effect as a massive stroke."

"Like I said. Dr. Dalton." Ed Vogel spoke again. "I'm glad you're here."

"Ready?" Rebecca asked quietly, when her thumb found the artery pulsation, and the others nodded.

"Now!"

"The heart's asystolic!" Ed Vogel's voice was suddenly tense, for the dancing line on the small monitor screen marking the heart currents had flattened out, indicating that the heart had stopped beating.

The tension in the room was palpable but there was no panic. Both doctors and the nurse were trained to cope with such an emergency and kept their eyes on their jobs, Ed Vogel and Mary Pearson concentrating upon the screen and Rebecca upon the now stilled artery beneath her left thumb, since she couldn't see the monitor. When she spoke, her voice was loud in the suddenly silent room.

"Get ready to start CPR, Ed," she said as the seconds ticked off with no sign of a resumption of the heartbeat.

Ed Vogel leaned across the bed and placed the heel of his left hand over the lower half of Ross McKenzie's breastbone, ready to push down and jolt the heart itself by pressing it between the sternum in front and the spine at the back. This time, however, the dramatic maneuver of cardiopulmonary resuscitation wasn't needed.

"There's a contraction!" Mrs. Pearson reported suddenly. "And another."

Ed Vogel quickly moved to where he could see the small monitor clearly and the flashing pattern of the electrocardiographic tracing that was now appearing.

"Those are ventricular ectopic beats," he said, but even

132

as he was speaking, the irregular line on the monitor suddenly shaped itself, as if by magic, into a normal pattern.

"By God, you've done it!" Vogel exclaimed. "The rhythm is normal again."

"Print the ECG pattern for me at the central console, Mrs. Pearson," said Rebecca as she moved around the bed. "I'd like to study it a little more closely before I decide what else to do."

As the nurse moved out of the cubicle, Ed Vogel wiped the sweat from his forehead with a handkerchief. At the same moment Ross McKenzie opened his eyes and a look of pleased surprise appeared on his face.

"I don't feel my heart beating in my throat any more," he exclaimed. "What did you do?"

"Dr. Dalton stopped your heart," Ed Vogel told him.

"And started it again?"

"*You* did that, Mr. McKenzie," said Rebecca. "But we were ready, if you hadn't saved us the trouble. You see, women doctors have their moments, too, in spite of what their critics say."

"Somebody call me a taxi." McKenzie started to push himself up into a sitting position. "I'm going home."

"You'll do nothing of the sort," said Rebecca sharply. "The attack of arrhythmia you just had is a warning, which is more of a break than most heart cases get. But it still didn't just happen and the next one could be really serious, so I'm going to keep you here a few days and find out why these things are happening. And I'm also going to put you on digitalis."

"What could be wrong?"

"At your age a reduction of blood flow to the heart muscle, rheumatic heart disease, high blood pressure, unusual exertion—almost anything." Rebecca picked up his chart and started from the cubicle.

VI

Ed Vogel was on his way back to the Emergency Room quarters of the night-duty Fellows about 3:00 A.M. after examining an oldster on the fourth floor who'd been given phenobarbital to sleep on and had promptly started seeing small animals crawling over the walls. Certain that he would be eaten alive, the patient had left his bed and padded down the hall to the chart desk, dragging a urine bag, an IV setup, and a tube in his common bile duct behind him, before collapsing in the doorway at the feet of a startled charge nurse.

Since any patient leaving his bed without permission under such circumstances had to be examined by a doctor to see how much damage he had done—in this case mercifully none—Ed had been called. As he was passing the door to the medical library, he noticed a light burning and went inside to turn it off, only to find Mike Raburn slumped over an open medical journal on the table before him, fast asleep.

"Wake up!" Ed shook the broad-shouldered surgeon.

Mike raised his head and blinked. "What time is it?"

"Three o'clock. You been in here long?"

"Since about ten-thirty. The last thing I remember, it was one o'clock and I'd just found what I was looking for."

"Which was?"

"How much do you know about exchange transfusion for serum hepatitis with hepatic coma, Ed?"

"You mean that business about using a baboon's liver to extract toxins from the blood? I thought it hadn't proved feasible."

"It didn't, there were too many bugs. This is a new method that's been worked out in an Air Force hospital in the Middle West. The patient's body is cooled to where it's almost in a state of suspended animation, while practically all the blood is pumped out and the entire circulatory system washed out with buffered Ringer's lactate solution, before it's filled again with fresh donor blood."

"You thinking of using it on the Cuban girl?"

"I'm *going* to use it on her, if I can convince the family that it's her only chance."

"That suspended animation business sounds pretty dangerous."

"Of course it is, but the risk seems to be justified." Mike picked up the journal he had been reading and followed Vogel to the door. "The guy who worked this out figured that you have nine minutes to get the whole procedure completed before permanent brain damage is likely from the cold and the lack of oxygen."

"Nine minutes from death? In addition to being a good title for a suspense novel, that's cutting it pretty close, my friend."

"The whole business has to go off without a hitch," Mike admitted. "But Dr. Dalton's had a lot of experience with open heart surgery on patients in hypothermia and on the pump oxygenator. This procedure shouldn't be any harder to bring off than that."

"I read a book once called *Seven Minutes*, but that had to do with making love. Good luck, Mike, I've got a hunch you're going to need it. And if you fail, just don't let the girl's death knock you the way losing those transplant cases did Ken Dalton."

Chapter 9

CAROLYN PAYSON hadn't slept well and it was a relief when dawn finally came. Getting out of bed as quietly as possible so as not to disturb Helga, who was fast asleep like the healthy and completely uninhibited female animal she was, Carolyn left the old hotel and walked along the bay front for a half hour before entering the hospital. It was a beautiful morning, particularly for one deeply in love who knew she was loved in return, but the knowledge only made the pain from the predicament in which Carolyn found herself all the more severe.

She arrived at the hospital cafeteria at half past six and ate a leisurely breakfast before going on duty and taking the morning report from Mary Pearson.

"The Cuban girl's temperature is still creeping up," Mary reported. "Mike Raburn was in here early to see her. He's talking about some new treatment, but if you ask me, he'll never save her."

"What about the baby Dr. Dalton delivered by section?"

"Since Dr. Henderson put Baby Hornsby on CPAP late yesterday afternoon, it's been responding well even in the middle of cold turkey, but I feel so sorry for it I could cry. Mr. Ross McKenzie was admitted about midnight—a heart case," Mary Pearson went on with the report. "Dr. Rebecca Dalton did a carotid body massage on him and slowed it down."

"Looks like you had a busy night."

"Just routine for the ICU. Well, I'll be going. See you in the morning."

"Not tomorrow. I'm off duty, Thursdays."

"Well, have fun." Mary was at the door, when she turned and came back.

"Could I ask you something, Carolyn?"

"Of course."

"Is it true that you've asked the God Committee to consider your father's case? One of the girls told me during the coffee break last night that you had."

"I asked Chaplain Hagan to arrange it."

"It's none of my business, but I want you to know I think you're being very brave."

"Brave? Why?"

"You know how people talk. But I don't care what they say, I think you're doing the right thing." Mary Pearson turned and hurried from the ward.

Carolyn sat for a long moment, staring at the door through which the other nurse had just disappeared. Mary's concern—and her avowal of support—could only mean that the hospital staff was already taking sides. Which could make it even harder for the Moriturus Committee to be strictly impartial in their deliberations, as well as for Carolyn herself to live with her own conscience, which had been troubling her ever since she'd begged the chaplain to request a meeting of the God Committee.

After a moment she called one of the other nurses to take her place at the nursing station which, as the very

136

heart of the ICU, was never left unattended, and went to the cubicle where her father was lying. Both side frames of the bed were raised, in case his constantly twitching muscles shifted his body sufficiently to make him fall out of the bed.

Richard Payson's eyes were open and, as on other occasions, Carolyn could almost convince herself that a light of recognition showed in them. As usual, too, the muscles of his lips and jaw were moving but whether without purpose, like the other contractions throughout his body, or in an attempt to speak, she couldn't be sure. Overcome by the surge of pity she always felt, when she saw her father thus and remembered how strong and happy he'd been only months before, Carolyn was turning away from the bed when a harsh croak came from Richard Payson's lips. She couldn't distinguish the words for certain but, as she moved closer to listen, they came again.

"Let me die." This time there was no doubting their meaning; it was the same refrain she'd heard so many times before, the cry of a soul tormented beyond bearing by its own deterioration and begging for the end that could bring peace.

"I promise," she whispered, putting her hand upon his. "Only a little while longer and you can be free."

She couldn't really be sure the spasmodic grasping of her hand by his fingers, a movement lasting only an instant, was not as purposeless as were the movements in the rest of his body. But it didn't really matter any more, for all her doubts about what must be done had been removed.

Gus Henderson was standing just outside the cubicle when Carolyn left it. Absorbed in trying to listen to her father and understand the words she was convinced he had spoken, she hadn't realized Gus was there. But at the sight of the craggy face with its unruly mop of reddish hair and the blue eyes that were always warm when he looked at her, she reached out instinctively to him for support.

Taking her hands, Gus held them between his own large-knuckled ones that looked awkward, as did the rest

137

of him for that matter, yet could be as tender as a mother's when handling a baby or, as Carolyn very well knew, the body of a woman.

"Morning." said Gus. "Are you okay?"

Carolyn nodded. "Seeing him like this always breaks me up for a minute or two."

"I know. That little preemie we've got on cold turkey damn near tears my heart out every time I look at him, too, jerking and twisting all the time."

"But the baby will be all right one day, while my father—"

"Are you still determined to bring him before the God Committee?"

"Yes."

"It will take a lot of courage—"

"Compassion, Gus, the same sort of compassion you feel for Baby Hornsby. And I'm only carrying out my father's wishes after all. If you could have heard him speak just now."

"I did hear." he said with an odd note in his voice. "Would it help any if I testify to that before the committee?"

"You'd do that, even if you're not convinced you heard him?" They were so close in their love that she could read his thoughts.

"I heard sounds that could have been 'Let me die.' If you tell me that's what it was, that's what I heard."

"No wonder I love you so much." She gave his hands a quick squeeze. "But he really did speak the words this morning, Gus, you can take my word for it."

"That's good enough for me—do you know yet when the committee will meet?"

"No. But I hope it's today."

They had been walking through the ward toward the nursing station while they were talking. Now Gus stopped beside the main console, whose battery of monitors, dials, and flashing lights made it look like a surrealist's dream of a machine for controlling life—and death.

"Don't expect too much from the God Committee, Carolyn," he warned. "After all, it's new and I doubt if the lay members on it understand what it means for a doctor

138

to deliberately let go of a life that's been placed in his hands."

"It's what Father wants, Gus. Even if I wasn't sure of what's best for him, I'd have to consider it seriously."

"Then promise you won't let it break you up if things don't go your way when the committee meets. They're only human too."

He shook his head, in frustration, she sensed, at not quite being able to put his thoughts into exactly the words he needed to express them.

"We call it the 'God Committee' facetiously," he added finally. "But I'm not sure anybody is cut out to be God. Will I see you tonight?"

"I don't know," said Carolyn. "At least not until I find out when the committee will meet. But I'm off duty tomorrow."

"I'll keep in touch," Gus promised, and reached out to give her hand a squeeze once again.

"Dr. Henderson, 131," the paging operator said. "Dr. Augustus Henderson, 131. Dr. Henderson, 131."

"That must be Professor McHale getting ready to make rounds," said Gus. "See you."

II

Mike Raburn was lucky enough to corral both Rebecca and Ken Dalton shortly after he left the Coffee Shop from breakfast for a conference about Carmelita Sanchez. They met in the physicians' office of the ICU, which was also equipped with a large monitor screen and a multiterminal switching unit. With it the essential parameters of information on any patient in the unit could be instantly studied without leaving the room, as well as the entire hospital record stored in the data bank. When Mike switched on the closed television circuit, a picture of the cubicle where Carmlita lay, with one of the ICU nurses watching over her, appeared on the screen.

"Obviously you didn't ask me to see her because any surgery is indicated, Mike," said Ken Dalton. "What's on your mind?"

"I hope to do an 'asanguineous hypothermic total body

139

perfusion,' otherwise known as TBW—'total body washout.' "

"Pretty new, isn't it?"

"So far I know of only about five successful cases. A TBW involves cooling the body to as low as 25 degrees Centigrade and a disappearance of all parameters."

"That's clinical death." The surgeon's tone was sober.

"I know. But it has been maintained for as long as nine minutes, with the patient's heartbeat returning spontaneously at the end of that period."

"Suppose you need more than nine minutes to complete the washout?" Rebecca asked.

"We don't know what will happen, of course, but I don't think it will take longer. One case—in Connecticut, I believe—was completed in seven minutes."

"Successfully?"

"Yes. TBW seeks to remove practically all the blood from the body and wash most of the hepatitis toxin from the circulation with a special Ringer's solution plus albumin precooled to a temperature of 5 to 10 degrees Centigrade."

Ken Dalton whistled softly. "No wonder you get such rapid body cooling and a total suppression of all clinical signs of life."

"When the washout is completed," Mike continued, "the only Au antigen left in the body should be what's in the intercellular spaces and the cells themselves, a fraction of what was there before. At that point, the heart-lung pump is filled with blood and plasma to which packed red cells have been added. The mixture is then warmed as it's forced through the circulation by the heart-lung pump until the patient's temperature reaches 35 degrees Centigrade. In both reported cases, heart action began spontaneously by the time that temperature was reached and recovery of consciousness was rapid."

"It sounded like too much of a gadget job to me when I first read the report," said Rebecca. "But I don't think so now, especially in your hands, Mike."

"Seems like you've got it worked out very well," Ken agreed. "But you're quite capable of putting in all the

140

cannulae needed in the procedure, Mike. Just where do I come in?"

"You've had far more experience working with the heart-lung pump and hypothermia in your open heart surgery than anyone in the hospital, Dr. Dalton. I'm hoping you'll work beside me and give me the benefit of your experience."

"That hasn't been too sanguine lately."

"You still did fifteen transplants without a surgical death—and innumerable open heart cases. I'd be very grateful if you'd help me."

"Have you talked to the girl's family?"

"They're due here at ten. They know we've exhausted all other means of treatment, so I don't think they'll object."

"Do you approve, Reb?" Ken asked.

She nodded. "Maybe not in anyone's hands except yours and Mike's, but I have confidence in both of you."

"When do you want to schedule it, Mike?" Ken asked.

"Tomorrow morning if the parents agree."

"Use the main vascular surgery operating room and the first team," Ken told him. "With a major new procedure like this, you'll need all the technical help you can get."

III

Shortly before ten o'clock Mike Raburn heard himself being paged and went to the telephone.

"Mr. Joe Gates is waiting to see you in the ICU waiting room, Dr. Raburn," said the operator.

In the small waiting room, Mike found the Miami Snappers star forward pacing up and down. As they shook hands he could see that the black athlete was considerably disturbed.

"Your boy's out of danger, Joe," Mike reassured him.

"I'd like to talk to you alone, Mike." The two men were old friends from college days and, besides, Mike had filled in a number of times as team physician for the Snappers.

"We'll go to my office in the Emergency Department," said Mike. "I think we can both get into it, even as big as we are."

Mike led the way to the office, strategically placed between the Emergency Room and the adjoining small Observation Ward, where patients could be watched for brief periods without actually admitting them to the hospital.

"Tell me what happened to Joey," said Gates when they were seated and Mike had closed the door.

"Shortly after noon yesterday, he went into a serious crisis with sickle cell anemia."

"Rachel told me that much and Joey's obviously coming out of it okay. But what about the future?"

"We believe we can prevent more trouble with small daily doses of a new drug. You really don't have to worry—"

"I didn't, as soon as Dr. Henderson told me you were looking after him."

"Then what's bothering you?"

"Myself. Oh, don't get me wrong. I'm not really afraid of sickle cell anemia, even though I know enough about it to realize that it's almost entirely confined to the black race."

"Something like ninety-nine per cent," Mike confirmed. "But all we need to do is test your blood to know whether you transmitted the inherited tendency to Joey."

"Maybe I'd better explain," said Gates. "You see, my contract with the Snappers has two more years to run and can't be broken by either the owners or myself—unless I'm found to have some chronic physical disturbance that wouldn't permit me to play."

"That puts a different light on things," Mike admitted. "But surely the Snapper management wouldn't want to bench you unless your physical condition didn't allow you to play."

"If I were found to have the sickling trait, would you advise me to play?"

"Maybe not. We could only decide that after a thorough medical study. But not everybody with the sickling trait develops symptoms, so it's quite possible that even if you have the trait you could still play basketball. We have experts on sickle disease on the faculty here and I could easily get an opinion for you."

"If the time comes, we'll do that," said Gates. "But what's involved right now goes deeper than whether or not I'm physically able to play. In San Francisco I was backstopping a group of athletes trying to form a professional players' union that can deal with the owners from strength."

"Surely *you* don't need—"

"*I* don't. But a lot of players who are not much in demand *do* need expert representation to negotiate the best possible terms, something they don't get now by bargaining piecemeal. I'm known to be working with the group on the West Coast, so the owners have ganged up on me."

"A blacklist?"

Joe Gates smiled wryly.

"No pun intended, of course," Mike assured the big athlete.

"I guess you could still call it that, since I'm at the top of the list," Gates conceded. "The owners can't do anything to me the way things are now. I've got a contract and they have to pay me so they're going to let me play. But if they could pin a physical disability like sickle cell disease on me and get a panel of doctors to testify that I'm physically disqualified, they could break my contract. And with it would go the best chance professional players in all sports have ever had to form a union."

"It's a dilemma, all right."

"So you see why it's vitally necessary that I not be diagnosed as having the sickling trait, at least not until after the last postseason exhibition game tomorrow night."

"*I'll* certainly not give out any information on you," Mike promised. "But I would like to test Rachel. If she should turn out to be positive, we'll have presumptive evidence that Joey got the sickling tendency from her side and not yours."

"Can you be sure?"

"Not absolutely. But if the trait came from both of you, I would guess that Joey would have developed severe symptoms much earlier."

Gates stood up. "I can't tell you how grateful Rachel and I are, Mike. She's pretty nervous right now, though, and I'd appreciate your waiting a few days before testing her."

"Certainly. We can always do it just before Joey is ready to be discharged."

"I'll send you a pair of ducats for the final exhibition game tomorrow night," Gates promised. "You and the chick of your choice will have box seats."

IV

Señor and Señora Rodrigo Sanchez were well known to Mike Raburn; he'd seen them many times when they were visiting their daughter. And as always with a very ill patient for whose recovery he could give the family little hope, he had felt genuine sympathy for them. They had once been in the upper levels of Havana's intellectual society, he knew. And like so many upper-class Cubans, who had fled rather than submit to Castro's regime, Rodrigo Sanchez had become an important business leader in the teeming section of Miami called Little Havana.

They looked up hopefully when Mike came over to the corner of the main hospital lobby where they were waiting.

"Sorry I'm late," he told them. "But I've found a new treatment that may help Carmelita and I wanted to discuss it with two other doctors before I spoke of it to you."

The sudden look of hope in their eyes was one of the most moving things Mike had ever experienced.

"This treatment, Doctor," said Señora Sanchez. "You say it is something new?"

"Very new," said Mike. And then, because he was fundamentally honest, he added, "And also very dangerous. I'll try to explain why."

As simply as he could Mike described how he proposed

to wash the toxin of serum hepatitis out of Carmelita's body. When he finished, Señora Sanchez particularly looked very concerned.

"Did I understand you to say that for nine minutes Carmelita will be dead?" she asked.

"Not dead—in the sense that you mean. But it is true that none of the instruments by which we measure life will show any signs of it."

"If Carmelita's heart does not beat and she does not breathe how can you say she will not be dead?"

Mike sought a way to explain what was actually unexplainable, and found it in one of the classic stories from the Bible.

"Do you remember in the Old Testament where Joshua was leading the Israelites into Canaan and the sun stood still?"

"Yes, but—"

"It will be like that with Carmelita."

"Do you mean that for nine minutes her life processes will stand still?" Señor Sanchez asked.

"I have every confidence that they will, " Mike assured them. "And that she will regain consciousness and be well."

"For always?"

"We think that once the poisons threatening her life are washed from her body, she will be able to overcome the infection."

"It would be like a miracle," said Señora Sanchez.

"Not *like* a miracle, but truly a miracle," said her husband. "We must go at once and make a novena for Carmelita." He stopped suddenly, and when he spoke again, his voice was troubled.

"Since our daughter will be so close to death, Dr. Raburn, would it disturb you if we asked our priest to administer the last rites?"

"Of course not."

"It would not be from any lack of confidence in you, Doctor," Señora Sanchez added.

"I understand. We will start tomorrow morning at nine o'clock."

At exactly eleven-fifteen Wednesday morning a red warning light flicked on at the CICU control panel before which Carolyn Payson was sitting, checking charts. The warning buzzer accompanying the panel light attracted her attention to it immediately and, with her left hand, she flipped the switch that kept Ross McKenzie's room in direct closed circuit television connection with the panel and the master screen before her.

Immediately a picture appeared upon it of the room where McKenzie was lying in bed. The nurse who was specialing him was bending over listening to his heart with a stethoscope and looking at her watch, quite unconscious of the remote observer.

"What's wrong, June?" Carolyn asked, by way of the small speaker on the wall, and saw the nurse jump, then turn and look at the camera with startled eyes.

"How did you know anything was wrong?" she asked, speaking into the two-way communication intercom set in the wall beside the bed.

"The computer just upstaged you again."

One of the sensors attached to Ross McKenzie's body after his admission last night to watch his blood pressure had been set to give a warning when it fell below a hundred millimeters of mercury in the higher, systolic phase, measuring the maximum force applied to the blood leaving the heart by the thick-walled muscular lower chamber called the left ventricle. The systolic reading was a sensitive indicator of heart function, second only perhaps to the pressure in the veins, also being faithfully recorded by the highly sophisticated monitoring system of the Coronary Intensive Care Unit.

Reaching for the Patient Selector switch, Carolyn pressed it, concentrating the tremendously intricate monitoring system upon Ross McKenzie's body. The Elapsed Time Indicator immediately began to record the number of seconds that had passed since the warning buzzer sounded and the Signal Delay started an endless-loop magnetic tape device, automatically recording the blood pressure for forty seconds, beginning ten seconds before the alarm, for playback when a doctor reached the CICU. Thus the cardiologist could tell whether the change was a sudden one, as in an acute disaster of some kind, or gradual.

At the same time, by depressing another switch among the battery facing Carolyn on the elaborate panel before her, she started the electrocardiographic printer, and a strip of paper tape, with a running account of the heart's electrical action recorded upon it by a moving stylus, began to spew slowly from the side of the instrument. CICU nurses were trained to interpret ECG tracings and, picking up the paper tape, Carolyn pulled it through her fingers, studied the pattern being printed there briefly, then picked up the direct line telephone to the paging operator and spoke into it tersely.

"Dr. Rebecca Dalton, CODE FOUR, CICU." The calm voice poured from loudspeakers all over the hospital. "Dr. Edward Vogel, CODE FOUR, CICU."

CODE FOUR indicated the need for the designated doctor at the indicated point immediately, but was less of an emergency than CODE FIVE, which sent the CPR team assigned to a particular area rushing to the spot.

Putting down the phone, Carolyn turned again to the battery of monitors and began to assay the information being reported there on Ross McKenzie's condition—blood pressure, both systolic and diastolic; venous pressure; ECG; pulse, respiration, and other data. The quick study of the ECG tracing had already told her that, in spite of the falling blood pressure, McKenzie's heart seemed to be following a normal pattern of action, as far as the various electrical components characterizing the individual beats were concerned. Most important of all, too, there was no irregularity of the beats, a sign which might have presaged a rapid disintegration of his cardiac condition.

Moving quickly, Carolyn covered the twenty feet or so from the nursing station to McKenzie's bedside. The patient, she noted, was snoring softly, which was fortunate. CICU patients were usually apprehensive in times of crisis and the arrival of several doctors, plus the inevitable

147

flurry of activity in the restricted area of the glass-walled cubicle, sometimes frightened them into a severe backset.

"Take over the station," she told the nurse who had been specialing McKenzie. "Did you notice anything else before the BP began to drop?"

"The change came all at once, Miss Payson. You can see the pressure curve on the graphic chart there."

Carolyn was already studying the record printed out by a pen against the slowly moving strip of graph paper. It gave little information, however, except what the sensitive electronic instrument had already observed, that the grower's blood pressure had suddenly started falling—for no reason that was immediately discernible.

"Do you have any idea what happened?" The student nurse was still at the foot of the bed, concerned whether she might have overlooked any sign that would have warned of the impending change earlier.

"Looks like cardiogenic shock." Carolyn was opening the stopcock of the intravenous drip so the fluid would flow more rapidly into McKenzie's veins. "His skin's beginning to turn pale, which means the peripheral vessels are contracting in order to send blood to the heart and the brain. Get to the nursing station and ask the operator whether she's located Dr. Vogel or Dr. Dalton. If not, tell her to call Dr. Raburn."

Picking up an ampule marked "Isoproterenol, one milligram" from a tray on a table beside the bed, Carolyn snapped off the blue needle cover protecting from contamination the needle attached to a sterile plastic syringe. Inserting tthe metal needle into the ampule, she drew the contents up into the syringe. Then holding the plastic tubing, through which the contents of a bottle of five per cent dextrose and water had been dripping slowly into Ross McKenzie's circulation through a tiny catheter in a hand vein, she injected the single dose of the powerful blood-vessel-constricting drug through the wall of the IV tube so it would flow directly into his circulation.

Ross McKenzie stirred and opened his eyes. "What the hell's going on?" he mumbled.

"Just giving you some medicine," said Carolyn cheerfully—one of the first characteristics of a good CICU nurse was that she didn't panic.

McKenzie closed his eyes and his lips puffed again in a faint snore.

On the graphic chart being traced by the indicator pen, the systolic blood pressure had started to rise as soon as the powerful drug began to exert its effect upon the tiniest blood vessels throughout the body. A vast network of circulatory channels, their opening or closing could markedly affect the blood pressure, literally allowing a patient in severe shock to bleed to death by loss of vital plasma from the bloodstream into the millions of tiny capillary blood vessels lying between the arterial system taking blood from the heart to the tissues and the venous system by which it was returned to the central pump.

Ed Vogel appeared at the other side of the bed, his eyes moving swiftly from the small monitor screen to the graphic chart of the blood pressure.

"Looks like cardiogenic shock," said Carolyn. "I put a milligram of Isoproterenol into the IV and stepped up the flow."

The cardiologist laid the diaphragm on McKenzie's chest, listened carefully for a moment, then moved it an inch or so and listened again. Repeating this process several times, he finally came back to the original position to the left and below the nipple, and listened awhile longer. Then, holding the diaphragm of the stethoscope in place, he took the rubber tips from his ears and handed that portion of the instrument to Carolyn.

She listened briefly to the sound, then handed him back the stethoscope.

"What do you hear?" Ed Vogel asked.

"A systolic apical murmur—pretty loud, and rather rough."

"Go to the head of the class."

"What could cause it?" Carolyn asked as they moved outside the cubicle.

"That kind of murmur means the mitral valve isn't closing completely and some blood is spurting back into the left atrium with every heartbeat. If I wanted to go way out on a limb, I'd say one or two of the *chordae tendineae*—do you remember what they are?"

"Fibrous cords attaching the cusps of the heart valves to the inner wall of the heart itself?"

"Right. If those cords—or the valves attached to them—are diseased, the valve cusps no longer close completely at the beginning of ventricular contraction and a backflow of blood occurs, hence the murmur."

"And beginning failure, as the heart tries to cope, causes the blood pressure drop?"

"Yes."

The telephone at the nursing station rang softly and the nurse on duty picked it up, listened a moment, then called to the cardiologist.

"Dr. Dalton for you, Dr. Vogel."

Ed Vogel spoke briefly with Rebecca Dalton, then came back to the cubicle where Carolyn was watching the patient and the various instruments recording important facts about McKenzie's general condition—especially the function of his heart.

"Dr. Dalton's busy arranging a meeting of a special committee for this afternoon," he said.

"The 'God Committee'?" Carolyn asked quickly.

"She didn't say. But it must be important, or she would have come here right away."

"Are you sure Dr. Dalton didn't say more about the committee meeting?" Carolyn asked.

"I'm sure." Vogel gave her an appraising look. "Your father?"

"Yes."

"You know some people will condemn you for it, don't you?"

"It's already started. But Helga says I'm doing the right thing."

"Our Helga's a pragamatist—about nearly everything. And also a very smart girl. By the way, Dr. Dalton said tell you she would like to see you in her office for a few minutes when you go off at three. If you can't make it, you can call her."

"I'll make it. What do we do about Mr. McKenzie?"

"You seem to have taken care of him, for the moment

at least. She asked me to request a surgical consultation stat with Dr. Kenneth Dalton."

"Does that mean Mr. McKenzie is liable to come to surgery?"

"What happens to his mitral valve and the left side of his heart in the next twenty-four hours or so should decide that question," said Vogel. "If they can adjust to that leak you heard in the stethoscope just now, he'll probably be okay, as long as he behaves himself. If not, somebody will have to go in and put a new valve in place of the defective one."

"Could he stand the operation? That change just now was pretty sudden."

"And pretty drastic," Ed Vogel agreed. "If McKenzie is going to need surgery eventually, it's better not to wait too long. But if he doesn't need it, anybody who operates would be subjecting him to a risk that wasn't necessary. I'm damned glad I don't have to make the decision."

Chapter 10

AS CHIEF of the two-technician team charged with operating the heart-lung pump—correctly labeled a pump oxygenator—that substituted for both heart and lungs during open heart surgery, Peggy Tyndall was a vital part of the highly skilled group who had contributed much to Ken Dalton's reputation in the field of cardiovascular surgery. When Mike Raburn came into the Cardiac Research Laboratory about ten-thiry Wednesday morning, Peggy looked up from the colorimeter she had been using to check blood gas determinations for a pulmonary function test.

"Dr. Rebecca Dalton called awhile ago and told me to drop everything and work with you, Dr. Raburn," she said. "What's up?"

"This."

On a table under a brilliant droplight, Mike opened the medical journal he was carrying and showed the diminutive physician's assistant the diagrams of the apparatus needed for performing Total Body Washout. Peggy studied it a moment and, when she looked up, her eyes were bright with interest.

"Looks like the kind of pump oxygenator Rube Goldberg might have designed. The word's out that you're going to try something new to medical science tomorrow. Is this part of it?"

"This is the heart of it. Can you make one for me?"

Peggy looked at the diagrams again for a moment, then nodded. "Essentially it's a Travenol-type bag oxygenator with a roller pump and side vents in some pretty odd places."

"Don't forget the heat exchanger. When the time comes, we'll be needing that in a hurry."

"You mean *if* the time comes, don't you?" Peggy had been scanning the article. "What I'm reading here scares the hell out of me."

"Me too," Mike admitted. "But it has to work."

"I'll start right away," said Peggy. "Where shall I work?"

"Dr. LeMoyne's turning over a workroom in the OR suite to us. She'll spend as much time with you as she can and I plan to be there most of the day too."

"I'll load a cart with whatever it looks like I may need from here and go right up to surgery," said Peggy. "The pump oxygenators are up there already and I'll start taking one apart."

"Dr. Raburn, 175," said the paging operator over the loudspeaker system. "Dr. Michael Raburn, 175. Dr. Raburn, 175."

Mike frowned. "That's Dr. Toler's extension. I wonder what he could want?"

"Whatever it is, you'd better answer," said Peggy. "See you upstairs."

"Mike," said Jeffry Toler over the telephone. "Can you come up here?"

"Certainly," said the Surgical Fellow. "Be there in a minute."

On the way up in the elevator, Mike couldn't help wondering what the administrator of the medical center could possibly want with him and was afraid it might be what he half expected it would. With the hospital already in the news because of the controversy with the Finance Committee of the County Commission over the budget, there was the possibility that Toler might wish to avoid possible public criticism over the use of such a largely untried and admittedly hazardous procedure as the TBW. Nevertheless Mike was determined not to give in to pressure—should it be exerted.

"I want to talk to you about the Sanchez girl, Mike." Characteristically, Toler came directly to the point. "What are her chances?"

"Without Total Body Washout—none."

"And with it?"

"I know of about five cases with detailed reports in the literature; two of those died but the rest are apparently cured. Admittedly, Carmelita Sanchez is in worse condition than I'd like to see her, but if it were any better, we might hesitate to use such a dramatic procedure. Are you worried about what losing her will do to the reputation of the hospital, sir?"

"Lord, no, Mike! I wouldn't think of imposing my professional judgment on that of the staff, when I haven't practiced medicine for fifteen years. I had a call this morning from Marcia Weston, a reporter for one of the local TV stations—"

"I know her. She covered Joe Gates's boy and also Baby Hornsby yesterday."

"And gave us a nice plug," said Toler. "Miss Weston has been after me for several weeks to let her do a TV profile on Rebecca Dalton—you know, the standard fem lib approach."

"I doubt that Dr. Dalton would like to be identifed with that movement, but her work certainly deserves recognition."

"Especially since yesterday, when she was made chief of the Cardiology Section and a full professor of medicine," Toler agreed. "When Miss Weston called this morning, I was sure that was what she wanted and was wondering how I could put her off with things the way they are between the Daltons."

"She couldn't have chosen a worse time, I'm sure."

"This time we're lucky. What Marcia Weston wants to do is a story on you—a day in the life of a dedicated doctor."

"Gus Handerson is taking care of both the cases she saw yesterday—"

"We're in a different ball game, Mike, plus a knockdown, drag-out fight with the County Commission on medical center finances. Right now we can use all the good will we can get."

"At least Mr. McKenzie will be out of action for a while. Ed Vogel just told me he may have to come to surgery."

"Lord, I hope not! But Ross McKenzie wouldn't let the way he's treated as a patient influence him, as far as knocking this hospital is concerned. No matter what happens to McKenzie, though, we'll still have to fight our battle before the County Commission."

"What do you have in mind, sir?"

"If it won't bother you during what is bound to be a delicate procedure, I'd like to let Miss Weston and a camera crew from her TV station film the—what did you call it?"

"Total Body Washout."

"The Cuban girl's father is one of the most important men in Little Havana. If we have to put a proposal for a separate medical center millage on the ballot in the fall elections, the Cuban vote could help us win."

"Suppose I fail tomorrow?"

"Everybody knows this is a last-ditch fight, but you could brief the Weston girl before you start the procedure, so she would emphasize that aspect of it in her commen-

154

tary. You're already a medical hero for saving Joey Gates, Mike. And, if you succeed tomorrow morning, you'll be the doctor of the hour."

"Tell Miss Weston to be here with her crew at eight-thirty, then," said Mike. "We're starting at nine but I don't want them walking in and messing up an operating room during the most important nine minutes in that girl's life."

III

Rebecca Dalton came into the cubicle in the CICU where Ross McKenzie was lying just as Ken finished examining the patient. The surgeon put the stethoscope he had been using back into the pocket of his long white coat and his expression was grave as he stepped outside the cubicle. Rebecca and Ed Vogel followed.

"Was the systolic murmur there when he was admitted?" Ken asked.

"Ed heard it for the first time this morning, when the pressure suddenly dropped," said Rebecca. "What do you think?"

"My guess would be that we're dealing with some changes in the mitral valve area, perhaps some involvement of the *chordae tendineae*."

"I agree," said Rebecca. "The echocardiogram might help us determine exactly what's happening but our instrument is out of order at the moment."

Even newer than tomorrow's space shuttle, echocardiography was a technique of bouncing ultrasonic sound waves off the heart and other organs and photographing the resulting wave pattern with a Polaroid camera. It achieved a degree of accuracy that could allow measuring even the thickness of the heart wall, but with the instrument not functioning they were deprived of a valuable diagnostic tool.

"He went into shock very suddenly about an hour ago," said Vogel. "I'm sure it would have been much more marked, if Miss Payson hadn't been right on the ball and given him Isoproterenol."

155

"The shock was probably a warning of the change in mitral valve function," Rebecca suggested.

"I'll buy that," Ken agreed.

Rebecca hesitated momentarily, then asked the question that was uppermost in her mind: "Do you think any surgical intervention is indicated, Ken?"

"Not at the moment, but what happened here is a definite warning. I'd like to see a record of at least three main physiologic correlates over the next six or eight hours: the level of heart muscle function, the tone of the blood vessels themselves, and an index of how much blood is being shunted because of the shock effect on the arteriovenous network in the lungs."

"Berggren's Equation should help us obtain that index," said Rebecca. "Ed can put in the necessary catheters and let us have the computer read-out when he gets it."

"Right," said Vogel. "Anything else?"

"I'd like to see what that mitral valve looks like," said Ken. "But we won't put him through a left heart catheterization unless there's more of an indication than we have now."

Rebecca asked the question that was foremost in her mind. "Do you think it's safe to wait as long as six hours?"

"I hope so," said Ken. "Trying to repair ruptured *chordae tendineae* is a pretty hopeless job; the tissues are usually so friable that sutures don't hold well. Of course if McKenzie does come to open heart surgery in order to put in an artificial mitral valve, it would be a lot better to do it before his left ventricle and the valve ring become stretched and thinned out from an acute dilation. But I'm not convinced yet that surgery is inevitable."

"Would you have any qualms about operating on McKenzie?" Rebecca asked after the two had left the cubicle and were beyond earshot of Ed Vogel.

"Qualms?" Ken frowned. "Why?"

"After what he said about you yesterday."

"Are you worried that it might affect my decision to recommend surgery, Reb? Or my operative technique?"

"Neither. I just wanted to be sure *you* weren't."

156

"The way you women manage men constantly amazes me." Ken shook his head a bit ruefully. "Most of the time we don't even realize we're being manipulated, until we've done what you want us to do—like last night."

"Maybe I did start out that way, but things sort of got away from me."

"From both of us." He lowered his voice. "Did I hurt you?"

She shook her head, her eyes warm with the memory. "Only the way a woman likes to be hurt by the man she loves."

He changed the subject abruptly. "Congratulations on your promotion, it's well deserved."

"I didn't ask for it."

"You wouldn't, and we both know the reason—because you don't want to put yourself before me. But holding back on your own professional advancement when you've earned it wouldn't change anything, Reb. We're both doctors and both naturally competitive, so our professional life is an important part of our existence, together or separate."

"I've always felt the same way," Rebecca agreed. "You've been successful with other transplants besides the heart and just because we haven't licked the problem of rejection yet doesn't mean you can't go on with your work in transplanting other organs, Ken. In fact, what you'd learn transplanting kidneys, the pancreas in severe diabetes, even the lungs, might one day help solve the heart problem."

"You're right, as usual," he admitted wryly. "I'd been up on the roof nearly an hour before you came up last night, thinking things out. When I failed to save the Hornsby girl yesterday afternoon, I was ready to call it quits—for good. Then Karen proved to me that she had been beyond saving—"

Rebecca stiffened at his words. "It was lucky for you that she ran the tests so soon after the patient's death," she said tersely.

"Yes, it was." He appeared not to have noted the change in Rebecca's voice, which had suddenly become harsh. "Actually the State's Attorney's office had asked

Karen for a quick report, so they'd know whether to arrest the man the Hornsby girl was living with for murder. It was a tactical mistake for me to let Ross McKenzie goad me into leaving the Executive Committee meeting yesterday afternoon, I knew that as soon as I was outside and had a chance to think about it. I also realized that McKenzie's accusations had been just what I needed to make me face up to the truth that I had almost reached the point of no return. Anyway, up there on the roof, I finally admitted to myself that, since you have already gone well past me in our professional careers, I have to catch up if we're ever to solve our own problems. If Karen hadn't—"

Rebecca's control suddenly snapped. "You're really saying that none of this talk about our remaining professional equals is the truth," she said harshly.

Ken looked at her in startled surprise. "What brought that on?" he asked.

"The real trouble between us hinges on the male ego," Rebecca continued on the same furious note. "You'll only be satisfied when you restore me to the same inferior professional status I occupied when you were a surgical god here, the same position most men insist on their women occupying."

She stopped for breath, color high and eyes hot with anger.

"That's absurd, Reb—"

"Is it? I've gone as far as I can, Ken." She knew she was being unreasonable and didn't care, though she would hardly have admitted that the real reason for the outburst was the fact that he appeared to be crediting Karen Fletcher with being more responsible than she for his decision to turn and fight at last.

"Go on, if you insist, and destroy your reputation as a surgeon, and as a man, over a shibboleth," Rebecca flung at him as she was leaving. "I can't hold back any longer, waiting for you to catch up."

She was gone, head high, cheeks flaming, her body stiff with indignation—and, he thought, more lovely, more utterly desirable, than ever before. But she had put her finger upon the tenderest spot of all, he couldn't help admitting—the simple fact that, until he had once more proved himself by gaining a lead, however small, in the professional world where they both moved and occupied responsible positions, he couldn't drop back to run beside her. All of which meant, he admitted somewhat ruefully, that she'd been correct in her evaluation of the real thorn in their relationship. And what was more, proving once again, if it needed proof, that women invariably understood the men they loved better than the men understood themselves.

When Ken came in, Ed Vogel looked up from the desk in the ICU doctors' office, where he was making some notes on a chart. The young doctor had seen Rebecca leave and realized she was in a huff, but he made no comment.

"Peggy Tyndall's tied up in the OR putting together a special pump oxygenator for Mike Raburn," he said. "But Miss Sundberg is putting a catheter tray together and we'll take Mr. McKenzie to the ICU treatment room when it's ready. You'll want them in both the subclavian vein and femoral artery, as usual, won't you, so we can determine the stroke work index?"

"I was just thinking that this would be an ideal case for that fiberoptic catherer I brought back from Boston a few months ago," said Ken. "The one they've been using at Peter Bent Brigham Hospital in the Harvard Medical School complex."

"It isn't sterile." Ed Vogel's tone was doubtful. "As I remember it, those fiberoptics are supposed to be sterilized in ethylene oxide at 60 degrees Centigrade and that will take a couple of hours at least."

"I'd still rather use it," said Ken firmly. "In Boston they say the information the fiberoptics give will let you predict which way a heart is going as much as twelve hours in advance."

"That's what we need," said Ed Vogel. "I'll get to work sterilizing the catheter right away and put it in as soon as it's ready."

159

Mike Raburn was working with Val LeMoyne and Peggy Tyndall in the OR suite setting up the necessary special apparatus for the TBW procedure in the morning, when the voice of the paging operator sounded from the loudspeaker in the corridor outside.

"Dr. Raburn, 161. Dr. Michael Raburn, 161. Dr. Raburn, 161."

"That's the Information Desk," said Mike. "What could they want with me?"

"Probably Marcia Weston wanting you to go over plans tonight for the TBW at her apartment," said Val. "That's what you get for pandering to famous people."

"Don't go away," Mike said as he left the workroom to pick up the wall telephone in the corridor outside. "We've still got a lot to do."

"Mr. Sanchez wants to talk to you about his daughter, Dr. Raburn," said the Gray Lady volunteer at the main desk in the lobby.

"Tell them I'll try to make it in ten minutes," said Mike. "I'm tied up right now."

"Carmelita's father is downstairs," Mike told Val and Peggy when he went back into the workroom. "He wants to talk to me."

"Think they're backing out?" Val asked. "The noon edition carried a story about what you're going to try tomorrow—emphasizing the danger element."

"I haven't had time to look at a paper for days. Dr. Toler is handling the publicity for this case himself, trying to put the screws on the Finance Committee of the commission. Maybe I'd better go down, though, and see what Sanchez wants."

"Peggy and I will check out that heat exchanger unit while you're gone," said Val. "It's got to work perfectly, or you'll never get that circulation refill of fresh warm blood and packed red cells into her in time to keep from damaging some of the brain cells from anoxia."

"Aren't you the encouraging one?" Mike said with a grunt. "I'll be right back."

Downstairs he found Señor Sanchez and his wife in one corner of the waiting room. With them was a tall, stern-looking man wearing the cassock of a Catholic priest.

"This is Father Junípero Cortez, Dr. Raburn," said Señora Sanchez. "He wants to talk to you."

"Would you like to come to my office, Father? It's on this floor."

"I think Carmelita's parents should hear our discussion, Doctor." Mike was a bit puzzled by the distinctly antagonistic note in the priest's voice, but couldn't imagine the reason.

"Perhaps we should all go to my office," he agreed. "It's more private than the lobby here."

The office was small but, with a couple of extra chairs, accommodated everybody. Father Junípero preferred to stand.

"Señor Sanchez has asked me to render last rites to his daughter, Dr. Raburn," said the priest. "Do I understand that you intend to perform an operation on her tomorrow from which you do not expect her to recover?"

"Of course not," said Mike. "I tried to explain what is involved to them—"

"Señora Sanchez tells me that for nine minutes during this procedure Carmelita will not be alive. The newspaper accounts this afternoon intimate the same thing."

"I haven't seen the papers, Father, but I assure you that she will be alive and that I have every expectation of her recovery. Else I wouldn't undertake an exchange transfusion."

"I am familiar with the use of exchange transfusions for jaundice in the newborn," said the priest. "Do you propose to do the same thing?"

"Not quite, but the difference is only in degree. Total Body Washout involves removing practically all blood from the cirulatory system, washing out the antigen and resultant toxins of serum hepatitis from the circulation, and replacement with fresh blood."

"The entire volume of the circulation?" the priest asked.

"As nearly as we can."

"Is that compatible with life?"

"In order to reduce the needs of the body tissues for oxygen to the point where they can survive for the nine minutes the procedure may take, we must chill them, particularly the brain, to a point where no sign of life actually exists because all body processes have been reduced to the absolute minimum degree of metabolism compatible with life."

"Then she will be clinically dead?"

"I suppose she could be declared so according to the now generally accepted final criterion calling for absence of all physiological evidence of brain activity," Mike admitted. "But I don't regard the state of suspended animation we obtain as representing clinical death."

"Can you be sure of it?" the priest insisted.

"No, I cannot." Mike was beginning to understand what was troubling the priest and from a theological point of view he could sympathize with Father Junípero's dilemma.

"Simply put, Dr. Raburn, if Carmelita will be physiologically dead for nine minutes tomorrow morning, what will be happening to her soul during that period?"

"I'm afraid that question is in your sphere, not mine, Father."

"Unfortunately, theology has no precedent by which to make a decision—just as this appears to be a medical procedure for which there is no precedent."

"Except that it has already been performed successfully several times."

"With full recovery?"

"As far as can be told at present, in two out of five cases. But now that you've brought up the subject, Father, a corollary question might also be argued that may be at the base of your difficulty in understanding. Before I decided to subject Carmelita to anything this new and potentially dangerous, I asked myself whether as a doctor I had the right to reduce a patient to a condition so near to actual death that it cannot be distinguished from death."

"I think it would help all of us if you could put into

words just what led you to assume such a responsibility," said the priest.

"Frankly it never occurred to me that a metaphysical aspect of what I propose to do existed," Mike admitted. "But I can see an answer."

"Please let us have it."

"No one can tell exactly how a particular person's body is going to react to any medical or surgical procedure, Father. Instant death under anesthesia doesn't occur very often, but it is a hazard; sometimes life ceases before the operation is even begun and medically we have no way of predicting it. Which means that every time I order the anesthetic started on a patient in preparation for surgery, I am in essence taking the responsibility for that life. The same goes for surgical procedures where occasionally, in spite of every precaution I take, my technique may fail to control hemorrhage or maintain life."

"I can understand that," Father Junípero admitted.

"What I plan to do for Carmelita tomorrow is certainly an extreme case, but it belongs in the same category, Father. The difference is only a matter of extent."

"Looked at that way, I can see your rationale."

"And you accept its necessity in Carmelita's case?"

"Yes."

"Then we are, to a degree, in partnership. By ministering to her spiritual welfare and giving her extreme unction, you are as I understand it, preparing her for death according to the tenets of your religious belief and hers, as well as insuring a continuation of life in heaven after death. In a different way, but with the same purpose, I am seeking to continue her life here on earth."

The Catholic priest smiled. "You are very persuasive, Dr. Raburn—and also very eloquent. If you will forgive my saying so, your profession produces rather fewer real philosophers than it should, but I am glad to meet one."

"Then you agree that, in Carmelita's case, the possible physical benefits justify the theological risks?"

"I'm sure they do, Doctor, although I was far from certain when I asked to speak to you. I shall be praying for you tomorrow. To use Señor Sachez' and my native tongue, *vaya con Dios.*"

"The whole apparatus checks out to a very handsome setup; Peggy here is a real expert," said Val LeMoyne when Mike came back to the room where they had been working on the TBW apparatus. "Is the family still willing?"

"Believe it or not, I've just been discussing theology with a very smart Catholic priest."

"Who came out ahead?" Peggy asked.

"I think it was a draw. He was troubled by the fact that Carmelita will be physiologically dead for nine minutes tomorrow, but fortunately we all agree that it has to be done. I've been looking at the whole question through someone else's eyes for the past fifteen or twenty minutes and it was an interesting experience."

"The priest didn't raise any doubts in your mind, did he?" Val asked.

"No," said Mike. "Every good surgeon learns early that he has to be two people: one is the guy who handles the scalpel in the sterile world of the operating room, the other is the one who on occasion has to withstand the buffetings of outrageous fortune."

Peggy Tyndall stood up and pushed the stool on which she had been sitting back from the worktable. "Miss Sundberg called a little while ago about sterilizing a fiberoptic catheter Dr. Ken Dalton wants put into Mr. McKenzie," she said. "If you'll excuse me for a few minutes, I'll run down to CICU and check on it."

"Sure, Peg," said Mike. "You and Dr. LeMoyne have done a fine job with the new pump.

"Not many women go into anesthesia for open heart surgery," said Mike as he was leaving the OR suite with Val LeMoyne. "I should think watching a patient for an hour or more on a pump oxygenator, with the heart and lungs not working at all, and knowing all the time that whether you win out or are credited with an anesthesia death depends solely on something as vulnerable as an electric motor or a mechanical valve inside the machine, must be pretty rough. How do you manage to stand up so well under it?"

"Because I long ago divided my life into two separate compartments, almost two separate existences," said Val. "When I walk through the front door into the hospital every morning, I'm stepping into the world of medicine, as a doctor. Just before I walk through it in the other direction in the evening, I shed my medical life. when I shed my hospital gown, and until the next morning I'm responsible to no one but myself. I think I'm the better anesthesiologist for it."

"I guess you are. At least I've never met a better one."

"Coming from a perfectionist like you, Mike, that's a real accolade."

"Maybe if I could separate my two lives I'd be better off, but so far I don't seem to be able to have but one."

"Stay just like you are, Mike. All of us need someone to cling to when one of our two worlds suddenly blows apart and it's nice to know there's at least one rock named Mike Raburn around."

V

"I hope you haven't had your lunch," said Jeffry Toler when Rebecca came into his office shortly after noon.

"I was on my way to the cafeteria for a bite when I got your call. Ken has just seen Ross McKenzie with Ed Vogel and myself in consultation."

"How is the old curmudgeon?"

"Sleeping most of the time. Ed Vogel is putting in some catheters to measure cardiac output."

"Has McKenzie accepted you as his doctor?"

"Apparently. Like he said last night, he doesn't have much choice."

"Just how severe a coronary attack did he have?"

"As far as we can tell, it isn't a coronary at all—unless there's a small infarct involving the area around the mitral valve. It looks more like he was already getting degenerative changes in the *chordae tendineae* that control the valve, and under strain some of them broke, letting the valve flap a little and causing enough mitral insufficiency to produce a fairly loud systolic murmur. If our echocardiograph was working we could get a clear picture of the valve and the rest of that part of the heart with ultrasonic waves. But the transmitter had to be sent back to the factory so we're deprived of one of our most important diagnostic tools."

"What's the prognosis?"

"Nobody can tell at this stage. If the valve breaks loose entirely, all the blood in the left side of the heart will be shoved back into the atrium and the pulmonary veins with each contraction of the ventricle, so the effect on the hemodynamics of the circulation could be pretty drastic. Fortunately Carolyn Payson, the ICU nursing supervisor for the morning shift, acted quickly this morning when McKenzie started into cardiac shock. We pulled him out of it before things went too far, but it could happen again at any time."

"Why not operate now?"

"If Mr. McKenzie does have an infarct from a blocked coronary, surgery would put a considerable strain on the heart. Besides, there's some chance that he may stabilize with partial function of the heart, at least until we can get him in better shape. Ken appears to be counting on that."

"And you don't agree?" Toler had not missed the change in her voice.

"Let's say I hope he's right—for Mr. McKenzie's sake and Ken's."

"I take it that the decision is a pretty ticklish one to have to make."

Rebecca nodded. "I don't envy Ken the responsibility, but no one else can assume it for him. Ed Vogel and I can get all the facts he needs but he has to make the decision."

"Do you think his emotional state is such that he's qualified to make it?"

He saw her hesitate and was immediately concerned.

"I—I'm not sure, Jeffry," she admitted.

"Yesterday you seemed much more optimistic. What happened to change your mind?"

"I think he should operate but he doesn't want to. And I'm afraid I just blew my top over it, which doesn't help any." She didn't mention Karen Fletcher, whose name had triggered her sudden explosion.

A white-uniformed waitress from the staff cafeteria came in just then with two trays.

"Put them on the coffee table over there in the corner," Toler instructed the waitress, then turned back to Rebecca.

"I hope you like ham sandwiches and coffee," he said. "I thought we could both save time by talking while we have a snack."

"Sandwiches will be fine."

He served her two sandwiches on a paper plate while she poured coffee for them from a Thermos flask.

"So what's the prognosis?" Toler asked as he put a spoonful of a non-dairy creamer in his coffee and emptied a small packet of artificial sweetner into it.

"I've already told you—"

"I mean about you and Ken."

"I don't know, Jeff; last night I shamed him into almost raping me." Her color heightened a little. "The first sign of a break between us was when our sex life practically disappeared, but last night he was as successful a lover as he was on our honeymoon."

"So he's not impotent, but surely you don't think going to bed with you once will cure his feeling of playing second fiddle to you professionally."

"Of course not. I was hoping Ross McKenzie would do that."

Jeffry Toler looked surprised. "Come again."

"As soon as Ken studied the information Ed Vogel and I were able to give him from our medical studies of McKenzie's heart, he made a diagnosis."

"The right one?"

"I'm sure of it. Right now we're using every tool at our command to stabilize Mr. McKenzie medically, but I think we're going to fail. If Ken has to operate, it will mean I have failed as a cardiologist, but if Mr. McKenzie lives, our marriage just may be saved."

"Suppose he does operate and Ross McKenzie dies?"

167

"I'm woman enough to believe Ken will succeed, Jeffry; in fact, I was staking my chance at happiness on it. But I'm afraid I pushed Ken too far this morning by intimating that I was convinced Mr. McKenzie would need surgery and that Ken is playing for time because he doesn't want to assure the responsibility for another serious open heart operation. He didn't agree—and I'm afraid my temper got the best of me."

Toler smiled. "Natural redheads aren't particularly noted for their even dispositions."

"I'm afraid I blew my cool just now."

"You took a long chance, Reb, in trying to run a squeeze play on Ken. But then I suppose a desperate situation can only be handled by desperate measures. Good luck."

"Thank you, Jeffry. Was that why you sent for me?"

"Good Lord! I was so worried about you two that I almost forgot," said the administrator. "Father Hagan tells me you're going to be the devil's advocate when the Moriturus Committee meets this afternoon, so I thought I should warn you that Judge Robie had to go out of town. He asked Anthony Broadhurst to take his place on the committee."

Rebecca didn't need to be told the reason for Jeffry Toler's concern. One of the trickiest aspects of the God Committee's activities was the fact that it had no legal status. In fact, according to existing law in most states, acceding to the request of relatives that the patient in question be allowed to die could make committee members technically accessories to murder.

Anthony Broadhurst was a brilliant and ambitious county prosecutor who was locally famous for holding accused and accusers to the strict letter of the law. So far Judge Robie's presence on the committee had given it quasi-legal status, but nobody could predict how Broadhurst would act in a God committee situation—except the certainty that he would bring to the deliberations very little of the broad understanding and humanity that characterized Judge Robie.

"Do you want me to postpone the hearing?" Toler asked.

"I can't answer that until I talk to Carolyn Payson," said Rebecca. "I've asked her to come to my office as soon as the shift changes at three."

"Will you let me know at once what she decides? The hearing is scheduled for six o'clock in the Board Room, so we don't have much time."

"I'll get a decision from Carolyn as quickly as I can," Rebecca promised. "Thanks for the lunch, Jeffry."

Chapter 11

AT 1:30 P.M. Wednesday afternoon the warning bell on the Regional Medical Program Network teletype in the Cardiac Research Laboratory at Biscayne General started ringing. Peggy Tyndall moved quickly to the network teletype printer as the message was typed out swiftly by flying keys:

"Dr. Harvey Boldt at the Veterans' Memorial Hospital in Marathon, Florida, requests ECG consultation with Dr. Rebecca Dalton re the condition of a patient, Mr. Kevin McCartney. Please expedite. Will start transmitting at 1:45 P.M."

Peggy was reaching for the telephone before the teletype keys stopped chattering. The fact that Kevin McCartney was in trouble could hardly mean anything except another rejection crisis, quite likely his last. Nor could it bode less than ill for the developing reconciliation between the Daltons, for both of whom Peggy felt a genuine fondness.

"Page Dr. Rebecca Dalton, please," she told the operator.

"What is it, Peggy?" Rebecca Dalton's voice sounded in the technician's ear a few minutes later.

"A teletype on the network, Doctor. Marathon wants to transmit an ECG at one forty-five. Dr. Boldt."

"I know Dr. Boldt. He's a capable general practitioner."

"The patient is Kevin McCartney. What do you suppose he was doing down in the Keys?"

"Fishing. He told me last night in the Dolphin Lounge that he wanted to go and I gave him permission, after he promised to report to you tomorrow morning for an ECG and blood work."

"I've got the requisition," said Peggy. "Can you make it in fifteen minutes, or shall I teletype Dr. Boldt to make it later?"

"I'll be there right away," said Rebecca. "You'd better ask Dr. Vogel to join us, too."

"Do you want anyone else?" Both of them knew very well whom Peggy meant.

"Not yet," said Rebecca. "Kevin's situation may not be too bad but make sure the ECG printer is in order. We want to get a clear picture."

The Cardiology Section of the South Florida Regional Medical Program had been organized by Rebecca herself a couple of years before. Joining eight smaller hospitals in a heart-monitoring network covering most of South Florida, the federally financed program gave doctors outside the medical center the benefit of expert help in diagnosing heart disease and in following patients, once the condition was fully diagnosed.

In the outlying hospitals, an electrocardiographic amplifier and oscilloscope recorded the electrical picture of the heartbeat as an electrocardiogram. This was transmitted over a leased telephone wire to the medical school, where the ECG was recorded on what was usually called a "slave" monitor equipped with another writer-recorder. In this way the pattern of the electrocardiographic tracing was reproduced at Biscayne General and could be visualized as well as recorded on moving paper strips by a conventional printer for permanent record. Simultaneous voice transmission was possible, too, all at a considerably lower cost and far more quickly than by transporting a trained cardiologist to the outlying hospital for consultation.

Promptly at one forty-five Rebecca sat down before the

network monitor, with Ed Vogel looking over her shoulder. At one side was a conventional telephone amplifier. When a small light on the amplifier started blinking, Rebecca pressed the button beside it.

"This is Dr. Rebecca Dalton in Miami."

"Dr. Boldt in Marathon, Dr. Dalton. A patient of yours named Kevin McCartney was brought here about an hour ago after he collapsed while fishing near the reef. His ECG worries us somewhat."

"I'm ready whenever you want to transmit, Dr. Boldt. How is Mr. McCartney's general condition?"

"He says he's having a rejection crisis."

"He ought to know. We've pulled him through four of them."

"He also insists that this one is his last. My technician tells me she's ready to transmit now, so I'll sign off for the moment."

A jumble of lines appeared upon the ground-glass screen and Peggy Tyndall fiddled with the controls of the oscilloscope until the picture cleared. When it did, Rebecca leaned forward to study the pattern of electric waves from Kevin McCartney's heart, roughly a hundred miles away across water, the Florida Keys in between and part of the Everglades.

Although the peaks of the tracing were low, indicating a decreased voltage of the current produced by the heart muscle, the beats were still fairly strong. The pattern at first seemed normal, although the rate was somewhat rapid, close to a hundred and twenty a minute when seventy or eighty would have been a more normal figure. But as Rebecca and Ed Vogel watched, subtle changes, discernible only to an expert eye, began to be noticeable.

"Print a ten-second strip for me, Peggy," said the cardiologist when the first abnormal beat appeared.

The technician pressed a button on the direct writer-recorder and the moving stylus that was the heart of the instrument began to trace out upon a paper strip the picture appearing upon the monitor screen. Picking up the tape as it came from the recorder, Rebecca studied it briefly.

"Dr. Boldt?" She spoke into the telephone beside her.

"Yes?" The other doctor's voice came back to her across the watery expanse of Florida Bay.

"How soon after Mr. McCartney was admitted did you start monitoring the ECG?"

"As soon as he told me he had received a transplant. Do you think those T-wave changes are significant?"

"I believe so," said Rebecca. "They're usually part of the rejection pattern."

"We took an X ray of his chest. The cardiac shadow appears to be considerably enlarged."

"That could be an accumulation of fluid around the heart inside the pericardium; it's part of the rejection picture too." Rebecca was dreading the task of breaking the news to Ken that his last transplant case was probably dying.

"Look at that!" Ed Vogel's voice broke into her reverie and she glanced quickly at the screen.

"What was it?" she asked, for the pattern seemed the same.

"Looked like a burst of atrial fibrillation, as if the left atrium had gone berserk for a moment."

"Dr. Boldt," Rebecca said quickly into the telephone, "have you noticed any disorders of rhythm?"

"That's another reason why I called you." The distant voice of the doctor in Marathon sounded disturbed. "There have been bursts of atrial fibrillation."

"There it is again," said Ed Vogel, and Rebecca reached for the button that started the writer-recorder printing a graphic record of the heart's action.

An irritable heart was, at least potentially, a diseased heart, vulnerable to any unusual strain or circumstance, and Rebecca's face showed her concern as she studied the ECG tape. The disorderly action phase lasted only about twenty seconds, however, then the normal rhythm was regained.

"I don't like the looks of these changes, Dr. Boldt," said Rebecca concisely.

"What do you suggest?"

"Have you injected Lidocaine?"

"No."

"I would suggest fifty milligrams intravenously and a hundred and fifty milligrams intramuscularly."

"That can be done immediately," said Dr. Boldt. "We have an IV drip going."

"We can monitor Mr. McCartney's cardiac condition continuously for you on the Regional Medical Program Network if you like," Rebecca offered.

"I'd feel a lot better if he was in Biscayne General with you watching his heart," said Dr. Boldt.

"We'll be glad to have him of course—if you think his general condition doesn't preclude moving him."

"It would have to be by helicopter. Do you think you can persuade the Department of Public Safety to send out of the county for him?"

"Give me a moment to check with them," said Rebecca. "Hang on, please.

"A specially equipped helicopter ambulance will be there in about an hour," she reported after conferring with the central Rescue Squad dispatcher. "We'll be able to monitor Mr. McCartney's heart while he's in transit and will be in constant communication with the firemen in the copter, so tell him not to worry. And thank you for getting in touch with me so quickly, Dr. Boldt. I'll keep you posted.

"Make arrangements to take Kevin directly from the landing pad on the rooftop to X ray for a six-foot film, Ed," Rebecca directed her assistant when the network lines were switched off. "This time I suspect we're going to have the fight of our lives."

"And Kevin's."

Neither of them added the postscript in both their minds—that the surgical career of the brilliant man who had given Kevin McCartney a new heart nearly two years ago might well come to a halt, too, if that heart stopped beating forever.

II

"Why don't you go home and take a nap?" It was ten after three and Helga Sundberg had finished taking Carolyn Payson's report on the previous eight hours in the Intensive Care Unit.

"I couldn't sleep." Carolyn was haggard from worry.

"Take a Valium or something."

"I might oversleep then and miss the God Committee meeting."

"I'll call you at five o'clock, if that will help you relax. Even with Dr. Dalton pleading your case, you need to be on your toes. They're liable to ask a lot of questions—"

"What troubles me most is whether I can make them understand that I'm not just trying to get rid of the burden of my father's care—or the finances."

"Anybody who knows you would understand that."

"But some of these people are laymen, Helga. Besides, if I can't convince Gus that it's the thing to do, how can I convince a total stranger?"

"Gus has only had to deal with babies, mostly mongoloids. They're enough to tear the heart of even a tough pro like me."

"Pull for me anyway, Helga. I'm going to see Dr. Dalton now. She wants to go over the strategy or something."

"Good luck," said Helga. "Now scat."

"Everything's ready for the catheterization on Mr. McKenzie," said Carolyn as she was leaving. "Ed Vogel wanted to do it an hour ago but we had to be sure the new catheter he's going to use was sterile."

Carolyn had to wait almost fifteen minutes in Rebecca Dalton's office before the cardiologist came in. The nurse could see at once that something was disturbing her.

"I'm sorry you had to wait, Carolyn," said Rebecca. "A helicopter is flying Kevin McCartney in from Marathon—"

"Another rejection crisis?" Carolyn asked quickly.

"A bad one from the looks of things. We'll know for sure when Kevin gets here."

"That's too bad."

"In more ways than one," said Rebecca crisply. "Now about the Moriturus Committee meeting this afternoon. It's scheduled for six o'clock but Dr. Toler wanted me to warn you that Judge Robie can't be here. The judge asked Mr. Anthony Broadhurst to substitute—"

174

"The State's Attorney?"

"Yes. And I might as well tell you that neither Dr. Toler nor I think it's a good omen for approval of your request that all treatment of any kind be stopped in your father's case."

"It isn't just that," said Carolyn. "I'm asking for positive action by medical authority to end his life."

"I understand that, but I don't know how Mr. Broadhurst and the other members of the committee will look at it. Dr. Toler felt you should be warned so you can withdraw the request if you wish."

"For submission later?"

"Possibly."

"Wouldn't that imply that my own convictions about the rightness of what I'm asking aren't very strong?"

"It could—yes." Rebecca gave her a quick, inquiring look. "Are you sure in your own mind that they are?"

"I'm absolutely sure," said Carolyn. "What's *your* advice, Dr. Dalton? After all, you're my law—my representative."

"If you're absolutely convinced that what you're asking is what your father wants, or would want if he were able to analyze the situation, I would go on as planned. If you aren't, I would wait and rethink the whole question."

"I have no doubts about what Father wants," said Carolyn firmly. "Or that I owe it to him to carry out his wishes any way I can."

"Then we'll go ahead. I have worked out a simple plan for presenting your case before the committee, but we'd better go over it before the hearing begins."

"I'll do whatever you say, except withdraw the request."

III

In the spotless tiled CICU treatment room, into which Ross McKenzie's bed had been pushed, Ed Vogel was just starting the catheterization of the grower's heart when Helga came in. Peggy Tyndall, who would normally have helped him, was making some last-minute changes in the TBW heart-lung pump before it was sterilized for tomor-

175

row's attempt to bring Carmelita Sanchez back from the very edge of the grave. Ross McKenzie was sleeping quietly from an injection of Demerol a half hour earlier.

"I'll stand by here, Miss Smith," Helga told the nurse who had been specialing McKenzie. "You can watch the nursing station."

"Welcome aboard," said Ed Vogel.

He had finished injecting novocaine into the skin at the front of the grower's elbow, where a fairly large vein could be seen. Picking up a scalpel from the sterile tray beside the bed, he made a small incision and, with a forceps, dissected out roughly an inch of the vein, slipping a small probe beneath it to make it more easily accessible.

Helga waited with a sterile pair of ring forceps in her hand, ready to hand the cardiologist anything he needed from a reserve table next to the wall. Upon it lay a somewhat larger instrument than was ordinarily used in vein catheterizations of the right heart, a procedure that had become almost standard in evaluating the status of seriously ill heart patients.

"That's quite a gadget," she said, looking down at the catheter.

"Would you believe that inside the woven outer covering on that fancy piece of tubing there are about a hundred cladded glass fibers?"

"The label on the package said it's a fiberoptic system, but you'll never make me believe you're going to look inside the heart with that little thing."

Ed Vogel laughed. "Not quite. Actually the catheter contains three individual systems, each with a different purpose. One is a wire electrode for recording ECG impulses from inside the heart or stimulating it with a pacemaker if it decides to quit."

"That we can do without."

"Another is a simple catheter for measuring venous pressure, injecting medications, taking blood specimens, or what have you. The third, and most complicated, part is really a pair of fiberoptic strands, one for sending pulses of light into the heart and the main pulmonary artery to the lungs, the other for returning the pulses of light picked

176

up on reflection from the red blood cells, after injecting a green dye, and transmitting them through the glass fibers to register on a detector."

"Sounds complicated."

"It really isn't. Using this gadget in conjunction with a second ordinary catheter beside it, we can measure right-sided heart pressure, record dye dilution studies for cardiac performance, determine oxygen saturation, cardiac output, and a few other things."

Ed Vogel had been working steadily while he was talking. Threading the fiberoptic catheter carefully through a small opening in the wall of the vein he had exposed, he worked it up the arm toward the heart through ever larger venous channels, by way of the connecting subclavian vein, where it entered the chest, and then on into the superior vena cava just outside the right atrium of the heart itself. When, from the height of the ECG pattern being recorded from the electric impulses of the heart itself by means of the wire terminal inside the catheter, he judged that the tip should be in the right atrium, he covered the small skin incision with a sterile towel.

"We'll check with an X ray now," he said.

The technician, who had been waiting outside with the portable X-ray machine, wheeled it into the room and positioned the tube over Ross McKenzie's chest. Only seconds were required to expose the film placed beneath his body, after which the machine was wheeled out again. While they waited for the result, Ed carefully positioned a smaller conventional catheter in the superior vena cava by inserting it through the same arm vein.

"When did Dr. Rebecca get the idea for this gadget?" Helga asked as they were waiting for the film to be developed.

"Oddly enough, it wasn't hers," said the cardiologist. "Dr. Ken brought a couple of these fiberoptic catheters back from Boston when he was up there months ago; they've been using them at Peter Bent Brigham Hospital in the Harvard Medical School complex. But he hasn't been doing much in the heart lately and she's a little more

177

conservative, so until today the catheter's lain in its box unused."

"If it does half the things you mentioned, it will make monitoring serious heart cases a lot simpler," said Helga. "Do you think this means Dr. Ken is getting a grip on things again?"

"Your guess is as good as mine," said the Research Fellow. "I'm pretty sure she thinks he's trying to avoid having to operate and I'd bet they quarreled over just that."

"You mean she favors surgery?"

Vogel nodded. "It's a tough decision for everybody."

"Why?"

"If she has to give her opinion, as the chief cardiologist for the hospital, that surgery is needed, and he refuses, this will be the final showdown."

"But he always left the decision of who should receive transplants up to her."

"And now he's blaming her, maybe unconsciously, but blaming her just the same, for the way things turned out."

"There's a man for you. When Eve gave Adam the apple, he didn't have to be persuaded to eat it. But when the Lord came around and caught him, after he did, the first thing he said was: 'The woman whom thou gavest to be with me, she gave me of the tree, and I did eat.'"

Ed Vogel shook his head admiringly. "You constantly amaze me, Helga. Where did you ever study the Bible?"

"When I was growing up, we had to go to Sunday school and church twice every Sunday, plus Wednesday night prayer meeting. In a way, it was fun though, especially once a year when we all went to what was called the Association. That was when a lot of churches got together and held a preaching marathon under a bush arbor to protect the people from the sun."

"Doesn't sound very exciting to me."

"That's what you think. You see, everybody camped out and, while the older people were being preached at, the young ones were making out in the bushes."

"Not much different from around here, would you say?"

Helga shrugged. "Maybe not but there was something about making love with pine needles and sandspurs pricking your backside that seemed to give sex a different flavor then."

The arrival of the X-ray film put an end to the conversation and Helga held it up against the light for Ed Vogel to study without contaminating the sterile gloves he still wore.

"The tip of the main catheter's in the right atrium," he said. "The question now is whether to go any farther."

"Let me study that a moment, please, Miss Sundberg." Neither of them had heard Ken Dalton approach the door of the treatment room. When Helga handed him the still wet film in the metal frame that had held it for developing, he examined it briefly, then gave it back to her.

"Was there any change in the ECG while you were putting the catheter in, Ed?" he asked.

"None at all."

"I'd like to get the tip through the right heart and into the pulmonary artery if we can. It could tell us how much pressure is developing in the lung circulation because of leakage through the mitral valve."

"I don't think I'll have any difficulty in putting it through into the artery, Dr. Dalton."

"Go ahead then. I'll stay around in case there's any trouble."

The procedure so far had been simple, but the next step involved threading the rather large catheter down through the right atrium and past the tricuspid valve separating the upper chamber from the ventricle below. From there it had to pass through the ventricle and the pulmonary valve leading into the main artery to the lungs, where it could be positioned in the midst of the stream of blood forced into the lung circulation with each stroke of the right heart. All went well here, too, however, and the chest X-ray film showed the tip of the catheter in excellent position.

"Nice going, Ed," said Ken Dalton. "They told me in

179

Boston that with a catheter like this danger signs will ordinarily show up fully twenty-four hours before any significant clinical warning can be detected. I want you to plot curves of the oxygen saturation, the pulmonary artery pressure and dye clearance rate every hour. With the information this type of catheter can give us, we can chart the cardiac output and the stroke work index, so it ought to be safe to watch McKenzie for a while longer. I'll be checking the first results on the computer as soon as you can connect the fiberoptic catheter to the bedside monitor unit."

"He knows exactly what he's doing," said Helga when Ken Dalton left the treatment room. "It could be that you and Dr. Rebecca have been selling him short."

"And the risk he's taking," Ed agreed.

"He wouldn't be the great surgeon he is if he didn't," said the blonde nurse cryptically. "I'd better get back to the console in case he needs any help."

"Tell him I've got the catheters connected here. He can start recording the data when he's ready."

Into the keyboard of the computer, Ken had already punched the figures representing the different values being fed to the main console from the bedside unit, while Ed Vogel checked the various new parameters made available by the sensitive fiberoptic catheter and the pulses of light flowing through it in both directions. Since Ken Dalton had first inserted into the computer circuits the fixed information about body surface, heartbeat, and other nomograms—normal values—the computer was able to calculate and display almost immediately the values for cardiac index, stroke volume, and stroke index. All of which were accurate indications of heart function which, prior to the development of the amazingly efficient single fiberoptic catheter, had required a number of separate and time-consuming measurements and analyses.

The surgeon studied the results, then compared them with previous estimates of Ross McKenzie's cardiac function made by more conventional methods.

"I don't see much change yet," he told Ed Vogel when the younger man came to the nursing station. "But the next six or eight hours ought to settle the question of whether to intervene surgically."

"I was hoping the new catheter would tell us something definite," said Ed.

"So was I. All of which goes to prove that, when you're working with the human heart, either physically or emotionally, you can never be entirely sure about anything."

Chapter 12

STRENGTHENED by one of the late afternoon thunderstorms making up to the south almost daily this time of the year, the normal sea breeze sweeping across the narrow island of Miami Beach from the ocean to the east was whipping the surface of Biscayne Bay into low whitecaps when Rebecca Dalton and Ed Vogel stepped out of the elevator that had brought them to the helicopter landing pad on the roof of the central hospital tower. They moved to a corner of the elevator housing upon the roof for protection against the wind and the additional blast from the helicopter rotors, when it settled upon the landing pad.

It had cost more than an extra hundred thousand dollars over the original estimated cost of the hospital tower to put the landing pad there with a special high-speed elevator to the ground-floor Emergency Room. But a half dozen lives had already been saved by the speed with which the two rescue helicopters of the Metro Fire Department had been able to shuttle serious accident and other emergencies to the hospital in the some six months they had been in operation.

With the quickened breeze, the helicopter was forced to make a second pass at the landing pad before it settled down smoothly, the whirling blades of its rotors adding to the wind sweeping across the roof of one of the two or three loftiest buildings in Miami. As the rotating blades came to a halt, a young man in a blue denim jumpsuit swung out of the cockpit and down to the pad.

"His ECG was skittering around considerably when we radioed you a little while ago, Dr. Dalton," he said. "But it settled down again."

"Looks like we taught you something, Sanders."

The young man, freshly returned from a two-year stint as medical corpsman with the Army and enrolled mornings in the new physician's assistant course operated jointly by the university and the medical school, was one of a new breed of paramedical personnel that was already increasing the efficiency of overworked doctors in many parts of the country.

The pilot came around to the side of the helicopter fuselage and the two men opened the wide doors that made entrance and exit easy with the basket stretcher used to handle patients.

"Hello, Dr. Dalton." Kevin McCartney could still smile, although his face was drawn from pain and his skin a sickly pallor in hue. "I'm sorry I couldn't bring you a fish."

"You brought one," Rebecca assured him. "Right now it looks like it's been out of the water too long, but we'll have you swimming again in no time."

The two men swung the basket litter down skillfully and transferred Kevin to a wheeled stretcher waiting beside the pad.

"We would have gotten here sooner," said the pilot, "but we had to fly around that storm."

"Thanks for making the trip," said Rebecca. "Kevin here is the only bartender in the world with a girl's heart inside his chest. We keep him around just as a curiosity."

Her fingers had moved to Kevin's wrist as he was being placed on the wheeled stretcher. His pulse was full, almost bounding in character, but regular and fairly strong, with none of the arrhythmia—at least for the moment—

that had made Dr. Boldt put his electrocardiographic tracing on the remote monitoring network.

"Travel seems to be good for you, Kevin," said Rebecca as she released his wrist. "Your heart's behaving better than it was before you left Marathon."

"The Lidocaine did that, I've had it enough times to recognize the effects. But a lot of my other equipment is running pretty rough." He grimaced with pain. "I never could understand why one of the first signs of heart rejection is a knot in your gut."

"Dr. Vogel is going to take you by X ray for a six-foot chest film," Rebecca told him. "But I'll ask Miss Sundberg to send a hypo for you from CICU."

Taken with the target of the X-ray tube six feet distant from the patient's chest, the film allowed exact measurements of heart size upon the film itself, giving a far more accurate picture than was possible from physical examination or an ordinary chest film.

"Peggy will take some blood and do an ECG, too, before we put you to bed on Intensive Care," Rebecca added. "Okay?"

"Whatever you say, Doc," said Kevin. "I never could resist a pretty woman—particularly one in white."

"Will you sign for him, Dr. Dalton?" The pilot had been eying the thunderstorm that was moving perceptibly nearer the landing pad. "I'd like to get off this tower before we're blown into the bay."

Rebecca scribbled her name at the bottom of the routing sheet on the small clipboard.

"Thank Chief Bates for me," she said as she handed back the board.

"He'll probably ask you to testify before the Commission Finance Committee," said the pilot as he swung himself up into the helicopter cabin. "The Fire Department budget is coming up for approval soon just like yours. Is it true that you've got old man Ross McKenzie in the hospital with a heart attack?"

"He's a patient," said Rebecca. "But we're not quite sure of the diagnosis yet."

"Do us all a favor and smother him before he can do

183

any more damage," said the pilot. "He's already got the salaries and the morale of the Fire Department so low that we're having trouble getting recruits."

Stepping into the elevator behind the stretcher, Rebecca pressed the button for "1" and the doors of the elevator closed smoothly, shutting away the roar of the engine, as the helicopter pilot gunned his motor to lift this latest and most sophisticated "Angel of Mercy" into the air once more.

II

Helga Sundberg had finished making rounds on the entire ICU section, after helping Ed Vogel with Ross McKenzie, when Mike Raburn appeared at the nursing station. She looked up from using the storage recall scope to check the orders Carolyn had punched into the computer date bank before going off duty.

"I didn't see you come in through the ER just now," said Mike.

"Don't tell me you were looking for me."

"I shouldn't admit it to a designing female, but I was. You assured me yesterday that you weren't interested in marriage for a long time, so I felt safe."

"A lot can happen in twenty-four hours."

"A lot happened between three and eleven yesterday, though I'm still not quite certain what it was."

"Neither am I," said Helga. "But maybe I should warn you that I plan to find out."

"We might make that a joint project starting, say, this weekend?"

"Why not, unless you get a swelled head from performing for television tomorrow morning. The grapevine has it that you'll be hitting the networks."

"Lord, I hope not," said Mike. "If I have as much trouble tomorrow as I've been having today, the program will be canceled."

"What's wrong?"

"Mainly blood. We'll be needing quarts of it tomorrow morning at the crucial point in the TBW, and unfortunately Carmelita's a Type A-negative. I've had to line up

184

the A-negative resources of every blood bank in town and it looks like we'll just make it even then."

"I'm sorry I'm an O," said Helga.

"Me too," said Mike. "Which would appear to be something else we have in common."

"Do you really only have nine minutes to complete the washout?" Helga asked. "That seems terribly short and you're bound to be under a considerable strain."

"Nobody has taken any longer than that so far, that I know of. And I certainly don't want to push my luck with my first case."

"You'll make it," she assured him.

"I wish I had your confidence. The more I think of all the things that could happen during those nine minutes, the more leery I get."

"Any surgeon who can quote Shakespeare at 11:00 P.M. after a long day's work must be something special. I've never seen you fail at anything yet that you had set your heart to."

"I was clobbered plenty of times on the football field— Joe Gates could vouch for that. And there always has to be a first time. Look at what happened to Ken Dalton; a year ago you would have said he couldn't even lose a patient, and now he is practically out of operative surgery entirely."

"Will you let it knock you tomorrow, if you fail to save Carmelita?"

"I don't know," Mike admitted gravely. "I'm way out on a limb this time, with a lot more than a girl's life, important though that is, at stake. Besides, if I make a mistake in the operating room tomorrow, everybody will know it, with those cameras grinding away."

"It's not too late to call off the broadcast."

Mike shook his head. "I can't let Dr. Toler and the hospital down; he's depending on this affair to be the finest public relations stunt anyone has ever brought off."

"I'm still betting on you." Helga's voice had a warm note which Mike didn't miss.

"Enough to help me celebrate this weekend, if everything turns out all right?"

"If you'll let me name the place and the time."

"Name it," he said promptly, and waited for an answer, but Helga shook her head.

"I won't tell you before tomorrow night, when you're sure you've won."

"And if I lose?"

"I'll let you cry on my shoulder as a consolation prize."

"Fair enough," he said. "Win or lose, I'll have a lot to look forward to."

III

Kevin McCartney had been taken directly from the X-ray room to the Cardiac Research Laboratory, on the special cardiac stretcher that allowed his condition to be monitored all the while by remote telemetry, the picture being received on the master screen of the ICU. He flinched a little as Peggy Tyndall stuck him with a rather large needle, so she could take enough blood for the tests Rebecca Dalton wanted run in addition to the regular CS-11 group, so called because the eleven tests could be run automatically by a fantastic machine that had taken over the work of several technicians.

After dividing into several test tubes the blood she had taken, Peggy taped a small dressing over the puncture wound on Kevin's arm and began to attach the leads used for a conventional ECG to his wrists, ankles, and the front of his chest.

"Dr. Fletcher says both you and she think Dale's getting more short of breath," said Peggy, as she started the machine. "I guess that's sort of a reflection on me as a mother."

"Did she say that?" Kevin demanded indignantly.

"Not in so many words. It was more like she was criticizing Dr. Rebecca for not watching Dale more closely."

"What's she trying to do? Cause trouble between Dr. Rebecca and Dr. Ken?"

"There's enough of that already," said Peggy. "But if

anybody's to blame where Dale is concerned, it's me. When I get to the apartment at night, I'm usually tired, so I guess I don't pay as much attention to him as I should."

"Dr. Fletcher and I could both be wrong," said Kevin. "When Dale comes to the lounge in the afternoon for his root beer, he's always panting from having run most of the way from Bayside Arms—"

"I've tried to slow him down," said Peggy, "but Dr. Rebecca says it's best to let him set his own pace, so he won't feel different from the other children. Dr. Rebecca's going to see him next week when the echocardioscope is fixed. By using it, she hopes he won't have to go through having a catheter put into his heart again."

"You can trust her to do what's best," Kevin assured the petite technician. "By the way, how is the work on the artificial heart coming?"

"The whole project has sort of stopped, since Dr. Ken and Dr. Rebecca aren't working together any more."

"Six months ago he told me he was about ready to implant an artificial heart run by atomic power in the chest of a calf. Every time I went to Mass, I said a prayer that Dr. Ken would get it perfected before the damn lymphocytes in my blood managed to kill me off. Now I'm half dead and you tell me it's a lost cause."

"I'm not any happier about it than you are, Kevin," said the technician. "After all, I've got a son with a heart that's all screwed up inside and he might need that pump one day too."

"Couldn't anybody else go on with the work?"

"Dr. Raburn could, I suppose. But Dr. Rebecca is still carrying the torch for her husband, and Mike's the busiest surgeon in the hospital."

"Meanwhile the one thing that might keep me going for another ten years or so is kaput. If you ask me, it's a hell of a way to treat a patient who depends on you."

Peggy gave him a quick, appraising look. "Have you told Dr. Ken that?"

"No. I figure he's got troubles enough of his own."

Peggy moved the sensor on Kevin's chest to another

187

position and a motor hummed while the ECG tape flowed smoothly from the machine.

"It could just be that you'd be doing him a favor by reminding him he owes you that much," she said.

"You might have something there, beautiful," said Kevin. "How does that ticker seem to be working?"

"I've seen worse. You'll probably outlast me, especially since you're not drinking the product you sell."

"When do I get a report?"

"When Dr. Dalton and Dr. Vogel finish examining you and the lab work is done, which means several hours." She disconnected him from the machine. "Meanwhile, I'll leave you to the tender mercies of your friend Miss Sundberg."

Picking up the telephone, Peggy called for an attendant to take Kevin and the stretcher to the CICU.

"And don't forget what I said about reminding Dr. Ken that you're waiting for him to perfect the artificial heart," she told Kevin in parting.

IV

It was almost four o'clock when Ed Vogel and Helga Sundberg finished connecting Kevin McCartney to the various monitoring instruments that would give a continuous picture of his vital signs. The narcotic administered by hypodermic before he was taken to the X-ray room and the Cardiac Research Laboratory had eased the pain that so often accompanied the rejection phenomenon and Kevin was dozing. But his breathing was rather shallow and the tracings of the ECG on the monitor screen at the head of his bed, as well as on the larger screen at the main nursing station console, were noticeably narrowed by the decreased voltage of the heart's electrical system.

At the storage data computer keyboard, Ed Vogel had completed punching in the standing orders and was dictating the findings of his physical examination into the red telephone in the CICU doctors' office that communicated directly with the typing pool.

"This is the worst rejection crisis Kevin's had, isn't it?"

Helga asked through the opening between the nursing station and the doctors' office adjoining it.

"So far. Actually each one is usually worse than the last until—"

"When you look at the ECG tracing, it's almost as if his heart were being squeezed."

"That's really what's happening," said the young cardiologist. "With lymphocytes attacking the conduction system and the heart muscle itself from the inside, plus fluid in his pericardium pressing from outside, his heart really doesn't have much of a chance."

"Since we're monitoring all possible parameters on both Kevin and Mr. McKenzie, I'm going to need all the visual channels available," said Helga. "The monitors on Mr. Payson don't tell us anything we didn't already know and, if you discontinue them, I'll have two more channels for Kevin and Mr. McKenzie."

"Write the order, I'll sign it."

Rebecca Dalton came into the CICU as Vogel was about to leave.

"Did you find anything new with Kevin, Ed?" she asked.

"His spleen is larger than it was on the last admission and there's some fluid in the abdomen, besides what's in the pericardium."

"I just glanced at the X rays. The cardiac shadow is considerably enlarged, too, but much of that could be fluid in the pericardium."

"Shall I aspirate it?"

"He's been subjected to enough diagnostic procedures for today. We can wait until tomorrow to remove the fluid."

"I've doubled the dosage of methyl prednisolone and ALG," said Vogel. "And also started heparin and Actinomycin D."

"Good," said Rebecca. "I'm going to be tied up from about five-thirty to six-thirty or seven with a committee meeting, but you can call me out of the Board Room if you need me. How's Mr. McKenzie?"

"The computer print-out on his stroke work index just

came through." Ed Vogel handed Rebecca a sheet of figures. "It seems to be holding up pretty well."

"Unless there's another sudden change." Rebecca had voiced the reservation that was in both their minds.

"Is Dr. Dalton coming up to see Kevin?" Ed Vogel asked on a casual note.

"This is one of his three afternoons on duty in the PDC," she said. "I sent word to him that Kevin was being admitted, so I imagine he'll stop by when he's free."

"I'll call his attention to the fact that Mr. McKenzie's index doesn't seem to be improving," said Ed. "The phonocardiogram appears to verify that, too."

He passed to Rebecca a strip of tracing paper upon which a continuous pattern of peaks and depressions somewhat resembling an ECG was recorded. A method of reproducing the heart sounds by photographing the conversion of sound waves into electronic impulses, the phonocardiogram was far more efficient than the conventional stethoscope. Even more important, it produced a graphic record which became part of the clinical data bank accumulated on the patient.

"The split in the second sound does seem to be wider than normal," said Rebecca thoughtfully. "The height of that apical third indicates an abnormally rapid left ventricular filling, too."

"Which means a larger stroke volume is needed to compensate for the amount of backflow into the atrium, when the ventricle contracts," said Ed. "So the amount of blood pumped out into his aorta with each heartbeat may actually be declining."

"Doesn't that mean his heart is failing at a faster rate than the clinical signs seem to indicate?" Helga asked.

"Possibly," said Rebecca soberly.

None of the three voiced the thought uppermost in all their minds: that if Ross McKenzie's heart function was actually declining, every hour that passed made surgical correction of the damaged mitral valve—the operation of choice, should surgery become necessary—more difficult and a successful outcome less certain. Or the fact that, by making the official request for surgery that Rebecca's position as chief medical consultant to the cardiovascular

190

service might require of her, she could be driving a final wedge between herself and Ken.

V

"I didn't see you come in, Carolyn." Helga Sundberg spoke from the door to the cubicle where Richard Payson lay, with Carolyn bending over him to smooth the hair back from his forehead.

"You were busy with Dr. Dalton and Dr. Vogel. I just wanted to spend a little while with Father before I go to the God Committee meeting."

"The whole hospital is waiting to see what the decision will be."

"No more than I am," said the other nurse. "Even though I'm pretty sure I already know."

Helga changed the subject, somewhat abruptly. "Dr. Rebecca and Ed Vogel were going over Mr. McKenzie's record just now. She seems to think surgery can't be postponed much longer without cutting down sharply his chances of coming through it. I guess it's a case of Hobson's choice for her, too."

Carolyn looked up. "Is that a reminder to me that I'm not the only one in Biscayne General with problems?"

"Everybody's got 'em," said Helga with a shrug. "Mike Raburn is risking the blame for Carmelita Sanchez' death tomorrow with a hazardous procedure he doesn't have to undertake."

"Mike wouldn't do the TBW if he weren't convinced that's the only chance she has."

"I know," said Helga. "That's the sort of a guy he is. But he's still taking a large risk."

Carolyn gave her roommate an appraising look. "Do you still feel the same way about him—after a night to sleep on the question?"

"More than ever," said Helga. "What's more, I'm going to test him this weekend—with the apple."

"His idea—or yours?"

"His, of course." Helga gave a creditable burlesque of outraged virtue. "What do you think I am anyway—a pushover? By the way, I asked Ed Vogel just now to write an order taking your father off the monitors when he's brought back later from the meeting upstairs."

"Why?" Carolyn asked.

"We need the extra channels for Kevin and Mr. McKenzie and your father's heart condition doesn't change anyway so there's no reason to keep detailed records." Helga's tone was casual. "His urinary output dropped some in the past twenty-four hours, too, so Ed ordered a continuous IV drop started later—also at my suggestion. That way we can be sure he's getting a full dose of chlorpromazine all the time to keep him relaxed. Besides, with the IV catheter in place, anything else he needs can be given quickly, too."

Carolyn didn't miss the change of emphasis Helga had given her last observation—or the reason.

"Thanks, Helga," she said. "I'm sorry if I was sharp with you just now."

"Forget it. What's a roommate for anyway except to lean on?"

"With everybody waiting to learn how the hearing will turn out, I wonder what the staff is saying about me for making the request."

"Who cares? You're doing what you think is right for your father and that's the only thing that really matters. Seen Gus lately?"

"No. I was pretty depressed when I finished talking to Dr. Dalton this afternoon, so I dodged him."

"He's in NICU now, checking on the Hornsby baby and the Gates boy."

"They were both doing fine when I went off duty."

"They still are, but Dr. Desmond read an article last night about the incidence of small lung emboli from clots forming around the ends of catheters left in blood vessels. He wants them taken out as early as possible, so Gus is trying to decide whether to let the catheters in Baby Hornsby's umbilical stump go another twenty-four hours, or risk taking them out now."

Carolyn managed to smile. "Around here it's nothing but decisions, decisions—all day long."

"Whatever the God Committee decides, just remember it isn't the end of everything for you," Helga urged. "Go on out with Gus this evening and forget everything else. Tell you what," she added. "I'll bunk with Magda Gatton tonight; her roommate's in the hospital with an acute mono."

"That's sweet of you, Helga, but—"

"There's a time when a woman needs a lover to hold her in his arms all through the black hours of the night and this is it for you. Be my guest."

"All right," said Carolyn. "Maybe tomorrow things will look different."

Gus Henderson was standing beside the crib, looking down at Baby Hornsby, when Carolyn came into the NICU.

"Take a look at our prize patient," he said, "sleeping like a cherub."

"No cherub ever had that much plumbing attached to it," said Maria Alvarez, who was specialing the baby. "Except maybe the Mannikin Pis."

"It's not even quivering," said Carolyn. "What happened?"

"Somebody used his head," said Gus. "Oh, it wasn't me. I was still set enough in my ways to believe cold turkey had to be cold turkey, instead of thinking of a simple thing like slipping enough methadone into the IV to take the edge off withdrawal."

"Who *did* think of it?"

"Some pediatricians in New York and another group in Philadelphia; one of the internes abstracted a medical journal article on their work at the weekly pediatric luncheon confab today. They found that babies born to addicted mothers on methadone did a lot better if they were breast-fed for a while because they kept on getting a small amount of methadone in the milk. So, I put one and one together and got the idea of adding a very small dose to Baby Hornsby's feedings."

"That was brilliant, Gus."

"The interesting part is that Baby Hornsby has not only stopped shaking like a leaf in a hurricane but his pO_2 has gone up sharply. If it keeps on like this for another twenty-four hours, we can take it off CPAP." He lowered his voice to a more intimate note as they moved to the

193

door, beyond earshot of Mrs. Alvarez. "Are you okay? About the committee, I mean?"

"I'll cope. Helga just reminded me that the world won't stop, even if the decision goes against me."

"That's my girl. You're going out with me tonight, aren't you?"

"If you want me."

"Don't you know I'll never stop wanting you?"

"That's nice to hear but I promise not to hold you to it." Her voice was a little husky. "See you about seven-thirty. Helga's spending the night in Magda Gatton's apartment—"

Gus's eyes lit up. "Say! That's great."

"I'll even cook your breakfast," she promised. "But I'd better run now. Dr Rebecca Dalton asked me to meet her in her office at five-fifteen so we can go up to the Board Room together."

Gus Henderson was thoughtful as he dictated a note for insertion into Baby Hornsby's record. When he finished, he stopped by the nursing station where Helga Sundberg was working on clinical charts with her ear always tuned to the frequency of the alarm buzzer that would signal any sudden change in the vital parameters of a half dozen patients being measured continuously on the monitors before her.

"I'd like to talk to you a minute, Helga," he said. "Can I buy you a cup of coffee?"

"And start tongues wagging from here to the helicopter landing pad on the roof? Let's have it in the lounge, nobody's in there right now."

In the small lounge provided for nurses and doctors who must stay within range of the monitor alarm buzzer, Helga poured two cups from the urn that kept a supply of coffee steaming twenty-four hours a day. Giving one to Gus, she spooned sugar into her own and stirred it vigorously.

"Do you ever worry about weight?" he asked.

"Never," said Helga. "It takes a lot of calories to keep this machine humming."

"I've never seen you worried either. What's your secret?"

"Whatever I'm doing, I give it everything I've got. That means I get everything there is to get out of it, too. So what's to worry about?"

"In my case, it's Carolyn," Gus admitted. "She said something strange to me just now. I'd asked her to go out with me tonight and she said she would if I wanted her."

"And you do?"

"Of course. But when I answered, 'I'll never stop wanting you,' she said, 'I won't hold you to it!' What do you suppose she meant?"

"Carolyn can't help wondering whether she's really doing the right thing in asking the God Committee to end her father's life, Gus. She's bound to be concerned that some people may feel she's wrong and turn away from her."

"But not me. Surely she knows that."

"Whatever happens up there in the Board Room this afternoon, she's going to need all the understanding and love you can give her. The best thing both of you can do tonight is to really hang on and try to forget the outside world."

Chapter 13

THE MONTHLY Tissue Conference for the surgical service met on Wednesday afternoon in the Pathology Amphitheater in the basement of the main hospital tower. Regarded as one of the most important teaching activities in the entire medical school, it was also rightly feared by the surgeons. During the hour, they were forced to watch while final evidence proving whether their diagnoses had been correct or incorrect was presented to a jury of their peers, either the results of autopsies performed on patients they had lost, or the diagnosis of microscopic slides from tissues removed.

Today the rows of seats were filled, for this was to be the first conference with Karen Fletcher presiding as acting head of pathology since Dr. Adrian Cooper, the ailing professor of pathology, had been felled by a stroke. The largely male audience was waiting to see how well she would be able to handle herself in the inevitable controversies that resulted, when the fat cats of the surgical staff were faced with the bald evidence of their failures.

At exactly four o'clock Karen Fletcher entered the open tiled space before the curving rows of seats, each row a little higher than the one below, so all might look down upon the specimens being exhibited. Behind her was Dr. Sam Toyota, resident in pathology, who was pushing a cart on which were several enameled trays covered with towels. A spattering of applause, mainly from the younger and brasher members of the house staff, greeted Karen's entrance but she ignored it coolly. Placing a hospital record upon the lectern, she looked up at the crowd through dark horn-rimmed glasses she affected as part of her rather severe workaday uniform and waited for the brief flurry created by her entrance to subside.

"The case to be presented for discussion this afternoon," Karen announced, "is from the Department of Obstetrics and Gynecology, the service of Dr. Jeremiah Singleton."

Jerry Singleton was sitting in the front row of seats, not more than six feet from where Karen was standing. At her words, he suddenly sat up straight.

"I received no notice that a case of mine would be discussed," he said stiffly.

"I was not aware that it had been Dr. Cooper's custom to notify the surgeons when their cases were to be presented," said Karen.

"Well, it wasn't," Jerry conceded.

"Of course, if you would like to put it to a vote, Dr. Singleton—"

"Never mind," said Jerry tartly.

"The case we are presenting is typical of many—except for the outcome," said Karen. "The patient was a thirty-eight-year-old housewife from an upper-income group and the mother of four. At the birth of her last child six months ago, she was instructed by Dr. Singleton to, in her own words, 'come into the hospital in six months for my birthday hysterectomy.' "

A round of laughter. from the audience greeted this familiar phrase and Jerry flushed angrily.

"In all fairness to Dr. Singleton," Karen continued, "I must concede that this custom has been becoming more and more frequent with gynecologists in recent years. In fact the number of vaginal hysterectomies in non-pregnant women with minimal or no indications for surgery, except to achieve sterilization, rose by 742 per cent in one Western medical center between July 1968 and December 31, 1970."

A murmur of astonishment from the onlookers interrupted Karen's presentation for a moment and she patiently waited for it to subside.

"The patient was operated upon the day after admission," Karen continued. "A conventional vaginal hysterectomy was performed, taking thirty minutes from start to finish, with the entire uterus, tubes, and ovaries being removed and some repair being made of the outlet."

Looking up from the summary, Karen added dryly: "I think most of you will admit that this feat is not only a tribute to Dr. Singleton's extraordinary skill but also proves that the uterus was not enlarged."

In his seat, Jerry Singleton was slowly turning a light shade of purple.

"The patient's recovery was complicated by a urinary infection," Karen continued, "but this seems to be almost a rule. In fact vaginal hysterectomy carries with it a morbidity rate of close to 22 per cent, most of it because of urinary complications. She was leaving the hospital on the sixth postoperative day, when she suddenly gasped and collapsed in her room. Attempts at resuscitation were futile and she came to autopsy with a clinical diagnosis of pulmonary embolism."

Slipping on a pair of rubber gloves, Karen removed the towel from a tray on the cart Dr. Toyota had wheeled into the room, revealing a human lung. Lifting it in her gloved

197

hands, she separated the two halves of a bisected lobe to reveal a blood clot filling a large section of the pulmonary artery.

"I think all of you can see the embolus, even from the back row," she said. "It was large and, as with such clots, instantly fatal. The slides, please, Dr. Toyota."

Sam Toyota switched on the projection microscope and doused the room lights with the same motion. Instantly a much-enlarged section of lung tissue appeared on the screen behind where Karen was standing. Picking up a pointer, she moved up the screen and began to indicate the significant findings.

"All of you can see the clots that fill the branches of the pulmonary artery," she said. "They form the classic picture of pulmonary embolism."

Dr. Toyota placed another slide beneath the microscope and a section of uterine wall appeared on the screen.

"You can also see," Karen said, "that the uterine muscle is quite normal in appearance and we found no significant changes in it. The pathological diagnosis, then, is a normal uterus and postoperative pulmonary embolism causing death.

"As both a pathologist and a woman," she continued as the lights went up and she peeled off the rubber gloves, before moving back to the lectern, "I can only deplore the tremendous increase in major surgery, particularly hysterectomy, simply as a means of insuring that the patient shall be freed from further childbearing. And lest I be influenced by personal prejudice, I have made a study of cases in such a category here at Biscayne General, plus many other reports throughout the country. The results are, to say the least, shocking.

"Leaving out, for the moment, the question of how much a human life is worth, the fact remains that, in the average case of simple hysterectomy, the hospital bill amounts to almost fifteen hundred dollars, to say nothing of the surgeon's fee. Balance this, if you will, against the use of laparoscopy—visualization of the interior of the abdomen with a fiberoptic instrument somewhat resembling a cystoscope—and occlusion of the Fallopian tubes with metal clips, a procedure that costs less than two hundred dollars. Or far less costly, the intra-uterine device known as an IUD which can be inserted into the cavity of the uterus as an office procedure, largely preventing pregnancy, at the cost of only one office visit to the gynecologist per year.

"Even more important, however, is the psychological shock when a woman loses an organ many of them consider the fountain of their own femininity, weeping as it does every twenty-eight days to remind them of it. In addition psychiatry has determined that, in a distressingly large number of cases, women unconsciously look upon hysterectomy as a castration procedure, naturally a profound shock."

"Excuse me, Dr. Fletcher," said Jerry Singelton, his tone heavy with sarcasm, "but aren't you gilding the lily a bit with all these horror stories?"

"I think not, Dr. Singleton," said Karen in the same even tone. "After all, less than 5 per cent of the surgery performed today can be called emergency in nature, nor can more than 7 per cent be considered urgent. Twice as many operations are performed in the average American city as in an English city of comparable size, so the conclusion would seem to be inescapable that almost half of the operations performed in the United States today are probably unnecessary. This means, of course, that a comparable number of deaths occur—some estimates run as high as thirty thousand a year—which could have been avoided if surgery had not been done. And high on the list must be the 'birthday hysterectomy' which resulted in the death of this patient from an embolus to the lungs. The case is now open for general discussion."

Jerry Singleton shot to his feet, spluttering with anger.

"Never, in this amphitheater or any other," he snapped, "have I heard a more biased presentation of a pathological report. You have heard in the case history that this patient recovered from surgery and was ready to go home when the embolism occurred. And I don't have to tell an audience of surgeons that pulmonary embolism

199

is a recognized complication of surgery which no amount of research so far has learned to prevent."

"Don't forget the bladder infection, Jerry," said a urologist in the front row. "You fellows drag a uterus out through an opening perhaps an inch and a half in diameter normally. But when the bladder becomes infected because you traumatized it, you turn the patient over to us."

"It's not my fault, Doctor, that God chose to put the birth canal between the waterworks and the sewer," said the gynecologist. "Besides, this opening you describe as an inch and a half in diameter is also capable of dilating to admit the passage of a baby's head. Infections of the urinary tract do occur after any kind of vaginal surgery, of course. But with adequate preoperative preparation and prophylactic doses of urinary antiseptics afterward, the number of such cases is considerably smaller than has been intimated.

"Getting back to Dr. Fletcher's shotgun accusations," Jerry Singleton continued, "more and more gynecologists today are convinced that halfway measures like laparoscopy to block the tubes and even tying them off immediately after delivery are a poor substitute for the full benefits to be obtained by hysterectomy, particularly by the vaginal route."

"You refer, I believe, Dr. Singleton," said Karen dryly, "to what is rapidly becoming known as 'hysterilization.'"

"Call it what you like, hysterectomy after the childbearing period has ended protects the patient from the uncertain menstrual future of the menopause and removes the possibility of cancer of the cervix or the fundus, among the most frequent sites of malignancy in women. And if the ovaries are removed, too, the danger of ovarian cancer is also eliminated."

"Leaving the psychological trauma of an early menopause."

"Which can be completely relieved with hormones by mouth."

"You will still find competent gynecologic opinion," Karen retorted coolly, "stating that it doesn't make sense to remove the baby carriage, leave the playpen intact, and think that everything is going to be all right."

The double-barbed sally drew delighted laughter from the audience. But even though Jerry Singleton had recognized by now that he was in retreat, he continued to fight back.

"With women today seeking to remove every aspect of femininity in favor of full equality, Dr. Fletcher, it would seem that the only completely liberated woman would be one who has had her uterus out."

Karen smiled tolerantly as if she were listening to a child. "I can only answer you, Dr. Singleton, with a quotation from *Planned Parenthood*. While devoted to the very principle you advocate of freeing women from the specter of childbearing at will, the organization still says regarding hysterilization: 'Preventive lobotomies for young people statistically at risk of developing violent psychoses, or ophthalmectomy for those populations found most likely to get cancer of the eye at some future time, have not been suggested by physicians writing in psychiatric or opthalmologic journals.' To which I might add that the widespread use of bilateral prophylactic mammectomy simply because the female breast is a frequent site of cancer would certainly detract considerably from what one might call the contour of society."

Another roar of laughter greeted Karen's retort and Jerry Singleton subsided in his seat, knowing he was beaten.

"I see that it is five o'clock," said Karen, "and since quitting time takes precedence over even the most learned discussions, this session of the surgical Tissue Conference is adjourned."

As she was leaving the amphitheater, Jerry Singleton loomed up beside her, causing her to look oddly fragile and defenseless against his height.

"What the hell were you trying to do, Karen?" he demanded angrily. "Crucify me?"

"Not at all, Jerry," she said. "I was merely doing what I considered to be my duty, as acting head of the department." Then she added, but in a lower tone, "But perhaps we should discuss it later—under more friendly circumstances."

And with the smile of a cat who has enjoyed its cream she left the room while, temporarily speechless, Jerry Singleton could find no words with which to answer her.

II

A sober group of people had gathered around the long gleaming table in the Board Room on the top floor of the hospital tower, when Dr. Jeffry Toler gaveled the meeting of the Moriturus Committee to order exactly at five-thirty. Moments earlier, an orderly and a nurse from the ICU had pushed into the room the narrow hospital bed upon which Richard Payson lay. An extra dose of chlorpromazine had been injected into his veins about a half hour earlier and under the influence of the powerful tranquilizer, the writhing of his muscles was not quite so pronounced as usual. He still did not appear, however, to be conscious of his surroundings.

Next to Jeffry Toler, who sat at the head of the table, was the State's Attorney who was substituting for Judge Robie that afternoon. Anthony Broadhurst was a stocky man of about forty-five, with a square jaw and a nononsense look about him. Watching him go into the Board Room as she sat outside alone, Carolyn Payson had felt her hopes for a favorable decision, never very high, start to fade even more.

Seated next to the attorney was Dr. Manning Desmond, chief of medical services, and beyond him, Dr. Angus McHale from pediatrics. Surgery was represented by Dr. James Karnes, associate professor of urology. On the other side of the table, Helen Gaynor, secretary of the medical center Board of Directors, sat at Jeffry Toler's elbow with the stenotype machine, upon which she would keep a running account of the proceedings, in front of her. Beyond her was Dr. Lewis Katz from psychiatry, Father Hagan, the hospital chaplain, and a guest expert, Professor Cecil Thorne from the Genetics Department of Biscayne University. At the end sat Dr. Peter Gross, the neurologist in charge of Richard Payson's case, and Rebecca Dalton, representing Carolyn Payson.

"I call this meeting of the Moriturus Committee to order," said Jeffry Toler. "Miss Gaynor will make a record of everything as usual.

"For the benefit of Mr. Broadhurst, who is here for the first time," he continued, "I might say that this committee came into being because of intense public interest in providing a way whereby patients who are hopelessly ill, with no prospect of a cure, may petition medical authority, as represented by this committee, either in person or through their closest relative, if the subjects are unable to speak for themselves, to allow life to be ended.

"One of the cases that brought this problem to something of a focus was decided some time ago here in the Miami area, when a woman patient in a local hospital with a terminal illness requested the physicians in charge of her case not to take measures to keep her alive any longer. In order to protect themselves against possible suits for negligence and malpractice, if they acceded to her request, the physicians and the hospital involved undertook legal action against this patient, seeking a final court opinion on the question of a person's right to make the decision not to be treated further and to be allowed to die.

"The judge in this case ruled that the patient's wishes could be obeyed by the physicians and the hospital without prejudice or danger of their being blamed for the consequences. The woman then received no more treatment for an advanced malignant condition and shortly died.

"I don't have to tell you, of course, that the very name we have chosen for this committee is a statement of the basic principle to which it seeks to adhere. *Moriturus* in Latin is part of the well-known salute of the gladiators before entering the arena: 'We who are about to die salute you.' " Jeffry Toler looked around the table. "Are there any questions?"

Only one member spoke, Anthony Broadhurst.

"Am I to understand that all patients brought before this committee are about to die?" he asked.

"That is a major criterion," Jeffry Toler conceded. "I might add that the appearance of similar committees in hospitals all over the country first came about largely as a result of the development of techniques for transplantation of the heart from one individual to another. Successful heart transplants require methods of keeping the body of a possible donor in what might be called a state of automatic functioning, even when death is inevitable and—"

"But has medical science reached the point where you can predict death absolutely?" Anthony Broadhurst inquired.

"That depends upon what you call death," said Dr. Katz. "From the philosophic point of view, physicians have always regarded death as occurring when the heart stops beating, the lungs stop breathing, and the patient no longer responds to any stimulus. More recently the determination of 'brain death' by means of the electroencephalograph has been added as the ultimate criterion."

"Exactly what is determined by that test, Doctor?" the attorney asked.

"Merely the cessation in brain tissue of the action currents which characterize all life," said the psychiatrist. "It must be said, however, that many investigators now believe real life ceases essentially with the ending of a person's ability to think, feel, reason for himself and maintain body functions consciously—in other words the end of consciousness permanently is the end of life."

"But can you measure the end of consciousness, as you describe it, any better than you can measure the brain's action currents?"

"Not as well," Dr. Katz admitted. "Which brings us back to the real dilemma—just what is death?"

"A court in Richmond recently heard a suit for malpractice against a group of physicians who carried out a heart transplant," said Toler. "The judge ruled there that death occurs when brain function ends, even though the heart still beats and the patient breathes."

"And a suit that ended yesterday against Dr. Kenneth Dalton came to practically the same conclusion," Dr. Katz reminded the committee.

"All of which brings us down to the basic truth," said Dr. Manning Desmond, "that the physician has to be the judge of what is best for his patient. With so many factors governing life or death decisions, no set formula is going to fit all cases. The ultimate criterion has to be based on commen sense and common humanity, just as it has always been."

"That may have been true before malpractice suits became so popular," Dr. James Karnes demurred. "But however much I may agree with Dr. Desmond, as a surgeon I must always bear in mind that, unless I take every possible measure to keep a patient alive as long as I can, and then use the most accurate method of determining death at my disposal, I am liable under present law. And with due respect to your profession, Mr. Broadhurst, some lawyer is usually waiting in the wings to take over and do everything he can do to wreck my career."

"Gentlemen," said Jeffry Toler firmly, "I believe this discussion has reached the non-productive point. Our committee, like those in most large centers today, was set up to remove from the individual physician the burden of responsibility for deciding whether a patient shall go on living under intolerable conditions or be let die. The patient before us today would appear to be a prime example of this purpose: he is Mr. Richard Payson, who has been on the neurological service for the past month under the care of Dr. Peter Gross, professor of neurology in the Department of Medicine. Dr. Gross, you have the floor."

The pudgy neurologist got to his feet and motioned for the orderly and nurse accompanying the movable bed on which Richard Payson lay to push it near the table so all could see him.

"The patient is fifty years old," he began. "Until the onset of the present illness, he was a successful architect. I have known the family for many years but the nature of his illness was only diagnosed about six months ago when he first consulted me, although some symptoms of Huntington's disease had been present for almost five years."

"Do you feel that there is any question of his having Huntington's?" Jeffry Toler asked.

"None at all," said Dr. Gross. "The case was discussed at a staff meeting last week and everyone there agreed."

Turning to the attorney, the neurologist continued: "Dr. Cecil Thorne is a world authority on genetic conditions, Mr. Broadhurst. I asked him to come here today and explain some of the pertinent facts about Huntington's disease, so I will defer at this point to superior knowledge."

"Huntington's disease," said the geneticist, "is a degenerative condition of the brain and nervous system transmitted solely by heredity. The gene for Huntington's apparently arrived in this country about the time of the American Revolution when several members of a single family—some reports say six, others only three—emigrated to America."

"You mean those few people have been responsible for every case that has happened in the United States since?" Anthony Broadhurst inquired.

"That is the general consensus," said the geneticist. "The Huntington gene is a Mendelian dominant characteristic transmitted without relationship to sex, so a fifty-fifty chance exists that a parent who has the gene will pass it on to the offspring. Other hereditary conditions follow a similar pattern, but what makes Huntington's such a deadly condition is the fact that every individual possessing the gene will eventually develop symptoms of the disease, if he or she lives long enough."

"But don't inherited diseases manifest themselves in childhood?" Broadhurst asked.

"Most of them do," Professor Thorne conceded. "With H-D, however, the symptoms of deterioration almost never begin before age thirty-five and usually later. By that time a person who does not know he possesses the possibility of having inherited H-D from a gene-bearing parent has probably already married and had children."

"With half of them certain to develop the disease?"

"Yes."

"My God!" the lawyer exclaimed. "Then this man's
206

offspring have had to go through life with the sword of Damocles suspended over their heads."

"Mr. Payson has only one daughter," said Rebecca Dalton. "The one who is bringing him before this committee."

"Did she know . . . ?"

"Not until a few months ago," said Dr. Gross. "Her father lived in Atlanta and managed to hide his real condition from Carolyn."

"She is determined never to have children," Rebecca added, "in order that this particular gene shall die in her father's body and in her own."

"Is there no possibility of a cure, Dr. Thorne?" the lawyer asked.

"Inherited conditions are never cured," said the geneticist. "All we can do is try to recognize them early, so they won't be passed on to succeeding generations. Fortunately a method of doing that has recently been discovered, but too late to help either father or daughter."

"Richard Payson knew what would happen to him," said Dr. Gross. "That's why he willed his body to the medical school here."

"Does anyone wish to question Professor Thorne further?" Dr. Toler asked and, when there was no answer, nodded to Dr. Gross. "Go on, Pete."

"There isn't much more except to show you the patient." The neurologist lifted Richard Payson's arm so all could see the continuous squirming and purposeless movements of the muscles, in spite of the heavy sedation that had been given to him. "He appears to be conscious at times but we cannot even be sure of that any more."

"Can you be certain that he doesn't know what's happening, Doctor?" the chaplain asked quietly.

"His daughter is convinced he still does at times," said Gross, "but I'm not at all sure I agree."

"What does she base that conviction on?" the attorney asked.

"Occasionally, but never except when she is with him, the patient makes sounds that could be construed to be words. In her opinion, they're always the same—begging her to let him die."

When there were no further questions, Dr. Gross helped the nurse and orderly push the bed from the room and called to Carolyn, who was sitting outside.

"Would you come in, please, Carolyn," he said. "The committee would like to hear you now."

III

At ten minutes before six o'clock the Patient Distress Alarm at the CICU nursing station sounded its two-second-interval beep and the small red bulb on the face of the alarm boxes in a half dozen spots scattered over the ICU floor suddenly began to glow. A glance at the master monitor screen told Helga the nature of the emergency, for the flashing pattern of the ECG tracing from Kevin McCartney's heart had suddenly become a flat line, indicating cessation of the heartbeat.

In one swift movement, Helga punched the red call button on the panel before her. But even before the taped call of "CODE FIVE—CICU" started sounding from loudspeakers throughout the hospital, she was across the main passageway separating the control panel from the glass-fronted cubicles in which the patients lay and into the one occupied by Kevin McCartney.

"Load a syringe with one c.c. of adrenalin and attach a long needle," she told the nurse who had been watching beside Kevin's bed.

"His heart just stopped, Miss Sundberg." This was the nurse's first day on CICU and her voice had a slightly hysterical note.

"I know. Get the adrenalin!"

Pulling down the sheet that covered Kevin's chest and jerking up his hospital shirt, Helga leaned over and started pounding with her fist upon the long scar of the transplant operation that bisected the skin over his breastbone, timing the blows to a one-second interval by an instinct generated by long practice. From a distance she could hear the monotonous taped voice calling: "CODE FIVE—CICU" over and over and knew that the nearest doctor on the CICU Cardiopulmonary Resuscitation team would be there at any moment. She didn't, however, wait for him to arrive.

"Strap a respirator mask on and start the oxygen going," she directed the nurse who was placing a syringe with a long needle and a cubic centimeter of adrenalin in the barrel on a sterile towel atop the bedside table. If a doctor did not appear in a few seconds, Helga would jab the long needle through Kevin's chest wall and into the now stilled heart, pumping the powerful stimulant adrenalin into the heart muscle.

At the sixth pounding stroke upon Kevin's chest—the skin was already taking on the dusky hue of cyanosis—a flicker showed up on the small ECG monitor beside the bed, revealing at least a tentative attempt by his heart to restart itself under the stimulus of the hammer blows. Meanwhile the other nurse, her slight touch of hysteria expelled by Helga's swift and skillful action in the routine of CPR, had strapped a mask tightly over his face.

When the respirator sighed into action, Kevin's lungs were inflated with pure oxygen for a moment, then allowed to collapse, when the pressure was released through the rhythmic action of the valve that was the very heart of the machine. Two more blows to the pallid chest and the faint pattern of an entire ECG tracing appeared upon the monitor screen, hesitating between beats, as if not yet certain that it really wanted to continue, but not quite ceasing again.

"Was there any warning, Miss Sundberg?" Ken Dalton, the first to arrive, spoke at her elbow.

"No, sir. The tracing just flattened out suddenly into a straight line."

Picking up the syringe containing the adrenalin, Ken plunged the long needle downward between the ribs until it was buried to the shank where it was connected to a plastic disposable syringe, the only kind used for injections in the hospital. When Ken pulled back on the plunger, dark blood spurted into the chamber of the syringe, telling him he was inside the heart, and he injected part of the contents directly into the heart. Then drawing the needle part way out, until blood could no longer be drawn into it—indicating that the point was now in the muscle of the heart wall—he injected about a third of the remaining dose before removing the needle.

On the monitor screen, the heart tracing leaped like a skittish horse under the powerful stimulus of the adrenalin. The height of the peak showing ventricular contraction had almost doubled, and the pallid hue to the skin was lessening rapidly too. When Ken Dalton pinched Kevin's cheek, a pink flush showed for a moment, the simple maneuver telling the surgeon that the oxygen flowing into the air sacs of Kevin's lungs, under the rhythmic pressure of the respirator, was already passing through the walls of the tiny capillaries surrounding those air sacs and streaming toward the brain and the other vital organs, which had been deprived of the vital gas for perhaps a minute by the sudden cessation of the heartbeat.

By now the corridor outside the cubicle was filled with people, but all was order and purposeful action, as each person went about the assigned activity with a skill born of repeated practice.

Ed Vogel pushed a pacemaker cart, ready to shock the heart into contraction if it was needed. The ICU interne carried a sterile cut-down tray, in case it was necessary to expose a vein through a small incision in front of the ankle and insert a catheter to start a second intravenous injection. And Val LeMoyne quietly moved into the cubicle to take over the respirator operation from the student nurse.

"Chalk up another victory for Miss Sundberg," said the surgeon. "We've got to do better, gentlemen. As I remember it, the nursing staff has beaten the CPR teams to the last four cessations."

"I got the first flicker of contraction with the sixth sock to his chest," said Helga proudly, then laughed. "I guess it's a good thing I'm a big girl."

"And an intelligent one," said Ken crisply. "Someday one of these little circuses is going to give me a heart attack, so remind me to ask for you to special me, Miss Sundberg."

He watched the small monitor screen for a full minute

and, when the ECG pattern showed no sign of failing, nodded to Ed Vogel.

"Release the team, Ed, but stick around," he said. "We're going to have to take some measures to keep this from happening again."

IV

"Please come up to the end of the table, Miss Payson, so the court reporter can hear you," said Jeffry Toler, when the door had closed behind Richard Payson's bed. "I believe you know everyone here, except perhaps Mr. Broadhurst and Professor Thorne."

"I consulted Professor Thorne at Dr. Gross's suggestion, after he told me Father's diagnosis," said Carolyn. "How do you do, Mr. Broadhurst?"

"I'm fine, thank you," said the attorney.

"Suppose you tell us just why you have brought your father before the Moriturus Committee, Miss Payson," said Toler.

When she first saw the sober-faced group around the long polished mahogany table and the secretary with her stenotype machine that gave the committee much the air of a courtroom, if not the reality, Carolyn had been intimidated for a moment. But she had herself fully under control now.

"I felt that I had no choice, Dr. Toler," she answered.

"Why do you feel that way, Miss Payson?" Anthony Broadhurst inquired.

"Because almost every time I see my father now, he begs me to let him die."

"Are you certain that he really knows what's happening?"

"Only at times, sir. The last few days, I've barely been able to make out the words because the deterioration in his muscular control seems to be involving the speech mechanism more and more."

"This is the usual course with Huntington's," Dr. Gross volunteered.

"But are you *sure* he wants to die?" Broadhurst persevered.

211

"Wouldn't you, if you were like he is, Mr. Broadhurst?"

"We're not here to question what anyone else would do under similar circumstances, Miss Payson, but to inquire into your own reasons. Is your father a financial burden upon you or other members of your family?"

"There are no other members of my family—and there never will be."

"Then he *is* a burden upon you?"

"Not yet, Mr. Broadhurst." Carolyn could see the trend the questioning was taking and also its possible implications, at least in the mind of the lawyer, but had no intention of denying the truth.

"My father's funds will last perhaps another week," she added. "But I have saved a few thousand dollars and that will be used as long as it lasts."

"And afterward?"

"If the committee does not choose to free him from what you can surely see is at best a hell on earth, I shall borrow what I can."

"May I ask whether you have considered transferring him to a state institution?"

"I brought Father here from Atlanta, where he had gone to a nursing home, Mr. Broadhurst, because I wanted him to be as comfortable as possible during whatever time he has left to live. And because I wish to be near him."

"In his present condition he could be committed to a state institution and the financial burden would be lifted from you," the attorney insisted. "My office would be glad to help with the details."

"Perhaps the financial burden but not the ethical one," Carolyn said quietly.

"Ethical?"

"As a little girl I was taught in Sunday school to honor my parents. My mother died when I was a little girl and Father brought me up. He is a very proud man and I know what having people—even me—see him as he is now must be doing to him."

"If he is conscious of it."

"He must realize it. Why else would he beg me to let him die?"

"You have a point there—if he is conscious of the state he's in," the lawyer conceded. "But as I understand it, mental degeneration is as much a part of this disease as are the obvious physical changes. Which means that, even if your father does know what is happening now, which I personally doubt, he probably will not know much longer."

"Have you visited a state mental institution recently, Mr. Broadhurst?"

"No."

"When I was a student getting my degree in nursing at the University of Florida in Gainesville, I spent several weeks at a large state mental hospital as part of my training. On the basis of what I saw there I have resolved that my father shall never have to be left in such a place."

"I can understand your emotional reaction, Miss Payson," Broadhurst conceded, not unkindly, "but I can't help believing a more pragmatic approach would be best for you."

"And for my father?"

"It could hardly hurt him—when he doesn't know what is happening."

"I want you to know that we all feel great sympathy for you, Miss Payson," said Dr. Jeffry Toler gently. "But I wonder if you really understand what you are asking of us?"

"I am asking the committee to take measures to end my father's life as quickly and as painlessly as possible."

"By starvation, Miss Payson?" Dr. McHale asked. "I'm sure you have seen some of the mongoloids with pyloric stenosis and meningoceles that have been let die."

"I have, Dr. McHale. That is why I would never approve of starvation."

"Just a minute." Anthony Broadhurst frowned. "I don't exactly understand what is involved in this question of starvation."

"Because of his muscular condition, Mr. Payson cannot

213

swallow without danger of aspiration—what you call strangulation—Mr. Broadhurst," Rebecca Dalton explained. "He is fed only through the tube you probably noticed running through one nostril."

"But starvation would be even more cruel than letting him live," the lawyer protested.

"I'm sure we all agree with that," said Rebecca. "Which really leaves us only two alternatives."

"What are they, Doctor?"

"A drug is probably the first choice, in a large enough dose to produce death. That would be painless, although several hours might be required before death occurred."

"And the other?"

"Air embolism."

"I'm afraid I don't understand."

"Air injected directly into the circulation through a vein blocks the flow of blood to the lungs and the brain and causes death rather quickly."

"Then it's true that a drop of air injected with a hypodermic can cause death?"

"Not a drop, Mr. Broadhurst. But a fairly large syringeful would do it."

"Either way involves what is technically murder," said the attorney bluntly.

"In a legal sense, I suppose you could only call it that," Rebecca agreed. "I prefer to think of it the way Miss Payson does, as an act of mercy."

"I can see that pulling the plug and stopping a respirator when the patient is not really alive might be defensible," Broadhurst conceded. "But euthanasia with the committee actually usurping a right possessed only by God is quite another matter."

"That's why the students call us the God Committee," Jeffry Toler said dryly. "Does anyone else wish to question Miss Payson? I'm sure all this is very painful to her.

"Thank you, Miss Payson," said Toler when there were no more questions of her. "Dr. Dalton will answer any other questions we may have about the case and will give you the decision of the committee. You may go."

Carolyn left the room, but there was no spring to her step. She hadn't really expected the God Committee to agree to her request and now she was convinced that it would be denied.

Even bringing her father before them had been futile, she was convinced. But it was a last and desperate legal resort, which had to be exhausted before anything else could be done.

Chapter 14

"I'M GOING to try something different, Ed," said Ken Dalton after the CPR team had left the CICU. "The presence of so much fluid inside the pericardium means the heart is probably being squeezed down, just as it would be by blood escaping through the wall in a stab wound of the heart itself."

"We can remove it," said Vogel. "But do you think that will have any lasting effect?"

"Not simply removing the fluid. We must remember that what's happening here is an invasion of lymphocytes triggered by the body's own protective mechanism against what it considers to be the threat of a foreign invader, in this case the proteins in the transplanted heart. But we do know that, when a cancer metastasizes to the heart area and effusion occurs, certain cell-destroying drugs can be injected into the pericardium with good effect."

"And lymphocytes in a rejection crisis could be considered a metastasis from the spleen and bone marrow?"

"Something like that."

"It might work," Vogel conceded. "And even if it doesn't, it's worth trying."

"Worth trying if for no other reason than because it's probably the only weapon we have left," Ken agreed soberly.

"What chemical agent will you use?"

"For a start, Thiotepa and Prednisone; with metastatic malignancy these chemotherapeutic agents sometimes produce remissions that last several months or longer. We have to remove the fluid anyway and by putting a heavy dose right into the space around Kevin's heart, we ought to get the best possible effect."

"Shall I get an aspiration tray, Dr. Dalton?" Helga had been listening to the discussion with considerable interest.

"Please," said Ken. "Have the pharmacy send up a single sixty-milligram dose of Thiotepa in two per cent procaine hydrochloride, as well as some Prednisone ampules. I'll want to inject the drugs as soon as I get most of the fluid out of the pericardium."

"I'll get the tray and order the medication." Helga vanished from the cubicle and Ken turned back to study the monitor screen beside the bed.

"There's not too much T-wave change, so I doubt if the heart itself has been badly damaged yet by the rejection," he said. "I'm gambling on much of this crisis being connected with the large effusion in the pericardium."

"At least we can hope," said Vogel.

"Any report on the blood work yet?"

"None on the record. I'll call Peggy Tyndall in the lab and see what she has for us."

At the nursing station, Ed rang the laboratory and Peggy answered almost immediately.

"I was just going to bring up the report," she said. "Anything new?"

"Kevin McCartney had a cessation, but Miss Sundberg got his heart started again."

"That was the CODE FIVE, wasn't it?"

"Yes. Have you found anything?"

"The enzymes are not significantly elevated, not even LDH-1."

"At least that's a good sign."

One of the first indicators of heart damage, whether by coronary thrombosis or by rejection, is an increase in certain biochemical agents in the blood, as the body seeks to absorb the damaged muscle. One in particular called

216

LDH-1 is elevated in severe rejection crises, when the heart muscle itself is literally cannibalized by the patient's own lymphocytes.

"Anything else?" Peggy asked.

"Dr. Dalton is going to put some Thiotepa and a slug of Prednisone right into the pericardium, but the pharmacy can supply that."

"At least he's doing *something* at last," said Peggy. "Is Dr. Rebecca there?"

"She had an important committee meeting."

"It's the God Committee about Carolyn Payson's father, but she's losing that battle."

"How in the hell would you know about that, if the committee is still meeting?"

"The attendant who took Mr. Payson to the Board Room was just in here with a cart of supplies. He says the D.A. who's sitting on the God Committee today in place of Judge Robie is giving everybody up there the third degree. And he isn't liking the answers he's getting."

"I've often wondered how the grapevine is able to find out things before they happen," said Vogel. "Now I know."

II

"Do you wish to make a statement before we vote on Miss Payson's request, Dr. Dalton?" Jeffry Toler asked, after Carolyn had left the room.

"I would like to put the philosophical aspects of this particular case into some sort of perspective, if I may," said Rebecca. "Admittedly as much for my own benefit as for anything else."

"Please do," said Toler. "I'm sure we can all benefit from your analysis."

"As I see it, the question here is one thoughtful people have asked themselves since the beginning of medical science: to what degree is a physician justified in assuming full responsibility for the life or death of a patient? I haven't studied the Aphorisms of Hippocrates lately, but I am sure we could find much in them that would help guide us in cases like this. Certainly we are all familiar with the profound principles of ethics set down for us in the Oath of Hippocrates most of us swore when we graduated from medical school. Largely because medicine is a challenge to overcome death by using our technical knowledge to prevent it, doctors naturally tend to regard the loss of a patient as a personal defeat. Thus we tend to elevate the principle of biological continuance of the individual to the status of an absolute, even to a point where we ignore what we may be doing to the dignity of that individual."

"Are you saying that physicians tend to take the view that their efforts are always helpful to the patient?" Anthony Broadhurst asked.

"Not only the view, Mr. Broadhurst; we must also be certain at all times that our efforts do not harm those under our care. It is a basic principle of medical ethics that *nolle nocere*—to do no harm—takes precedence even over doing good through treatment. And with that view in mind, we must ask ourselves whether we will not in fact be doing harm to Richard Payson's status as an individual, his personal dignity, by letting him live longer in the condition he is in now."

"I admire your eloquence and grant at least part of your logic, Doctor," said the lawyer. "But I am not sure they apply to the case in point."

"I was just coming to that."

"Please forgive the interruption, then."

"The first successful transplantation of the human heart occurred less than ten years ago, in December 1967, to be exact. As you may know, my husband has been severely criticized for continuing to perform heart transplants after it became evident that in most cases the process of rejection severely limits the chances of success with the operation. As Dr. Toler said, a long and painful case of alleged malpractice in one transplant case ended day before yesterday with exoneration of my husband."

"During which, I believe, he did not defend himself?"

"Yes," she conceded, "the reason being a matter of conscience on his part. My husband and I worked as a team during the transplant program and, as a cardiologist,

I was largely responsible for selecting the cases. Few, if any, of the patients he operated on would have lived more than a few months without surgery, most of them as cardiac invalids and all in great pain. Yet after transplantation of another heart, some lived as long as eighteen months in relative comfort, and don't forget that some of them had previously even begged for death."

"Euthanasia?"

"That's the technical term; 'mercy killing' has caught the public interest even more. But there can be two forms of euthanasia. In the 'active' form the patient is given an agent that produced death painlessly and as quickly as possible, for example the air injection mentioned earlier. In 'passive euthanasia,' however, the patient is given sufficient medicine to relieve pain, even if his life is shortened. Or, as is more usually the case, where pain is intractable or brain damage irreversible, supportive measures such as the use of a respirator or cardiopulmonary resuscitation are simply stopped with the same result. Did you know a magazine survey recently showed that ninety-one per cent of the readers responding to a questionnaire felt that a terminal patient should be permitted to refuse treatment which would prolong life artificially?"

"I am familiar with the survey, Doctor," said Broadhurst. "And also the fact that a similar survey among parents of severely handicapped children overwhelmingly rejected euthanasia. Obviously the passive form has to be rejected in Mr. Payson's case, since it could only be accomplished by slow starvation. As his daughter's representative before this committee, do you recommend the active form?"

"That is what his daughter is asking," said Rebecca.

"And yourself?"

"I don't know. If I had seen several of the patients my husband operated upon successfully before heart transplantation was a fact, I would have been strongly tempted to recommend stopping their medication. But, as I said, some of them lived fairly comfortably for as much as a year and a half after surgery. One is still alive."

"Aren't you saying, Dr. Dalton, that in a sense you and

219

your husband performed mercy killing in the end—by recommending them for surgery?"

"My conscience is clear on that score, Mr. Broadhurst."

"But not your husband's? His failure to defend himself at the trial would seem to prove that."

"I think you can begin to see some of the ethical questions a doctor must ask himself, Mr. Broadhurst," Manning Desmond interposed. "Particularly when treating people who are seriously, perhaps even hopelessly, ill. But in justification of Dr. Dalton and her husband, even their failures have helped immeasurably in our understanding of how to combat rejection in the case of other organs."

"Such as?"

"Specifically kidneys, which are far easier to transplant than hearts. And we hope with other organs as well."

"Surely you don't argue that Mr. Payson's death can contribute anything to science?"

"I am not at all certain that it will not, Mr. Broadhurst," said Professor Thorne. "Huntington's is relatively rare and the opportunity to study cells from the patient's tissues could be valuable. Knowing the importance of post-mortem examinations in the study of medicine, I'm sure Miss Payson would agree—"

"If Mr. Payson should die under anything resembling suspicious circumstances, Professor Thorne," Broadhurst interrupted, "be assured that my position as attorney for the state would require me to order a post-mortem, whether his relatives permitted it or not."

"I've already reported that the patient has willed his body to this medical school," said Dr. Gross. "So the question of its disposition after death is academic."

"The point I am making," Rebecca said firmly, "is that in Mr. Payson's case we are dealing with an absolutely incurable disease, one that proceeds inexorably from the beginning of symptoms to the death of the individual."

"Over what period, Doctor?"

"Dr. Gross can answer that better than I."

"In most cases death occurs in a few years. But some

220

have lived as much as ten years after the major symptoms of H-D appeared and a few even longer."

"With no possibility of a cure?" the attorney asked.

"Absolutely none," said Professor Thorne.

"So if there ever was a case where active euthanasia is justified, this is it," said Rebecca.

"And yet you have just refused to advocate it, Dr. Dalton," said Broadhurst.

"We seem to have come to an impasse," Jeffry Toler said firmly. "Do you have any other points to make, Rebecca?"

"Only to remind the committee that Carolyn Payson is making what seems to her a reasonable request and that she is perfectly sincere in her belief that, by arranging her father's death, she will be carrying out his wishes."

"Does anyone doubt that statement?" Toler asked.

"I am convinced that Miss Payson firmly believes what she is asking is best for her father," said the attorney. "Nevertheless one court case, in which a patient who was in command of her faculties insisted that no further treatment be carried out for what was a terminal condition, does not constitute a precedent for euthanasia, especially the deliberate killing of a patient by a doctor or a hospital. Therefore I must warn you that, if I am outvoted here today and you approve the death of this patient, you will be opening a Pandora's box that can only damage the reputation of this hospital and yourselves as physicians and teachers, at a time when the institution is already under fire by certain forces in the community."

"Thank you, Mr. Broadhurst," said Jeffry Toler. "I think we might hear from Father Hagan before we take a final vote."

"I am greatly in sympathy with both Miss Payson and her father and, as you all know, I initiated proceedings before the committee at her request," said the old priest. "But I agree with Mr. Broadhurst that we have no right to give official approval to what can hardly be called by any other name except euthanasia."

"Or murder," said the attorney bluntly.

"I think we are ready to vote," said Jeffry Toler. "If you approve Miss Payson's request that her father's life

221

be ended, please write 'Yes' on the small writing pad before you. If you do not approve, write 'No.' Dr. Dalton and Professor Thorne are not members of the Moriturus Committee and cannot vote. Please do not sign your ballot and be sure to fold it so no one else can see your vote. They will be tabulated by Mrs. Gaynor."

The secretary collected the ballots and examined them at one side of the room.

"There was one vote of 'Yes,' Dr. Toler," she reported. "The rest were all 'No.' "

"The request is denied and the ballot slips will be destroyed," said Jeffry Toler. "I need not remind the committee members that everything done or said here this afternoon is strictly confidential and must not be divulged to anyone, except that Dr. Dalton is authorized to inform Miss Carolyn Payson of this decision."

He tapped the polished block of wood upon which the gavel lay. "The meeting is adjourned."

III

Helga Sundberg pushed the small table containing the aspiration tray into the cubicle where Kevin McCartney lay and Ed Vogel helped her move the bed to one side. While Ken Dalton was putting on a pair of sterile gloves, Helga opened the tray, folding back the sterile covers to reveal its contents.

Upon it was a fifty-cubic-centimeter syringe, needles, and a metal stopcock by which the fluid being aspirated could be drawn up into the syringe, then, simply by turning the handle of the cock, expelled through a section of plastic tubing into the large basin she placed on the bed beside Kevin's chest.

With quick, skilled movements, Helga painted the still somewhat pallid skin of Kevin's chest with a crimson-colored antiseptic, then stepped back so Ken could place a sheet about two feet square, with a small window cut into it, over the bartender's chest. Feeling through the sterile drape, the surgeon counted ribs by pressing upon them, then centered the window on a spot in the lower chest, a little to the left of the surgical scar that extended from the top of the sternum to the bottom.

"I'm going in low so as to drain the entire pericardium if I can," he explained. "Please watch the monitor, Ed, and speak out if there is any change."

Watching the syringe in Ken Dalton's hand, Ed Vogel saw the slight perceptible hesitation as the point of the needle touched the crimson skin. It was only momentary, however, before the needle was thrust firmly between the ribs and into the chest. Drawing back on the barrel of the syringe, he removed about twenty c.c. of fluid before pushing the needle deeper, so it would remain inside the pericardium while the tough membranous sac itself was being emptied.

The fluid was thin and cloudy, but flowed easily through the needle. As the process of emptying the pericardial sac continued, the level of the cloudy fluid in the basin Helga was holding to collect it grew steadily higher.

"Must be close to a liter," Ed Vogel observed. "No wonder his heart had trouble beating."

"I guess our concern for Kevin and our assumption that this might be his last bout of rejection made us fail to realize that this amount of fluid could have crippled the heart enough to produce the picture he showed," said Ken. "All of which should teach us not to jump to conclusions too easily."

The aspiration completed, Ken injected the two drugs carefully into the sac around the heart, taking longer with the Thiotepa, which could have an irritating action.

"No change in the ECG," Ed Vogel reported from his observation of the small monitor.

Ken stepped back after removing the needle and Helga strapped a small dressing over the puncture wound.

"Let's hope the medication will slow down the attack of the lymphocytes upon his heart," he said. "If it does, we could have won this skirmish."

"Maybe it will buy time enough to help win the battle, too," said Helga. "This place somehow wouldn't be the same without Kevin behind the bar of the Dolphin Lounge."

223

Carolyn Payson was sitting patiently in the small alcove just off the Board Room when Rebecca Dalton came out. One look at Rebecca's face told Carolyn her mission had failed.

"I'm sorry," said the cardiologist. "The decision went against us."

"I knew it would, the moment I walked into the room and saw Mr. Broadhurst."

"You mustn't blame him entirely, Carolyn," said Rebecca. "As State's Attorney, he must view something like this differently from the ~~way we would.~~" She hesitated, then added: "The real stumbling block was the fact that we weren't asking simply that your father be given the right to die in peace, but that someone be the active agent in what can hardly be called anything but euthanasia. I'm afraid neither the medical profession nor the public are ready for that, so under the circumstances we could hardly expect any other decision."

"I don't feel any resentment, Dr. Dalton," said Carolyn. "Not against the committee, or anybody."

"It's not the end of the world, you know," said Rebecca gently. "Dr. Gross thinks your father can't live more than a few more months."

"Thank you for pleading my case, Dr. Dalton. It wasn't really fair of me to ask you."

"I'm sorry I wasn't able to do a better job," said Rebecca. "Dr. Toler has asked that the decision of the committee not be made public, and I assured him that he could rely on our discretion."

"You can be sure of that. Thanks again—and goodby."

Rebecca stood in the hall outside the Board Room, watching the lithe, erect figure of the girl as she marched to the elevator and into it without so much as a backward look.

"How did she take it, Reb?" Dr. Peter Gross came out of the Board Room and stopped beside Rebecca.

"Very determined. You know, Pete, I believe she was

sure from the start that it would turn out this way but felt she had to bring it up, if for no other reason than to convince herself she had done everything she could."

"That's a reasonable enough thought—under the circumstances."

"But somehow I can't help believing it's not the whole thought. And I'm not even sure I want to know what the rest is."

"When you spoke in the Board Room just now about the philosophy and ethics of this situation, I couldn't help remembering some phrases from the Hippocratic Oath we all swore as a part of the medical school graduation ceremony," he said, "particularly the part that goes:

"So far as power and discernment shall be mine, I will carry out regimen for the benefit of the sick and will keep them from harm and wrong. To none will I give a deadly drug, even if solicited, nor offer counsel to such an end.

"It's pretty sobering, when you think of it," Gross added. "Doctors have been swearing that oath for more than two thousand years and it has been the guiding principle of our profession. But when we start deciding not only who can exercise the right to choose when to die, which conceivably might fall within our province where the patient himself initiates the action, but also undertake to bring about the death of another human, the whole thing begins to get to you."

"It got to me just now, and I don't mind telling you I was happy not to have a vote. The single 'Yes' vote just now was yours, wasn't it, Pete?"

"Yes."

"Mind telling me why?"

"I'm not quite sure myself. When I looked at Richard Payson I thought, 'There but for the lack of one single gene go I.' And I knew that, if I were in the same fix, I'd want somebody to shoot a gram or so of morphine into my veins."

"Or that you would have the courage to do it yourself?"

225

"There I think I would chicken out. How about you?"

"When Ken and I first separated, I was so depressed that I would have welcomed the decision of someone to intervene in my life—"

"You're too young and there's too much ahead for you to even think of that, Reb. The kind of knowledge you possess and your skill in helping other people isn't something you can willfully destroy, just because you're only thinking of yourself."

"I finally saw that," said Rebecca. "But I can't help wondering whether an oath I swore ten years ago can have much real meaning for me, now that I know what it is to want to die."

v

When she left the Board Room floor, Rebecca Dalton was strongly tempted to visit the CICU to see what decisions Ken had made about Kevin and Ross McKenzie, but resisted the urge. She had already done everything she could medically for Kevin except perhaps to remove the fluid from his pericardium and she was planning to do that tomorrow. Or rather to suggest that it be done, since Kevin was technically Ken's patient, as the surgeon who had operated upon him.

Ross McKenzie, however, was in an entirely different category. As the doctor in charge from the beginning, she was responsible for the politician until he was transferred to the Cardiovascular Surgery Section. And if she became convinced that Ken was unduly delaying surgery and thereby seriously endangering Ross McKenzie's already sharply decreasing chances, she would have no alternative except to make an official demand from the medical service for action by the surgical service.

Such a demand would either require Ken to act or lead to the case being assigned to another surgeon from the faculty, perhaps to Mike Raburn, whose skill in the field of heart and blood vessel surgery was not far behind Ken's own. Mike, however, was quite preoccupied with preparations for the TBW on Carmelita Sanchez and it wasn't fair to involve him in the inevitable controversy such a move on her part would cause—unless she became convinced that McKenzie's life was being endangered greatly by further delaying a mitral valve replacement.

Soberly evaluating the consequences of such a last resort as she rode down to the cafeteria floor on the elevator, Rebecca faced up to the fact that a demand for surgical intervention by her could only mean the end of her marriage to Ken. And after last night, she knew that in spite of her brief flare-up that morning she must avoid that eventuality, unless she was faced with a possible choice between the life of her marriage and that of a patient who had entrusted himself to her care, leaving her no alternative. Bemused with the thought, she almost ran into Ed Vogel, who was hurrying from the cafeteria.

"Well, I got it in and it's working," he said jubilantly.

"I thought you'd inserted the brachial and femoral catheters for determining Mr. McKenzie's cardiac function long ago."

"Then you didn't know?"

"Is Mr. McKenzie being prepared for surgery?" she asked quickly—even hopefully.

Ed looked puzzled. "Didn't you and Dr. Dalton decide to use the fiberoptic catheter right after you left the CICU? I saw you talking in the corridor and right afterward he came back and told me to get the fiberoptic catheter ready. But it had to be sterilized in a special way with ethylene oxide and that took a couple of hours. I just finished putting it in a little while ago."

"He must have thought about it after I left him." Rebecca covered up her irritation as best she could but she was sure Ed Vogel realized it was there. "How's the catheter working?"

"Like a Swiss watch," said the younger cardiologist. "You can calculate the stroke work index in less than half the time it took with catheters in both an arm vein and the groin. They've been using it at Peter Bent."

"I read the journals," Rebecca said, a little tartly. "But thanks for telling me."

She marched into the cafeteria, leaving Ed Vogel star-

227

ing at her rigid back. Then, shaking his head, he turned toward the elevators.

Angry, both at Ken for not mentioning the special instrument, and at herself for being irritated when she knew perfectly well that she had been tied up with the God Committee and therefore not available for him to notify her of the change in Ross McKenzie's program, Rebecca hardly noticed the dishes she chose as she passed through the busy cafeteria line, until Jerry Singleton called to her from his place back of her in the line.

"May I join you, Rebecca?" he asked.

"Certainly, Jerry."

"Go ahead and pick a table," he said as she was leaving the cash register and, choosing one in the corner somewhat separated from the rest of the large room with its din of conversation, Rebecca put down her tray.

"Congratulations on your promotion," said the gynecologist as he brought his own tray to the table and pulled out a chair. "I had to call a special meeting of the Faculty Personnel Committee Monday afternoon so we could approve it for action by the Hospital Board. Ken's on the committee, too, but I managed to keep him in the dark."

"I'd forgotten you were the chairman; thanks for taking the trouble," she said. "But how does it happen that you're dining with the hoi polloi? I thought your evening routine always included beautiful women and *coq au vin.*"

"Right now I feel more like a plucked chicken," the surgeon admitted wryly.

"What's happened?"

"For one thing, I've got to wait a couple of hours here for the daughter of a rich casino owner who's being flown over from Nassau with a suspected ruptured ovarian follicle that may turn out to be only a premenstrual bellyache. I told him over the phone that any surgeon in the Bahamas could operate on her, but I took care of his wife some years ago and he won't let anybody else touch her."

"That should make you feel good."

"Sic transit gloria." Jerry Singleton shrugged. "You mean you haven't heard how Karen Fletcher raked me

over the coals at the Tissue Conference this afternoon before the entire surgical service? And all because I lost an elective hysterectomy last week from a pulmonary embolism nobody could have foreseen."

"The Moriturus Committee met this afternoon and I was tied up with a case I was presenting until after six. But why did Karen pick on you?"

"I'm asking myself the same question—and not getting any answer," Jerry admitted. "Most gyn. specialists are doing a lot more elective hysterectomies on women who've had as many children as they'd planned and don't want to be bothered with taking the pill or putting in a diaphragm whenever hubby—or the boy friend—starts getting romantic."

"Maybe I'm prejudiced because I seem to be sterile—"

"I've never been able to find a reason for that either."

"Go on, Jerry. I'm sorry I interrupted."

"The point I'm making is that this whole question was thrashed out a few years ago at a meeting of the American College of Obstetrics and Gynecology—with the consensus overwhelmingly in favor of elective hysterectomy, particularly by the vaginal route, in such cases. Then I lost a simple case last week, for no reason I could be blamed for, and Karen Fletcher chooses to rake me over the coals before a jury of my peers. Don't get me wrong, I'm in favor of peer review. But the way she put it, I was practically a murderer."

"Karen can be very effective when she wants to be, and she's as smart as a whip." Rebecca gave Jerry a quick sidelong glance. "You haven't been ignoring her lately, have you?"

"Ignoring?" he spluttered. "She always looks so unapproachable that I've never even made a pass at her."

"Did it ever occur to you that you may have just put your finger on the reason she cut you down this afternoon?"

"You mean . . . ? Hell, Rebecca! Doctors don't mix sex and love with medicine; it would be unethical."

Rebecca laughed. "For a medical Don Juan, you're really very naïve, Jerry. Women doctors are still women."

229

Then she sobered. "I know because I've found myself doing something like that lately."

"Really, Rebecca," he protested, "I find that very hard to believe—maybe of Karen because, come to think of it, there have been times when I couldn't be certain I wasn't receiving signals but didn't believe it at the time."

"I don't know why. You're very attractive."

"Then why would she deliberately cut me down, knowing it would make me mad as hell?"

"Aren't you more conscious of Karen right now than you were three hours ago?"

"Conscious of her! I'd like nothing better than to wring her neck."

"It's a very lovely neck—or hadn't you noticed?"

"Of course I've noticed. What man on the faculty hasn't?"

"One, I hope." Rebecca's voice was suddenly sober. "But I'm afraid I'm wrong there too."

Jerry looked at her in surprise. "Ken—and Karen? You're talking through your hat."

"Maybe. But she went to the trouble yesterday of running a special test right after the patient Ken did the Caesarean on died to prove that heroin killed her. And she called him down to her private laboratory to show him the results."

"What was wrong with that?"

"Those lab reports don't usually come through for several days, Jerry. Pathology is one department that takes its time."

The surgeon shook his head unbelievingly. "If anybody else but you had told me women doctors would mix sex and medicine, I wouldn't have believed it. But come to think of it, maybe you're right. And I guess it's inevitable, with women taking over so much of the medical field these days."

He glanced around the dining room, which was largely filled with women, most of them in white uniforms. "When I was in medical school they hadn't moved into very much, but from the looks of this cafeteria, there must be a half dozen of 'em for every doctor in the place."

"Anybody connected with medicine knows women in white just about rule the medical world these days, in numbers at least," Rebecca agreed. "I guess it's not surprising that so many emotional relationships develop and so many marriages go on the rocks."

"Like mine," Jerry agreed. "But surely not yours, Rebecca?"

"Ken and I are on a collision course, Jerry. And I don't know what to do."

"You could try telling me about it. I was headed for a career in psychiatry a long time ago, until I figured out that I could straighten out the female world about as effectively as a gynecologist as I could being a shrink."

"Suppose you were married to a woman doctor who tried to force you into an operation you were afraid to do, Jerry?"

"Afraid, Reb?" His tone was grave now. "That's a serious charge to make."

"Especially against someone you love."

"I think you'd better tell me more about it. You and Ken are fellow members of the faculty, besides being my friends. If it comes to a controversy between you, people will start taking sides and that could easily tear the school apart."

In a few terse sentences, Rebecca gave him a summary of the course of Ross McKenzie's illness since his admission to the hospital around midnight.

"How certain can you be that McKenzie is losing ground?" he asked.

"He's not gaining—the stroke work index Ken seems to be depending on indicates that."

"How much of your conviction that the patient is failing because of an incompetent mitral valve could be attributed to the fact that you don't trust this new catheter Ken is using?"

She gave him a startled look. "What makes you think that?"

"I could hear it in your voice just now, when you spoke of the fiberoptic instrument. My guess would be that you unconsciously resent Ken's decision to use it without consulting you. Isn't that true?"

"I don't know, Jerry. I've been so concerned with what might happen to Ken if I put him on the spot by demanding that he operate, I haven't stopped to analyze my motives."

"I suspect a certain amount of ambivalence."

"Ambivalence?"

"It's only natural for you to be concerned for Ken's career and for your marriage, but you're tops in your field, too. If this new gadget should turn out to be more accurate in determining heart function than the traditional methods you've been using, with a catheter threaded through an arm vein into the right side of the heart and another directed upward from the groin through the femoral artery into the left, it's bound to reflect a little on your skill as a cardiologist."

"I can't accept that agrument." Her tone was somewhat cool now.

"I read the medical journals—particularly the JAMA. The article on the catheter Ken is using first appeared there, and quite a number of cardiologists are also becoming disenchanted lately with the femoral route. You'll have to admit that the incidence of complications like clot formation and embolism have been found to be much higher when that route is used."

"That is true," she conceded.

"Then if this fiberoptic catheter inserted through an arm vein really accomplishes the same thing with much less danger, it will end up being the procedure of choice."

"Do you expect me to stand by and watch the optimum time for replacing the mitral valve pass without saying anything, and then have McKenzie's death on my conscience?"

"You can always withdraw from the case."

"Would that make me any less guilty of a patient's death?"

"Perhaps not, being you."

"What does that mean?"

"Simply that both you and Ken are too conscientious for your own good, so naturally you blame yourselves for the failure of the transplants."

"Ken blames me, I'm sure of that."

"Perhaps he does—unconsciously," Jerry agreed. "When we get in trouble we always hunt for a scapegoat."

"And he *did* take over the McKenzie case."

"So we're back where we started." Jerry shook his head sadly. "And it looks like I've only made the situation worse by trying to help two people I like very much. Maybe next time I'll keep my fool mouth shut, but at the risk of making the same mistake twice, I'll give you one last piece of advice, Reb."

"What's that?"

"Be patient. In spite of all our sophisticated monitoring gadgets, surgeons sometimes have to depend on instinct alone in making a decision, particularly when they're not sure of themselves. And in a surprising number of cases, a well-trained instinct turns out to be more reliable than a computer." He stood up. "Excuse me, please. I've got a job to do before that case from the Bahamas gets here."

VI

Mike Raburn had decided to stop by the ICU to check on Carmelita Sanchez before going to dinner. The local six o'clock news was on the color TV set in the small ICU staff lounge and he stopped briefly to watch.

Sports came on last and he'd started to leave when he heard Big Joe Gates's name mentioned and turned back. The station sports director was delivering a television editorial. And as soon as Mike heard the first words, he knew the campaign Joe Gates was expecting to be launched aginst him had already begun:

"Local backers of the Miami Snappers professional basketball team are asking themselves whether their star forward, Big Joe Gates, has been entirely candid with them. While Joe was busy in San Francisco, helping promote a players' union for all participants in professional sports, his son, Joe, Jr., barely missed dying at Biscayne General Hospital from a crisis associated with sickle cell anemia.

"It's no secret, of course, that sickle cell disease is hereditary, and limited mostly to the black race. So the question this reporter feels hasn't been answered is: Did Joe Gates know of this tendency in his family before the crisis that threatened to take the life of his son? If so, there is a strong question whether Joe has played fair with backers and fans, or with the betting public, in not warning them that he, too, might be incapacitated at any time and not be able to play.

"In question, too, is whether Big Joe has the right to help organize a union of professional players without prior permission by the group of sportsmen who have spent large amounts of money to bring big-time professional basketball to Miami. In the opinion of this reporter, Joe Gates owes both the owners and the public an answer to one question: *Are you or aren't you a possible victim of sickle cell anemia, Joe? Your followers have a right to know!*"

"The dirty sonsabitches," Mike muttered as he turned down the sound on the color set.

Helga Sundberg had appeared in the door of the lounge in time to hear his last words. She was supporting Rachel Gates, who was weeping softly.

"Are you cussing somebody or just muttering to yourself?" Helga asked.

"Anything wrong, Rachel?" Mike asked in quick concern.

"One of those people you were just talking about was in the ICU waiting room and upset her by saying something nasty about her husband," said Helga. "I'm busy getting a cardiac stroke work index reading on Mr. McKenzie, Dr. Raburn. Could you take care of her?"

"Sure." Mike took Rachel Gates's arm and led her to a chair. "Wait here, I'll get you something—"

"A cup of coffee will be enough, Mike. It was foolish of me to get so upset."

"You're under a double strain—with Joey in here and the big guns opening up on Big Joe," Mike assured her. "Didn't Joe tell you he was expecting this sort of thing?"

"No." She accepted the coffee he gave her. "Joe's been pretty nervous since he got in from San Francisco. What does all this mean, Mike?"

"The owners don't like the idea of a players' union and they know how much your husband's supporting the players who want to organize one can mean. So they're trying to shut him up."

"Could Joey have really gotten the sickle cell thing from Joe?"

"Possibly. How old is Big Joe by the way?"

"Thirty his last birthday. Why?"

"If he had the sickling tendency, I'd have expected him to develop symptoms earlier."

"Like Joey's?"

"Maybe not as bad, but much the same thing. Before we learned the new treatments we're using with your son, not many black males with an inherited sickling tendency got beyond twenty without showing the disease. And a lot of them didn't live much longer."

Rachel Gates shuddered. "I'm just beginning to understand how much I owe to you and Dr. Henderson for—"

"Forget it," said Mike. "We were just doing our jobs. Besides, you and Joe and Joey are friends and, if you can't help friends, who can you help? But I hope you won't let this TV campaign worry you too much. Once Joe went into labor politics, it was inevitable that he would be attacked. The newspapers will be on him next."

"I can take it, as long as I know what it's all about, Mike. But I wish Joe wasn't so nervous. He's playing tomorrow night in the last postseason game, then we were going across the country in our Winnebago. But now—"

"Joey's going to be all right," he assured her.

"Are you sure?"

"Sickle cell disease is really a medical condition and Joey's a pediatric patient, but Dr. Henderson tells me all the signs are good. My only role was in getting oxygen to him fast in the hyperbaric chamber."

"And saving his life."

"I doubt that it was in quite that much danger."

"You kept his brain from being damaged by lack of

oxygen. Dr. Henderson and Professor McHale both told me that."

"Will you do me a favor, Rachel?" Mike asked.

"Of course."

"I'd like to take a blood specimen from your finger."

"To look for sickling?"

"Yes."

"Joe told me if any of you asked me, not to let you take it."

"I'll only have to prick your finger and that won't show, so Joe doesn't have to know anything about it. Then if you show the sickling trait, it will tell me how to handle this campaign against your husband, when it comes to a showdown."

"Please do it then."

"The ICU lab is across the hall," he told her. "We won't even make an official record of this, until the right time comes."

In the laboratory, Mike pricked Rachel's finger and touched the blood on it with the surface of a glass slide, dropping a thin cover slip upon it in what was known as a "fresh preparation." Placing this under a miscroscope, he focused the controls until the biscuit-shaped red blood cells of the preparation sprang into sharp focus.

It took him several minutes to find what he was looking for, several cells whose outlines were ragged and a few that were even shaped like a quarter moon. Their shape was practically diagnostic of a carrier of the sickling trait or tendency, though not necessarily the disease itself, which depended upon the formation of masses of elongated cells large enough to block important small blood vessels.

"You have the trait," he told Rachel. "We'll double-check it with Sickledex, of course, but there's no doubt as far as I'm concerned."

"Then Joey inherited it from me?"

"Almost certainly. Of course, Big Joe could have the trait too. But if both of you possessed the tendency, I doubt that Joey would have lived through more than the first two or three years of life."

"Shouldn't I call Big Joe now and tell him?"

236

"I don't think so," said Mike. "Joe's determined to play this thing his way, and part of his chance of success depends on how much the owners attack him. My guess, judging from the way the TV station went after him tonight, is that he'll be under heavy attack in the newspapers tomorrow. But that's what he wants."

"I still can't see why."

"Joe's giving the owners a lot of rope, Rachel, in the hope that they'll hang themselves, so to speak. First he'll let the heat build up for a day or so, long enough to show how vicious some people can be to gain their own ends. Then he'll cut the rug from beneath them by letting himself be tested for sickle cell anemia. When it turns out that he doesn't have the sickling tendency at all, he can show up the owners' attack for what it is, an attempt to keep lesser-known players under their thumbs. The public is almost certain to react unfavorably to such tactics so the owners will be over a barrel as far as the players' union is concerned."

"But Joe isn't absolutely certain that he doesn't have sickle cell anemia, Mike."

"Are you sure?"

She nodded. "He doesn't tell me much but I know when Joe's worried about something. And from what little he does say, I can tell that he's troubled by the possibility that he's positive too."

"Then he really is taking a long chance by letting this campaign against him go as far as it already has," said Mike.

"But what can you—or anybody—do?"

"Play it by ear, I guess."

Rachel shook her head. "This is all too complicated for me to understand, but thank you for taking so much trouble with us." She reached for her handbag. "Goodness! I almost forgot that Joe told me to give you this."

She handed him an envelope; inside were two box seats for the final exhibition game between the Snappers and the Lakers Thursday night.

Chapter 15.

KAREN FLETCHER finished her daily thirty laps of the Bayside Terrace swimming pool and, climbing from the water, put on the short terry cloth robe draped over a beach chair. Slipping her feet into a pair of fiber scuffs, she rubbed her hair dry with a towel as she crossed the grassy plot to the back door of the terrace. By the time she took the elevator to her floor and pushed open the door of her apartment, the silver pile of hair about her shoulders was beginning to dry. Moving into the apartment, she closed the door and started across the small living room, dropping the terry robe on a chair as she passed and leaving her only garment the black nylon tank suit that failed to hide even the taut thrust of her nipples through the thin fabric.

"Very lovely," said a masculine voice from across the room where Jerry Singleton was sitting in a wing chair, smoking a filter-tip cigarette.

At his voice, Karen turned quickly but did not reach for the robe. In fact, to a really close observer, it would have appeared that she was hardly surprised to find him there, but Jerry seemed not to have realized it.

"How did you get in?" she asked, crossing to a mirror and starting to brush her still slightly damp hair with long, practiced strokes.

"Walked in, the door was open."

"I ran down for a quick swim."

"You could get into trouble that way. A man could be waiting for you——"

Brush in hand, she turned to face him and laughed. "It seems that one is."

"You could be attacked."

Karen moved across the room and took a cigarette

from the small table beside the chair where he was sitting, but when he reached out to touch her thigh, she moved away casually.

"I'm an athlete, Jerry. And I also hold the black belt in karate."

"Is that a warning?"

"I only use karate on enemies, not on friends. Which, by the way, are you?"

"Until you came in just now, I felt like an enemy. But now—"

"There's no reason for us to be enemies, Jerry. Just because I did my duty as head of the Pathology Department and presented a case of embolism at the Tissue Conference—"

"But did it have to be mine?" His voice had taken on a slight edge.

"It was the only death from pulmonary embolism we've had in the past six months. And the younger members of the surgical staff need reminding periodically that embolism can complicate even the simplest surgical operations."

"Rebecca Dalton thinks you may have chosen me as the target because I haven't paid much attention to you—"

"Really? It would seem that I have underestimated Rebecca."

"I haven't heard you deny the allegation."

"Perhaps because I don't." She shrugged, a highly stimulating action in the thin tank suit.

"Then?"

"You're a very attractive man, Jerry—with quite a reputation as a woman chaser." She surveyed him coolly but he didn't miss the glint in her eye nevertheless. "As such you're legitimate prey for every attractive unattached woman around."

"Mind telling me why you deliberately chose to attack me?"

"When you know me better, Jerry"—she was back brushing her hair again—"you'll know that everything I do is deliberate."

"I still don't see why it had to be today."

"I just told you. The case I presented was the first fatal embolism at Biscayne General in six months and the only one I can remember happening to one of your patients. It was ideal for my purpose."

"Which was?"

"Don't you know?" She laughed and the throaty tone in her voice made the short hairs along his spine rise in a reflex as old as life itself, as well as set his heart to pounding. "If you don't, you're really not as sharp as I credited you with being, Jerry."

He was halfway across the room toward her when a thought stopped him dead.

"You planned all this, didn't you? Even to leaving the door open."

"Really, Jerry." Now her tone was purely sensual. "Do you have to use so many words? I'm beginning to think what I've been hearing about you as a lover was exaggerated."

The sarcasm in her words released him, even though he knew the answer to his question without her having to speak it. But before he could touch her body she moved back.

"Just a minute," she said. "These tank suits are hard to find—and expensive."

With a sinuous movement that somehow reminded him of the graceful rhythmic sway of a cobra to its master's flute, she slipped down the straps of the tank suit and, peeling the damp fabric swiftly down over her breasts, hips, and thighs, stepped out of it, leaving a small pile of black nylon on the thick white pile of the rug. Jerry's eyes bugged at the perfection of the lovely nude body facing him, a perfection so complete that he was reminded of an alabaster statue of a Grecian goddess—except for the sudden glow of fire in her eyes.

II

Carolyn Payson opened the door of the apartment she shared with Helga at Gus Henderson's first ring. She was fully dressed, even to make-up, which, he noticed, was heavier than she usually wore.

"Could we have a drink in the Dolphin Lounge before we go out to dinner?" she asked. "I've had a pretty rough day."

"I heard about some of it. Sorry things didn't go your way."

"Let's not talk about that. Helga said the best thing we could do tonight is to hang one on and for once I feel like drowning my sorrows."

At the long highly polished bar in the Dolphin Lounge, they had bourbon highballs. Gus was surprised when Carolyn asked for another; she usually didn't go beyond a limit of one drink, but he sensed that tonight she was in a different mood. Both were feeling fine when they came out of the lounge and went to his car.

"The place doesn't seem to be the same without Kevin McCartney," said Gus. "No matter how low you were feeling, you could come in there and tell yourself how much better off you were than somebody with a time bomb ticking away inside his chest."

"Do you know how Kevin is tonight?"

"Not too good. He had a cessation a couple of hours ago but Helga got him started before Ed or Dr. Ken could get there."

"Helga's been like the Rock of Ages these last few days to me. I don't know what I'll do without her."

"You always have me," Gus assured her. "Have you decided where you want to go to dinner?"

"Any place that's gay, and bright. And where we can dance, too."

"There's a Polynesian restaurant on the North Bay Causeway. We might try it."

III

Ken Dalton was having a hamburger and coffee in a booth at the far end of the nearly deserted Coffee Shop when Rebecca stopped at the cashier's desk to get change for the newspaper vending machine outside. When he beckoned to her, she came over to the booth and slid into the seat across from him.

"How about a piece of strawberry pie and a cup of coffee?" he asked. "I was just about to order it."

"I've already had dinner—with Jerry Singleton."

"So?" Ken's eyebrows rose. "I've been wondering when he would go on the make for you."

"Jerry's lonely, Ken."

"About as lonely as a single bull in a pasture of young heifers. He's having a ball."

"You could, too, if you wanted to."

"Not a chance." His voice was suddenly sober. "Once you've had a glimpse of heaven, Reb, you don't settle even for paradise. And I had a good look at both down in Florida Bay."

"Stop it! You'll have me bawling."

"You didn't have dessert with your dinner, did you?"

"No."

"Two strawberry pies and some coffee for Dr. Dalton, Maggie," he called. "And some more coffee for me, too."

"Comin' right up, Doctors," said the waitress.

"You'll ruin my figure," Rebecca protested.

"As I remember, it can stand a pound or two more."

"I hear you were busy while I was tied up with the God Committee meeting," said Rebecca.

"You mean the fiberoptic catheter?"

"That." With an effort Rebecca kept her voice even. "And other things."

"Kevin almost went out on us, but Helga got his heart going again before the CPR team arrived. That girl's a real tower of strength in this hospital."

"She's absolutely unflappable."

"You've taught her a lot since she came here. I used to think you were the only completely self-sustained individual I ever saw, Reb, but our Helga has you beaten."

"Did you know she and Carolyn Payson spent a year nursing at a hospital in Northeast Brazil, just after they got their nursing degrees at Gainesville?"

"Helga a missionary? She's better equipped to play the part of Sadie Thompson."

Maggie brought their pie and filled the coffee cups.

"By the way, what was the verdict of the God Committee?" Ken asked.

"It's not supposed to be broadcast, but Carolyn and I lost."

"What now?"

"She'll just have to make the best of it and hope her father doesn't last long. She was terribly tense before but I somehow got the feeling afterward that the committee meeting only crystallized something for her. She thanked me—and told me good-by."

"The girl was and is under a terrible strain. I wouldn't try to read anything special into what she does or says under these circumstances."

"Jerry just read me a lecture on trying to pressure people into doing what I think they should," Rebecca admitted. "But nobody would know that better than you do."

"I don't think many people resent the pressure, Reb." Ken's voice was entirely sober now. "It's just that you're always so infernally right. Take this business of trying to get me to go on with heart transplants—"

"I've sworn off that." Rebecca raised her right hand. "Scout's honor."

"Maybe so, but you got under my skin the other night."

She smiled. "I'm still reminded of it occasionally."

"I was lashing out at you, so I guess I did treat you pretty rough. But it started me thinking about the way you've been pressuring me to go back into research on that plastic heart pump I was working on, so I started looking up the literature and right off I found some things I didn't know. Do you realize that a Frenchman has been living nearly five years with a transplanted heart?"

"Where did you find that?"

"A publisher in Paris has brought out a book about him. If you want to read it, you can find it in the medical school library, the title is *C'est pour ce soir*. My French is pretty lousy, but I understood enough to know the patient is doing very well."

"Did you find any concrete reason why?"

Ken shook his head. "My own idea is that he belongs to

243

a class of people who might be called hyporeactive—the unflappables like Helga Sundberg. They can stand almost anything and bounce right back, because something inside them, maybe the endocrine system, doesn't go pumping a lot of stress-produced hormones into their bloodstreams at the slightest excuse."

"But you can't select only that kind of person for major surgery."

"Which is why surgeons are always going to have failures," he agreed. "What we can do, though, is pay more attention to the emotional make-up of our patients, knowing that the hyperreactives, like you and me, are going to develop all the complications possible—and take measures accordingly."

"It's an interesting theory."

"And worth exploring."

"Then you're going back into research?"

"Maybe. I won't know until I've studied other people's results."

"Meanwhile there's no reason why you can't do other types of surgery, like Ross McKenzie, for example."

"Have you already decided he's going to need it?"

"Everything looks that way, doesn't it?"

"Not to me."

"What more evidence do you need with his mitral valve flapping like a sail in the wind?" Rebecca tried to curb her instinctive irritation at what she considered to be his stubbornness. "If you replace it with an artificial one now, the chance of his coming through the operation okay should be almost certain."

"Nothing is certain when you're doing open heart surgery on a man who's sixty-five years old, Reb. Besides, I examined the arteries in his eye grounds, and they're considerably more tortuous and sclerotic than his age seems to indicate."

"B-but—"

"How many congenital floppy mitral valves have you diagnosed in the past couple of years, since you've had the echocardiograph to work with?"

"More than we ever knew existed." Rebecca had the strange feeling that she was being backed into a corner, and it wasn't pleasant for one whose judgment, in matters concerning the function of the heart, was rarely challenged.

"Every one of them leaks a little blood back through into the atrium each time the left ventricle contracts," he said. "Yet most of those hearts aren't even noticeably enlarged, although some of them have been leaking since the patient was born. Isn't that true?"

"Y-yes. But I thought—"

"I couldn't have lived with you ten years without knowing something about your thought processes, Reb. Plus the fact that you have your share of an essentially feminine psychological quirk that allows you to convince yourself without much argument that, in dealing even with someone as close to you as a husband, the end justifies the means."

"I didn't know you had a degree in psychiatry." She was stung at last into tartness and Ken's slightly mocking grin only made it worse, just as Jerry Singleton's analysis of her emotions had done a little earlier.

"When Ross McKenzie was brought in last night with the story of some sort of heart attack after pretty strenuous exertion, you found a dysfunction of the mitral valve and made a brilliant diagnosis of ruptured *chordae tendineae* attached to the valve, keeping it from closing completely."

"You agreed. Remember?"

"Of course, I agree. Because you were, and are, right."

"And he *did* go into cardiogenic shock."

"No doubt about that, either. Unless I miss my guess, the first thought that popped into your mind was that, if you could persuade me to operate on McKenzie and replace the damaged mitral successfully with an artificial one, you'd be giving me back my confidence."

"Was anything wrong with that?"

"Only one thing, it just could be that you weren't doing what was best for the patient. And when a doctor loses sight of that, the seeds of real trouble are being sown."

"Have you thought of the possibility that you're emphasizing the hazards of cardiac surgery on Ross McKenzie because you're not sure of your own ability to perform it successfully any more?"

When she saw him wince as the angry words went home, she knew she hadn't been fair to him—but it was too late now to recall them.

"Et tu, Brute?" he said wryly, rising to his feet.

"Ken, I—"

"I guess all along I've been telling myself you didn't really feel that way, Reb, and ignoring an obvious truth. If it's your medical decision that Ross McKenzie can only be saved by replacing that mitral valve, you have an obligation to put in an official request that someone else be assigned to do it. I have no intention of operating on him until I'm convinced there's no other alternative."

"Nobody ever accused me of letting my own wishes interfere with a medical decision before."

"And I know you couldn't be charged with it this time, if your desire to help me wasn't so strong. But have you studied the incidence of cerebral artery block lately from clots forming on artificial heart valves and then breaking loose?"

"No."

"It's far more frequent than any of us ever thought would happen, just as we're seeing a lot of failures we didn't expect after coronary by-pass surgery. It was a nice try, Reb, and I appreciate the thought behind it. But I'll have to work myself out of this the only way I know how—by being stubborn."

He moved toward the cash register. "Are you going to request surgical intervention?"

"I don't know," said Rebecca soberly, conscious that they had come at last to the very brink of disaster in their marriage. "The only thing I can do now is go over the case again in detail, then do what I have to do."

IV

Mike Raburn was on the way to the cafeteria for a belated dinner when the paging operator called his name. Stepping into his office in the Emergency Department, he picked up the telephone from the desk.

"This is Dr. Raburn. Did you want me?"

"You have an outside call, Doctor. Mr. Joe Gates."

"Put him on, please. . . . Looks like you called the shots right, Joe," said Mike. "That sports editorial on TV really slammed into you."

"Tomorrow morning's paper will be worse; one of the sports writers just called to warn me."

"That figures."

"They think they've got me over a barrel because of Joey."

"Dr. Henderson has taken the catheter out of Joey's arm vein. He's taking his medicine by mouth, now, and asking when he can go home."

"That's good. Did Rachel give you the tickets?"

"She did but I'm not going to be able to use them. I'll be watching a special patient all day tomorrow and we won't know which way it will go for her much before midnight."

"That's too bad," said Joe. "The team physician came down with a strep throat this afternoon and we don't have a doctor for the game tomorrow night. I was hoping you'd come and bring a medical bag."

"Come to think of it, Ed Vogel has tomorrow night off. You want to hold the phone while I find out whether he can go? Or shall I call you back?"

"I'd better hold. I'm supposed to go out on the court again in five minutes to practice."

On the wall beside the door to the Emergency Department, Mike took an inside phone off the hook and asked the paging operator to ring Ed Vogel. The cardiologist answered almost immediately.

"I've got a couple of box seat tickets for the Snappers-Lakers game tomorrow night, but I can't go," said Mike. "Joe Gates is on the telephone now wanting to know if someone from here can bring a medical bag. The team doctor has a strep throat."

"I'll use 'em," said Ed Vogel promptly. "I've got a date but the game will be over before eleven, leaving the shank of the evening."

At the other phone, Mike found Joe Gates still on the line.

"Dr. Vogel will be glad to go tomorrow night, Joe; he's a cardiologist and will bring his own medical bag. By the way, Rachel was pretty upset over that six o'clock broadcast but I told her it wasn't nearly as bad as it sounded."

"I'm not used to this sort of thing either and it's given me a bad case of the jitters," the athlete admitted. "If I don't play any better tomorrow night than I did in the first half hour of practice tonight, the Snappers will probably trade me to Slippery Rock."

"Want me to phone you a prescription for a sedative?"

"Doc Moriarity gave us all some pills for emergencies like this during the season. If I'm still shook up tomorrow night, I'll take one or two of 'em."

V

The moon was shining brightly when Carolyn and Gus Henderson took the causeway toward North Bay Village and Normandy Shores, turning the surface of the bay into a vast sheet of rippling molten silver. At the restaurant Gus surrendered the car to a parking attendant wearing a colorful pareu and they went inside through a somewhat garishly decorated passageway of bamboo framing interlaced with palm fronds.

The décor was authentic enough to allow the diners, especially after several tall drinks called Tahiti Trips, to imagine they were in the South Seas. The food was exotic and the floor show exciting, with hula dancing, in which the guests joined, and a fire walk by the parking attendant doubling in brass—in which they didn't.

Carolyn seemed to be enjoying herself, with a hectic, almost fervid gaiety Gus had never seen in her before. He was happy to see it, however, because it seemed to mean she had decided she could do nothing about her father's condition, now that the final termination of life had been refused by the God Committee, and should live her own life to the full with no thought of the horror later years might bring.

Kevin McCartney opened his eyes and tried to focus them on the shadowy white-clad figure standing beside the bed but the oxygen mask got in the way. He could hear the rush of gas as it bubbled through the water bottle that gave an index of its flow and also added moisture to keep from drying out the mucous membrane lining of his lungs.

"What happened?" he mumbled.

Helga Sundberg moved around the bed and shut off the flow of gas before removing the mask.

"Think you can breathe on your own?" she asked. "Or are you still too lazy?"

"Hello, beautiful, I thought for a while I was in heaven and you were an angel."

Helga chuckled. "That's sweet, Kevin, but not very practical, I'm afraid."

"Mind telling me what happened?"

"You tried to quit this life and I had to knock you around a bit with CPR."

"So that's why my chest feels like it's been stepped on by an elephant?"

"I got your pump started up again and Dr. Dalton took about a quart of fluid out of your pericardium."

"Is that why I don't feel like my heart's being squeezed to death any longer?"

"That, plus some drugs he left in there to discourage any more fluid from forming, plus the stuff we've been shooting into your veins to overcome the rejection."

"So I'm going to make it this time?"

"If you don't you'll have to answer to me," Helga promised him. "Now do you think you can keep functioning on your own while a student sits with you so I can get back to where I'm supposed to be?"

"I promise," said Kevin. "Do you suppose Dr. Ken will be back tonight?"

"I'm not sure. Why?"

"I want to talk to him, something important."

"We're watching another patient of his pretty closely, so he'll probably be in later."

"In that case I think I'll take another nap. Be sure to wake me when he comes around."

"Will do," said Helga. "And just to be sure you don't get lazy again, I'll be watching you on the big screen. One cessation a night is about all my nervous system can stand."

VII

In Apartment 1011 at Bayside Arms, Peggy Tyndall finished giving Dale his bath and rolled him dry in a nubby towel, before helping him into his pajamas. Was the dusky hue of cyanosis his skin had shown since birth really more marked than before as Dr. Karen Fletcher thought? She asked herself—and couldn't be sure of the answer. Mrs. Taylor, the baby sitter who watched the boy, thought so too, but she hadn't counted the times Dale was forced to squat for a moment each day to get his breath, though she had promised to do so from now on.

Warm, tired, and sleepy, Dale reached up to hug Peggy when she bent down to kiss him in his youth bed. Then, gathering the Teddy bear he always slept with in his arms, he turned on his side as she pulled up the small blanket he, like so many small children, insisted on having around him when he slept. Gently Peggy lifted the small hand and examined the fingers but, aside from the clubbing tendency that characterized children with congenital hearts, she couldn't be sure of any change.

"Honey," she said, "are you having any more trouble keeping up with the other children than you used to?"

"Maybe. Jack Peters can run faster'n me—but he's bigger." Dale squirmed farther under the small blanket. "Nighty-night."

"Good night, darling." Peggy leaned down to kiss him again but he was already asleep and she smoothed the dark hair from his forehead instead, gently squeezing his ear lobes, where the telltale bluish tint from the cyanosis of oxygen lack was most apparent.

A full checkup meant catheterization of the heart again

to study it with the X ray and she was reluctant to put this small reminder of the husband who had died in Vietnam in a chopper accident to even that not entirely innocuous procedure. Meanwhile, there was the alternative of waiting for the echocardioscope, with its amazing ability to explore the interior of the heart with reflected sound waves, to be repaired. Dr. Rebecca Dalton felt that it was safe to wait and that was almost enough to reassure Peggy—almost but not quite.

VIII

The bedside clock said ten minutes before eight when the electronic pager in Jerry Singleton's coat pocket emitted its sharp, high-pitched "beep," awakening him. Beside him in the bedroom of the apartment, Karen Fletcher stirred beneath the sheet that partly covered her but left an arm, a shoulder, and one lovely breast bare. She did not awaken when Jerry got out of bed and moved to the chair over which he had draped his coat. The electronic pager, capable of transmitting its signal for ten miles or more, was carried by all the staff while on call outside the hospital and inside as well after nine o'clock, when the loudspeaker call system was turned off so as not to disturb the sleep of patients. When Jerry pressed the switch on the side of the cigarette-pack-sized instrument, telling the operator he had answered, her voice came to him, somewhat tinny from the electronic transmission, but perfectly distinguishable.

"Mrs. Valenti was just admitted to Private Gyn, Dr. Singleton," she said.

Jerry switched off the pager, letting the operator know he had received the message without, however, betraying his whereabouts. As he dressed hurriedly, he glanced toward the bed, where Karen still lay, her face flushed from their love-making and her hair tousled upon the pillow. For a moment Jerry Singleton debated awakening her to tell her he would be back, then put the idea from him.

If the patient flown as an emergency to Biscayne General from the Bahamas was indeed hemorrhaging internally from a ruptured ovarian follicle, where an ovum had burst from its nest on the surface of an ovary, after undergoing maturation to the point where it was ready for fertilization should a live spermatozoön be encountered on its way down the reproductive tract, he might be quite busy for the next couple of hours. And remembering, with a stir of his own pulse, how the lovely perfect body beneath the silken sheet had responded to his own, like the highly tuned instrument for love-making it was, he knew he could no more resist coming to her again than he could have stopped the progress of the blood clot she had demonstrated that afternoon. Loosened from its source in a leg vein and floating free in the rush of blood through ever larger veins until it was swept through the right side and into the lung circulation, where it had shortly blocked a large branch of the pulmonary artery, the clot had caused instant death, giving Karen Fletcher the lure that had drawn him here as surely as if it had been foreordained.

What difference did it make that Karen had actually been the aggressor, from the moment she had attacked him before the surgical Tissue Conference? The important thing was that she had been attracted to him strongly enough to execute such a clever plan for bringing him to her bed. It was a heady thought, almost as heady as the prospect of their next coming together. And with that in mind, he finished dressing and left the apartment.

The click of the lock released Karen from the enforced rigidity she had maintained since she, too, had been awakened by the sharp beeping tone of the pager. Throwing back the sheet, she moved to the door and made certain that it was locked. Then, still nude, she moved across the living room to a bookcase and, pulling down a copy of the Biscayne University Medical School Directory, leafed through the pages until she came to the listings for the Faculty and Administrative committees. Running her finger down the page, she stopped at the Personnel Committee and, beneath it, the Subcommittee on Faculty Promotion.

"Dr. Jeremiah Singleton, Chairman," she read silently.

Picking up a pencil from the desk beside it, she carefully made a ring around the name. Then, moving down the Personnel Committee list, she came upon the name of Ken Dalton and, after a moment of hesitancy, carefully penciled a ring around it, too, confident that her move in performing an immediate test for heroin yesterday and demonstrating the result to Ken had put him in her debt.

The next two names were faculty nonentities who could be counted on to vote with the majority. The bottom name on the list of five was that of Val LeMoyne and Karen chewed on the eraser while her mind moved rapidly, deciding upon the course of action that would insure her the third vote needed when Jerry Singleton presented her name for promotion to full professor. After a moment she nodded and closed the directory.

Everything was working out fine, she told herself as she put the book back into the bookcase and moved to the bath for her shower. She had no intention of suggesting to Jerry, even obliquely, that she should be promoted, until the retirement of Dr. Adrian Cooper was a fact. The important thing there was that, when her promotion to the rank of full professor was approved, her appointment as chief of the Pathology Department should accompany it. Jerry might need some softening up before he would go that far out on a limb in one action but Karen was in no hurry. And in the meantime there was the prospect, not at all unexciting in itself, of future evenings like this one, evenings in which Jerry would no doubt be fully as adequate as he had been tonight.

As for Val LeMoyne, Karen had already decided upon a simpler, less devious way. But one that would be equally effective—for her purpose.

Chapter 16

SHORTLY AFTER nine o'clock Rebecca Dalton called Ed Vogel from her office on the medical floor. "Can you meet me on the CICU right away, Ed?" she asked.

"Certainly, Dr. Dalton, I was just up there. Is anything wrong?"

"I'm considering requesting immediate surgery on Mr. McKenzie."

When there was silence at the other end of the line, Rebecca spoke again, impatiently. "Did you hear me, Ed?"

"Yes. Will Dr. Kenneth Dalton be there?"

"I presume not. He told me about an hour ago that he refuses to operate on the patient." Rebecca's voice became more brusque. "You can see, of course, that his refusal leaves me no alternative except to request that another surgeon be assigned to the case. We can't let a patient die because the Cardiovascular Surgery Section refuses to operate."

"I'll go to CICU right away."

"If you get there before I do, you can be getting together the data I need to call an emergency meeting of the executive staff."

"You'll have it," Ed promised. "Are you going to call them first?"

"What difference does that make?" Rebecca's patience at what seemed to be the Cardiology Fellow's reluctance to support her decision broke through the grip she was maintaining upon her emotions.

"None, Dr. Dalton." Ed Vogel spoke hurriedly. "I'll get going right away."

At the CICU nursing station, the younger cardiologist studied the curve of the stroke work index being recorded every half hour as an indication of Ross McKenzie's condition; the line was moving upward slowly, but definitely. In McKenzie's cubicle, he checked once again, too, the findings being reported by the fiberoptic catheter in his pulmonary artery, the smaller conventional tube in the vena cava just outside the heart, and the various other parameters being constantly measured. All showed slight, but definite, improvement over the patient's condition some six hours before, when Ed had started inserting the special catheter.

Ross McKenzie opened his eyes while the young doctor was fiddling with the bedside unit that transformed the information furnished by pulsations of light through the fiberoptic catheter into electric voltages which could be assimilated and reported upon by the control console for the master information center at the main nursing station.

"When are you going to take that damned tube out of my arm?" the politician demanded. "You've got me tied to so many boards I might as well be crucified."

"Keep on the way you're going and it won't be much longer," Ed promised. "Are you feeling better?"

"How could anyone feel better with all these gadgets hanging from him? No wonder it costs so much to run this damned hospital."

"I'm glad you've had a chance to see where the money goes, Mr. McKenzie."

"What about that fellow McCartney? I heard one of the nurses say he almost died this afternoon."

"Kevin had a close shave, but he's a lot better now," said Vogel. "His heart stopped but Miss Sundberg got it started again."

"If you ask me, the nurses around here know more than the doctors."

"That could be, Mr. McKenzie. That could be."

II

When Rebecca Dalton came on the ward about ten minutes later, Helga was working at the control panel and Ed Vogel was in the doctors' office adjoining it, with the

255

entire monitor bank visible through the large counter-topped opening between the two.

"Your hus—Dr. Kenneth Dalton ordered hourly calculations of the stroke work index," Helga told Rebecca. "I just finished plotting the most recent one on the chart."

She handed Rebecca the graph but the woman doctor didn't pause to study it.

"I want to make my own examination," she said brusquely.

"Certainly, Doctor." Helga was not flustered in the least by the terse note in Rebecca's voice. "I'll get the examining basket."

On every ward, the instruments for physical examination not ordinarily carried by doctors in making rounds were kept in a basket. They included a combined ophthalmoscope-otoscope for examining eyes, ears, and nasal passages, an extra stethoscope, a blood pressure manometer, reflex hammer, and other paraphernalia for a neurological examination, plus a few special instruments used only on the ward in question. Picking up the basket on the way to Ross McKenzie's cubicle, Helga stepped inside and drew down the sheet, exposing the grower's chest, with the cardiac sensors attached to the skin.

Using the personal stethoscope she always carried in the pocket of her long white coat, Rebecca listened carefully over Ross McKenzie's chest. Then, moving around the electrodes attached to his skin, she tapped on his chest to percuss the outlines of his heart, marking them with a wax pencil upon the patient's skin. This finished, she carefully located the edges of his liver and his spleen below the lowest ribs on either side, marking them, too, with the wax pencil. Finally she took the ophthalmoscope from the basket and switched on its tiny light.

"Look at the ceiling, please," she told the patient. "I'm going to examine your eyes."

The inner lining of the eyeballs showed bright pink as Rebecca studied the pattern of the retinal arteries. They were tortuous from arteriosclerosis, as Ken had said, which didn't improve her temper any more than the fact, obvious even from her clinical examination, that Ross

McKenzie was unquestionably holding his own and probably gaining as well.

Helga pulled the sheet back up over the grower's chest when Rebecca finished. He'd been silent during the examination. Now he spoke and his words startled them all.

"Twelve hours ago, I would have said you'd be pulling that sheet up over my face for good before now," said the grower. "Think I can go home tomorrow, Doctor?"

"Not unless you want to commit suicide," said Rebecca dryly, but much of the brusqueness that had been in her voice when she came on the ward was gone. "You had a pretty close shave, Mr. McKenzie."

And so did I, she said—but not aloud.

"Don't you think I know that?" said McKenzie. "If that day-time nurse hadn't been on the ball this morning, I wouldn't be here."

"I'll see you in the morning," said Rebecca. "Good night, Mr. McKenzie."

"Good night, Doctor."

Kevin McCartney was sleeping soundly and a glance at the ECG tracing being recorded on the small bedside monitor told Rebecca all she needed to know about him. At the nursing station, she carefully studied the records Helga gave her on Ross McKenzie's progress, then turned to face the other two.

"You've just witnessed something that I hope never happens again," she said. "A woman doctor who almost allowed the woman in her to make a fool of the doctor."

Neither Helga nor Ed Vogel spoke, for there was nothing really to say.

"Are you going to tell him that?" Helga asked finally with a twinkle in her eye.

Rebecca smiled. "Not if you two don't."

"We women have to stand together," said Helga promptly, and two pairs of eyes were turned on Ed Vogel.

"You gave me my job, Dr. Dalton, and you could take it away," he said with a shrug. "What sort of a fool would I be to buck you?"

Ken Dalton came on the CICU about a half hour after Rebecca and Ed Vogel left. Helga was working at the nursing station as usual, when no critical emergency existed with any of the patients.

"How's Kevin?" he asked.

She answered by flicking a switch on the master console so the tracing of Kevin's heartbeat would appear on the large monitor screen.

"The voltage is holding up well," the surgeon observed. "Have you noticed any T-wave changes or arrhythmias lately?"

"Only very occasionally and then it's barely noticeable. He's been sleeping most of the evening."

"No point in bothering him then." When he hesitated, Helga answered the question which, she sensed, was foremost in his mind.

"Your wife left not over a half hour ago," she said.

"I suppose she examined Mr. McKenzie."

"She went over the whole case with Dr. Vogel—and Mr. McKenzie."

"He was awake then?"

"And asking to go home."

Ken Dalton laughed. "He's a tough one—thank God. Did she leave any further orders?"

"No, Doctor. But she made a note for the record. I punched it into the data storage bank right after she left."

Reaching across to the end of the console, Helga pressed the keys on the portable keyboard. The printed words appeared immediately on the data storage monitor screen, extracted from the infinitely complicated electronic channels of the main computer.

PATIENT IMPROVING, CONTINUATION OF PRESENT EXPECTANT MEDICAL TREATMENT INDICATED. R.D.

"Looks like you made a first down, Dr. Dalton," said the statuesque blonde nurse. "And I think you're going to win the game."

"You need your sleep, Mike—for tomorrow."

"Then promise me you'll ask one of the security guards to walk over to the Arms with you."

"All right. But I still don't—"

"I've got a whole weekend invested in you, woman—the most important weekend in my life."

"Go to bed, you big lug." Helga's voice was husky. "Before I start a hospital scandal by swooning in your arms like a love-sick schoolgirl—with that damned computer watching every move and recording it for posterity."

At the door, he paused. "The word's out that the God Committee turned your roommate down. Is she okay?"

"I haven't seen Carolyn since around five o'clock but she really didn't expect them to agree to her request. It was just something she had to get out of the way first."

"I can understand how she would feel the way she does," he said soberly. "But whatever she has decided, you're not going to be involved, are you?"

"Some things people have to do for themselves, Mike. I guess this is one of them."

V

The clock over the central switchboard showed five minutes to eleven and all through the tightly organized city-within-a-city women in white were busy with last-minute chores before going off duty. Except for the supervisors, who were giving reports to their night-shift counterparts, most of those going off were busy in the ward nurses' lounges, applying lipstick, combing hair, smoothing uniforms rumpled from bedside sitting or more active nursing care, quite conscious that, outside, husbands, sweethearts, and just hopeful male admirers waited for the exodus of dozens of young and old, a nylon brigade in retreat to mark the end of the afternoon shift.

At the main nursing station of the ICU unit, Mary Pearson, buxom, gray-haired and wise from long experience in the eleven-to-seven activities characterizing the vertical city that was Biscayne General, listened while

Helga recited the salient occurrences of the past eight hours.

"There goes the night!" she exclaimed when Helga told of Kevin McCartney's cessation.

"He seems to be a lot better. And so does Mr. McKenzie."

"Any time there's been a crisis like a cessation during the day, we're certain to have a bad night," said Mary. "Hearts will be skipping all over the place."

"I've noticed that too. Dr. Rebecca says she thinks it's because in the daytime, when they're fully conscious or even dozing, heart patients and other really sick people are subconsciously controlling the rate of their heartbeats."

"But when they go to sleep the control is lifted? Could be."

"I see a lot more heart rhythm changes on the monitors while people are sleeping than when they're awake," Helga added. "Sometimes it looks like all the tracings get St. Vitus' Dance and Dr. Rebecca says a lot of the people who die in the hospital for no apparent reason are killed by their nervous systems."

"Scared to death?"

"When they're asleep, they can't keep their circulations under conscious control. The result is a skittering heartbeat, followed by collapse of the circulation, and before we can get to 'em and start beating their chests, Bingo! They're gone."

Mary Pearson's eyes swept the bank of smaller monitor screens on which the ECG tracings of nearly a dozen critically ill patients were being constantly recorded.

"Who's tonight's candidate, would you say?" she asked.

"Nobody, I hope. If there's anything that bugs me, it's coming on duty and finding an empty bed that housed somebody I thought was making it okay the night before."

Mary Pearson glanced at the small monitor screen where Carmelita Sanchez' heart and temperature patterns were being recorded electronically.

"If what Mike Raburn is going to try is as chancy as it

262

sounds, you might just do that," she said. "Is it true that they're going to have TV cameras in the OR tomorrow watching the whole TBW?"

"That's the plan. If all goes well, you and your husband can watch on the six o'clock news."

"If it doesn't come on, I'll know Mike lost—and that's going to upset me a lot. I love that boy like I would my own son, if I had one."

"So do a lot of people around here," said Helga. "And not all of 'em as a son."

Mary Pearson gave the tall nurse a surprised look. "How long has this been going on?"

"Since yesterday afternoon at three o'clock. And don't tell me the real thing couldn't happen that fast, because I can hardly believe it myself."

VI

Kevin McCartney was awake when Mary Pearson made rounds about eleven-thirty.

"Where's Dr. Ken?" he asked. "I told Helga I wanted to see him tonight."

"You were asleep when Dr. Dalton made rounds. What did you want to see him for?"

"I'm getting over this crisis, ain't I?"

"Every sign we're monitoring says you are."

"Then I'm going to lay it on the line with him. He gave me a new lease on life by putting that girl's heart inside my chest. Now it's up to him to see that I keep going—if necessary with one of them plastic pumps he was working on for a while."

"I thought he'd stopped the artificial heart project."

"I'm going to insist that he start it again. He can't just operate on me once and save my life a second time, like he did this afternoon with that needle, then throw me aside like I was an old shoe. It's not ethical."

"Go back to sleep now," said Mary. "Dr. Dalton is helping Dr. Raburn with the Sanchez girl tomorrow morning but he's sure to make rounds after that's finished. You can tell him then."

"All right, slave driver. But be sure the alarm is set on

263

that monitor. I don't want my pulse to stop beating and nobody discover it until Carolyn Payson comes on duty in the morning."

"Don't look for her. She has the day off."

"And Helga's off for the weekend. Who's going to look after me the next few days?"

"You just finished telling me you're getting well."

Turn the little monitor around then, so I can see it and call you, if my heart quits. It's too much trouble trying to watch the reflection in that glass pane over the door."

"You mean you've been watching all the time?"

"I discovered I could see it right after I was admitted. When I saw the line flatten out with that cessation this afternoon, I only had time before I blacked out entirely to pray that somebody at the main panel would see it right away—or wait so long it couldn't be started again. The last thing I want is to be one of them human vegetables with a brain that's been cut off from oxygen too long. The next time I see that line flatten out, I'm going to use all the strength I've got left calling somebody before I go out. But between God hearing me in time to do something about it and Helga Sundberg, I'd rather take my chances with Helga."

VII

"Let's go back the long way, Gus, I haven't seen Miami Beach in ages." They had left the Polynesian restaurant and were waiting for the car to be brought from the parking lot.

"Sure, darling. This is your night."

Carolyn hardly spoke as they negotiated the miles of brilliantly lighted Collins Avenue southward to the Mac-Arthur Causeway, but he couldn't fail to notice that she was scanning the luxurious shops and hotels along the famous thoroughfare almost, it occurred to him, as if she were seeing them for the last time.

"I want to go home now," she said, settling back in the seat as he turned westward on the causeway toward Miami itself.

In the small apartment in Bayside Terrace, Carolyn

came into Gus's arms as soon as the door was closed. The desperate urgency with which she made love stirred an answering passion within him that demanded an explosive relief. When the first need had been sated, they lay close together in the half-darkness of the room, her body pressed against him as if she couldn't bear a moment's separation.

"You made love that time like you thought Congress was going to make it illegal, darling," he said.

"Did I shock you?"

"Surprised is a better word, like a child expecting one present who gets two."

"That's how much I love you."

She reached up to pull his head down so their lips could meet once more. And almost as soon as they touched, he felt her mouth grow avid beneath his own and her body start to move against him with the onset of passionate demand. It was after two when, exhausted, they finally drifted off to sleep, still in each other's arms.

Sometime during the night the whine of an ambulance siren pulling into the emergency entrance to the hospital, plus the pain where her head pressed against his arm, woke Gus. Carolyn didn't awaken when he moved slightly to ease the pain, but he could feel the dampness of her tears against his cheek where her face had been pressed.

He put her strangeness tonight down as an emotional reaction to the ordeal before the God Committee the previous afternoon and wished he could help her in some way other than the sharing of their bodies. But he couldn't—for even in her passion tonight he'd sensed that she'd been seeking something he hadn't been able to bring her.

Chapter 17

WHEN THE ALARM CLOCK jangled its strident summons a little before seven, Carolyn got out of bed at once.

"Snooze a few minutes more while I get a shower," she told Gus. "Then I'm going to fix you some breakfast."

"My cup runneth over," he said. "Are you all right?"

"Sure." She was opening the venetian blinds at the window that looked toward the hospital tower. "Why?"

"You cried sometime during the night."

"See you in a minute," she said, stepping into the bathroom.

Gus didn't obey her suggestion and go back to sleep, however. She'd given no explanation for weeping and obviously didn't intend to, but that didn't stop him from worrying.

She spent only a few minutes in the shower and, when she came out, pink and glowing, Gus thought he'd never seen anyone so beautiful. But as he started to get out of bed she quickly moved to a closet and pulled down a negligee.

"Wait till I get something on," she said.

"Leave it off and I'll go without breakfast."

"No, you don't. I've got a lot of running around to do today while I'm off duty, and you have early morning rounds with Dr. McHale on Thursdays. Go shave and shower while I get your breakfast."

It was ready by the time he finished dressing: orange juice, bacon, eggs, toast, and coffee, arranged on a small table before the window through which the sun was streaming. They sat at the table like any married couple, he thought with a sense of pleasure that left a lump in his throat, eating breakfast and watching the seven-thirty news.

"Will I see you today?" he asked as he was leaving about ten minutes to eight.

"I doubt it, I've got some things to do."

When she kissed him good-by, she held onto him for an instant with a grip that actually brought pain to his arm.

"Go to work now," she said, shoving him out the door. "We've got eternity before us."

Going quickly to the window, she stood watching until she saw his tall form cross from the apartment building to the hospital, stopping for a moment to get the morning paper from a vending machine, and turning to wave just before the automatic doors opening into the lobby moved apart for him.

As she waved back, Carolyn felt the tears she'd managed to control until then begin to flow. Nor did she make any attempt to stop them for a long time.

II

Ed Vogel was already on the CICU when Kenneth Dalton stopped by there about eight-fifteen, on the way from the staff cafeteria, where he'd had breakfast, to the operating room.

"You look bushed, Ed," he said. "Night off?"

"Night on, which is sometimes worse," said the Cardiology Fellow. "With that TBW coming up this morning, I figured Mike needed all the sleep he could get, so I took emergency calls."

"Rough, eh?"

"Mary Pearson told me once that, whenever there's a crisis during the day in any part of the ICU, hell is sure to break loose here at night. Now I know she's right."

"Any trouble with Kevin or Mr. McKenzie?"

"The really sick ones have been okay. McKenzie's stroke work index curve has been moving up steadily. Kevin's having soft diet for breakfast and griping because it isn't steak."

"That's good."

"But there have been arrhythmias all over the place, plus a coronary admitted at 3:00 A.M. that I had to start on heparin. By the way, Kevin's awfully anxious to see you about something."

Ken looked at his watch. "I've got about a half hour before I start scrubbing. Might as well see him now."

Kevin McCartney was sitting up in bed, eating soft-boiled eggs—with obvious distaste.

"What the hell have they got me on soft diet for, Dr. Dalton?" he asked. "I need a breakfast steak to combat all them cell-destroying drugs you're piping into me."

"Yesterday you were settling for five per cent glucose intravenously, and liking it."

"That was before you pulled me out of the grave and injected that Thiotepa around my heart."

"How did you learn about that?"

"Helga said if you hadn't gone to bat for me in a hurry yesterday afternoon I wouldn't be here."

"Did she tell you she started your heart before the CPR team could get here?"

"I figured that, when she said she was the one that pounded on my chest." Kevin put down the spoon with which he had been eating the eggs. "I told Helga to wake me if you came around last night, so I could pick a bone with you. But she was pretty busy, with that new catheter in Mr. McKenzie and all, so she probably forgot it."

"Do you want to tell me what's bothering you in five minutes right now? Or would you rather wait until I have more time? I have to scrub—"

"I know—with Mike Raburn for that Sanchez girl. Everybody's excited about it."

"Nothing's secret in a hospital."

"Including the fact that you psyched out your wife with that new catheter Dr. Vogel put into Mr. McKenzie and Dr. Reb was a bit miffed about it."

"You're using up time with hospital gossip, Kevin."

"I'll give it to you straight then, Doc. You've saved my life twice already so you probably don't have over one more chance left. I just want you to know that, the way I figure it, you've been layin' down on the job of looking after my future by not keeping on with that research you were doing on a plastic heart before everything started going to pot."

268

"I hadn't really proved anything, Kevin."

"Peggy Tyndall told me you were just about ready to put an atomic-powered artificial heart into a calf when you stopped the research about six months ago. What I want to know is when are you going to get back to work on that thing?"

"I've been thinking—"

"Thinking isn't enough; I've lost six months and maybe my third chance at living, while you were out of action. How about going to work again before it's too late?"

Ken gave Kevin an appraising look. "Did my wife ask you to put the bite on me, Kevin?"

"Absolutely not. I swear it."

"You may well be right about the artificial heart program. I'll see what I can do."

"You don't resent my saying it?"

"Nobody should resent hearing the truth, Kevin, even about himself. I guess in a way I *have* been pretty selfish, thinking only of my own feelings." Ken glanced at his watch. "I'll have to run. We'll talk about this again another time."

"Maybe over a bottle of Cold Duck soon—with Dr. Rebecca? I remember just how you like it and the way I feel now, I'll be back tending bar in a few days."

"You might be right—on both counts," Ken told him. "Who can tell?"

III

Peggy Tyndall was in Operating Room Two by eight-thirty, in a green scrub tunic and wearing cap and mask. She was fussing over the elaborate pump oxygenator setup when Hans Brokaw, the other pump technician, came in.

"Damnedest-looking gadget I ever saw." Hans was a German male nurse who had married an Army nurse during her tour of duty and emigrated to the United States when she returned. Trained by the manufacturer of the pump oxygenerator they were using, Hans was wholly without imagination and inclined to regard any modifica-

269

tion of the basic machine as heresy. "Think it will work?" he added.

"Of course it will work," said Peggy. "Get busy and help me cool this Ringer's solution."

Hans helped her pour crushed ice into a small tub and pile it around a large flask containing the solution that would take the place of Carmelita Sanchez' blood for the brief period during which the toxins of hepatitis would, hopefully, be washed out of her circulation.

"That Ringer's looks a little opalescent to me," he observed. "Are you sure you're using the right solution?"

"Dr. Raburn decided to add some albumin and heparin to it. We had to make up a fresh solution and sterilize it while you were off yesterday afternoon."

Hans Brokaw studied her for a moment, then shook his head in bafflement. "The way you're jumping around, you'd think you were performing this operation instead of Dr. Raburn, Peg. What have you got the ants about?"

"Guess you're right." Peggy controlled herself with a visible effort. "After I finished making the changes in the pump oxygenator yesterday afternoon, with Dr. LeMoyne and Dr. Raburn, I took some journal articles home with me last night to read up on TBW. And I discovered that this same method of inducing deep hypothermia is being used a lot in operating on children with congenital hearts while they're very smell."

"Dale having more trouble?"

"I can't be sure. But from what I read last night, it's possible to correct some of these mixed-up hearts in kids during the first weeks of life, by cooling their bodies the way Mike Raburn's going to do with this girl and operating on a stilled heart."

The other technician dumped more ice into the tub and piled it around the flask of Ringer's solution.

"You know what you're saying, don't you?" he asked.

"It's not Dr. Ken's faul—" Peggy said quickly. She stopped, then burst out, "Damn you, Hans. You trapped me."

He shrugged and went on with his work.

270

"One thing I did learn, though," she continued. "They're not real sure the technique works too well with tetralogy of Fallot, so maybe Dr. Ken is only playing it safe by trying to carry Dale until he's old enough to do the complete job with an open heart operation."

"You'll be better able to decide whether to ask for another consultation after you see how this case goes." Hans voiced the thought that was uppermost in Peg's mind. "I'd better check the temperature of the blood Dr. Raburn will be putting back into the patient's circulation —if she lasts that long."

IV

Mike Raburn had almost finished scrubbing when Ken Dalton came into the scrubroom adjoining Operating Room Two. The older surgeon was wearing operating pajamas and a cap and held a mask in his hand.

Operating Room Two was especially equipped with a full range of monitoring instruments, as well as a small adjoining laboratory where rapid blood gas and other tests could be performed. The very last word in operating theaters, the room was used for all heart and blood vessel surgery at Biscayne General. Tying on his mask, Ken moved to the door leading into the surgery itself.

"Looks more like a TV studio than an operating room, Mike," he observed.

"I don't particularly like it," Mike admitted. "But Dr. Toler is very anxious for this procedure to be publicized as widely as possible."

"If you bring this off, it should certainly improve the hospital's image—as well as yours."

"The first part I can see a reason for, the second makes no difference," said Mike. "Fortunately we'll be making only two incisions, neither of them very large or very deep, so we should be able to avoid infection, even with the increased possibility from the cameras and the extra people around."

"I wasn't being critical, Mike. It takes a lot of guts, as well as ingenuity, to try something as new as this. Good luck."

"Shall I go ahead and make the incisions while you're scrubbing?" Mike asked.

"This is your show. I'm just assisting."

"It's still a lot of comfort to me that we'll be working together, Dr. Dalton."

"Just how are you handling the TV side?" Picking up a sterile brush from a bowl filled with them on a shelf above the long sink that ran almost the length of the scrubroom, Ken started scrubbing his hands and forearms.

"The TV crew positioned the two cameras you see at the back of the OR on platforms. I wouldn't let them come any closer to the actual field. The highest one will be focused on the patient so the technique of the washout will be photographed at all times. The second camera is centered on the bank of monitors against the wall. Both of them of course will record on videotape."

"It's quite a setup."

"I added a timer, too—at Miss Weston's suggestion."

"Like the ones the TV cameras always show during a launch?"

"Yes. NASA flew one down here from the Kennedy Space Center yesterday afternoon."

"Then all you need now is Walter Cronkite." Ken's smile robbed the words of any sarcastic intent.

"I'm afraid I'll be a poor substitute." Noting Mike's tone, Ken gave him a sharp glance.

"All of us are a bit jittery the first time we have to do an entirely new operation, especially when it's liable to be touch and go," he said. "It's like the stage fright all good actors feel just before a performance; I've had them tell me that if they don't experience it they usually louse up the show. You'll be okay by the time the pump starts humming."

"I'd better be," said the younger surgeon. "Else you'll be doing the first TBW in the history of Biscayne General."

Through the open door to the operating theater, Ken glanced up at the packed gallery that allowed as many as two dozen observers to watch an operation closely, with no danger of contaminating the wound, while the action was described by the surgeon over the closed circuit sound and TV system with a microphone hanging around his neck beneath the gown. The closed circuit TV cameras also enabled the operation to be watched on large screens in the teaching amphitheater across the hall.

"You've got a full house, Mike," Ken observed as he turned back to the scrub basins, where Mike was soaking his hands in a large basin of antiseptic.

"Miss Weston will be in the gallery," said Mike. "I dictated sort of a script for her, so she'll know what's happening as we go along. She can fill in from time to time in addition to my own description—all on tape, of course. The sound will be recorded separately from the taped television picture and dubbed in this afternoon."

"Sounds complicated to me."

"Me too," said Mike. "But Miss Weston thinks there's a good chance that part of the procedure, at least, will go to the network—if everything turns out all right, of course."

Lifting his hands so the antiseptic ran down his forearms and dripped from his elbows, thereby removing the possibility of contaminating his scrubbed forearms from the unscrubbed area of his elbows and arms, Mike moved into the OR. Accepting a sterile towel from a waiting scrub nurse, he dried his hands and forearms carefully, then dropped the towel into a waste container before donning a sterile gown. Only moments longer were required to put on sterile gloves, while a circulating nurse was tying the strings of the pale green garment.

As Mike moved to the center of the room, where Carmelita lay with at least a dozen wires connecting the bank of monitor screens to the sensors Val LeMoyne had applied to her body, a "dirty" nurse, so named because she was not scrubbed, picked up the wire trailing behind him from the throat microphone he wore and plugged it into a jack on the floor connecting him to the gallery and amphitheater PA systems, as well as to the tape recorder brought by the TV crew.

Val LeMoyne sat at the head of the table, an anesthetic machine beside her. The hose from it ran to an intratracheal tube she had inserted through Carmelita's larynx into her windpipe to attain a closed system between her

273

lungs and the breathing bag of the anesthetic machine. The bag was emptying and filling in a regular, though somewhat hastened, rhythm and the respiratory rate was also being indicated by a small flashing light on one of the monitors.

"Did you have any trouble with the tracheal tube, Dr. LeMoyne?" Mike asked as he took the long forceps the nurse waiting at her small sterile instrument table handed him and dipped it into a sterile bowl of light brown antiseptic solution.

"The pharyngeal reflex was slightly active but a local anesthetic spray took care of that," said Val. "I don't want to give her any anesthetic unless I have to, so I'm carrying her on oxygen alone."

"I don't believe we'll need a general anesthetic," said Mike. "I'll infiltrate the skin with xylocaine before I make the incisions to put in the artery and vein catheters, just to make sure."

Across Carmelita's body Mike could see the heart-lung pump, with Peggy and Hans Brokaw, whose responsibility it was to operate the machine, busy making final adjustments. Unlike open heart surgery, where the pump must act as both heart and lungs for the patient while the heart was open and was therefore charged with donor blood, the pump reservoir now contained a solution that was almost as clear as water, except for the hint of opalescence caused by the small amount of albumin which had been added. A mixture of blood and packed red cells—obtained when the plasma was separated from donor blood—waited at one side, warmed and ready for the moment when the Total Body Washout was completed and replacement of the circulatory volume could be started.

As he began the familiar task of painting an area on Carmelita's groin with antiseptic in preparation for inserting two of the three cannulas that would connect her to the heart-lung machine, Mike lifted his eyes to the gallery. And he felt his tense nerves steady when he saw Helga, in the front row of seats across the glass-fronted gallery, lift her hand with thumb and forefinger joined in a salute of victory.

"The patient is a twenty-two-year-old laboratory technician who contracted Australian antigen hepatitis, ordinarily called serum hepatitis, while taking blood from a patient with this disease," he told the onlookers by way of the PA system. "She has become progressively worse during the past two weeks with a marked degree of jaundice, which the television audience may be able to see in the color picture as a deep ocher tint to her skin.

"Serum hepatitis is a far more serious illness than ordinary contagious hepatitis, which runs a predictable course, usually with complete, or near complete, recovery and the prognosis is consistently poor. We therefore advised this patient's family that an asanguineous hypothermic total body perfusion—more easily pronounced as Total Body Washout and further shortened usually to TBW —should be performed.

"Until recently TBW was an experimental procedure and only a small number of human cases have yet been treated with this method. It involves, as you will shortly see, the reduction of body temperature to a point where the ordinary life processes cease to be recorded on our monitoring systems, plus the removal of as much blood as possible from the entire circulation.

"With the toxin-containing blood removed, the circulatory system is then washed out with previously refrigerated Ringer's lactate solution containing sodium, potassium, calcium, chloride, and lactate ions in approximately the same concentrations that occur in the liquid portion of the blood called plasma, plus small amounts of heparin and albumin to prevent clotting. During the TBW Ringer's solution will actually subsitute for the patient's blood—a medical procedure known as perfusion—so you will hear us refer to the solution as the perfusate.

"The purpose of the entire procedure, of course, is to wash out of her blood vessels as much of the hepatitis antigen as possible, after which the circulation will be replenished with blood and packed red blood cells and the body warmed.

"The longest period so far recorded during which a living human body has been kept in what is essentially a state of suspended animation during TBW is nine minutes. Four minutes is generally considered to be the longest period that brain cells can ordinarily live without oxygen, but by dropping the entire body temperature, including the brain, to a very low level, the need for oxygen by all body cells is very much reduced. We still don't know whether it is safe to maintain a state of suspended animation longer than nine minutes, even with refrigeration, but we hope, of course, to accomplish our purpose in less than that time.

"Since the patient's heart will not be beating during that period and she will not be breathing, the heart-lung pump you see on Dr. LeMoyne's left will take over as soon as removal of the blood and lowering of body temperature begins. Needless to say, we will be watching the patient by every available sensor to observe her condition. But once the procedure is begun, it must be carried to completion as swiftly as possible, preferably in less than the nine-minute period already established, but certainly not more.

"You will note that Dr. LeMoyne has already inserted several small catheters into the patient's arm veins to measure blood gases and pressure, while we proceed with the TBW," Mike continued. "If you glance at the monitors on the wall, you will see representations of these parameters, along with the more familiar electrocardiographic and electroencephalographic tracings measuring the activity of the heart and the brain respectively.

"Prior to surgery, Dr. LeMoyne passed an electronic thermometer into the patient's esophagus and with it a tiny microphone that can pick up the heart sounds without interfering with our work. You can hear those sounds when she increased the volume on what is called the phonocardioscope."

Valeria LeMoyne moved a rheostat control on the panel beside her and the steady, though hurried, "lup-dup, lup-dup" of a normal heartbeat echoed from the speakers.

Dropping the ring forceps he had been using into a basin, Mike carefully placed sterile towels around the groin area where he planned to make the incision. Then taking the windowed sheet handed him by the instrument nurse, he gave one end to the interne across the table

276

from him, who had scrubbed earlier. When they opened the sheet, the rectangular window in its center fitted neatly over the area of skin left bare by the covering towels, while the drape covered the lower half of Carmelita's body.

Moving then to her neck, he painted an area just above the collarbone with antiseptic and draped it to make a small area there available for surgery, the two sterile sheets now covering her body completely. While the scrub nurse was moving the table containing the instruments and dressings into place cross Carmelita's sheet-covered form, Mike spoke again to the listeners in the gallery and the nearby surgical auditorium:

"Another electronic thermometer has been inserted into the lower part of the digestive tract, allowing us to watch very accurately the temperature inside the body itself, sometimes called the core temperature. When you hear the parameters being reported and see the temperature readings on the monitors, please remember that they are being registered on the Centigrade scale, where 0 degrees is freezing, 100 degrees is the boiling point of water, and the normal body temperature is roughly 37 degrees. When you consider that the temperature of the solution we will use to wash out the patient's circulation will be as near 5 degrees Centigrade as we can keep it, you will understand how rapidly her body temperature will be lowered during TBW."

While he talked, Mike had been injecting areas of skin in both the groin and lower neck with a local anesthetic solution. The injection completed, he handed the syringe to the scrub nurse and took the scalpel she gave him.

The bright lights of the operating theater were reflected from the thin, sharp blade, giving it almost the appearance of a flash of light as it moved swiftly across the groin for a distance of about four inches, laying open the skin and subcutaneous tissue down to the glistening white fibrous layer of the fascia enveloping the deeper muscles. Dropping into a basin the scalpel he had used for the incision, Mike began to clamp small bleeders in the fatty layer beneath the skin. Only the larger ones were tied off with fine catgut ligatures by the interne who was assisting him;

the rest would be closed by the pressure of the hemostatic forceps used to seal their mouths.

Into the incision Mike now inserted a self-retaining retractor, two rakelike arms separated by a ratchet device, spreading the edges open so he could get at the deeper structures. With curved scissors, he split the fascia downward from a round opening through which a fairly large vein emerged.

"The vessel you see is the great saphenous vein," he told the watching audience. "It will guide us to the femoral, which it joins at a deeper level."

Dissecting carefully now, he uncovered the femoral vein, a dark blue tube in the depths of the muscles. Slipping a curved hemostat beneath the vein, he gripped the end of a piece of narrow cloth tape the interne placed between its jaws and pulled the tape through, isolating the vein where it could easily be lifted up. A similar maneuver isolated the femoral artery, a whitish firm-walled tube about the size of his little finger lying beside the vein.

By the time Ken Dalton, now gowned and gloved as Mike was, moved into the position vacated by the interne at his approach, Mike was ready to insert the catheters through which Carmelita's blood would be removed. When they were in place inside the femoral artery and vein, Ken allowed the backflow of blood to fill them until it dripped from them, then clamped the outer ends. Meanwhile Mike had moved to the neck, exposing the jugular vein through a smaller incision, and placed a catheter inside it, clamping it off too, like the others.

Only a few moments were required to attach the outer ends of the three catheters to tubes leading to and from the heart-lung pump where Peggy Tyndall and Hans Brokaw were waiting. When it was finished, only the clamps shutting off the ends of the vein and artery catheters separated the girl's circulation from the heart-lung pump and the five-degrees-above-freezing Ringer's solution that would substitute for her blood during the long minutes of Total Body Washout.

"We have just finished connecting the patient to a standard heart-lung pump unit, such as is used in open heart surgery," Mike explained to the watchers. "You will note, however, that a side vent has been placed in the circuit from the femoral and jugular veins so the body can be drained of blood through it, while refrigerated Ringer's solution is pumped into the circulation through the femoral artery catheter. When the circulatory system is empty of blood, it will be flushed with Ringer's, then refilled with warmed blood. The heat exchanger you see between the roller-head pump that substitutes for the heart and the femoral artery catheter leading back into the circulation will further warm the replacement blood and with it increase body temperature."

He paused and glanced around the table, checking each item as he described it, then spoke to Val LeMoyne.

"Give us the preperfusion parameters, please."

On the monitor TV screen behind Val LeMoyne, a picture of the bank of dials and controls appeared.

"Hematocrit, 29 per cent," she read them off. "Esophageal temperature, 37 degrees Centigrade. Rectal temperature 37.4 degrees. Blood pressure, 120 over 75. Arterial pO_2, 150. pH, 7.34. Blood urea nitrogen, 70. Alkaline phosphate, 72. SGOT, 237. Perfusate temperature, 5 degrees Centigrade. Flow rate, 0."

"The patient's general condition is satisfactory," Mike summarized the findings. "The blood chemistry changes are what you would expect with an advanced case of impending hepatic failure."

He looked at Ken Dalton, who nodded without taking his eyes from the heart-lung pump. Moving swiftly then, Mike unclamped the three catheters.

"Open the side vent," he said.

Peggy quickly turned the stopcocks shutting off the tubes connected to the catheters and blood immediately began to flow from the open end into a container placed beneath it.

"Start the pump, please."

Hans Brokaw, whose duty it was to watch the vital machine at all times, pressed a switch and the roller-head pump hummed into action.

"Rate of flow, 3000 milliliters per minute." Mike's voice was even and controlled but the listeners could sense the underlying tension in it as, under the force of the pump, the flow of blood from the open side vent suddenly spurted and the pattern of the blood pressure tracing on one of the monitor screens began to trend downward.

The removal of poisoned blood from Carmelita's veins and arteries had begun.

Chapter 18

ED VOGEL hadn't missed Helga Sundberg's victory signal to Mike, as he slipped into a seat beside her on the front row of the gallery. Wearing slacks and a soft woolen sweater with a turtleneck, Helga was attracting almost as much attention from the largely male audience as the drama whose first act was just beginning on the stage of Operating Room Two below them.

"How long has this been going on?" he asked in a whisper.

"What?"

"You're as tense as a bride. Is it over Mike?"

She nodded but did not look up.

"Does he know it?"

She nodded again.

"Well I'll be damned," said the young cardiologist.

Mike's voice filled the gallery as he began to explain what he proposed to do, shutting off any answer Helga might have given.

"I never saw you dewy-eyed before," said Vogel in a tone of wonder. "It's positively nauseating."

"Shut up," Helga told him, without taking her eyes from the stocky form of the surgeon.

"You still didn't tell me how long this has been going on," Ed reminded her.

"Forty-two and a half hours, give or take a few minutes."

"I still don't believe it." Ed looked down at Mike, then back at the lovely blonde girl beside him. "Yeah, I guess I do," he admitted. "Does Mike know how lucky he is?"

"Not quite," said Helga. "But he will."

"Just be sure this time." The cardiologist's tone was dead serious. "Mike's not the kind that can take something special like you—or leave it. He's big but in a lot of ways he's like a little child—inclined to trust people and easily hurt when they turn out to be something less than he expects."

"Don't you think I'm as worried about that as you are?" said Helga.

"If you lead him on—and then drop him, I'll wring that beautiful neck with my own two hands."

"You won't have to. If this doesn't work out, I'll wring it myself." Helga looked up from the scene below and, as her eyes swept the gallery, stiffened suddenly.

"Miguel Quintera's on the back row, Ed," she said.

"The firl's fiancé?"

"Yes. He's only a first-year med student at the University of Madrid and, from the way he looks, this may be too much for him."

"Want me to take him out?"

"Not right now. But you can be ready in case he passes out."

II

Maria Alvarez, subbing for Carolyn Payson on the morning shift, was at the main ICU nursing station when Rebecca Dalton came into the ward shortly after nine-thirty to make rounds.

"Is this Miss Payson's day off?" Rebecca asked when she saw the plump Cuban nurse at the control station for the ward.

"Yes, and she really needed it," said Maria Alvarez. "I saw her right after the God Committee refused her request yesterday afternoon; she looked like she was taking it pretty hard."

281

"The committee decisions are supposed to be secret."

"If you can find a secret around here that isn't on the grapevine before it stops happening, I'll be surprised," said the nurse. "Sometimes everybody even knows what's going to happen before it really does. Would you believe there's a pool going right now on how long it will be before Carmelita wakes up?"

"But the TBW just began."

"Like I was just saying, Dr. Dalton, the grapevine is like the Shadow used to be on the radio a long time ago, it knows everything. But this time it's in the bag. Around here, Mike—Dr. Raburn—can do no wrong."

"I know," said Rebecca, but did not add that sometimes she couldn't help wishing she could say the same thing about herself. . . . "Could I have the chart on Mr. McKenzie?" she asked.

"Right here." The nurse handed Rebecca a bulky chart. On the front was the graph sheet upon which the night's readings of the cardiac stroke index calculations by the computer had been plotted earlier by Ed Vogel in preparation for Rebecca's morning visit. "He was asking for breakfast this morning."

In Ross McKenzie's cubicle, Rebecca listened to the grower's heart carefully, then percussed out its size. The measurements were somewhat smaller than the day before, when the heart had appeared to be dilating to accommodate the extra blood spurting through the incompetent mitral valve with each ventricular contraction. Nor was there any doubting that McKenzie had shown steady improvement in the some eighteen hours since Ed Vogel had inserted the remarkably versatile fiberoptic catheter into the right side of his heart and on into the pulmonary artery on Ken's orders.

"How much longer do I have to keep this damn tube in my arm, Dr. Dalton?" McKenzie demanded when Rebecca finished examining him.

"Probably another twenty-four hours. Dr. Kenneth Dalton will have to decide that."

"What the hell has he got to do with deciding how I'm to be treated? I'm your patient, not his."

"For your information, Mr. McKenzie," Rebecca said

evenly, "I was ready yesterday at noon to demand that you have open heart surgery, but Dr. Dalton didn't agree and had this special catheter put into your circulation instead. As late as last evening, I was still inclined toward surgery, but the new catheter is telling us more about your heart than we could possibly have learned in any other way."

"I could have told you I was better," McKenzie grumbled. "But nobody took the trouble to ask me."

"You could hardly have predicted twelve hours in advance what your heart action would be like. That's what this new instrument did."

"How much extra are these gadgets you're using going to cost me?"

"I don't have the least idea, Mr. McKenzie. But I can tell you it's a lot less than surgery would cost, and a lot safer."

"Just how much trouble am I going to have when I get out of here?" McKenzie asked.

"You'll be able to live a normal life—for a man of your age."

"Hell! I might as well be dead."

Rebecca laughed. "Maybe if you didn't stay mad all the time you wouldn't put such a strain on your heart, Mr. McKenzie. My assistant will get another ECG later this morning and I'll see you again this evening. Maybe tomorrow we can talk about taking the catheter out."

"Are you going to give me something to eat besides pap?"

"That's another area where you'll have to practice a little more moderation. The arteries in your eye grounds show quite a lot of hardening, so those of the heart have probably undergone much the same changes too. I'll give you detailed instructions about diet and several other things before you leave the hospital. We're going to want to check up on you about every three months, too."

"Damn nuisance," McKenzie muttered.

"I'll put you on a light diet for the time being," she promised. "But animal fat for you is a thing of the past."

Kevin McCartney was watching television, an old

Humphrey Bogart movie. He flicked it off with the remote control switch when Rebecca came into the room.

"Hi, Dr. Reb," he said. "How about me getting out of here?"

"All at once, everybody wants to leave. First Mr. McKenzie and now you."

"Don't let him go unless he agrees not to cut down the hospital budget. The fact that you just saved his life doesn't make any difference to that old goat."

"That would be blackmail—or something."

"I'm still glad he's had a chance to see what the taxpayers' money is spent for around here. Think it will change him any?"

"I doubt it," said Rebecca. "Besides, I almost flubbed his case. And we almost lost you, too, because I failed to realize how much the fluid in your pericardium was crippling your heart. Actually, you have Miss Sundberg to thank for your being here at all."

"I've already thanked her, me 'n' Helga are buddies. And I read the riot act to Dr. Ken, too, when he was in here early this morning."

"Why?"

"Because he almost let me down."

"You've been through enough rejection crises to know the only reason why you're coming out of this one so fast is because he injected antilymphocyte drugs into your pericardium yesterday after he removed the fluid."

"I give him credit for that," said Kevin. "But I told him I wasn't going to stand for him laying down on the job no more with that plastic heart project he used to work on. One of these days I may need that gimmick and I want him to have one ready by the time I do."

"I can understand that."

"I also told him he took on the job of keeping me alive when he put that girl's heart into my chest, so it's up to him to stay on the job."

Rebecca didn't ask the question that was foremost in her mind, because she was afraid of what the answer might be.

"He didn't promise me anything, just said he'd have to see about it," Kevin continued. "But I think he's going to start back on his research. And you know what that means, Dr. Reb?"

"Yes, Kevin." Rebecca's eyes were warm with appreciation—and with hope. "I do know."

III

"Increase the pump rate to 3500 milliliters a minute, please."

Mike Raburn's voice sounded loud in the stillness gripping those in the operating room and the observers in the gallery, as they watched the blood pouring out of Carmelita Sanchez' jugular and femoral veins and the flow of Ringer's solution into her body through the femoral artery. Already the blood spurting from the side vent draining the joint circuit of the two venous catheters was noticeably paler, as the Ringer's solution mixed with the remainder of the blood still inside the vessels.

"Parameters, please, Dr. Le Moyne?"

"Esophageal temperature, 30 degrees. Rectal, 32 degrees." Val LeMoyne's voice was calm. "Respiration, 20. Blood pressure, 100 over 70. Arterial pO_2, 100. Perfusate temp, 10 degrees."

"Everything seems to be going well," said Mike.

"Couldn't be better," Val agreed.

On the monitor screens the height of the ECG tracing was already sharply diminished and the voltage represented by the waves from the brain's action currents was also noticeably less than before the side vent had been opened and the blood tainted by the Au antigen of hepatitis allowed to leave her body.

"Time since pump activation, five minutes," Peggy Tyndall reported from her station at the pump oxygenator.

"You will notice that, as the toxin-containing blood is removed and replaced with the refrigerated perfusate, the indices of body metabolism represented by the ECG and EEG tracings are decreasing steadily," Mike said for the benefit of the television and gallery audience. "These indicate that our intended purpose of reducing metabolism and oxygen use by the body cells to as near zero as possible is being rapidly attained."

"Pulse, 160. Blood pressure, 90 over 60," Val LeMoyne reported. "Arterial pO_2, 70."

"The human body is a remarkably well-balanced machine," Mike continued, as if he were lecturing an audience of students. "When not enough oxygen is being received by the red blood cells, the heart rate increases in order to pump the blood through the circulation more rapidly. This accounts for the steadily increasing pulse rate, as the blood inside the vessels of the body is thinned by mixture with the perfusate solution."

On the monitor screens, the ECG had become so rapid in the past several minutes that the separate heartbeats could hardly be distinguished from each other and the tracing was now little more than a rapidly vibrating pinpoint of light. On the EEG tracing, too, the waves were so low that they could hardly be seen.

"As you can see from the monitors, the heart is now beating so rapidly and with such a low voltage in the action currents registered by the ECG tracing that it can almost be considered to have stopped," Mike continued. "The same is true of the brain's action currents recorded by the EEG on the monitor screen."

"Esophageal temperature, 25 degrees. Rectal, 26 degrees. Arterial pO_2 no longer measurable," Val LeMoyne reported. "Blood pressure cannot be obtained. Pulse cannot be counted."

"We are now approaching cardiac standstill known in medical terms as asystole." Mike's voice had taken on a somewhat strained note as the crucial period approached swiftly. "Since our time limit from standstill to replenishment of the circulation is nine minutes, time will be counted in half minutes from my signal. Those of you who can see the patient's face will note that it is quite pallid, indicating that almost no blood remains in her circulation. We will continue pumping the perfusate solution through the circulatory system after asystole, however, in an attempt to wash out the largest possible amount of the hepatitis antigen before replenishing the circulation with blood."

"Esophageal temperature, 20 degrees. Rectal, 22 degrees." The voice of the anesthesiologist was still calm, the only such in the room. "Patient is asystolic."

"Now!" said Mike tersely, and the counter began to tick off the seconds, while one camera watched it. "Pump speed, 4000."

The hum of the pump as the rate was increased and the click of the timer were almost the only sounds in the room. The breathing bag on the machine through which Val had been administering oxygen had long since stopped its motion, since the heart-lung pump had taken over not only the heart's function of pumping blood through the arteries and veins but also the task of oxygenating what blood remained in Carmelita's body by exposing it to an atmosphere with a high concentration of the gas before it was pumped back into the body. At the moment, however, the almost clear Ringer's solution substituting for blood could carry no oxygen.

"One half minute since asystole." The voice of the nurse watching the counter was high-pitched with tension.

"You will note now that there is practically no color to the perfusate being drained from the jugular and femoral veins," Mike pointed out to the audience, "indicating that we have already removed as much of the circulating blood as it is possible for us to remove. We will continue to pump the perfusate through the vessels a little while longer, however, in order to wash out all the toxins we can."

"One minute since asystole," the nurse announced.

"Parameters, please, Dr. LeMoyne?" Mike's tone was also tense.

"Esophageal temperature still 20 degrees. Rectal, 21 degrees." Val's voice was calm. "Arterial pO_2 and all other parameters not obtainable. This patient is clinically without metabolism. Early resuscitation advised."

IV

In the observation gallery looking down upon Operating Room Two only the low voice of Marcia Weston, the television reporter, intruded upon the tense silence, as she spoke into the microphone of a small tape recorder describing the scene below, while the TV cameras in the operating theater recorded the event on videotape:

"This is surely one of the most remarkable, and moving, moments this reporter has ever experienced," she was saying. "The patient upon the operating table now shows no sign of life and you just heard the anesthetist announce that metabolism is absent, the same thing as saying she is clinically dead. Actually the only thing about the patient even simulating life at this moment is the roller-pump of the heart-lung machine forcing a clear frigid solution through her blood vessels to wash the greatest possible amount of the hepatitis toxin from her body.

"As I watch, I cannot help asking myself whether any procedure that so remarkably simulates death isn't too dangerous to justify its use? And whether a clinically dead person can be resurrected, the only name that can rightly be given to what will happen here, if Carmelita Sanchez does indeed live again?"

At the back of the gallery, Miguel Quintera had been watching the scene below with growing apprehension and horror. Now a sudden sob of anguish drowned out the voice of the reporter as, stumbling to his feet, the young Cuban lurched from the gallery, the sound of his sobbing suddenly cut short when the door slammed behind him.

"Poor devil," said Ed Vogel. "Looks like it was too much for him."

"It's almost too much for me." Helga's voice was shaky. "Can you imagine what Mike is going through down there now, wondering where he can draw the line between possibly saving her from a liver death and damaging her brain cells beyond any return of consciousness, even if the hepatitis is cured?"

"I hope I never have to make such a choice." Ed Vogel's words were more of a prayer than a statement.

V

Miguel Quintera staggered through the door of the first-floor Coffee Shop and into an empty booth.

288

"Coffee!" he managed to gasp.

Seeing how pale he was, Maggie McCloud, who was working the morning shift for another waitress, quickly drew a cup, picking up a glass of ice water as she passed the tap on the way to the booth.

"Drink this," she commanded, and he gulped the scalding brew obediently.

"What happened?" she asked.

"Carmelita's dead!"

"On the operating table?"

"Yes. I was watching, but I had to leave."

"We've all been pulling for her," said Maggie sadly. "I'm so sorry. And Dr. Raburn worked so hard."

"He killed her." The Cuban's voice was shrill with hysteria from strain. "He drained all the blood from her body! Then he just stood there and watched her die."

Quintera buried his head in his arms and started sobbing again. But when Maggie tried to pat him on the shoulder in an instinctive gesture of sympathy, he shook off her hand angrily. Pushing his way out of the booth, he knocked over the glass of water and almost spilled what remained of the coffee.

"Dr. Raburn killed Carmelita!" he shouted as he lurched through the door that gave access to the garden outside.

A business office clerk, coming to the Coffee Shop for her morning break, heard the words and saw Miguel Quintera lurch from the shop.

"What's wrong with him, Maggie?" she asked.

"The Sanchez girl just died on the operating table. They're engaged and he was watching."

"My God! What a tough break!"

Death in one or another of its myriad forms was a constant dweller in a hospital, but none of its masks was so dreaded, so fraught with utter defeat, as death on the operating table. In the surgical theater, more even than on the Intensive Care Units, all the forces with which death could be fought were available, all needed expert help immediately at hand.

A highly trained anesthesiologist like Valerie LeMoyne was the ultimate expert in resuscitation. Surgeons with the experience of Mike Raburn and Ken Dalton were highly qualified to carry out such a dramatic procedure as opening the chest to massage the heart, although more recent techniques of resuscitation had made this desperate measure rarely necessary any more. And so the triumph of death over all the forces arrayed against it represented the ultimate defeat, particularly in one so young and so beautiful as Carmelita Sanchez.

Moving across the lobby, the clerk paused beside the desk of the hospital receptionist.

"Did you hear, Mrs. Peters?" she asked. "Carmelita Sanchez just died on the operating table."

"How do you know?"

"Her fiancé saw the whole thing. He just ran outside shouting that Dr. Raburn killed Carmelita."

"Poor things." The receptionist was gray-haired and a grandmother. "They're both so young."

The telephone on the receptionist's desk rang and she picked it up.

"Biscayne General—Patient Information, can I help you? Oh, it's you, Evelyn. No, I can't take my break yet. The Sanchez girl just died—on the operating table."

Dr. Jeffry Toler's secretary knocked softly on the door of the administrator's office before going in.

"The Sanchez girl just died on the operating table, Dr. Toler," she said when he looked up inquiringly from his desk. "I thought you'd want to know."

"When did it happen?" Jeffry Toler's shock at the news showed on his face.

"Just now, apparently. Mrs. Peters called from downstairs to tell me. The girl's fiancé just came down from the OR."

Toler reached for the telephone, then drew his hand away. "No use bothering Dr. Raburn and Dr. Dalton now. They'll be busy breaking the news to the relatives."

In the lobby downstairs, Mrs. Peters dialed an outside number and spoke into the phone softly, so she couldn't be heard in the rest of the room.

"I thought you could use the news, John," she said, "maybe between records. You know the Sanchez case, the one that's been on TV and in the newspapers the last day or two. Well, Dr. Raburn was doing a very dangerous operation on her, draining all her blood and replacing it and she just died on the operating table. No, I don't have any details, but I thought this would be a real scoop for you—son."

From the radio station Mrs. Peters had just called where her son was a disc jockey, the excited voice of the announcer broke into the music:

"We interrupt this program to bring you an exclusive bulletin. Most of Miami and much of the country has been waiting to hear the outcome of the daring surgical procedure being carried out this morning on Carmelita Sanchez, the Sleeping Beauty of Biscayne General Hospital. She has been in coma for several weeks with a severe form of hepatitis, and this morning doctors at the hospital resorted to a desperate measure in an attempt to save her, involving a new and largely untried surgical operation designed to wash the poisons of hepatitis from her body. Key to success was to be the critical period of nine minutes in which the patient was clinically dead, after which she would be revived by replacement of her blood volume with a fresh transfusion.

"What was hoped to be a gift of life for Carmelita Sanchez this morning turned out to be the grim stroke of death, however. Word has just come from a reliable source inside the hospital that she died a few moments ago on the operating table, while the desperate surgical operation was being attempted."

On the CICU, Maria Alvarez had answered the telephone moments before. Now she hung it up and looked bleakly at the console before her.

"Poor Carmelita," she said. "And poor Miguel. I guess I'd better wait for Dr. Raburn to tell the family."

No more than five minutes had elapsed since Miguel Quintera lurched from the observation gallery of Operating Room Two. Yet in that time the news had raced through the twenty floors of the hospital by the elaborate communications network known as the grapevine, from Dr. Jeffry Toler's office on the twentieth floor to the Pathology Laboratory in the basement, alerted there by a technician who had brought coffee for the morning break to Dr. Karen Fletcher and Dr. Sam Toyota and picked up the information from Maggie in the Coffee Shop en route.

Rebecca Dalton heard the news when she called the main laboratory to request a multi-lead ECG tracing on Ross McKenzie. Putting down the phone, she stared unseeingly at the framed certificate on the wall indicating that she was fully qualified as a specialist in cardiology. Ken had merely been backstopping Mike Raburn that morning, she knew, but he was present in the operating room during the TBW and must therefore accept some of the onus for the girl's death—in his own mind at least. And just when she had dared to hope he was on the point of regaining the confidence in himself he must possess if he were ever to go back into cardiac surgery and research.

"I'm going to OR Two, Ellen," she told her secretary.

"It's tough luck for Dr. Dalton and Mike—Dr. Raburn," said the secretary.

Rebecca stopped short. "Were you listening to my telephone conversation, Ellen?"

"Oh no, Doctor," said the secretary, somewhat intimidated by the note of coolness in Rebecca's voice. "I got it about two minutes ago, when the record librarian brought up some charts for you to sign."

"And you didn't tell me?"

"I guess I did wrong, Dr. Dalton," said the girl. "But it *was* bad news and I thought—"

"I know what you thought, Ellen—and why. But I would have heard about it soon anyway."

When she came into the observation gallery above OR Two and looked down upon the scene below her, Rebecca frowned. Carmelita certainly could be dead, judging from the pallor that marked the skin of her face, the only part of her body Rebecca could see. But none of the activity in the operating theater faintly resembled the sort of frenzied order that usually characterized a last-ditch attempt to bring life back to a seemingly dead body.

Moving down the steps to where Ed Vogel and Helga Sundberg sat watching the scene below intently, Rebecca took a seat on the row behind them made available by a student who recognized her.

"What's happening?" she asked in a whisper.

"They're getting ready to recharge the pump with blood and packed red cells," said Ed Vogel. "Want to come down here?"

"No. I'm fine here. Is everything going okay?"

"Like a Swiss watch." Ed turned and, seeing Rebecca's face, asked quickly, "Is anything wrong?"

"Somebody started a rumor that the girl died on the operating table. I even heard it on a patient's radio set on the way here."

"Miguel!" Helga exclaimed.

"Who's that?"

"Carmelita's fiancé—a first-year medical student at the University of Madrid. He was here at the beginning of the TBW, and I could see that he was quite disturbed. When Mike—Dr. Raburn—drained out all the blood just now and Miguel saw only the Ringer's solution going through the heart-lung pump, with no heartbeat and no other sign of life, I guess he panicked. Anyway, he ran out."

"You never saw anything like the way the story that she died on the table has traveled," said Rebecca. "It's all over town by now, from the radio broadcast."

"Excuse me, Dr. Dalton." It was Marcia Weston, the TV reporter. "Did you say you heard a broadcast on the radio saying Carmelita was dead?"

"Just a few moments ago."

"Do you know what station?"

"No. I was passing a patient's room on the way here and the radio was on."

The reporter looked anxiously at her watch, then down at the scene in the operating room.

"This is the climax of the TBW," she said. "I'd give

anything to be able to warn my own newsroom, but I can't leave here now."

"Neither can I," said Rebecca. "Give me a rundown on what's happened so far, Ed."

Chapter 19

"FIVE MINUTES since asystole." The nurse's voice was a little unsteady as she read the figures on the steadily ticking clock.

"Esophageal temperature, 20 degrees. Rectal, 21 degrees." Val LeMoyne's voice was still calm as that of a highly trained anesthesiologist should be in a grave emergency. "No other parameters obtainable."

"Perfusate clear, pump rate, 4000 milliliters per minute." Peggy Tyndall looked at Mike and had all she could do to keep from urging him to start returning blood to Carmelita's circulation.

"Blood and packed red cells ready?" Mike asked quietly.

"Yes, Doctor," said the operating supervisor, a tall nurse whose nerves were like steel from weathering many crises.

"Oxygenation tank—"

"Ready. Oxygen, 95 per cent. CO_2, 5 per cent."

"Five and one half minutes since asystole," the nurse reported.

"Don't push your luck, Mike," Ken Dalton said softly, and the younger surgeon nodded.

"Clamp the femoral artery catheter, please, Dr. Dalton," he said, and Ken quickly closed off the catheter through which the almost freezing-cold Ringer's solution had been pumped into Carmelita's circulation.

"Open side vent to drain system," said Mike.

Peggy moved quickly to obey and, with the pump still

running but no more of the perfusate being forced into Carmelita's circulatory system, an almost clear stream began to spurt from the side vent of the system. The level of perfusate in the pump reservoir diminished rapidly as it was emptied through the vent and in a few seconds the flow of Ringer's solution from it became a mere trickle, indicating that the pump reservoir had been emptied.

"Pump off!" said Mike.

"Pump off," Peggy verified as Hans Brokaw threw the switch.

"Recharge system with blood and packed cell mixture."

Peggy and Hans Brokaw worked rapidly and efficiently together, as a highly trained team should, pouring the warm mixture of two parts transfused blood to one part of packed cells in plasma into the pump reservoir.

"Start pump, 3000 milliliters," said Mike. "Leave side vent open."

"Seven minutes since asystole," the nurse watching the timer reported, as the pump started humming and blood started flowing from the open side vent. Mike did not order it closed immediately, however, for bubbles could be seen in the stream of flow.

"We are allowing oxygen and CO_2 to be removed from the tubing in order to prevent embolism," he explained to the audience, watching the flow from the side vent closely as he spoke.

"Unclamp the femoral catheter," he ordered when the flow of blood had cleared and no more bubbles could be seen.

"We are now starting to refill the patient's circulatory system with a fresh mixture of blood and red cells," he told the audience as the color visible through the walls of the catheter in the femoral artery darkened, indicating that blood was flowing through it.

"Heat exchanger on," Mike ordered before speaking again to the audience:

"The rate of oxygenation of this blood will be kept as high as possible, so as to provide an oxygen-rich supply to the body tissues which have been without oxygen now for about nine minutes," he said then. "With luck, most of the Au antigen of viral hepatitis was removed with the blood drained from her circulation plus the further washing out of the entire circulatory system with refrigerated Ringer's solution. The rapidity with which she awakens from coma, possibly as early as twelve hours from now, will tell us how successful we have been.

"You will note, too, that with the blood being warmed as it flows into the body, the technicians are now adjusting the rate of flow through the pump about 2500 milliliters per minute. This level will be maintained during the rest of the procedure, since it closely approximates the normal output of the human heart."

"Esophageal temperature, 30 degrees. Rectal, 31 degrees," Val LeMoyne reported "Arterial pO_2, 50 and rising."

There was silence as the pump hummed, sending blood circulating through Carmelita's body, then Mike spoke again:

"By adding 5 per cent CO_2 to the 95 per cent oxygen concentration in the pump chamber, we hope to stimulate spontaneous respiration and, of course, a beginning of heart function as quickly as possible."

"Esophageal temperature, 32 degrees. Rectal, 33 degrees," said Val. "pO_2, 68."

"Flow rate, 2900," the technician at the pump reported.

"Step up the heat exchange rate a little, please," said Mike.

"Nine minutes since asystole," the nurse at the clock reported.

All eyes in the room and the gallery were now centered upon the ECG monitor. Only a moving pinpoint of light traveled across the ground glass of the screen, but the watchers knew the entire success of the procedure depended upon whether or not the heart would resume its spontaneous beat under the influence of the warming of the blood and the steadily rising oxygen tension in the arteries.

"pO_2, 90 millimeters," Val reported. "Urine excretion resumed."

"That's the best sign we've had so far," said Mike in a

tone of deep satisfaction. "It means that the kidneys withstood the lowered temperature. Now if the ECG and the EEG come through on time, we'll be okay."

The electroencephalographic tracing had shown no sign yet of brain waves. But as those gathered around the operating table and in the gallery watched—plus the crowded surgical auditorium where everything that happened was being reproduced upon the teaching monitors of the closed circuit TV receivers—the spot of light indicating heart action suddenly darted upward in an attempt to form the QRS complex that was the center of every heartbeat pictured on the screen.

"It's trying to start," said Val.

"We may have to use the pacemaker, sir," Mike told Ken Dalton. "Would you drop out and take charge of it?"

"Certainly." Moving to the other side of the patient, Ken picked up the electrodes used to apply an electrical stimulation to a balky heart or, by switching to the defibrillator current, still an unruly one.

"Spontaneous respiration established," said Val LeMoyne as the light on the small screen monitoring respiration started to blink. At the same instant a corresponding wave appeared upon the ground-glass face of the screen in the respiratory channel.

"Say when," said Ken. "We're ready."

"Hold a second more, please. The pump seems to be handling heart function very well."

As if to corroborate his words, Val reported: "Arterial pO_2, 90 millimeters and rising."

The dancing pinpoint of light suddenly darted up, down, and up, forming a QRS pattern. On the heels of that contraction came another, this time preceded by the small P-wave signifying contraction of the auricles and the begining of a full heartbeat cycle.

"Cardiac function resumed." Nobody could mistake the joyous note in Val LeMoyne's voice now and a somewhat shaky laugh ran through both the operating room and the gallery.

"Congratulations, Mike," said Ken. "You made it."

"We all made it," said the younger surgeon. "If there ever was a team play, this was it."

II

In the gallery, Marcia Weston moved toward the door.

"Can anybody tell me where's the nearest outside phone?" she asked.

"Tell the nurse in charge of the floor nursing station just outside that I said you could use the inside phones, Miss Weston," Rebecca Dalton answered. "Dail 9 for outside."

"Thank you, Doctor." The TV reporter disappeared through the door.

"Mike's over the first hurdle," said Ed Vogel as he, Helga and Rebecca were leaving the gallery. "The next will be to see whether the girl regains consciousness."

Rebecca stopped at the ward nursing station to make sure Marcia Weston had been able to get an outside line.

Ed Vogel looked at his watch and whistled. "Can you believe it's only nine-thirty? I could have sworn that TBW took an hour instead of nine minutes."

"It was the longest nine minutes in my life," said Helga. "And I'm sure in Mike's."

III

From the operating room, Ken Dalton took the elevator down to the CICU. Maria Alvarez was at the central console.

"Kevin's SGOT is still elevated some, Dr. Dalton," she reported. "But Mr. McKenzie's is almost back to normal. Here are the latest lab reports."

Ken studied the laboratory report sheets and the last multi-lead ECGs that reported on the heart from several angles, registering a picture of its action in sections, so to speak.

"Looks like they're both pretty close to being out of the woods," he agreed. "Has my wife seen these?"

Maria noted the absence of hesitation when he spoke

the word "'wife'"; it was the first time in many months that he'd failed to stumble over the word when he happened to mention it.

"Not yet," she said. "It's a shame about Carmelita, isn't it?"

"What do you mean?"

"It's been all over the hospital that she died on the table about ten minutes ago."

Ken stared at her blankly. "Whatever gave you that idea?"

"Maggie in the Coffee Shop said the girl's fiancé told her. He was there." A look of horror came over the nurse's face. "You mean she didn't . . . ?"

"The patient was doing very well when I left the operating room less than ten minutes ago."

"Oh, my God! Mrs. Peters at the reception desk is telling it all over the hospital. And it's on the radio, too."

"How could that happen?"

"Mrs. Peters told me once that her son's a disc jockey on a local radio station."

"I'd better warn Mike." Ken Dalton reached for the telephone. "He'll want to talk to the family immediately and assure them the girl's okay."

Valerie LeMoyne answered the telephone in the operating room. "Mike's gone down to the first floor to talk to the girl's parents, Ken," she said.

"How is she?"

"Fine. All the parameters are returning to normal, some more slowly than others, of course."

"Did you know that for the past ten minutes or so the whole hospital and half of Miami has believed the girl was dead?"

"What?"

"It was even broadcast over the radio."

"That's the weirdest thing I ever heard of."

"Well, if Mike's talking to the family he probably knows about it too, by now. Thanks, Val."

"Where's Carmelita's family?" Mike asked Maria Alvarez.

"They're not in the ICU waiting room?"

"No."

"They must have gone to the main waiting room. Or maybe out in the garden. They were pretty up—"

Mike was already through the door leading to the main lobby and the gardens so he didn't hear the last two words. He had no trouble finding the Sanchez family, however. The furious babble of Spanish and the sound of sobbing coming from the center of the garden told him where they were.

He was halfway across the open space around the fish pool when Miguel Quintera saw him. Leaving the others, Miguel ran toward Mike, who just had time to throw up a hand and set himself against the unexpected attack, when the younger man piled into him, flailing with his fists and sobbing.

"Murderer!" the Cuban shouted. "You killed Carmelita."

Mike held the slight Cuban off as best he could without actually striking him, for Quintera was much lighter and shorter than he, the while he looked for the familiar face of Mr. Sanchez to bring some order out of the melee. Then he saw the priest sitting on a bench talking to Mrs. Sanchez, whose head was bowed.

"Father Junípero!" he called. "Get this madman away from me."

The priest moved then and Mr. Sanchez, too, appeared, accompanied by a gray-haired man with a clipped mustache. Together they pulled the young Cuban away, still shouting, "Murderer!"

"Will somebody tell me what's going on here?" Mike snapped.

"Dr. Raburn!" Father Junípero's voice was sharp. "You have no reason to speak like that to grieving relatives."

"Grieving?" Mike was thoroughly irritated now. "What kind of people are you anyway?"

"It would be more appropriate for me to ask you that, Doctor." The priest's voice was icy.

Mike shook his head, baffled and angered by behavior he couldn't understand.

"The minute I could leave the operating room, Father, I came down to tell Carmelita's family she came through the procedure in excellent condition. And I get attacked by this young man—"

"You mean she's still alive?" The priest's tone was incredulous.

"I just finished telling you Carmelita came through in excellent condition. Of course she won't be conscious for—" Mike stopped, a partial comprehension of what had happened starting to dawn upon him. "You mean you thought . . . ?"

"The family were told Carmelita died on the operating table. It was even broadcast—"

"Nobody but the doctor in charge has the authority to tell a patient's family that. Who did it?"

For a moment there was silence.

"It was I," Miguel said brokenly. Then he broke into a torrent of Spanish Mike couldn't understand.

Señor Sanchez translated.

"Miguel says he saw you drain the blood from Carmelita's body," Sanchez explained, "and when her heart and her breathing stopped, she was dead."

"Where did he see all this?" Mike demanded.

"I am a student of medicine at the University of Madrid." Miguel Quintera was speaking English again. "One of the internes at the hospital directed me to the gallery of the operating room."

"Mr. Sanchez," said Mike, "I explained to you yesterday how we would drain the blood from your daughter's circulation and wash out her heart and blood vessels with saline before putting in fresh blood. I thought you understood."

"It seems we have all done you an injustice, Dr. Raburn," said Father Junípero. "I hope you will be charitable and forgive us."

"It was on the radio," said Señor Sanchez. "Are you sure Carmelita will get well now, Dr. Raburn?"

"Her chances are at least a hundred times better than they were two hours ago."

"When can I see her?" young Quintera asked.

"I'm going to keep her in the recovery room on the operating-room floor for several hours, so Dr. LeMoyne can watch her," said Mike. "But she should be back in her room on the Intensive Care Section by midafternoon."

"Thank you, Dr. Raburn, for saving my daughter's life," said Mr. Sanchez. "I'm sorry we caused you so much trouble. It was all a mistake, thank God."

"*You* suffered because of it, not me," said Mike. "Why don't you all have some coffee or something in the Coffee Shop? Just keep the receptionist informed as to where you'll be."

V

Peggy Tyndall and Ed Vogel were busy when Rebecca Dalton came into the Cardiac Research Laboratory shortly before noon. Spread out on a long laboratory table was an assortment of odd-looking pieces of apparatus, much of it plastic in various shapes.

"Looks like you've been cleaning out the storage closet," said Rebecca. "Why all the sudden activity?"

"Dr. Dalton called me right after the Sanchez operation," Ed explained. "He wants us to start working right away on that plastic heart."

"The one he thought of implanting in a calf?" Rebecca felt a sudden surge of excitement and hope.

"He's stopped thinking about it and is going ahead. Wants the first one ready next week so he can put it in before he leaves for Paris." Vogel looked at her questioningly. "When did he decide that?"

"There's a transplant patient in France who's still living five years after the operation." Rebecca was careful to keep the exultation she felt out of her voice, not wanting the others to know Ken's sudden decision was as much of a surprise to her as it had been to them.

Or was it? she asked herself. She'd never admit—to him—that Ken was right, of course, about the way she had been gently nudging him toward a renewal of his very promising experimental work. And his decision to resume it could actually be a result of Kevin's bald reminder that Ken was now responsible for his life, a final stimulus that had carried him over the barrier represented by the failure of the other transplants. But whatever the cause, he seemed on the point of going back to work again, the first and most important step toward the resumption of their marriage.

"Dr. Rebecca Dalton, 275." The voice of the paging operator poured from a loudspeaker. "Dr. Rebecca Dalton, 275."

"That's his number," said Peggy. "I forgot to tell you he said he would call you as soon as he could."

Rebecca dialed the extension and Ken himself answered.

"I'm in the Research Lab," she said.

"That's what I wanted to talk to you about, Reb. Would you have time to look over that last experimental work we did and give me an opinion on its present status?"

"Certainly. I remember most of it, Peggy and Ed can fill me in on the rest."

"I've got to work in the PDC this afternoon and Jeffry has called a meeting of the Executive Committee for five o'clock. I could meet you in the cafeteria at six, though, unless you have other plans."

"I don't have any other plans," said Rebecca. "I hear you're going to be traveling."

"I want to talk to you about that, too. Six o'clock?"

"Right. 'By."

As she was hanging up the telephone, Rebecca saw Peggy looking at her with a speculative light in her eyes. But when she turned back to the table where the tiny physician's assistant and Ed Vogel were working, their attention was once more directed to the apparatus scattered before them.

"Get me the data on that last experiment we did with the plastic pump, Peggy," said Rebecca. "Dr. Dalton wants me to look over it and give him an opinion tonight at dinner."

"Right," said Peggy happily. "I can tell you one person who'll be glad to hear about this, too—Kevin McCartney."

"He may be responsible for its getting started again."

"I know," said Peggy. "I practically had to break Kevin's arm to make him tell Dr. Ken that it was up to him now to keep him living, but he must have come through."

"Kevin told me about it this morning but not that you had put him up to it."

"Never underestimate the power of women when they put their heads together." Ed Vogel chuckled. "Especially women in white—God bless their conniving little souls."

VI

By one o'clock that afternoon all parameters being recorded on Carmelita Sanchez were approaching the normal range and Val LeMoyne allowed her to be wheeled from the recovery room on the surgical floor to her own cubicle on the ICU. Val was still busy with the heavy OR schedule so Mike came up from Emergency, where he had been busy since completing the TBW, to watch the transition.

"It's hard to believe she's the same person," said Maria Alvarez, as they were attaching the sensors to the girl's body. "If there ever was a medical miracle, this is one."

"The bilirubin level in her blood has dropped from 31 to 3 since early this morning," said Mike.

"You can almost see the jaundice decreasing," the nurse agreed. "Did Miguel Quintera really attack you, Dr. Raburn?"

"He tried, but I suppose it was a natural mistake for anyone as worked up as he was. I don't mind admitting I was pretty tight inside myself during those nine minutes."

"I was talking to Helga at lunch. She said it was the most exciting thing she ever saw."

"If Helga was excited, it must have been something." Mike straightened up from attaching a sensor and pulled the sheet up across Carmelita's breast. "I don't think we can expect her to become conscious in much less than twelve hours, but please make a note that I'm to be called if Carmelita shows the slightest sign. I'm going through PICU to see about Joey Gates and after that I'll be in the Emergency Department all afternoon."

Rachel Gates was sitting in Joey's cubicle. The boy was sleeping quietly but she looked haggard and rather worn.

"You look like you could use a shot of Java," said Mike. "Shall I get it, or will you be my guest?"

When she looked hesitantly at the boy, he added, "Joey's doing fine, I just checked his record."

"Okay," said Rachel. "If you don't mind having coffee with a member of an oppressed minority."

"You're the wife of one of the finest athletes this country has ever produced," he said. "I'm the one who's honored."

"You wouldn't think so if you read the morning paper."

"I missed it this morning." Mike waited for her to slide into an empty booth in the Coffee Shop, then took the opposite seat himself. "Had other things on my mind."

"So I heard. They're after Joe again, Mike—in full cry."

"He asked for it, you know—by taking up the cause of less famous athletes."

"But I'm sure Joe never thought the owners and the media would be this vicious."

"Nothing is more vicious than a man with money who thinks somebody else is trying to take it away from him. But if somebody doesn't stand up for the rights of the little man, the way Joe is standing up for the other players, the guys with the monopolies will have everything their way."

"That's what Joe says. I guess he could have stood that all right, too, if Joey hadn't gotten sick."

"Joey's out of the woods as far as this attack is concerned, Rachel. And from all the evidence we have now about sickle cell anemia, Joey may never have another crisis, if you keep up the medication Dr. Henderson will prescribe."

"It's not just that, Mike. Joe's scared stiff that he has the sickling trait, too."

"I can settle that question quickly enough. Have him come by and I'll take some blood."

"He isn't going to do it, at least not now."

"Why not?"

"You know how it is when people develop a fear of something, Mike; they don't think rationally any more. Joe knows that if he does have the sickling trait no basketball team in the country would hire him, for fear he'd have one of those cramps in the legs like I—"

She stopped but not before Mike was alerted by something in her voice.

"How bad are the ones you're having, Rachel?"

"What's the use of trying to fool you?" She shrugged. "I've had them for a long time, but I didn't have any idea what it was, until you did the test the other night and found sickling. I'm not worried about myself, though; it's that guy I'm married to that's driving me crazy."

"You still can't afford to take a chance, Rachel. I'll get Gus Henderson to figure out the dosage of potassium cyanate you need for your weight and you can start on it tonight. Did you tell Joe your test was positive?"

She nodded. "I thought it might help him but it only made things worse. I tell you, Mike, Joe's scared absolutely stiff over this thing. He knows ninety-nine per cent of the people with sickle cell anemia are black, so he won't have the test because he's sure it will be positive and that will be the end of his career."

"Don't sweat this so much." Mike put his hand over hers and gently uncurled her fingers, which were clenched. "The important thing is that Joey's safe and you'll be too, as soon as we get the medication started. How much do you weigh?"

"A hundred and thirty-four."

"I'll get the prescription filled for you and bring it up to Joey's cubicle. We'll get the blood for Big Joe's test somehow, too, if I have to slug him and take it while he's unconscious."

306

"That will be the day, even for somebody as big as you." But she could laugh, which was what he wanted.

VII

Gus Henderson came to the main ICU nursing station as soon as Helga Sundberg finished taking the afternoon shift report from Maria Alvarez; it was five minutes past three.

"Seen Carolyn today?" he asked.

"Just for a few minutes when I went to the apartment about eight-thirty to dress before I came to watch Mike do the TBW." Helga's tone was casual. "She said she had some errands to run. Why?"

"I figured she would probably come by to see her father and left word with Mrs. Alvarez to call me," said the pediatrician.

"Carolyn's probably shopping. With only one day off a week, plus the time she spends with her father, a lot can accumulate that needs to be done."

"I'm worried about her, Helga. She didn't seem to be herself when I left her this morning."

"The God Committee meeting yesterday afternoon was bound to upset her. Give her time, Gus."

"Do you think she'll come to the hospital for dinner?"

"Would you eat in a hospital cafeteria if you had a chance to eat out somewhere?"

"I guess not, but I can't help being worried about Carolyn. If she does come over to see her father, be sure to call me."

"Of course," said Helga soothingly. "And don't worry."

When Gus Henderson left the section, Helga started on her rounds. Her first stop was the cubicle where Carmelita Sanchez lay sleeping. Miguel Quintera was sitting beside the bed, but rose when the tall nurse came into the small room.

"This morning I made a fool of myself, Miss Sundberg," he said. "Dr. Raburn should have slugged me."

307

"He's a very gentle man, Miguel, and a very fine surgeon."

"I know that. But when I saw Carmelita lying there, with no life, I guess I went—"

"Berserk?"

He nodded. "I felt so helpless that I was like a child who flails out at those who would help."

"You must love her very much," Helga said gently.

The anxiety and embarrassment were suddenly erased from the young Cuban's face by a warm smile. "You cannot know—"

"I think I do." Helga's voice was soft for an instant, then once again became conversational. "Have you two been engaged very long?"

"Since we were children. I wanted us to be married before I left for medical school in Spain. But Carmelita said I would need to think only of my studies so I would make high grades and do well on the examinations I will have to take before coming back to the United States as a doctor."

"I've seen a lot of fine doctors who were trained in foreign medical schools. And I understand that the University of Madrid is one of the best."

"It is rated so. But I'm not going to leave Carmelita behind when I go back this time."

"It may still be months before she'll be well enough to travel."

"Then I will stay out of medical school a year and work here, perhaps as an attendant."

"Even then, she may not be entirely well for a long time."

"I will look after her. I almost lost her this time and I will never let us be separated again."

"You are both very young, and very much in love." Helga's voice was warm. "Don't let anything—or anyone—ever take that from you."

Chapter 20

SHORTLY AFTER four o'clock the telephone rang in Val
LeMoyne's office in the surgical suite. It was Karen
Fletcher.

"Do you have a few minutes, Val?" the pathologist
asked.

"Sure. What's on your mind?"

"I'll tell you when I get there. Five minutes?"

"Whenever you say. I'm through for the day—with
luck."

Karen arrived in four minutes, and shut the door of the
office behind her when she came in.

"I hear you and Mike Raburn covered yourselves with
glory this morning," she said.

"It was a team effort, Mike said so himself."

"I guess I've missed something by going into pathology.
Nobody in a morgue ever talks back."

"Have you ever regretted the choice?"

Karen shook her head. "There aren't many women
pathologists in the country."

"And even fewer who are board-certified in forensic
pathology," Val observed, and Karen gave her a startled
look.

"How did you know that?"

"I'm on the Faculty Personnel Committee as well as the
Subcommittee on Faculty Promotions—or didn't you
know?"

"As a matter of fact, I did." Karen decided to come
directly to the point. "Which is why I came to see you."

"If you knew I was on the subcommittee, you must
have known that Jerry Singleton is the chairman."

"I did."

"Then was it a good idea to tear into Jerry the way you did at the surgical Tissue Conference yesterday?"

"It must have been." Karen smiled. "He came to see me last night."

Val studied her for a moment, then nodded slowly and somewhat admiringly.

"In other words, you took a calculated risk and it paid off."

"It will, I think. Do you blame me?"

"No. I guess when you come down to it we're somewhat alike, Karen. We both know our business and what we're worth—"

"And we intend to get everything we'e entitled to out of it," Karen completed the sentence. "Except, I think, that you have principles and I don't."

"I suspect you have more than you've admitted—at least where medicine is concerned."

"I don't mix my personal life with my professional life any more than you do," Karen said with a shrug. "Except, of course, where the two seem to coincide, as they do now. You've already gotten where you want to be, Val—a full professorship and head of your own department."

"I saw Adrian Cooper in Rebecca Dalton's PDC clinic the other day," said Val. "He'll never be able to come back to work and Jerry has already spoken to Ken Dalton and myself about putting him up for early retirement. Which means you'll head the Department of Pathology eventually, with the rank of full professor."

"If eventually, why not now? After Adrian is retired, of course." Karen leaned forward intently. "With you a full professor and department head and Rebecca in a similar status, I'm the only woman associate professor who's eligible for promotion. And I intend to get it."

"You'll have my support," Val assured her. "We'd have a hard job finding anyone else in your field as capable as you are—male or female."

"Thanks, Val. I was sure I could depend on you."

"But after yesterday afternoon, can you depend on Jerry?"

"When the Tissue Conference ended, he wouldn't have

approved anything less than my being fired," Karen admitted. "But I think I convinced him differently later. He's quite a man, Val—everything you've heard he is, and more."

Val had been studying the other woman thoughtfully while she was talking. "Are you saying Jerry's enough for both of us?"

Karen laughed. "I'm glad we understand each other. But there's no need to tell Jerry that, is there?"

"None at all," Val agreed. "You might say this is just between us girls."

Karen got to her feet. "Thanks for saving me the trouble of beating around the bush. I always prefer the direct route. You're off this weekend, aren't you?"

"Yes. Jerry has invited me to go to the Keys with him—for scuba diving."

"Go by all means, Val. I'm sure you'll enjoy yourself. 'By."

"What about the post of medical director that will be vacant when Adrian Cooper is retired?" Valerie asked as Karen was reaching for the doorknob. "Are you going for that too?"

"Of course. As you said, only a few women in the country are certified in forensic pathology—a *very, very* few."

"And I suppose you already have plans for getting that post too?"

"Tentative plans, yes. I'll have to play that one by ear, though, so it may take more time."

When the door closed behind Karen Fletcher, Val lit a cigarette and sat smoking it thoughtfully for a while. Then, picking up the telephone on her desk, she dialed an inside number.

"Jerry," she said when a familiar male voice answered, "I've decided to take you up on that weekend offer. Shall I bring my own scuba gear?"

"Just bring yourself, Val." She heard his delighted, and triumphant, laugh over the wires. "I'll supply everything else."

As she hung up the telephone, Val LeMoyne didn't need to put a finger to the artery at her temple where anesthetists were trained to take the pulse, to know hers was beating much more rapidly than usual. Karen Fletcher was obviously experienced when it came to judging the capability of a lover. So it just might be that in Jerry Singleton's arms she would find relief from the steady build-up lately in a craving she'd learned to fear, even while another part of her welcomed the excitement it always brought.

The very thought was so stirring that her hands were trembling as she unlocked the top drawer of her desk and shook a yellow Valium tablet from the bottle there, before going to the adjoining lavatory for a cup of water with which to wash it down.

II

Six o'clock was a slack period on all the wards. The dinner trays had come and gone, and the regular chores of evening care for the patients wouldn't start for another thirty minutes. As many of the ICU nurses and attendants as could be spared had been released for dinner: in the cafeteria, the Coffee Shop, or from the bank of vending machines just off the main lobby, where everything from hot coffee to submarine sandwiches were available to possessors of a sufficient store of dimes and quarters. One machine would even take dollar bills but was usually out of order.

Helga Sundberg glanced up momentarily when she saw Carolyn Payson enter the ward, then looked down again at the chart she was updating. Nor did she lift her eyes when Carolyn passed the nursing station though she could have almost touched her.

Only one nurse was working in the general section and she was watching Carmelita Sanchez, so no one besides Helga noticed Carolyn enter the cubicle where her father lay, with the glucose solution from a bottle hanging upside down from a tall stand beside the bed dropping slowly through the glass chamber of the intravenous setup, as the fluid nutrient flowed into his veins.

The relatively heavy sedation Dr. Gross had ordered before Richard Payson was taken to the Board Room for the meeting of the God Committee yesterday had been continued by orders of the pudgy neurologist and the patient was fairly quiet. He opened his eyes when Carolyn reached down to smooth back the hair from his forehead and a travesty of a smile—although perhaps no one else could have interpreted it as such—showed briefly on his face, tearing at her heart.

The large syringe used to inject liquid food every four hours through the nasal tube leading to Richard Payson's stomach lay on the table beside the bed. The metal adapter by which its glass tip was decreased in diameter, so it could slip easily into the end of the nasal tube, was still on the syringe, as it had been when Helga injected his liquid dinner into the nasal tube shortly before six. A fairly large needle lay beside it but, looking at the syringe, Carolyn thought with a surge of sudden panic how small it appeared to be, considering the purpose she had been steeling herself over the past twenty-four hours to accomplish with it.

Nobody knew for sure just how much air would have to be injected into a vein to bring about the merciful instant death by air embolism that was the last duty she could perform for her father. But more would be required, she was certain now, than the few bubbles most people considered sufficient to act as the lethal agent of air embolism, a sudden blockage of blood to the lungs as air flowed through the veins to the right side of the heart and thence into the pulmonary circulation. Or, if it got through the lungs and into the left heart, blocking the circulation to the vital centers in the brain.

The intravenous drip afforded an easy route by which the air could reach her father's veins; she had only to inject it through the plastic wall of the tubing between the glucose bottle hanging from its stand and the catheter in an arm vein, using the syringe and the needle beside it. But, whether the amount she could inject in the time available would be sufficient to cause death, or merely turn Richard Payson into more of an inert vegetable than he already was, she had no way of knowing. Nor was there time to waste for, although she had not missed

Helga's studiedly ignoring her presence, another nurse might appear at any moment and see her there.

Then Carolyn's eyes fell upon the oxygen tube hanging in a coil from a hook on the panel attached to the wall at the head of the bed and she suddenly remembered Helga describing in detail just how she had connected an oxygen tube to a needle-catheter setup and used the central supply piped throughout the hospital to save the child in the Emergency Room only a little more than forty-eight hours ago. And remembering Helga's graphic description of the technique, she also knew the answer to her own immediate problem.

Picking up the needle from the bedside table, she quickly worked the end of the oxygen tubing over the flanged coupling for receiving the top of a syringe. The tubing fitted snugly over the large end of the needle and, when she reached up and opened the valve that shut off the main system until oxygen was needed, the gas hissed through the smaller shaft of the needle.

Glancing outside, she saw only Helga's blonde head still bent over the desk at the nursing station. And, picking up the intravenous tubing below the drip chamber that measured its flow, she thrust the point of the needle through it, then shut off the tubing above the needle puncture with the thumb and forefinger of her left hand, to keep the oxygen stream from flowing back up into the glucose bottle, and sent the gas pouring through the small tubing.

It made a faint bubbling sound as it cleared out the glucose solution ahead of it in the lower part of the IV setup, then surged under pressure directly into Richard Payson's arm vein. Watching for some sign of a leak or blowout of the needle connection from the pressure of the gas, Carolyn saw the vein into which a small nylon catheter had been inserted, when the intravenous was started last night, suddenly swell. At the same moment the transparent plastic catheter lost its normal bluish tint, as the blood that had filled it seconds before was pushed ahead of the column of oxygen flowing rapidly into Richard Payson's bloodstream.

A sudden gasping sound made Carolyn look quickly at

314

her father's face. She half expected it to be convulsed with agony, for the stream of gas had certainly reached his lungs through the pulmonary artery by now, driven there by contraction of the right ventricle of the heart. But instead, his eyes were open and a smile of utter peace had settled upon his features. It remained, too, even when he no longer breathed and she could feel no pulse in his wrist.

Only when she was sure his heart and respiration had stopped did Carolyn shut off the oxygen valve and remove the needle from the plastic tubing wall, noting with satisfaction that, even though the needle was larger than was ordinarily used to inject medications through the wall of intravenous tubing, there was no leakage.

In her haste to remove all signs of how death had come to Richard Payson, Carolyn accidentally dropped the needle to the floor as she disconnected it. She wasted no time looking for the needle, however; at the moment it was more important to replace the oxygen source so no one would realize it had been used.

Looping the oxygen supply tubing expertly into its previous position, she hung it on the hook in the panel at the head of the bed. Only a few additional seconds were required to milk the gas still inside the IV setup back into the glucose flask, removing the last external evidence of how his death had been accomplished. Except that Richard Payson's body no longer writhed in the tortured movements of H-D and his features were more peaceful than Carolyn remembered seeing them in years, nothing about either him or the room appeared to have changed.

Only the probing scalpel of the pathologist at autopsy would reveal the fact that the blood vessels of his lungs were filled with oxygen, as were many of the vessels of the brain. And unless the post-mortem was done reasonably soon, even that evidence might dissolve during the interim into his body tissues where it could never be discovered.

Although intent only upon an act of mercy, Carolyn Payson had also discovered the perfect agent for murder.

Helga's head was still bent over the desk when Carolyn passed it on her way out of the ward. Only when she heard the door to the ICU waiting room outside sigh shut did Helga look up. Going to a window that looked out upon the circular drive in front of the hospital, she watched until she saw Carolyn come out and step into one of the taxis that were almost always waiting at the stand halfway around the circular drive from the marquee. Nor did she need to hear Carolyn's voice tell the driver, "International Airport," to know the other girl's destination, more than two thousand miles to the south. Returning to the nursing station by way of Richard Payson's cubicle, Helga glanced inside just long enough to note that his chest no longer moved in respiration and that the intravenous had stopped running.

"I noticed that Mr. Payson's intravenous has stopped, Miss Garth," Helga told the student nurse who was the first to return from dinner some ten minutes later. "He seems to be quiet, though, so why don't you give him evening care last tonight? I'll restart the IV then."

"Yes, Miss Sundberg," the young nurse said. "I guess it's not going to make much difference to him whether he's first or last."

"No difference at all now—or ever," Helga could have assured her, but lowered her eyes to the chart on which she had been working instead. Nor was she surprised to find that she had been writing gibberish.

Helga waited until another of the regular ICU nurses came back from dinner, then picked up her handbag from the shelf beside her desk, where she had placed it when she came back from an early dinner in the cafeteria.

"Watch the station for me, please, Helen," she said. "I've got to make a private outside call. Mr. Payson's IV has stopped but he's quiet, so I wouldn't bother him until Miss Garth finishes his evening care. I'll restart the IV later."

"Sure, Helga," said the other nurse. "See if your friend's got a friend."

316

In one of the telephone booths off the main lobby of the hospital, Helga dropped in a dime and dialed a number she had looked up in one of the directories outside.

"International Airport Information," said a pleasant voice with just a hint of an accent. "Can I help you?"

"Could you tell me when the next flight to Brazil leaves? And by what airline?"

"What day, please?"

"Today."

"That would be Varig Flight 803, leaving for Rio at 8:00 P.M. Anything else?"

"No, thank you."

Outside, Helga glanced up at the clock above the receptionist's desk. It said six-thirty and an hour and a half was a long time to keep hidden the fact that a patient on ICU was already dead. But she had to string it out long enough to keep the State's Attorney from learning of it much before 8:00 P.M. and starting to wonder just what had been the cause.

IV

Mike Raburn had been tied up in the Emergency Room with a fracture case from the daily six o'clock traffic jam on the Miami Expressway system so it was six-thirty before he received a note to call Marcia Weston at her home.

"Oh, Lord!" he said when he was handed the call slip. "She's going to ask what I thought of the way she handled the TBW on the news tonight and I'll have to admit that I didn't even see it."

"Neither did anybody else," said the three-to-eleven Emergency Room supervisor. "We had a portable TV on in the office but they barely mentioned the most exciting thing that's happened around here in a month of Sundays."

Marcia Weston herself answered the telephone. "I called to apologize," she said, "but you know the worst by now."

"I got tied up with a case and didn't even see the news."

"I'm glad you didn't have a chance to be disappointed then. We had trouble editing the tape, there was so much material that the station manager decided to use just a flash of it on the evening news."

"Then it came out all right?"

"It's beautiful, just beautiful. We're going to show a bit more at eleven—the part the 'Today' show will use in the morning—and the rest will be edited into a half-hour special. I don't know when we'll show that but I'll give you a ring well beforehand. Thanks again for all that suspense."

Mike laughed. "One thing you can be sure of, it wasn't contrived. I was sweating all the way."

"So what happened?" the ER head nurse asked when he hung up the phone.

"You'll never believe this," Mike told her, "but I'm so big they couldn't squeeze me into the small screens everybody watched the six o'clock news on while they eat dinner. They're going to make it a half-hour special—for big screens only."

"I should have known I'd never get a straight answer out of you," said the veteran nurse. "But at least they won't be drafting you for 'Emergency Hospital.' And that's something to be thankful for."

"They're going to remake 'Medic' instead. I'm playing Richard Boone."

V

Rebecca Dalton was ten minutes late getting to the cafeteria. Ken was waiting outside the entrance when she arrived, breathless, flushed and, he thought, lovelier every day.

"You should have gone on and gotten your dinner before the best dishes are gone," she said as they took their places in the single line that was serving late-comers. "Peggy Tyndall stopped me to ask whether I knew when the echocardioscope would be back from the factory. We're going to check Dale with it as soon as it comes; Peggy is pretty sure the boy is getting more cyanotic lately."

"That could mean an early operation."

She looked at him quickly, wondering instinctively whether his failure to identify himself with the operation had any meaning.

"If the echoscope isn't ready by the last of next week, I suppose we'll have to bring Dale in and study him with conventional catheterization of the heart," she said. "But I was hoping we could spare him the discomfort."

"And the danger. Even in the hands of an expert like Ed Vogel, there's always a chance of cessation. I hope the machine gets back in time."

"What was the big deal with the Executive Committee?" she asked.

"Jeffry Toler is working out the problems connected with putting a separate millage for the medical center on the ballot in a referendum at the next election. But not everybody is satisfied that it's a wise thing to do."

"Couldn't the Hospital Board budget more effectively if a probable veto by the Commission Finance Committee wasn't hanging over it?"

"Yes. But if we go to the people with a referendum and lose, the Finance Committee and Ross McKenzie will have been handed a big stick. And the first order of business will be to clobber the Hospital Board."

"Is there much doubt about how the vote would go in a referendum?"

"Andrew Graves thinks so. It's going to be interesting to see whether Ross McKenzie keeps after us, now that he's had a chance to see why it costs so much to run a hospital."

"He already knows how close a call he had, I laid that on the line," said Rebecca. "Also the fact that, if you had gone on and operated when I wanted to, he'd be on the surgical ICU right now and a lot sicker than he is."

"It's not that simple, Reb. When you first asked me to see McKenzie, I was just as certain he was going to need surgery as you were—and scared to death into the bargain that I would have to be the surgeon and lose him. My happening to remember their telling me at Peter Bent that, by using the fiberoptic catheter, you could anticipate a major change in cardiac function as much as twenty hours before it happened was really an act of desperation."

"There you go, low-rating yourself again."

"It's true, Reb. When I had Ed put in the fiberoptic catheter without telling you, I was afraid I'd have to fight you—and not at all sure I'd be right."

"And I almost made a fool of myself by getting my back up because you went ahead and put it in without consulting me."

"I guess that's part of where we get into trouble," he admitted. "We were unconsciously competing with each other—"

"Not entirely unconsciously," Rebecca corrected him. "At least not on my part."

"Or mine, which means we've each got to give a little. But you're already ahead of me there."

"I don't see—"

"When you admitted to Ross McKenzie that you misjudged his case."

"That was the truth."

"Truth is sometimes the hardest thing to face—as I've discovered twice today."

"I don't understand."

"The first time was when Kevin told me early this morning that I was responsible for his life from now on and he expected me to keep him going a long time. He wasn't kidding, either."

"I know. Peggy confessed that she put him up to it."

"I'll have to thank her," he said. "But the real crisis for me came when I stood across that Cuban girl from Mike Raburn and watched him drain all the blood from her body and then let Ringer's solution wash through her circulation, when every half minute was a lifetime. I'm telling you, Reb, that took guts—"

"The same kind of guts you showed when you did those fifteen transplants without losing one."

"And then lost, when my courage failed and I turned yellow because you held your head up, while they were dying one by one, and I couldn't face the fact that you were a better doctor than I was."

"But I'm not. You proved that."

"Let's say I was lucky. Both with Kevin and in realizing that, if I didn't start scratching again, Mike Raburn was going to show me up for a failure by being a better surgeon than I am—if he isn't already."

"As much as I like Mike, I doubt that," said Rebecca. They had finished the meal and Ken went back to the coffee urn and filled their cups again.

"Nothing's really settled completely until I prove that the emotional turmoil of the past six months hasn't dulled my surgical skill," he admitted. "Writers run dry, you know, and I've already proved that something like it can happen to surgeons."

"But you're cured."

"Perhaps—but I still can't risk a patient's life to prove it. That's why I asked you to look over that plastic heart experiment I was working on before I developed the acute attack of what you might call 'surgeon's slump.' Did you have time this afternoon?"

"That's another reason why I was late for dinner," she confessed. "I spent an hour in the Research Lab going over the whole thing with Peggy and Ed and didn't get to the PDC until almost three o'clock."

"What do you think?"

"I'm not sure the model you stopped work on over six months ago is going to be the one that makes history. But by putting what you already have in a calf—" She stopped suddenly. "That's the way you're going to prove you've regained your skill, isn't it?"

He nodded. "If I can successfully replace a calf's heart with an artificial one, I'll know I'm cured."

"Dr. Rebecca Dalton—Operator, please. Dr. Dalton—Operator, please. Dr. Rebecca Dalton," the loudspeaker at the corner of the large room intoned, interrupting Ken's final word.

Rebecca pushed back her chair and moved quickly to a telephone in a corner booth. When she came back not much more than a minute later, however, her expression was grave.

"That was Peggy," she said. "Dale has disappeared and the security guards have started a search of the grounds."

June afternoons in South Florida are extra long, thanks to Daylight Saving Time, and little boys playing in the hot Florida sun become very thirsty. Dale Tyndall often went to meet Peggy when she came from her work in the Cardiac Research Laboratory. He was almost to the hospital entrance when he remembered that Kevin McCartney should be on duty at this time of day and would have a cold root beer in the refrigerator for him. Detouring to the lounge, he climbed up on a stool but was so winded that he had to lean his head on his arms against the polished surface of the bar for several minutes to get his breath. Finally the bartender—a man he didn't recognize—came to the end where he was sitting.

"What do you want, little boy?" he asked, not unkindly.

"Beer?" Dale managed to gasp.

"What?" Then the bartender laughed. "You must be the one Kevin told me about—that drinks the root beer."

"That's me. Where's Kevin?"

The bartender opened a bottle of root beer from the refrigerator and poured in into a frosted mug, sliding the mug along the bar to where Dale was sitting.

"Kevin's sick. They had to put him in the hospital yesterday."

"Kevin's got heart trouble, like me." Dale put down the mug and wiped his mouth on his arm. "I was a blue baby."

"Well, what do ya know?" The bartender put his elbows on the bar. "You're still blue, ain't you?"

"A little," said Dale. "But when I'm old enough, Dr. Dalton is going to operate on me and then I won't be so blue any more. And I can run and play like the other children."

"That's nice. When will this be?"

"Mommy says when I'm eight or ten. I start to school next year."

"You're a smart little fellow," said the bartender as Dale finished his beer. "Come in any time."

"Maybe tomorrow?" said Dale hopefully.

"Sure."

"Good-by, Mr. Bartender. You're almost as nice as Kevin is."

"Thanks, kid. That's saying a lot."

The bartender stood watching the little boy as he left the lounge, then shook his head as he lifted the empty mug and wiped the polished surface.

"That's a smart kid, but he sure is blue," he told a customer who came up to pay his tab just then. "Says he has heart trouble, and I can certainly believe it."

Outside in the sunlight, Dale walked a dozen steps, then suddenly squatted. He had no way of knowing, of course, that filling his small stomach with an ice-cold drink, when his heart was already laboring to keep up with the demands for oxygen from the body tissues, had placed a heavier burden on it than the structurally disarranged organ was capable of bearing very long.

Getting up again, he took a short cut behind a huge bougainvillea that fanned out between several ficus trees. They made a natural screen, hiding him from immediate view, and thus no one saw him when he tumbled into a flower bed.

There, a hospital security guard taking part in the search found him almost an hour later—unconscious.

VII

Rebecca Dalton started to turn right as they left the elevator that had taken them to the first floor but Ken caught her by the arm.

"Where are you going?" he asked.

"To help search for Dale Tyndall. What else?"

"The hospital security force can take care of that," he said. "You and I need to be in the Emergency Room when they bring him in—"

"You're right, of course," she said. "He must be unconscious somewhere from not getting enough oxygen through to his blood—"

323

"It's more like not getting enough blood to his oxygen," said Ken. "With the pulmonary artery almost closed, as it is in most tetralogy of Fallot cases, the boy could die of asphyxiation in a crisis, simply because not enough oxygen from the air he breathes is absorbed by the hemoglobin in his blood and gets to the brain. On second thought, I'll go to the Emergency Room and backstop Mike. You'd better get Val LeMoyne. If Dale is in a cardiorespiratory crisis, Val can intubate him and start pressurized oxygen."

Rebecca nodded and turned toward the elevator. But neither of them voiced the thought that was foremost in both their minds—that Ken might very well have to start operating again and considerably sooner than either of them had expected.

VIII

"Miss Sundberg!" Miss Garth, the student nurse who had been giving evening care to the patients not ill enough to require constant specialing, was standing just inside Richard Payson's cubicle. "Come here, please!"

Helga glanced at the clock on the control panel. It said seven and, if the Lord was in His heaven and all was right with the world, Varig Flight 803 would soon be moving up to the loading tunnel preparing to take on passengers for Rio.

"No wonder Mr. Payson's intravenous stopped and he was so quiet," the student nurse added, a little shakily. "He's dead."

"Help me get the pacemaker that's outside Mr. McCartney's door into Mr. Payson's room." Helga spoke quickly. "Then call the operator and ask her to sound CODE FIVE on the PA system. And on the way back you can bring a Mark VII respirator."

"Right," said Miss Garth as she followed Helga to where the pacemaker, on its mobile cart, had been standing beside Kevin McCartney's door since he'd had the cessation the day before.

"Hey! What's up?" Kevin asked when he saw the cart moving.

"Mr. Payson. And don't try to help," Helga called over her shoulder. "A CPR team will come through here like the thundering herd in a minute or two and I don't want you to be run over."

In Richard Payson's cubicle, Helga moved quickly, attaching the terminals from the pacemaker to the skin of the dead man's chest with rubber suction cups. Plugging the power cord into a baseboard socket, she set the controls and switched on the machine. Immediately, as rhythmic jolts of the shocking current surged through circuits thus formed between Payson's body and the machine, his chest muscles jerked. The pulse at his temple took up a visible regular beat, too, indicating that the heart was being stimulated to contract, sending blood surging through his arteries and veins. While Helga was working she could hear the call from the loudspeaker outside, muted somewhat here where the usual strident summons might disturb already apprehensive patients:

"CODE FIVE—CICU. CODE FIVE—CICU."

Working quickly and protected against electric shock from the pacemaker by the rubber-soled shoes she wore, Helga disconnected the nylon catheter in Richard Payson's arm vein from the IV set, noting that blood still flowed from the open end of the catheter. Lifting the glucose bottle from the stand attached to the bed, she dropped tubing, drip chamber, and partially filled bottle into a wastebasket. Meanwhile, the student nurse—only seniors worked in the ICU—had slipped a curved plastic airway into Richard Payson's mouth to hold his tongue back and connected him to the respirator kept on the floor for just such an emergency.

Since the catheter was still patent, Helga quickly injected an ampule of Isoproterenol through it, completing the routine of CPR.

Mike Raburn was the first doctor to appear. He took in the scene with one glance, as well as the fact that, between the pacemaker, the Isoproterenol Helga had just finished injecting into the venous catheter, and the click of the respirator valve as Richard Payson's lungs were being rhythmically inflated with oxygen and then allowed to deflate, the situation was well under control.

"Any sign of spontaneous resumption?" Mike asked, his voice somewhat muffled as he reached down, apparently tying a shoe.

"No," said Helga.

"Why the pacemaker and not routine CPR?"

"Miss Garth thinks he may have been dead awhile and this looked like a standstill arrest, so I thought electric stimulation seemed to offer more hope."

"You're probably a better cardiologist than I am," he said. "Where's Carolyn?"

"I haven't talked to her since early this morning." The statement was literally true.

The rest of the CPR team had arrived by now but there was nothing to be done at the moment except watch the pacemaker stimulate the heart and the respirator inflate the lungs.

"Cut the current, please," Mike said after some five minutes with no visible result. Reaching for Richard Payson's wrist, he held it for ten seconds while listening over the chest with a stethoscope, then dropped it.

"You can start the respirator again," he said as he put the stethoscope back into his pocket. "But I think it's too late even for heroic measures."

"Shouldn't I continue pacemaker stimulation for a while longer, just in case?" Helga asked.

"It can't do any harm, since you've already chosen this method of resuscitation."

"No need to hang around," he told the rest of the CPR team.

The others left, but Mike stayed at his post near the foot of the bed watching the rhythmic contraction of the patient's chest muscles, the pulse in the temple artery that followed each time, and the inflation cycle of the respirator breathing bag.

"Interesting thing about blood," he said casually. "It's still liquid enough for an hour after death, maybe even longer, to be pumped around the body, if the heart can be made to contract. Different parts of the body die at different times, too, depending on whether they get oxygen through the circulation."

At his words, Helga glanced quickly at the oxygen

326

tubing hanging from the panel on the wall at the head of the bed. When the tubing came from Central Supply, it had been coiled, with a strip of transparent tape holding the coils together so it could be hung out of the way from a hook beside the oxygen valve on the wall but still instantly available, merely by jerking it down and pulling the coils apart to loosen one end of the tape.

The coil was hanging where it should be, she saw, but the tape had pulled loose and hung by one end.

"Somebody down in Central Supply didn't check this." Mike reached up and pinched the coil together, so the short strip of transparent tape could easily encompass it again, and Helga suddenly understood the method Carolyn had used to bring instant death to her father. More than that, she knew Mike Raburn had also figured it out—except that he probably attributed the final act of mercy to Helga herself.

"I don't think we can accomplish anything more with this," he said after some ten minutes had passed.

Reaching past Helga to the switch, he turned off the current to the pacemaker and pulled the plug to the respirator. Returning, his hand brushed against the side pocket of Helga's white nylon uniform. But that it wasn't simply the kind of exploring pass so many men tried she knew at once when she felt something drop into the pocket.

"I'll certify Mr. Payson while I'm up here," said Mike. "What time did you say death occurred?"

"I looked in about six forty-five and saw that his IV had stopped. But he was quiet like he is—was—when asleep, so I thought I wouldn't disturb him by starting the IV again until after Miss Garth had given him evening care."

"Could he have been dead then?"

"I guess so," Helga confessed. "I just glanced at the drip chamber of the IV the way I do all of them whenever I pass the door of a cubicle, but didn't go inside. Looks like I goofed, doesn't it?"

"Nothing you could have done would have mattered, I suspect, but I'll put the time of death down as seven. And

I'm glad to see you goof occasionally. It proves you're not perfect."

"Is that supposed to be a compliment?"

"Very much so. You haven't had time to notify Carolyn, have you?"

"No."

"She'd rather hear it from you, I'm sure. Why don't you call her while I fill in the front of the chart?"

He went into the small doctors' office adjoining the nursing station and Helga sat down before the desk phone. She let the telephone in the apartment ring for at least a minute, then hung up.

"Carolyn's not there," she called through the opening between the control station and the office. "She probably went out to dinner somewhere, she's been off all day."

"You can get her later, she knew this would happen before long." Mike handed Helga the chart with the front sheet filled in. "While I'm here I'll stop by and see Joey Gates and Carmelita."

"Carmelita's been moving her arms and legs spontaneously. I put some water on her tongue just now and she made swallowing movements, too."

"That's good news." He glanced up at the screen that displayed the parameters being monitored continuously on the sleeping girl. "The way her pulse has slowed certainly looks good and the pO_2 is close to normal."

"I'm betting she'll regain consciousness before I go off at eleven."

"Then we'll have to celebrate." His eyes hadn't left hers. "Have you decided where?"

"I'm betting she'll regain consciousness before I go off tonight."

"Fair enough," he said. "When you've waited for something all your life, a few hours more can't be too bad."

"Dr. Raburn—Emergency Room," said the paging operator, and Mike started for the door. "They must have found Dale Tyndall," he called over his shoulder as he left the ICU, a stocky figure that possessed, Helga knew, the solidity of Gibraltar in spite of the almost delicate grace with which his hands moved, when encased in surgeon's gloves.

328

Then Helga's hand went to her pocket. And when she found there the large intravenous needle Mike had dropped into it, she understood fully just what she had come to mean to him in some fifty-two hours—and he to her. In the desperate need to get the blood moving in a dead man's circulation and thus dissipate in the body tissues the oxygen that had brought about his death, where Carolyn had no doubt dropped it when she pulled off the tubing. But Mike had seen it and, although he had almost certainly decided already that Helga herself had accomplished Richard Payson's death, he had still picked it up so no one else would know, taking that measure to protect her even though he must have thought she had violated one of the basic obligations of their profession, to save life with every means at her disposal.

If there had been any doubt in her mind—and there had not—she knew now that what had happened to both of them in an incredibly short period of time was something they must hold onto for the rest of their lives—at all cost.

Chapter 21

THE SECURITY GUARD who found Dale Tyndall in the flower bed hadn't waited to call for help. Lifting the small form in his arms, he carried the boy directly to the Emergency Room, where Mrs. Connor placed him on the examining table in the specially equipped cubicle. Noting the dangerously deep cyanosis of Dale's skin, the veteran nurse began to administer oxygen with a face mask, while the student nurse on duty called Mike and Dr. Valerie LeMoyne, who was also on emergency call for cases of apparent respiratory failure.

Word that the child had been found spread quickly. Peggy Tyndall, who had been helping with the search, came into the Emergency Room just as Mike and Val LeMoyne arrived, followed quickly by Ken and Rebecca Dalton, who had been standing by.

"I think we'd better intubate Dale and put him on oxygen under pressure, Dr. LeMoyne," said Mike.

Val had brought emergency equipment with her and wasted no time in discussion. Opening the case, she removed a small laryngoscope and intratracheal tube, while Mike was sliding Dale's head off the end of the examining table in order to facilitate direct visualization of his larynx.

With the child in deep coma from oxygen lack, his pharyngeal reflexes were already gone and Val had no trouble inserting the tube. Connecting the outer end to the hose from an anesthetic machine with a metal adapter, she began to administer oxygen under pressure to the gasping patient. Meanwhile Rebecca Dalton started percussing out the outline of his heart on the small chest. When she looked up, her face was grave.

"It's starting to dilate," she said, speaking directly to Ken, who was standing by, and her words confirmed what everyone there already knew, that the case was now in his hands—or Mike Raburn's.

"Gus Henderson used a new gold-tipped electrode inserted into the umbilical artery on Baby Hornsby the other day to measure oxygen tension continuously, Dr. Dalton," said Mike, speaking to Ken. "It worked beautifully and gives the readings much more quickly than the laboratory can do with routine blood gas determinations."

"Is it still in the Hornsby baby?"

"No. Gus told me he took it out yesterday, but it was sterilized in case he needed to use it again."

"You'd better expose the radial artery then and slip the electrode into it," said Ken. "We're going to need all the help we can get."

Rebecca had lifted the stethoscope, with which she had been listening to Dale's chest, in time to hear the last words. "The picture hasn't changed, except for the enlargement of the heart," she reported. "And that could be

330

because it's trying to pump more blood and step up the tissue oxygenation rate."

She didn't have to explain further to any of those present the significance of the enlarging heart, or the danger of failure if it was not able to stand up under the increased demands upon it. At five, Dale was small for his age, his growth slowed by the lowered concentration of oxygen in his body tissues due to the congenital heart defect called the tetralogy of Fallot. The most common abnormal heart condition found in children at birth, its greatest danger to life lay in an extra opening between the right and left ventricles, the main pumping chambers of the heart, allowing blood from the right side to pass directly to the left without going through the lungs and thus not receiving its quota of oxygen.

Second in importance was a marked narrowing of the pulmonary artery itself, by which the right heart normally pumped blood directly through the lungs. This obstruction served to increase the pressure in that ventricle and to force more blood through the abnormal opening between it and the left side. With these two defects also went an enlargement of the right ventricle and, in most cases, a displacement of the aorta, the large artery carrying blood from the left heart to most of the body. Normally arching to the left as it leaves the heart, the aorta in tetrad cases often arches to the right.

A not uncommon congenital abnormality, the tetralogy of Fallot is usually recognized quite easily from the loud murmur heard over the heart as blood rushes back and forth between the two ventricles, and the marked decrease in the blood oxygen concentration, the pO_2. Moreover, it is one of the most successfully correctible congenital abnormalities by surgery, in most cases after age six when the heart and vessels are larger than at birth and more amenable to suturing.

Mike Raburn had put on a pair of sterile gloves while Mrs. Connor was opening one of the surgical trays kept at all times in the ER supply closet for any emergency. Through a small incision on the thumb side of Dale's wrist, he now quickly exposed the radial artery there, easily identifiable by its palpable pulsation. Meanwhile,

Mrs. Connor had ordered the gold-tipped electrode sent down from the operating suite supply room and, when it came, removed the sterile cover and dropped the slender electronic sensor on the tray where Mike could easily reach it.

"The electrode will be inside the artery in a few minutes," Mike promised as he began to slide it into the small opening he had made in the wall of the rapidly pulsating radial artery. "With it we should be able to determine pretty quickly whether pressure breathing is getting any more O_2 into his blood."

"I don't think it is," said Val LeMoyne quietly. "The degree of cyanosis hasn't lessened."

Ken moved over to the corner of the room where Peggy Tyndall was sitting on a stool, watching the scene of hurried, though purposeful, activity with eyes that were bleak from pain and worry.

"Feel like telling me what happened, Peg?" he asked gently.

"The sitter usually stays until I get home, Dr. Dalton," she said, "but today she had to leave at five-thirty. Dale likes to play with the other children and I let him because I don't want him to feel that he's different. Usually, if his breath gets short, he just squats, like most children with congenital hearts do, but sometimes, unless somebody stops him, he plays until he drops. I wasn't there to stop him at the usual time because I worked late getting out that plastic artificial heart you're interested in—"

She broke off speaking, with a look of horror in her eyes as she realized she had implied that Ken had been responsible for her working late, then added quickly: "I don't mean that you—"

"It's all right, Peggy, I understand." He reached out to touch her shoulder reassuringly, but she seized his hand and held it between her two smaller ones, while her shoulders shook in a sob.

Mike had finished inserting the oxygen electrode and closed the small skin wound with two Teflon sutures. He applied the surface electrode to Dale Tyndall's skin, completing the circuit, and connected both to the accompanying meter and continuous strip recorder on a bedside cart.

"Blood oxygen tension is 40 millimeters of mercury, Dr. Dalton," he reported as the reading was recorded on the moving paper strip.

"He's been getting 100 per cent oxygen for ten minutes," Val LeMoyne added. "So it looks like no more is being absorbed by the hemoglobin in his RBC than before we put him on positive pressure breathing."

"Watch him, please, Val," said Ken. "We'll be in Dr. Raburn's office close by."

When the others, including Peggy, were in the small office adjacent to the nursing station, Ken pressed the keys of the portable keyboard connection and began to retrieve the salient facts of Dale Tyndall's medical history from the data storage bank deep in the heart of the main computer in the basement. Line by line, the story of the boy's birth, clinic record, and two previous admissions flashed upon the ground-glass screen as rapidly as the words could be read, including the notes Rebecca had made after her last examination of him in the Private Diagnostic Clinic. When the screen was blank, Ken switched off the computer connection and put down the small hand retriever.

"I'm afraid we have no choice except to operate right away, Peggy," he said. "I don't have to tell you how serious this is, either. Or that I feel personally responsible for its happening."

"Please, Dr. Dalton. I didn't mean—"

"All of us knew Dale would one day come to surgery. If the circumstances were different, we would have chosen a more auspicious time, but they aren't."

Peggy voiced another question that had been in all their minds: "You'll operate yourself, won't you, Dr. Dalton?"

"If you want me to."

"Oh, I do."

"I'll talk to Dr. LeMoyne," said Ken. "It isn't safe to wait, with the pO_2 as low as it is."

Val LeMoyne didn't question the wisdom of immediate surgery either. Trained to evaluate the condition of a patient and, weighing the chances of life or death, act swiftly and effectively, she was able to recognize the gravity of the emergency.

"Hold this mask, Mike," she said. "I'll call the OR and get things started.

"OR Two is clear," Val reported when she came back from the nursing station a few minutes later. "I know you like to use it because of the monitors, Ken, so we'll do the boy there, starting thirty minutes from now. You understand, of course, that I'll have to carry him as light as possible; he may even squirm when you make the incision but he won't remember it."

"You're the boss in that area, Val." Ken turned to Mike. "Can anyone cover Emergency for you?"

"Ed Vogel's off and so is Nolan Gaither, so I think I'd better stay available. But Ned Green is in his room, he can assist you." As chief surgical resident, Green was just below Mike himself in the non-faculty surgical hierarchy.

"Ned will be fine," said Ken. "Let's get Dale up to surgery."

II

Rebecca Dalton didn't follow the others when Dale Tyndall was moved to the operating suite on the special cardiac stretcher that had its own oxygen supply, allowing the vital gas to be given under pressure without interruption. Even greater than her desire to watch Ken while he operated was the fear that her presence there, and the knowledge of how much depended upon his having retained all his skills during the months of relative surgical inactivity, might put him under additional tension when he needed every faculty for the task at hand.

To occupy herself meanwhile, Rebecca decided to make evening rounds in the CICU. She stopped by the nursing station just as Helga was gathering up the records that were to go to the morgue with Richard Payson's body.

"I was tied up when the CODE FIVE sounded a little

while ago," Rebecca told Helga. "It was for Mr. Payson, wasn't it?"

Helga nodded. "You couldn't have done anything, Dr. Dalton. All the monitor channels were being used, so we didn't even realize he was dead for a while."

"When the operator told me Dr. Raburn was with the CPR team that responded, I figured I'd just be in the way," said Rebecca. "Not that he's so big, of course."

"I guess there are more ways of being big than just size." Helga's voice was soft and Rebecca looked at the nurse in surprise.

"Mike is most of them," she agreed.

"I'll remember that," said Helga. "Are you sure you don't need me on the floor, Dr. Dalton? I can stay but Miss Garth is helping and I always hate to send a student to the morgue."

"Don't start now, please," said Rebecca. "I remember well my first day in anatomy. Do you have any idea what happened to Mr. Payson?"

"Apparently a standstill arrest."

"With so many varied stimuli reaching his muscles from a disordered brain, it's not surprising that those going to the heart would get involved enough to literally tie it into a knot and bring about arrest. Was Carolyn much upset?"

"We haven't been able to get her," Helga admitted. "She was off duty today."

"She couldn't have done anything anyway. And it will be a greater relief to her when she finds it's all over."

"I'm sure it will," said Helga.

"Go ahead and take Mr. Payson's body down to the morgue," Rebecca told the blonde nurse. "I want to see Kevin and Mr. McKenzie but if I need any help I'll call one of the other nurses."

Ross McKenzie didn't speak while Rebecca checked his heart, had him cough so she could listen over his lungs for the fine râles of congestion, and checked his ankles for any sign of edema, the swelling that would perhaps have signaled the beginning of a failing heart.

"Do you feel like talking a little, Mr. McKenzie?" she asked him when she had finished the examination.

"I feel like getting out of here, if I could get rid of some of this plumbing and electric wiring you've got attached to me."

"We will probably remove the catheter from your arm tomorrow. It did its job by telling my husband about twenty hours in advance that your heart was adjusting and surgery would probably not be necessary, at a time when I felt certain that it would be."

"Where did he learn about this gadget?"

"Doctors attend medical conventions and visit other clinics regularly to keep themselves informed on new things. He's going to Paris soon to try and discover why a heart transplant case in France is still living, five years after his operation."

"Does that mean Dr. Dalton's going to start transplanting hearts again?"

"That's possible. We know a lot more about rejection than we did a year ago."

"I suppose you learned from the ones who died."

"Partly, but work in that area is being done in a lot of laboratories besides ours."

McKenzie studied her for a moment. "Do you love your husband that much? To assume responsibility for his mistakes?"

Rebecca flushed. "To keep fifteen people alive for as much as two years longer than they would have lived otherwise can hardly be called a mistake, Mr. McKenzie."

"That cute little technician of yours—"

"Peggy Tyndall?"

"Yes."

"She's a physician's assistant, not just a technician."

"What's the difference?"

"Medical schools that rain PA candidates usually require them to have had around two thousand hours' experience in some aspect of the medical field before acceptance. Most of those we have trained as PAs here are former corpsmen and technicians from the armed services. Peggy had three years as a *Wave* corpsman in one of the largest naval medical centers in the country. After her husband was killed in Vietnam, leaving her with a newborn baby, she put herself through the PA course under the GI Bill. She deserves a lot of credit, Mr. McKenzie."

"She tells me Dr. Dalton has started to work again on an artificial heart."

"He has—but I don't know how far he'll be able to go, if you succeed in cutting the appropriation for the hospital."

McKenzie shrugged. "That was a low blow, Doctor."

"No lower than your accusing him of contributing to the death rate of older people in the hospital, Mr. McKenzie. Right now he's getting ready to operate on Peggy's little boy for a serious heart abnormality."

"And she's letting him?"

"She asked him to do the operation."

He shook his head, as if baffled. "I'll never understand women. You have admitted you were ready to demand that I be operated on by your husband, when I didn't need it."

"Would you have agreed?"

"Of course, if you had said it was necessary. And incidentally, your husband passed up a fine chance to perform a brilliant operation on me that would have made all the local newspapers at least, proving he wasn't all washed up. Even if it failed, he could always have claimed you had made a mistake in diagnosis, so why didn't he operate?"

"Because he's a dedicated doctor and not an opportunist," said Rebecca. "Now I'd like to ask you a question, Mr. McKenzie."

"Fire away, then."

"You've said you would have submitted to surgery yesterday if I had told you it was necessary to save your life. Suppose I had recommended a transplant and a donor had become available. Would you have let my husband operate?"

"Of course."

"You trust us that much?"

"I didn't." Ross McKenzie smiled and Rebecca realized that she was seeing a side of him she—nor anyone else, she suspected, except perhaps someone very close to him

337

—had never seen before. "But that was before I was brain-washed—by an honest female doctor and a bartender named Kevin McCartney."

III

Helga herself went down to the morgue with Richard Payson's body, remembering very well the time when, a timorous probationer, she had accompanied the first corpse she had ever been close to—drumming up her courage as best she could while half expecting to feel icy fingers close around her throat at every corner.

"Miss Sundberg!" Dr. Sam Toyota, the resident in pathology, looked up from the desk where he had been dictating an autopsy report, his eyes beaming behind thick lenses. "We don't see much of you down here, worse luck."

"This is my roommate's father, Mr. Richard Payson."

"The Huntington's disease case?"

"Yes."

Toyota came over to the stretcher and pulled back the sheet that covered Richard Payson's face.

"There's something you hardly ever see," he remarked.

"What's that, Doctor?"

"Somebody who looks like he welcomed death. There's even a smile on his face, but I guess he had reason to smile at that. H-D is a pretty horrible fate. His cheeks are pink, too."

"Anything significant in that?"

"Death was sudden, probably a cessation. Didn't your monitors show it?"

"Our channels were tied up with two severe heart cases, so Dr. Vogel took him off the monitors yesterday."

Dr. Toyota shrugged. "It was just as well, he couldn't have had anything to live for."

"I guess not," said Helga. "Will you let me know if you find anything?"

"Sure. Come to think of it, I've got a note from Dr.

Fletcher on him somewhere here." He rummaged through some papers on the desk. "Here it is: *'Autopsy to be performed immediately after death.'* Hmm!" He looked up. "By request of the State's Attorney."

"Mr. Broadhurst?" Helga hoped the Japanese pathologist didn't notice the apprehensive note in her voice.

"Yes. I wonder why?" He reached for the telephone. "I'd better call Dr. Fletcher."

"I haven't been able to get in touch with Mr. Payson's daughter; she's off duty today and must have gone out for the evening." Helga was playing for time. "You'll need her permission for the post, won't you?"

"Not for a coroner's case." Dr. Toyota glanced down at the note again. "Besides, it says here that Mr. Payson willed his body to the medical school."

Defeated, Helga was turning toward the door when she heard the pathologist say into the telephone: "Mr. Payson just died, Dr. Fletcher. Want me to get started with him—drugs? Sure, I'll be on the watch. See you later."

In the corridor outside the Pathology Laboratory, Helga stopped beside a cooler and filled a cup with cold water, drinking it down without even feeling the chill. She'd been counting on Richard Payson's body being treated like any other routine autopsy on a patient who died during the night. Usually they were put into one of the long refrigerator drawers to await post-mortem in the morning. But Anthony Broadhurst was apparently as thorough as she'd heard he was and had anticipated the possibility that, after the God Committee refused to take the responsibility for ending her father's life from Carolyn, she would undertake it herself.

There was one ray of sunlight, however. If the medical examiner looked for a drug as the possible death agent, he'd find nothing but chlorpromazine. And the hospital record would show that the powerful tranquilizing agent had been given regularly for most of the time Richard Payson had been in the hospital.

Helga's watch showed eight o'clock and Carolyn's plane was presumably just taking off, so she'd be safe. But seeing a pay telephone on the wall of the empty corridor,

Helga stopped and searched in her purse until she found a dime.

"International Airport—Information," a bored voice said in her ear.

Helga looked quickly up and down the corridor but could see no one near enough to hear. Nor did she hear any footfalls on the steps.

"International Airport—Information," the bored voice repeated. "Can I help you?"

"Could you tell me whether Varig Flight 803 has departed?"

"One moment, puh-lease. Yes, Varig Flight 803 departed Miami on schedule at 8:00 P.M."

"Thank you." Helga started to hang up the phone, but froze beside it with the receiver still in her hand when an angry voice said in her ear:

"Now tell me what the hell this is all about, Helga."

It was Gus Henderson.

IV

Ned Green had finished scrubbing and was soaking his hands and arms in antiseptic, when Ken Dalton came into the scrubroom, adjoining Operating Room Two, where final preparations for surgery were going on rapidly.

"Hope we didn't interfere with any other plans you had for the evening, Ned," said Ken. "I was hoping not to have to operate on this boy for another few years, when we could do a complete repair, but it looks like we were a bit too conservative."

"I was just brushing up on anatomy for the American Board exam, Dr. Dalton," said the resident. "I notice that his hematocrit is pretty high."

"Too high—for comfort," said Ken. "These Fallot children compensate for not getting enough oxygen into the red blood cells by making more cells—which is all right if the RBC count and the blood viscosity, as measured by the hematocrit, don't go too high. When Dale was examined in the Cardiac Research Laboratory six months ago, the hematocrit was 50 per cent, but just now it was up to

80, which explains why he had the severe attack of anoxia."

"Shall I drape the operative field?" Ned Green asked as he lifted his hands and arms from the antiseptic basin.

"Please. The catheterization we did, when Dale first started having the spells of anoxia, shows that the aortic arch is to the left, instead of reversed like it is with so many of these children. We'll go in through the third right interspace."

"Right," said the resident, and moved into the operating theater.

When Ken came in some five minutes later and began to remove the antiseptic from his hands and forearms with a sterile towel handed him by the scrub nurse, Dale Tyndall's small body was already covered by a voluminous sterile sheet leaving only a rectangle of skin, bright red from the antiseptic, exposed on his upper chest.

"How is he, Val?" Ken asked as the circulating nurse was tying the strings at the back of his gown.

"The pO_2 is a little better since the blood's been diluted by the IV."

"I considered bleeding him to reduce the number of red cells in his circulation and lower the hematocrit a little. Maybe I should have."

"Benjamin Rush would approve, at least. According to the history books, he must have bled practically everybody in Philadelphia about the time of the Revolution. I'm still carrying Dale very light, mostly oxygen."

"Good." Ken moved to the table. "I'm hoping this won't take very long."

Watching from the gallery, Mike Raburn wasn't even sure he detected an instant of hesitation before the surgeon made a fairly long incision outward in the space between the third and fourth ribs on the right. But if there had been any hesitation, it was only before that first cut through the skin, for Ken Dalton's movements as he opened the chest cavity through the muscle layer between the ribs were as sure and as skilled as ever.

No more than fifteen minutes after the first cut, a rib

spreader was in the wound, opening it wide to expose the small heart beating rapidly but regularly in its protective sac, which in some instances—as it had yesterday with Kevin McCartney—could also be a threat to life itself.

The picture that presented itself in the almost square frame of the incision maintained by the rib spreader was one Ken Dalton—and Mike—had seen many times: the right ventricle thickened in an attempt to raise pressure in the right heart and supply the lungs adequately with blood; the purring vibration called a "thrill"—easily felt when the heart itself was touched as blood rushed through the opening between the ventricles which had failed to close as it should by birth; the markedly constricted pulmonary artery, literally exerting the effect of a tourniquet upon the flow of blood to the lungs—all were part of a classic picture of congenital heart disease.

Lifting his eyes to the gallery, Ken spoke over the surgical suite PA system.

"Except for the fact that the aorta is not reversed, this is a classic case," he said. "We can feel the thrill as the blood moves from the right ventricle to the left and you may even be able to see the small size of the pulmonary artery compared to what it should be. If the patient's hematocrit wasn't so high and this wasn't an emergency, I'd choose to put him on the pump. Then I could open the left ventricle, repair the opening, and enlarge the strictured portion of the pulmonary artery by means of a Teflon patch. But everything considered, I'm going to do a simple Blalock-Taussig shunt between the subclavian artery and the pulmonary."

In the gallery, where about a dozen of the hospital staff and students were watching, Mike Raburn nodded agreement. Communication with the theater was only one way, but he understood that Ken's words had been a message for him to transmit to Rebecca Dalton and Peggy that the relatively simple operation of shunting blood from a major artery, the subclavian, which also supplied the arm, into the lungs where it could be adequately supplied with oxygen, was almost certain to be a success.

Leaving the gallery, Mike stopped at the OR suite

342

nursing station and dialed the hospital operator. "Do you know where Dr. Rebecca Dalton is?" he asked.

"She was on CICU a few minutes ago, Dr. Raburn," said the operator. "Shall I call her?"

"Don't bother," he said. "I'm going to the first floor, so I'll stop by there."

V

Ed Vogel was enjoying himself immensely, and the evening had hardly begun. The two seats at the Coliseum for the final postseason basketball game between the Miami Snappers and the league-leading Lakers were in the owner's box right at mid-court. And the redhead beside him, a teacher from Vero Beach attending summer school at the University of Miami, was gorgeous—and probably impressed.

"I've never been to a real professional game before," she confided. "Imagine sitting in the owner's box. I could love you to death, Ed."

"I'm liable to hold you to that, Beautiful," said Vogel happily. "Now just pray nobody gets injured and I have to make a house call."

"Can I go, if you do? Anything about medicine excites me."

"I wouldn't leave you behind for the world," he assured her, allowing the arm he had casually placed across the back of the adjoining seat to drop, so his hand touched the warm pink skin of a lovely shoulder left bare by a sleeveless dress.

"Umm!" She shivered and moved closer to him. "I'm so excited from all this, I must have goose pimples."

"I haven't found any but I'll be glad to—"

"Oh! Oh!" The girl stood up suddenly, along with practically everybody watching the game, almost tumbling Ed, who hadn't been watching the game at all, out of his seat.

"Wha—what happened?" he asked.

"It's Big Joe Gates. He's down."

"Hell!" said Ed in disgust. "Now I'll probably have to be a doctor. And just when I was—"

"Dr. Vogel!" It was the Snappers' coach, calling up from the bench. "We need you on the floor—right away."

VI

Joey Gates was watching TV on one of the small portable sets allowed in the ICU when Mike stopped by the room, after giving Peggy and Rebecca, who were sitting together in the ICU waiting room, the good news about Dale.

"How's the game going, Joey?" he asked.

"Great, Dr. Mike! Just great! Dad's shooting more baskets than the rest of the Snappers put together. And guess what?"

"I give up."

"We saw Dr. Vogel just now—in the owner's box."

"I know. Your dad sent me the tickets but I couldn't go. Dr. Vogel's substituting for the team doctor."

"He's also enjoying the company of a stunning redhead," said Rachel.

"Ed knows how to pick 'em."

"Daddy just shot another basket," Joey exclaimed.

"My husband is showing off, Mike. He's been saying all day that he was going to make the owners realize they can't write him off, so he's really putting on the heat tonight."

"Nobody can do it better."

"Let's go outside," she said. "I want to talk to you, but I can't hear myself think with Joey jumping around."

"Maybe turning on the heat tonight will be good for Joe," said Mike as he followed her out into the corridor. "It might even help him get the worry out of his system."

"By getting hopped up on Dex?"

"Joe?" Mike stared at her unbelievingly. "He's got better sense than that."

"Ordinarily, yes. But when you're scared to death that you have an incurable disease, and at the same time afraid the owners are going to discover it and dump you"—she shrugged—"you're liable to do anything."

"At least he seems to be getting away with it. And the

344

way he's going, he'll burn up a lot of amphetamine before the game's over."

"Mommy!" Joey's voice, anxious and afraid, drew them back into the room.

"What is it?" Rachel asked but they needed only to look at the TV set to see.

"It's Daddy! He's down! And he must be hurt bad, 'cause he ain't moving."

"Oh, my God! That big fool has gone and killed himself."

Chapter 22

"DAMMIT, GUS!" said Helga. "You scared me half to death. Where did you come from anyway?"

"Miss Garth told me you had brought Mr. Payson's body down here. I just got out of the elevator but you were so busy phoning the airport, you didn't hear me."

"Don't talk so loud, or *everybody* will hear you. Come on. I know a place where we won't be overheard."

She led the way to the end of the corridor, turned right, and opened a door at the end of a side passage. The room was small, with a cot, a chair, a small table, and a half bath attached.

"What's this?" Gus demanded as she pushed him in and shut the door. "I didn't even know it was here."

"Quarters for the night pathology technician. But they don't have one just now."

"What happened tonight?"

"Mr. Payson died about seven-thirty."

"Where was Carolyn?"

"I don't know. I've called but she doesn't answer."

"Maybe because she's on Varig Flight 803?"

"Could be."

"Going where?"

"The first stop that flight makes is Rio. And Brazil doesn't have an extradition treaty with the United States."

"Then it's true? She did kill him?" The tall pediatrician sank into the chair before the small table, the stricken look on his face that of one who has just seen a nightmare become reality.

"I haven't spoken to Carolyn since early this morning," said Helga.

"But how could she do anything so foolish?"

"It was an act of love—"

He shot to his feet, his face flushed with anger. "Was it an act of love to risk shattering our whole life together—and my career—by having a charge of murder brought against her?"

"If it's right for a man to kill a dog he loves, when the dog's in pain and can't recover, Gus, why isn't it right for a daughter to help a parent she loves by putting *him* out of his misery?"

"It's not the same thing, and you know it," Gus snapped. "You put her up to it, Carolyn never would have had the courage to do it alone." He wheeled suddenly. "How do I know you didn't do it yourself?"

"Because then I'd be flying to Brazil tonight instead of Carolyn."

"God, what a mess!" He threw up his hands in a gesture which, Helga suddenly realized, was more exasperation than grief or despair. "She'll be charged with murder now for sure."

"You're probably right. I didn't know it until I brought the body down, but Mr. Broadhurst—"

"The State's Attorney?"

"Yes. He had left a note with the medical examiner that, if Mr. Payson died, his body was to be posted immediately. I think he expected Carolyn to use a narcotic. Sam Toyota's going to start the autopsy in a few minutes and he'll be looking for evidence of a narcotic overdose."

"What will he find?"

"Nothing, I hope. Mike Raburn put down the cause of death as 'Cardiac Arrest, Cause Undertermined.' "

"How did she do—no, don't tell me. Then if they subpoena me I'll have to admit that I know."

Helga studied the tall doctor for a moment thoughtfully.

"What are *you* going to do, Gus?" she asked. "About Carolyn, I mean?"

"How do I know? She deliberately ran away—"

"From a charge of murder. Not from you."

"She couldn't have been thinking much about me to risk—"

"Carolyn didn't really care very much what happened to her, Gus. The way she looked at it, she was doomed from the day she was conceived. The thing that did concern her was that, if she stayed here and faced the charge of murder Anthony Broadhurst would probably bring against her, you might still be loyal to her and become involved, with all the damage that could do to your career."

She was looking at him speculatively as she spoke, waiting for the indignant explosion her deliberate use of the words "you might still be loyal" should have elicited. And when it didn't come, she let out her breath in a sigh, though whether of relief or disappointment, she wasn't quite certain.

"*Your* choice now," Helga added, "is between accepting her sacrifice or deciding that the fifteen or so years you and Carolyn could have together, even if she does develop H-D later, plus your natural wish to stand beside someone you love in a time of trouble, are worth giving up your immediate plans for the future."

"How could that be?" She could hardly have missed the note of wariness in his voice.

"Brazil's a big country. I'm still not going to tell you where Carolyn will be by tomorrow or the next day, depending on flight schedules, until I'm sure you're going there too."

"You want me to bring her back? When you just said Broadhurst is likely to place charges against her?"

"Not bring her back, Gus. Stay with her."

"You're out of your mind, Helga."

"I guess I am," she said wearily. "But I owed it to

Carolyn to give you at least a glimpse of what you two can have together down there, if you go to her the first of July instead of joining the faculty here."

"I already know—professional suicide."

"That's where you're wrong, Gus. You'd be working in a modern hospital that serves an area of over a million people, with only one doctor for every eighteen thousand. The infant mortality is over a hundred and fifty per thousand live births, where the U.S. is around twenty."

"Twenty-two."

"Children under five account for more than half the deaths in the area, so if there ever was a place needing a fine pediatrician, that's it. And even if Anthony Broadhurst is politically ambitious enough to bring charges against Carolyn, the whole thing will be forgotten in three to five years, with public opinion on the 'right to die' question changing the way it is. Then you two could come back to the United States. Or you could stay in Brazil and have a very rewarding life together."

"For God's sake, Helga," he exploded. "You know I can't make a decision like that on a moment's notice."

"No, Gus, I guess you couldn't. But I doubt that you felt any hesitation in sleeping with Carolyn the first time you had a chance."

"When did you get to be such a damned moralist?"

"Touché." Helga looked at her watch. "I go off duty at eleven. If you decide to go to Carolyn, let me know by then and I'll tell you where she'll be. If not, I'll expect you to forget that this conversation ever occurred. Excuse me, please. I've got a ward to watch upstairs."

II

Joe Gates had been hot, hotter than he ever remembered being, even when he'd played forward for the Lakers in '70 and handled more rebounds than anyone else in the league that year. As the ball left his hands from his favorite position in the corner of the court, he'd sensed that it would arch in a curve as beautiful as anything ever revealed by a bikini, right through the basket without touching metal.

348

It had, too. But even before the ball cleared the fringes of the net Joe was already halfway down the court, legs pumping, heart pounding until it threatened to come out of his throat, moving fast to be ahead of the tall black Laker forward with the goatee who was the season's high scorer.

With the Snappers ahead by ten points before the quarter was over, Joe knew he was the hottest thing on the court—and so, he hoped, did the owners. Convinced that tonight could be crucial, he'd taken no chances on being anything less than at the top of his form—plus a little more. And from the very first tip at center, he'd been maintaining a pace far more taxing than even a veteran like Joe Gates should try to maintain.

And so, when the ball came into play on a long pass intended for the tall Laker waiting for it under the enemy basket, Joe had to beat it to the man for whom it was intended. Straining every muscle of those famous legs to the utmost of its strength, Joe went up, up, until his outstretched fingers touched the ball just before the Laker forward, tipping it to a Snapper player racing down the court.

Even as his body started downward, Joe had felt the black-out coming and fought to keep a hold upon his senses. But the effort had sent so much blood to his legs, leaving so little for his brain, that something had to give— in this case the brain.

The blackout lasted only an instant, but the Snappers' coach called time even as one of his own players caught the tipped ball. When Big Joe regained consciousness moments later, shaking his head to clear his vision and trying to sit up, a young doctor whose face was vaguely familiar pushed him back without much effort.

"Lie still." The doctor's finger reached for Joe's wrist, and when he felt the pulse, a startled expression came over his face.

"What is it, Doc?" It was the coach, anxious—both about Joe and about maintaining that ten-point lead. "It looked to me like he was tripped."

"Tripped over his own heart most likely," said Ed Vogel. "I can't even count his pulse and it's skittering all

349

over the place. Let's get him off the court and into the locker room."

Joe tried to rise again but Ed Vogel pushed him down once more.

"Get some help and carry him," he told the trainer who was kneeling beside them. "This man's in no shape to walk."

Willing hands lifted Joe and carried him to the locker room, but he didn't hear the burst of applause that accompanied his departure from the court, having blacked out once again. When he came to, he was lying on a rubbing table and the trainer was waving a crushed ampule of ammonia beneath his nostrils. The young doctor had ripped open his jersey and was attaching something that grabbed the skin over his chest.

"What's that thing, Doctor?" Joe heard the trainer ask.

"It's called a ventricular impulse detector; you can transmit an electrocardiogram to a central monitoring station by telephone with it. Besides, it's got a built-in alarm and its own computer."

A faint but perfectly audible sound came from the small unit, interrupting the speaker. It continued for perhaps eight seconds before shutting off.

"That's the alarm," Vogel explained. "It means his pulse is either a little below fifty, above a hundred and fifty beats per minute, or that he's having more than seven abnormal ventricular contractions per minute."

Glancing at his watch, the cardiologist picked up Joe Gates's wrist again.

"The rate's about one-forty now," he said at the end of a half minute. "That's not high enough to set the alarm off, so he must be having enough ventricular contractions to do it."

"What does that mean, Doc?" Joe was able to ask, as Ed Vogel was inserting the tips of a stethoscope into his ears.

"It means you're damn lucky you didn't drop dead out there on the court."

"But I was hot—"

"That you were. That you were."

"I can go back in the second half, can't I?" Joe asked, but somehow didn't seem to have enough breath to say any more.

"Not in the second half of *this* game," said Ed Vogel crisply. "You're going to the hospital."

The tiny buzzer sounded its warning again.

"Call the Rescue Squad," the young cardiologist told the trainer, as he applied the flat diaphragm of the instrument to Joe's chest over the heart. "And tell them to be sure to bring a cardiac ambulance.

"All right, Joe," said Vogel when the trainer disappeared into the adjoining office where the telephone was located and the two of them were alone. "What did you take?"

"I don't know what—"

"Don't try to con me, I've seen too many kids high on bennies not to recognize what they can do even to an athlete's heart. How much?"

"Seventy-five milligrams of Dexedrine."

"Jesus Christ! Were you trying to commit suicide?"

"This is an important game, Doc. My whole career could depend on it."

"You chose one helluva way to save it then. God only knows what you've done to your heart."

"A lot of fellows take the pills before the game, even the hard stuff," Joe protested. "They say it gives them a lift."

"If you'd taken any more, it would have given you a lift—right through the Pearly Gates or wherever it is you're trying to go."

"The ambulance is on the way, Doc," the trainer reported when he came back. "The dispatcher said it ought not to be more'n five minutes."

"Good." Ed Vogel opened his medical bag and took out a plastic syringe and a small sterile pack. Opening the pack swiftly with skilled fingers, he reached in and pulled out two ampules, swabbed them with an alcohol sponge, knocked the tops off, and drew the contents of both up into the syringe. Pulling up the hem of Joe's shorts, he rubbed the skin with alcohol and jammed the needle deep into the muscle, pumping in the contents of the syringe.

351

Moving then to the adjoining office, he dialed Biscayne General and was immediately connected with Mike Raburn.

"I'm sending Joe Gates in with a heart that's spraying premature beats all over the place," Ed reported.

"I was outside Joey's door talking to Rachel when the boy saw him fall on TV. He says Joe was tripped."

"Seventy-five milligrams of Dexedrine tripped him, when his heart rate got past 150. I put a VIDA on him and it sounded like a fire alarm. He'll be there in a few minutes but you'd better have Dr. Rebecca see him, Mike. This guy could go into acute dilatation any minute."

"I'll get her. Things are sort of humming around here, too. Peggy Tyndall's little boy, Dale, overexerted and went into acute oxygen insufficiency. Ken Dalton is just starting to do a shunt on him."

"Is Dr. Dalton operating himself?"

"Yes. Ned Green is assisting."

"I hate to think what losing Dale would do to Peggy."

"Or Dr. Dalton," said Mike, "but it looks like the kid will be okay. The worst part is that, if Peggy hadn't been working late in the laboratory on that plastic heart project, she'd have been home and this might not have happened."

"I hear the ambulance siren outside," said Vogel. "Unless you need me, I won't come in."

"We saw that redhead on TV, too," said Mike. "Good luck, fellow."

III

In the teaching theater of the Pathology Department, located in the basement of the Biscayne General tower, the glaring lights shone down upon the nude body of Richard Payson, laid out on the marble top of the autopsy table. Dr. Sam Toyota stood beside it, a razor-sharp knife in his gloved hand, his body protected from accidental spattering by a large rubber apron.

"Ready to go, Sam?" Karen Fletcher had just come into

the room, wearing a long white coat over beige slacks and shirt, and a matching bandeau restraining the silver-tinted hair.

"All set, Dr. Fletcher."

"You might as well begin. I got in touch with Mr. Broadhurst, and he'll be here by the time you get to the internal organs."

Karen moved nearer to the table as the Japanese pathologist made his initial incision, a sweeping curve that began under one armpit, swung down to about four inches above the navel, then up to the opposite armpit.

"That blood look overoxygenated to you, Sam?" she asked.

"It's certainly oxygen-rich, but then he's only been dead a little over an hour. He died very suddenly, too, from cardiac arrest and the hospital record says he was on a pacemaker and a respirator for fifteen minutes or so."

"I guess that explains it, though I've never seen blood that highly oxygenated before. We'll check the pO_2 on the blood itself, so be sure and save enough for that and all the other tests Mr. Broadhurst is going to insist that we make."

"That will be no trouble, the blood's still pretty liquid."

Dr. Toyota dissected up the large flap he had made, exposing the rib cage and the upper part of the abdomen. When he finished, he casually turned up the flap, covering the dead man's face.

"It's really remarkable how much variation there is in blood liquidity after death," Karen observed. "An embalmer for a large mortuary once told me he sometimes finds it liquid as much as four or five hours afterward."

Reaching for a pair of rib shears, Sam Toyota began to cut through the rib cage on either side of the chest, exposing the organs of the thorax.

"Why is it I always seem to come in when you're doing that?" Anthony Broadhurst spoke from the doorway. "Even though I've heard that blade crunch ribs at least fifty times, it still gives me the willies."

"Wait in my office, if you'd rather," said Karen. "We'll call you if anything significant turns up."

"Unh! Unh! I'd just come back about the time Sam starts in on the skull with that damned saw, and it gets to me worse than the rib shears. Find anything yet?"

"No," said Dr. Toyota. "Mind telling us what you suspect?"

"During that God Committee meeting yesterday afternoon, I got the distinct impression that, if the committee didn't allow her father's life to be ended, Payson's daughter would do it herself."

"So all you're going on is a hunch?" Karen asked.

"Being a nurse and on the same ward where her father was, that girl could easily have given him a massive injection of morphine."

"That's pretty flimsy circumstantial evidence. Besides, the nurses have to account strictly for all narcotic drugs."

"Come now, Dr. Fletcher. We all know that an addict has been employed as a nurse more than once, either because she's worked out a clever trick or because she's a bona fide nursing graduate. Some of them even manage to supply themselves with morphine from the hospital supply for months."

"Not with a computer keeping watch, the way it does here," said Karen.

"At the committee meeting yesterday," said Broadhurst, "it was suggested that a quick method of euthanasia would be the injection of a large amount of air into a vein."

"Air embolism can easily be fatal," Karen conceded. "How about it in this case, Sam?"

"I think not, but we can certainly find out." Picking up a lung he had just removed, the Japanese pathologist sliced the organ open and examined the cut surface carefully.

"No air bubbles in the larger vessels," he reported, then squeezed the soft spongy lung, forcing bright red blood out of the cut surface. "This blood is highly oxygenated, too, and it wouldn't be if enough air had been injected to drive much of it out of the lung vessels."

"Can you be absolutely sure he didn't get a large dose of morphine?" Broadhurst insisted.

354

Karen had been studying intently the cut surface of the lung Sam Toyota had exposed and the blood he had squeezed out of it. Now she looked up.

"If Carolyn Payson had managed to give her father a lethal dose of a narcotic, his respirations would have failed gradually from the effect of the drug on the respiratory center of the brain," she said. "The proximate cause of death would then have been a decrease in the oxygen supply to the brain cells below their life tolerance and the blood would be dark from cyanosis, not red the way it is here."

"How about a heart drug?"

"Did you have any particular one in mind?"

"I read a novel last year about a pharmacist who killed a man by putting a powerful poison in beer and paralyzing his heart."

"I read the same story," said Karen. "The drug was aconite."

"If that made the heart stop suddenly, wouldn't the blood show oxygen?" Broadhurst asked.

"Yes. But aconite is easy to detect chemically in body fluids and even in tissues."

"She could still have given him something like that, couldn't she?"

"It's a possibility, except that aconite is hard to come by," said Karen. "We almost never use it in medicine and it wouldn't be in the hospital pharmacy—or any other one I can think of offhand."

"Could she have used another drug?"

Karen smiled. "I can see why you win so many cases, Mr. Broadhurst. Be sure and take plenty of blood for testing, Sam. And sample all the major organs, too. We don't want to let the DA catch us napping."

"Another thing," said Broadhurst. "Before I came over here, I tried to call Carolyn Payson at the hospital and the operator gave me her apartment number but nobody answered. I wanted to warn her to stay put, until you could determine the cause of death. I also questioned the security man at the front door when I came in just now. He remembers seeing her go into the hospital around dinnertime and Payson died not long after that."

"Are you going to put out an APB?" Sam Toyota asked.

"Not unless you can find a cause of death tonight that could involve her," said the attorney. "With all this public agitation and discussion over the 'right to die,' I'd be a fool to arrest and charge the nurse unless you can nail down the cause of death. That's why I asked that Payson be posted immediately, in case he died soon after the Moriturus Committee meeting yesterday afternoon."

"It's going to take awhile to finish the autopsy," Karen told the attorney as she picked up the bulky hospital record. "Why don't we wait in my office? That way you won't have to listen to the saw, and Sam can call us if he finds anything suspicious."

In Karen's office, Broadhurst lit a cigarette and relaxed in a comfortable chair while she took the one behind the desk.

"Anything new in Dr. Cooper's condition?" he asked.

"Dr. Desmond is going to recommend retirement for him soon. There's been no improvement in the paralysis since the last major stroke, so it's not likely that he will ever be able to work again."

"If you don't mind my asking, where does that leave you?"

"Dr. Jacob Barrows' retirement from the medical service because of angina was approved by the Hospital Board Tuesday afternoon. Dr. Rebecca Dalton was promoted to full professor and made chief of the section at the same time."

"So why not you as head of Pathology?"

"And professor," said Karen. "I'm pretty sure both will happen after Dr. Cooper's retirement. Or don't you approve?"

"I have nothing against women lawyers," said Broadhurst. "Some of the smartest ones I know are women. So why should I object to women doctors?"

"Thanks for the vote of confidence." Karen swiveled her chair so she could look directly into his eyes. "Now what about a woman as county medical examiner?"

Broadhurst looked surprised. "So that's the way the wind blows?"

"Any reason why it shouldn't?" Karen's eyes had never left his.

"Probably not, I just hadn't thought about it." He put down his cigarette. "It can be a pretty messy job sometimes."

"So can this one," said Karen. "I'm the only board-certified forensic pathologist in the county besides Dr. Cooper. And I've been his deputy for the past year."

"You want that post pretty badly, don't you?"

"I've set my heart on it. And what I set my heart on, I usually get."

Anthony Broadhurst's eyes had begun to glow with a light Karen recognized and quite understood. "Does the fact that you will probably be the only woman medical examiner in the country have anything to do with that ambition?"

"Of course—for the same reason you expect one day to be governor of Florida. Or do you deny that?"

Anthony Broadhurst shook his head and Karen decided that now was the time to make her real play, the clincher so to speak.

"If there's any doubt in your mind about my being fitted for the job of medical examiner," she said, "I'll tell you how the death of Richard Payson was almost certainly accomplished—for a price."

He leaned forward eagerly. "How was it done?"

"I said for a price—remember?"

"My support of you when the question of Dr. Cooper's successor comes up?"

"Yes."

"How do you know I wouldn't have given you that anyway?" he asked, and Karen knew with a surge of exultation that victory was only one step away—a step she was quite prepared, even eager, to take.

"I think you would have," she admitted. "But it never hurts to be certain and I rarely leave anything to chance."

"We're in agreement there. Now give—"

"You noticed how red Richard Payson's blood was out there just now, didn't you?"

"Yes. But then—"

357

"You can take my word for it that the redness was abnormal."

"So what does that prove?"

"That he was killed with an embolism—"

"But Dr. Toyota said not."

"Sam said there was no sign of *air* embolism. But that doesn't mean it couldn't have been *oxygen* embolism."

"What is this, anyway? Some Perry Mason type of trick?"

"It's clever enough to be worthy of one of Mason's best cases," Karen conceded. "Let me explain the sequence of events, as I believe they happened."

"Please do."

"Every room in this hospital has an oxygen supply of its own connected to a central source. Payson was getting an intravenous, too." She picked up the chart and turned up the top sheet of the nurses' record. "It was started yesterday."

"What has that got to do with—"

"Let me finish, please. With a catheter used for continuous intravenous injection of glucose already in place in an arm vein, it would have been a simple matter to connect the end of the oxygen tube hanging on the wall of every room to the outer end of the catheter. Or simpler still to put a needle on it and inject the oxygen through the intravenous tubing. A lot of medication is given that way to patients getting intravenous injection."

"But Sam Toyota said just now that air in the veins would have been detectable. Why not oxygen?"

"For a very simple reason. Oxygen is absorbed by the hemoglobin in the red blood cells all the time, but air is four fifths nitrogen, which is inert, though some is dissolved in the blood. The record shows that the patient was put on a pacemaker and his heart kept beating for at least fifteen minutes after there was no sign of respiration or heartbeat."

"Surely the Payson girl couldn't have—"

"She didn't need to," said Karen. "In an ultramodern hospital like this, with respirators and external pacemakers on every floor, nobody gets to die in peace. They're pumped and shocked until the CPR team gives out. While

Payson was on a respirator, oxygen was going in and out of his lungs in simulated breathing. And with the heart beating, blood was circulating in his arteries, veins, and the capillaries in his body tissues, so the oxygen injected into his circulation was quickly absorbed by the hemoglobin in his red cells."

"But he was dead."

"Was he really? We don't know just how long different tissues live after what we call death, for lack of a better word. Actually his brain tissues may have been alive all the time, along with some others. But whether he was dead or alive, blood was circulating in his arteries, veins, and capillaries and some chemical changes were going on."

"It's an interesting theory," said Broadhurst. "And a clever one. If it all happened the way you say, you've just discovered the perfect way to accomplish a murder without detection." His tone changed suddenly. "But can you prove it happened that way?"

"Not a chance," said Karen. "If you put me on the stand and I tried to explain how a person could be killed by an element that not only passes freely into the body in one form and out of it as CO_2 in the next breath, a lay jury would be lost before I got started. And a defense lawyer wouldn't even have to be clever to tear the whole thing down with one question."

"I can figure that one out, at least," said the attorney. " 'Do you mean to tell me, Doctor, that something as vital to life as oxygen would also kill?' "

"Exactly," said Karen.

"So Dr. Toyota isn't going to find anything that would let me bring a charge of murder against Carolyn Payson?"

"Not a thing."

The telephone on Karen's desk rang and she picked it up, listened a moment, then handed it to Anthony Broadhurst.

"It's Police Headquarters. They want you."

Broadhurst listened for a short time, asked several terse questions, and then hung up.

"Seems like you called the shots," he said. "The Payson

girl left for Brazil tonight on Varig Flight 803—first stop Rio. And Brazil has no extradition treaty with the United States."

"You weren't going to indict her anyway."

"I might try—now that she ran away." He shrugged. "But it wouldn't do any good, unless she tried to come back."

"I'm not an attorney," said Karen, "but I don't think you could make that bit of circumstantial evidence stick either."

"By now, I'm sure you're right," said Broadhurst. "But I'd like to know how you arrived at that conclusion."

"You're a very positive man, Tony, that's what I particularly like about you." Karen's voice had taken on a warm, throaty note that set the lawyer's hackles stirring. "According to the scuttlebutt, you threatened to investigate if Richard Payson died soon after the meeting, so Carolyn Payson knew—"

"But she wasn't there when I warned the Board."

"Rebecca Dalton was the girl's representative, wasn't she?"

"Yes."

"Rebecca's very conscientious and would consider it her duty to warn Carolyn Payson about what might happen. Carolyn must have been fairly certain the method she used to kill her father wouldn't be discovered, but she couldn't afford to take any chances and left the country."

"Proving she was guilty."

"Not necessarily. You see, she must have realized that even if you were able to bring her back she could claim that, when her father died, she was so afraid of what you might do that she left the country. So she has you buffaloed either way."

"I'm damned glad you chose medicine instead of law," said Broadhurst on a note of pure admiration. "The best defense lawyers I know couldn't hold a candle to you."

"It's nice to be appreciated," said Karen. "Are you going back on our bargain because I can't prove what happened and Carolyn Payson got away?"

"Not at all," said the attorney. "I'm beginning to think

tonight marks the beginning of a profitable—and I hope pleasant—relationship between the State's Attorney and the soon-to-be new county medical examiner. If you're free for a while, we might cement that beginning with a drink."

"It might be best if we aren't seen together in public until after my actual appointment," said Karen as they left the office. "But I have some excellent Wild Turkey bourbon, if you'd care to drop by my apartment."

Anthony Broadhurst chuckled delightedly. "You're not only beautiful and smart, Karen, you also have ESP."

IV

Surrounded by the scientific paraphernalia of the Coronary Intensive Care Unit, Big Joe Gates was beginning to be alarmed. The effects of the massive dose of Dexedrine he'd taken before the game were beginning to subside, too, bringing on the inevitable reaction of depression.

"How am I, Doctor?" he asked when Rebecca Dalton and Mike Raburn finished examining him.

"It appears that you escaped without serious effects, Mr. Gates—"

"I told Dr. Vogel I was all right, but he—"

"Dr. Vogel is one of the finest young heart specialists we have ever trained here, Mr. Gates." Rebecca's voice was sharp. "You may well have escaped severe heart damage because he recognized your condition and took action immediately to counteract the effects of the drug you took."

"But, Doctor—"

"If you want to wreck your heart, that's your privilege. But don't expect me to praise you for being a fool."

Joe looked at her and knew she meant every word of it.

"All right, Doctor," he said. "I apologize to you and I'll apologize to Dr. Vogel. What do I do now?"

"We'll keep you here a day or two and make a complete study of your heart function. By the way, how often have you been taking amphetamines?"

"Tonight was the first time in years, not many professional athletes take 'em. Team doctors are usually pretty strict about drugs. But the coaches and trainers see that they're available if you want 'em. It's the amateurs who really go for stimulants, from the Olympics right down to the Little League. Doctors sometimes even give bennies to their sons, when they're trying out for high school teams."

"I've seen several of those," said Mike. "Every time there's a tight series, we can count on having high school athletes and some college ones, too, in the Emergency Department half the night. We try to calm 'em down so they can go home and sleep it off but the really bad part comes when some football hero wins the game while he's high and takes his girl home—by way of the Florida Turnpike and West Palm Beach, at a hundred miles an hour. If the two of 'em are lucky, I spend a couple of hours later that night putting them back together, after the car hits a tree or another automobile. But a lot of 'em end up in the basement—under refrigeration."

"An athlete that takes drugs is only doing what's expected of him—so he figures why not?" said Joe Gates. "Take me, tonight: if I hadn't taken that last jump to try to get the ball, I might have finished out the game and been a hero. But now what do I have to look forward to?"

"A good night's rest from the hypo Miss Sundberg is waiting to give you," said Mike Raburn. "Turn over."

The needle was barely out before Joe Gates began to relax from the powerful dose of Demerol Mike had ordered. About thirty minutes later he roused up in the half-darkness when he felt the prick of a needle in his arm.

"Hey!" he mumbled. "Whatcha doin'?"

"Just a routine test, Mr. Gates." The technician was a vague figure in white. "You can go back to sleep now."

Chapter 23

AN HOUR after the initial incision, Ken Dalton stepped back from the table and washed his gloves in the sterile basin of water beside the operating table. During that hour Dale Tyndall's subclavian artery, by which blood was normally channeled to the right arm, had first been severed and the farther end tied off. Next the cut end nearest the heart had been connected to an opening Ken had made into the side of the pulmonary artery, the main blood supply to the lungs, above the constriction that had almost closed the artery even before Dale was born. Fortunately the body provided its own collateral arterial supply almost everywhere like backup circuits on a space capsule, so blood in an adequate amount still flowed to the arm, even though the main supply was no longer open.

Moving back to the table, Ken examined the rows of delicate sutures surrounding the new opening, and felt a warm sense of pride and satisfaction at the realization that they were as neatly placed and tied as any he'd ever done.

"I'm going to remove the clamps and test the suture line," he told Val LeMoyne.

"Good. He can use the extra oxygen."

Two clamps had blocked the arteries while Ken had been suturing the shunt. As he prepared to remove them, Ned Green's gloved left hand was poised above the operative field with a gauze sponge between his fingers, ready to stop any sudden geyser of blood that would have indicated a leak in the suture line. Ned's right hand held a lighted plastic spatula that had not only helped expose the small blood vessels Ken had been working on but also flooded the area with light.

Gingerly, Ken loosened the clamp that had occluded the channel of the cut subclavian artery. It slipped away easily and, when not even a drop of blood appeared along the suture line, he drew a deep sigh of relief. Dropping the forceps to the instrument table, he loosened the second clamp that had blocked the pulmonary artery and removed it, too. As he did, he could feel the rush of blood into a vessel that had never known an adequate flow before, while above the anastomosis the walls of the artery swelled with the surge of blood into the lungs and began to pulsate in rhythm with the beat of the small heart visible in the depths of the operative wound.

"There's no sign of leakage." No one could mistake the thrill of satisfaction in Ken's voice.

"The pO_2 has already started to rise and his color is distinctly better." Val LeMoyne looked around the small tent of draperies that separated her from the operative field. "May I say that it's nice to have the not-so-old master back on the job again? Welcome home, Doctor."

II

When Mike Raburn came into the ICU laboratory about nine-thirty, the night technician looked up from the microscope, where she had been studying a preparation of the blood she had removed from Joe Gates's veins on Mike's instructions.

"The preliminary Sickledex test is somewhat equivocal, Dr. Raburn," she reported. "It's positive in some forms of non-S hemoglobin besides the regular S-compound of sickle cell disease. Just to make sure I added some three-molar urea to one sample and ran two through the autoanalyzer simultaneously in order to measure the difference in light transmission between urea and non-urea Sickledex solutions."

"What's the verdict?" he asked.

"There's no question about it; Mr. Gates does *not* have either sickle cell disease or the trait."

In the doctor's office adjacent to the nursing station of the central ICU, Mike took a slip of paper from his pocket and dialed the number he'd written on it when he talked to Marcia Weston earlier. She answered, but sounded sleepy.

"I hope you hadn't gone to bed," he said.

"I usually get in bed by eight-thirty, when I'm not going out, and read or look at TV until after the eleven o'clock news, but that show you put on this morning was so exciting I was worn out. If you hadn't called I would probably have slept right through the eleven o'clock news and missed your segment."

"Joe Gates was brought to the hospital this evening—"

"I saw his accident on TV before I fell asleep. Was he injured badly?"

"It wasn't an injury. Joe's been under quite a strain lately, what with the owners in full cry after him and his son's close shave with a sickle cell crisis. He overexerted and had a spell of arrhythmia."

"That's tough."

"It may have been the best thing that could have happened for him and his family. Since the newspapers and other media started insinuating that he's the carrier of the sickling trait that almost got Joey, he's been convinced he has it and that his career is over. I hadn't even been able to get him to let me test his blood for sickle cell disease, but tonight I got a specimen under the guise of a routine admission test."

"That's interesting. What did you find?"

"The test proved absolutely that Joe has neither the sickling trait nor the disease."

"Then how did his son get it? Isn't sickle cell anemia hereditary?"

"Rachel, Joe's wife, is the carrier. I've already started prophylactic treatment and she shouldn't have any trouble—"

"You never fail to amaze me, Dr. Raburn. I think I'll ask the station to let me title the half-hour show we'll be putting together from those tapes we made this morning 'Superdoctor.'"

"I look more like King Kong," Mike chuckled. "But right now I'm more concerned about getting the truth that Joe absolutely does not have the sickle trait publicized at

365

rapidly as possible, along with the fact that he's going to be okay. Is there any newsman on the eleven o'clock news I could depend on to broadcast that information?"

"Jim Long is sports director. He called the Snapper game tonight, so he'll also be doing the sports segment at eleven. I know he hasn't approved of this campaign that's been going on against Joe Gates and our station hasn't carried any of those editorials the owners of the team have been planting. The game's over by now, so you can call Jim at the station."

She gave him the telephone number and Mike jotted it down. When he hung up the telephone, he saw Helga looking at him across the counter separating the nursing station from the adjoining doctors' office.

"Sounds like you and the willowy Marcia have a thing going," she said. "Should I be jealous?"

"She wants to call me Superdoctor in the special they're doing on the TBW. How could I help loving her?"

"With those shoulders of yours, it's going to be awful close quarters changing into tights in phone booths."

Mike had been dialing the number Marcia Weston gave him. When he asked for Jim Long, a man with a deep voice he recognized from TV newscasts answered.

"This is Dr. Mike Raburn from Biscayne General."

"*The* Dr. Raburn? Superdoctor?"

"That's Marcia Weston's idea, not mine. If she goes through with it, the Medical Association will blacklist me for unethical publicity."

"From the little I saw of the tape Marcia and her crew made at the hospital this morning, you deserve the title, Dr. Raburn. What can I do for you?"

"I admitted Joe Gates earlier this evening—"

"One of our young floor reporters interviewed Dr. Vogel at the game. He said Joe should be all right with a day or two of rest and some sedation. We're going to run the interview with Dr. Vogel again on the eleven o'clock news. By the way, how is Joe?"

"Fine. Like Dr. Vogel told you, it was just a case of anxiety over Joey's illness and overexertion—"

"I think we can stop there, Doctor. I've seen enough of what happens to kids who get hopped up before high

366

school games to know what really sent Joe's pulse skittering. But I'm pretty sure this was his first offense—"

"It was, at least since high school."

"So we'll not condemn him. But thanks for the information that Joe is okay—"

"If you'll help me, I'm sure we can settle this business the media have been pushing about Joe's having sickle cell disease," said Mike. "He wouldn't let me have the blood for a test before, because he was convinced that he's responsible for Joey's having it. But I sneaked up on him tonight and got a specimen. The test is absolutely negative, Joe Gates doesn't have a trace of the sickle cell trait—"

"Which means he couldn't have given it to his son or have it himself?" Jim Long sounded excited.

"There is absolutely no possibility that Joe Gates could ever have the disease or pass the trait to anyone."

"Do you mind if I quote you, Dr. Raburn?"

"If you think it's best."

"It's not only best, it's the best time in the world to lay this ghost that's been haunting one of the finest athletes America has ever produced. Hold the phone while I get us connected to a tape recorder. We'll run your statement right after the segment on the miraculous operation you did on that girl this morning. If the public doesn't believe you after that, they won't believe anything."

"Isn't that featuring me a little too heavily?"

"You might as well face the fact that, as of this morning, you're the hottest news item in the medical sphere. With your authority behind it, a statement that Joe Gates is free of the sickle trait will have twice the punch it would otherwise have."

III

Ken Dalton telephoned Rebecca at her apartment just after ten o'clock. She'd gone there after Dale Tyndall, recovering rapidly from surgery and already conscious, had been taken to PICU by Val LeMoyne.

"I'm sorry to be late," he said.

"I hear you did a beautiful job on Dale."

367

"Dr. Alfred Blalock and Dr. Helen Taussig deserve the praise for working out that shunt idea at Johns Hopkins a long time ago. Can you meet me in the Dolphin Lounge in fifteen minutes, Reb? I want to ask you a couple of questions."

"Certainly, I didn't undress because you said you would call. Besides, I was busy with Joe Gates."

"See you there," he said. "Whichever of us is first can hold a table."

IV

Rebecca sat for a moment on the bed after cradling up the telephone, which was on a bedside table. She could feel the pulse beating more rapidly in her throat at the thought of what Ken's questions could mean, and wondered if she should let herself hope she already knew the answers. Then suddenly realizing that she was still wearing the sweater and skirt she customarily wore under the long white coat that was the working uniform of the medical school faculty—except the surgeons, who often wore operating suits, and the house staff in stiff white duck—she stood up and quickly peeled them off.

There was no time for a shower, so perfume and an anti-perspirant would have to suffice. But she did select a canary-yellow dress with a swing skirt she remembered he'd always particularly liked. Brushing her hair, putting on fresh make-up, and heightening the color of her lips a little more than the shade she customarily wore on duty, she took the elevator from the penthouse down to the ground floor of Bayside Terrace.

Ken was sitting at a table in the corner of the Dolphin Lounge when she came in. He got up and came across the room to take her hands.

"I'm glad you remembered that I always liked that dress," he told her. "You look lovely in it."

"Careful, or you'll turn my head with all this flattery. Don't forget that we're a couple of hard-working unemotional doctors."

"Maybe that was part of our trouble, Reb," he said as he seated her and took the chair across the small table

368

from her. "We worked too hard and had too little time for emotion—among other things."

"There *were* other things. And I was just as guilty of them as you were, Ken, maybe more. I suppose when a husband and wife are pursuing careers in fields as closely related as ours are, there's bound to be competition between them and I'm willing to admit that at times I carried it too far."

The waitress appeared with a bottle of Cold Duck surrounded with ice in a silver bucket and placed it on a corner of the table, with a pair of wineglasses.

"Shall I open the wine now, Dr. Dalton?" she asked.

"Just leave it and the opener, Evelyn," said Ken. "We'll have it a little later."

When the waitress was gone he turned back to Rebecca.

"I decided definitely tonight that I'm going to take that trip to San Francisco and Paris I've been thinking about," he said. "And I want you to go with me."

The suddenness of his words made her catch her breath, although this was what she had been hoping for. And for a moment, the tension in her throat kept her from speaking.

"I don't blame you for hesitating about resuming a relationship that brought you a lot of pain and unhappiness," he continued. "This probably isn't the right way to tell you I want us back together again either, and I know there's a long list of omissions and some commissions I should plead guilty to at the same time. But you can be sure of one thing, Reb: since I first fell in love with you that day, when you insisted on doing your own dissection in Anatomy I, there's never been anyone else."

"If there's anything in the world I'm sure of, darling, it's that." Rebecca found her voice at last. "And I guess when the two lists of misdeeds are totted up, mine is as long as yours."

"Then you'll go?"

"If Jeffry will give me the time off. How about you?"

"I've been a fixture around here for so many months, hardly anybody will miss me. By next week we ought to have a version of that plastic heart I stopped work on six months ago developed to a point where I can implant it in a calf out at the university's Animal Husbandry Department. Ed and Peggy can be checking it while we're gone; as I remember it, our passports are still in order, so we should be able to leave in ten days at the latest."

"I'll need clothes—"

"You can buy them in Paris. Maybe we can even spend a few days on a houseboat on the Seine."

Rebecca laughed. "Not dressed like we were most of the time in Florida Bay, I'm sure."

"This calls for a personal celebration," he said. "Shall I open the wine?"

Rebecca looked around the room, which was almost filled with people.

"Let's take it with us, darling," she said. "We've got a lovely penthouse that's certainly a lot more appropriate place than this for a private celebration."

V

At twenty minutes to eleven, Helga Sundberg was punching the orders for the eleven-to-seven shift into the computer data bank with the small hand-held keyboard when a light beside the monitor screen reporting the information coming into the main nursing station from the sensors on Carmelita Sanchez' body started flashing.

A quick glance at the screen itself told Helga none of the parameters being reported by light tracings across the ground-glass surface of the screen, or upon the recording meters at one side of the monitor, were abnormal. Pressing the communications switch, she spoke into the microphone beside her.

"Anything wrong, Helen?" she asked the nurse who was specialing Carmelita.

"Nothing wrong, Miss Sundberg. I think she's about to regain consciousness."

"I'll be right there."

Inside the narrow cubicle where Carmelita lay, Helga turned up the light and leaned over to lift an eyelid. The girl's skin was already perceptibly lighter in color than it had been that morning, further proof of the sharp decrease in the concentration of bile pigments in her blood achieved during the nine climactic minutes of the TBW.

The pupil of the lovely dark eye contracted immediately from the light and Carmelita tried to move her head to escape the stimulus upon her retina. One arm was held down by the intravenous catheter through which fluid and glucose were dripping into her body, but with the other she reached up and tried to push Helga's hand away.

When the blonde nurse pressed upon one temple with her thumb, causing a mild pain stimulus, the sleeping girl opened her eyes and grimaced, frowning slightly as she stared at Helga. Her lips moved too, but the sound was so faint that neither Helga nor the younger nurse could distinguish the word she spoke, until she tried a second time—and whispered, "Miguel."

"Do you know where her fiancé is?" Helga asked.

"He was in here ten minutes or so ago. Said he was going down to the Coffee Shop."

"I'll call Dr. Raburn and see if I can get Miguel too. They'll both want to be here for this.

"Please page Dr. Raburn and have him call the ICU," Helga told the telephone operator when she returned to the nursing station.

Mike called back in a few minutes. "What's up?" he asked.

"Carmelita seems to be coming out of coma. I thought you'd want to know."

"You'd better alert the family, if any of them are there."

"Miguel Quintera's in the Coffee Shop. The rest of them went home."

"I'm on the ground floor," said Mike. "I'll bring Miguel up with me."

As Helga hung up the telephone, she heard the door of the ward open and saw the shadow of someone going into the ICU waiting room. Moving to the door, she saw Miguel Quintera in the act of picking up a magazine.

"Carmelita seems to be regaining consciousness," she told him. "I thought you'd want to be with her when she awakens."

371

The young Cuban's dark-skinned face lit up like that of a pilgrim who has just witnessed a miracle. "I—I—" Words failed him.

"Go on into the cubicle," Helga told him. "She spoke your name just now, so she may awaken at any moment. I'll wait for Dr. Raburn."

Helga had just finished punching the orders for the eleven-to-seven shift into the computer when Mike Raburn came into the main ICU and stopped at the nursing station.

"You bet me she'd regain consciousness before you went off duty," he said. "What did you do? Give her a shot of psychic energizer?"

"I live right—and usually win my bets."

Miguel Quintera started to his feet when Mike came into the small cubicle, but the broad-shouldered doctor waved him to his chair.

"Any more signs of consciousness?" Mike asked the student nurse, but she shook her head.

"Not yet, Doctor," she said. "At least nothing we could be sure of."

"Maybe a little oxygen would help bring her out. Hand me the mask and breathing bag, please."

Taking the oxygen mask and bag from the hook where it was hanging, Helga opened the valve to the main oxygen system and the bubbles started flowing in the water bottle that allowed the flow to be visualized and measured. Mike let the bag fill, then put the mask over Carmelita's mouth and nose and opened the small valve that let the stream of gas flow from the bag into her lungs.

For perhaps a dozen breaths nothing happened, then the Cuban girl opened her eyes and reached up with her free hand to push the mask away. Closing the valve between mask and breathing bag, Mike removed the mask from her face and nodded to Helga to shut off the main supply.

Carmelita looked around dazedly but did not close her eyes again.

"Why don't you stand on the other side of the bed?"

Mike said to Miguel Quintera. "She can see you better there."

When the young Cuban came within the girl's range of vision, the response was immediate. A happy smile broke over Carmelita's face. Her lips moved too and this time they had no trouble distinguishing the words they spoke.

"Miguel!" she cried. *"Querido mio!"*

"This is Dr. Raburn, Carmelita," Miguel managed to say. "He saved your life."

The girl seemed not to hear, however; all her senses were tuned to the single fact of her fiancé's presence and her happiness because of it. She reached out her hand and, when Miguel took it, pulled him down to kiss her. And when she released him, tears were streaming from Quintera's eyes.

"God will surely bless you, Dr. Raburn," he said brokenly. "You have given her back to me."

Turning without speaking, Mike left the room and Helga followed. But when he started to leave the ward, she touched his arm.

"Why don't you watch the eleven o'clock news on the TV in the staff lounge?" she said. "Maybe I can finish the report in time to watch your part of it with you."

"I'd forgotten all about it," he admitted, but turned into the small lounge. "I guess I'm just a sentimental slob after all," he admitted as he poured a cup of coffee for himself from the urn there. "The way those two love each other sort of got to me."

"It should happen to me that way." Helga's voice was a little husky as she left the small lounge for the nursing station.

And she could just as well have added: "I'm quite sure it has."

VI

"You're just in time to see the debut of 'Superdoctor,'" said Mike when Helga came back into the lounge. "If you laugh, I'll slug you."

"I still think you ought to wear tights." She settled

down on a hassock beside him and, when his hand groped for hers, wasn't at all surprised to discover how comfortable her slender fingers felt with his much larger ones around them. The brief scenes from the morning's drama had been well chosen; they covered most of the climactic minutes while the blood was being washed from Carmelita's veins and replaced with a fresh supply.

"I'll call Marcia Weston at the station tomorrow morning and tell her they can come out any time and tape the wrap-up, now that Carmelita is conscious," said Mike.

"With her fiancé beside her, it will go over big in Little Havana, when it's time to vote on the Hospital Authority referendum."

"They make a handsome pair."

"Miguel's going to take Carmelita back to Spain with him," she said. "He told me about it this afternoon."

"She may not be ready to go very soon."

"I told him that. He says if she isn't he's going to skip a year and work in the hospital."

The news closed with Jim Long's story about Joe Gates and Mike's taped statement exploding the accusations that Joe was a carrier of the sickling trait. As the closing commercial was coming on, Mary Pearson came to the door of the lounge.

"A flash just came over the grapevine from the Dolphin Lounge," she said. "Dr. Ken and Dr. Rebecca have taken the elevator to her penthouse."

"*Their* penthouse," said Helga.

"I guess you're right at that, they were carrying a bottle of Cold Duck in a silver bucket."

Helga looked at her watch. "It's eleven-thirty. Looks like Gus Henderson isn't going to make the deadline I gave him, so I might as well go home."

"I'll make sure you get there safely," Mike told her. "Besides, you haven't told me how we're going to celebrate the success of the TBW."

At the front door to the hospital, they took the walk heading to Bayside Terrace and the Dolphin Lounge. But where the graveled walk debouched toward the apartment hotel, Mike took Helga's arm and guided her along a winding side path that ended on the bulkhead marking the bay.

"Did you really think Gus would come?" They were standing on the bulkhead but neither was looking at the bright wall of lights marking the Miami Beach hotels across the bay.

"Not after he didn't jump at the knowledge that I could tell him how to join Carolyn." Helga looked up at the sky where an airplane, homing in from the sea for the airport almost directly west of the hospital tower, angled downward, its running lights blinking rhythmically. "Poor Carolyn," she said. "She's going to be lonely in Brazil."

Mike looked at her quickly. "Then it really was Carolyn—not you?"

Helga nodded. "I thought I would die those five minutes or so she was in her father's room, wondering whether one of the other nurses would come back early from dinner and find Carolyn there."

"I saw Sam Toyota just before you called me for Carmelita," said Mike. "He told me they weren't able to find a thing to justify any charge against Carolyn."

"Does that mean there won't be any prosecution?"

"To prosecute for murder, you need a *corpus delicti,* with medical proof of the cause of death. Broadhurst has the body, but not the proof, so he can't do anything."

"I wonder what the verdict will be here in the hospital."

"I'd say most people will believe Carolyn engineered her father"s death, but I doubt if many who knew her well will hold it against her. Do you think she'll come back?"

"I hope she doesn't—not for quite a while," said Helga. "With Gus feeling as resentful as he does, what was between them has to be at an end and she'll get over it a lot quicker with two thousand-odd miles between them. Besides, Carolyn is the sort of girl who needs to be needed and down there she will be. Promise me something, darling—that someday we'll fly down to see her. It's a lovely place."

"Of course we will," he assured her. "Now tell me how her father's death was really accomplished."

"I can't, Mike."

"Why?"

"That would make you an access—" She broke off as he reached into her pocket and took out the large needle he'd picked up from the floor of Richard Payson's cubicle when he stooped down several hours before, ostensibly to tie his shoe. The rays of a floodlight shining through the fronds of a palm near where they were standing were reflected from the metal as he threw it far out into the bay where it struck the water with the faintest of plops and disappeared.

"Now I *am* an accessory," he told her. "So give.

"I thought that must be the way it was done," he said when she finished.

"Mr. Broadhurst would have had a case, wouldn't he, if I hadn't made the mistake of using the pacemaker and driving the heart to contract immediately and disperse all the oxygen throughout the body, where it would be absorbed into the tissues?"

"Mistake, hell!" Mike chuckled. "The minute I saw it, I told myself Helga wouldn't choose a pacemaker instead of the CPR that's SOP in a standstill arrest—unless there was a reason. And when I really looked for it, there was the presumptive proof—at least—in a poorly coiled oxygen tube."

"Which you promptly fixed so no one could tell it had been used," said Helga softly. "Why?"

"I couldn't let you go to jail as an accessory." He pretended indignation. "Have you forgotten that you're committed to helping me celebrate a successful TBW this weekend?"

"I hadn't forgotten. But—"

"You also promised to tell me what we're going to do."

"I had in mind a weekend on Grand Bahama; there's a plane out at five o'clock every Friday afternoon and we could have been there in time for dinner." She turned and put her hands on his arms in a pleading gesture. "Would you believe I've got cold feet?"

"I believe it," he said. "Because I was getting them myself."

"I can't come to you a virgin, Mike; they're pretty scarce nowadays. But I don't want us to start our life together as if it were a casual affair."

"There's an answer," he said, and his voice assured her that everything was going to be all right.

"Tell me, Mike—"

"A boat leaves Palm Beach late every afternoon for Grand Bahama; if we drive up tomorrow afternoon, we can make it. The ship crosses international waters, too, even though the trip takes only a few hours, so the captain could marry us. Are you game?"

"Thank you, darling." She slipped her arms around him and kissed him. "And since we're being so square, let's spend our two-day honeymoon at the Holiday Inn. There's a big one on Grand Bahama."